So good to have met you at the Decatur ... M.K.
Sept 02, 2012

Coming in 2013

Fitzwilliam Darcy
A Man in Want of a Wife

Other books by M. K. Baxley

The Regency Pemberley Series

The Mistress's Black Veil: A Pride and Prejudice Vagary

The Modern Pemberley Series

The Cumberland Plateau: A Pride and Prejudice Modern Sequel

Dana Darcy

Fitzwilliam Darcy A Man in Want of a Wife

Raven Books

M. K. Baxley

Fitzwilliam Darcy: A Man in Want of a Wife is a work of fiction. All other characters are either from the author's imagination, or from Jane Austen's novel, *Pride and Prejudice*.

No part of this book may be reproduced without prior permission.

mkbaxley@bellsouth.net

ISBN-10: 1468136135
ISBN-13: 978-1468136135

© Copyright by M. K. Baxley

All rights are reserved.

First Edition:

Cover and internal design © M. K. Baxley 2012

Part One

A Man in Want of a Wife

Jane Austen's Pride and Prejudice from Fitzwilliam Darcy's Point of View

Told by M. K. Baxley

This book is dedicated to the memory of *Jane Austen* who has inspired so many with her creations. After nearly two hundred years, she is still loved and revered.

Acknowledgements

I would like to give a special thanks to all those who helped me with the proof reading of this story, and especially to the girls at www.darcyandlizzy.com. Ladies you're the best.

Chapter 1

It is a truth universally acknowledged that a single man in possession of a good fortune must be in want of a wife, especially if said man feels as if he holds the weight of the entire world squarely upon his broad shoulders. With the responsibility of one younger sister more than ten years his junior and a large estate to manage, a single man of fortune cannot be too careful…or can he?

~*~

26 August 1811
London

Fitzwilliam Darcy moved past the servants in the great hall making his way in haste to his study where he knew his cousin would be waiting. He was more than an hour late. After a short stop at his solicitor's establishment to settle his affairs with Mr. Wickham and Mrs. Younge, he had gone by once more to call upon his sister at their aunt and uncle's house on Brook Street in Grosvenor Square and found her yet again in tears, unable to forgive herself for her moral failure and betrayal of her brother. He had sat in her dressing room, cradling her to his chest like a small child. Georgiana had cried all afternoon, and it had been all he could do to comfort her, especially when he had no soothing words to express what he felt would be appropriate for a young girl of fifteen to comprehend. So distraught had she been that he had been hard pressed to leave her side and had, therefore, remained longer than he had intended which had made him late for this appointment.

To say Darcy was upset would have been an understatement. He was more than a little upset. He was angry…and he was frightened. Since his father's death five years previously, he had held the burden, along with his cousin, Colonel Richard Fitzwilliam, of the care and upbringing of his sister. He did not mind the responsibility, for it was a burden of love. However, he had failed to fathom what that duty would entail and felt that he had neglected his sister in regards to Mrs. Younge. Having been recommended by none other than his aunt, Lady Catherine de Bourgh, he had not been as thorough as he should have been in checking her references. Lady Catherine had always prided herself on being useful to others, but this time she had failed miserably. In fact, his confidence in his aunt had almost cost him everything he held dear.

As Darcy reached his office, he put his hand to the latch and hesitated. He already knew what his cousin, waiting within, would say. Darcy took a deep breath and braced himself for what was to come. Turning the latch, he entered the room.

~*~

A Man in Want of a Wife

Colonel Fitzwilliam paced back and forth, a glass of brandy in one hand and a poker in the other. Stopping only long enough to stoke the fire for the umpteenth time, his mind wandered as it had done quite often over the past few days. This incident with Georgiana had been close—too close. They had barely avoided a disaster and now it was time to press Darcy to do what they both knew he must. It was time for him to take a wife—one who could not only be a companion to their young charge but also guide her through these problematic years that were proving far too difficult for two lone bachelors to undertake. As he waited, Fitzwilliam prodded and poked as anger and frustration coursed through him, wondering where Darcy was. Suddenly his thoughts were interrupted.

The Colonel looked up at the sound of the latch turning. It was about time his cousin arrived. Had it taken any longer, he had been of a good mind to go in search of him. Tossing the metal rod aside, he stood erect and faced his cousin.

"It's about time you got here, Darcy. You will soon need another log on the fire."

"Never mind the log. Jennings will see to it soon enough."

"What took you so long?" Colonel Fitzwilliam asked.

"I was delayed."

"Mr. Mann or," the Colonel paused, "Georgiana again?"

Darcy sighed. "The latter."

The good Colonel shrugged his shoulders as he ambled over to the drinks cabinet and took out another tumbler. Giving his cousin a cursory look, he enquired, "Care to have a brandy, old man? You look as if you need one."

Darcy slumped down into the oversized chair behind his desk and glanced up at his cousin. "Pour me a double. I need more than one."

Running his fingers over the smooth, mahogany finish, Darcy took a deep breath. His father's desk seemed more imposing than ever as he tried to fill the chair in which the former Master of Pemberley had sat while he conducted estate matters. George Darcy was a giant of a man who always seemed to have the answers even before the questions were asked, or so it seemed to his son. His father had given him good principles, always stressing duty and honour, and the care which must be taken of those whose welfare depended solely upon him. But in the case of his sister, Fitzwilliam Darcy had failed miserably—almost—but not quite. As Darcy saw it, Georgiana was none too worse for the wear. She was not ruined, at least not in the physical sense. Her virtue and her fortune were still intact. But as to her mental state, on this point he was very much concerned.

The Colonel took the seat crossways from him and slid the glass across the sleek mahogany. "So, Darcy, Wickham swindled another two thousand from you, did he? And Mrs. Younge? How much did you pay her?"

Darcy raised the drink to his lips and took a large swallow of the amber liquid, wincing at the fire running down his throat. "Yes, I gave the reprobate two thousand. He demanded more, but I told him he was lucky to get what I had agreed to give." He paused and caught his cousin's piercing gaze. With a sigh, he continued. "As for Mrs. Younge, she received nothing short of a warning and one month's wages. If she so much as mentions one word of this to a dormouse, I will hunt her down, and she will rue the day she was born."

Colonel Fitzwilliam raised one eyebrow. "Darcy, you narrowly avoided disaster this time. You know we should have checked those references more carefully. But no, you said Lady Catherine's word was recommendation enough; therefore, you let it go, shirking your responsibility."

Darcy's gaze shot up. "And I suppose you bear no responsibility in this affair? Why did you not check them if you felt so strongly about it?"

"It just so happens that I did...after the fact, that is." Colonel Fitzwilliam paused, glancing at the floor before raising his eyes to meet his cousin's gaze which was firmly fixed on him.

"And?" Darcy motioned with his hand. "Out with it!"

"It seems that Mrs. Younge was at one time in the employ of *Mrs. O'Kelly*."

Darcy stiffened in his seat.

"I thought that would get your attention. As you are perfectly aware, Mrs. O'Kelly is the most notorious brothel keeper in London's East End, a woman who takes young virgins—desperate women of little to no means without protection and ruins them. I highly doubt Georgiana would have met that fate, but Wickham's intentions were not honourable. Once he had married her, you would have been powerless to protect her, much less her fortune, from his greedy claws. Then Georgie would have been left in disgrace once the money was squandered away. That is the way young women are ensnared in the life Mrs. Younge represents. How she managed to fool Lady Catherine, I've no idea, but at least all is now well. How fortunate for Georgie, and us, that you felt inclined to call upon them at Ramsgate."

"Indeed," Darcy said, taking another sip of brandy. "Are we agreed that this is not to be discussed with anyone, not even Lady Catherine? All she is to know is that Mrs. Younge found employment elsewhere, for should our aunt discover the truth, she may try to seize control of Georgiana, and I will not have that."

"No, and neither shall I. Mother is sworn to silence, and the Earl will present no problem as he is away in the West Indies seeing to our interests there. It should prove to be an extended visit of some duration as there are problems with the governor on one of the islands."

"And what about Wex? Does he have any inkling as to what has happened?"

"No. He is abroad. But you know perfectly well how he feels about Georgie. Even if he were to know, he would protect her with his life. She is as much a sister to him as she is to you. Cassie will protect Georgiana as well."

"Good! The three of you are more like brothers and a sister to me as well. When you can, give Lord Wexford my regards," Darcy said. "And now that this is behind us, we must go about finding a new companion."

"No! It is time for you to take full responsibility and do your duty as a brother and as the master of—"

Darcy raised his hand to stop his cousin in mid speech. "We've been through this time and again. I will not hear it yet another time! Women simpering and fawning, seeking my attention without one jot of sense or the ability to string two intelligent words together to form a complete thought. Their conversations always reflect what they think I want to hear and never what *they* think—if they think at all. Even our cousin Anne is very dull. I will not have it. When and *if* I choose to marry, Cousin, it will be on my own terms and to someone of my own choosing. She must possess attractive qualities: intelligence, musical talent, frankness, and the capacity to love deeply. She must also share my artistic and cultural sensibilities, and I am afraid there are few women of our acquaintance who do. Fitzwilliam, I will not be leg-shackled to some woman seeking to elevate herself in society by my means. The endless circuit, running the gamut of invitations to first one soirée and then another, all grander than the last. I despise it all. You'd do better to find a wife for yourself and Wex than to trouble yourself over me."

A Man in Want of a Wife

Colonel Fitzwilliam rolled his eyes and shook his head. Passing his hand over his face, the Colonel tilted his head and paused for reflection. "It is not Wex or I who have the responsibility that is thrust upon *you*. We will marry in good time."

A moment of silence passed between them, both staring at the now dying fire in the hearth. Finally, the Colonel spoke.

"Cousin," Fitzwilliam said at last, "you have the wrong opinion of marriage. Women of our sphere are there to be seen, to set a fine table, to entertain our friends and connections, and to bear our heirs. They are not to be companions of like mind or even lovers. They have not been bred for that role. That is what we have our clubs and mistresses for. If you are looking for love, Darcy, I'm afraid you will be sorely disappointed amongst the *ton*. It is simply not the way of things in our circle. You cannot have such high expectations, and you must think of Georgie. Georgiana needs a sister to guide her, and you, my cousin, are in need of a wife to continue your line." Colonel Fitzwilliam gave him a knowing look, one that Darcy knew well.

He snorted in disgust. "A paid companion will do for Georgiana. When I reach a point where I *must* have an heir, then I will attend the season and pick one from among the many eligible smiling young ladies present—one of good breeding who can at least set a fine table, as you say, or maybe I will choose Anne. She has about as much sense as any other. For the most part, I find women to be pretentious, overly ambitious, and completely exhausting to listen to with little, or no, thought for the improvement of their minds. Allow me to choose *when* and *if* I so desire. Perhaps I might be fortunate to find one with at best half a brain to recommend her, though she might resemble a horse." He smiled. "Then again, my horse looks better than most women of the *ton*."

"Darcy, you astound me! You know perfectly well what is expected of you. What are you waiting for; the perfect little Miss Mary Lou *slipper bottom* to bat her lashes at you and win you over with some éclat of a proverb to impress you of her self-worth and understanding? You are now seven and twenty. You do not have forever and neither does Georgiana. She cannot remain with Mother forever lest Father and Lady Catherine discover what has befallen her. Time is of the essence. You must select a wife, Darcy. You do not keep to the standard of our forbearers nor do you—"

"Then let me keep to the standard of my choosing." Darcy downed his drink and slammed the glass upon his desk. "I am *not* in want of a wife—not yet, at least. And only when I am, will I take one. Do not forget, Fitzwilliam, I am my own master. I owe obedience to no one."

"As you wish." The Colonel released a long held sigh as he reached for the decanter of brandy and poured another round. "But I will find the companion this time, and I will check her recommendations before she is even given an audience. Mother already has an older woman, a widow, in mind, a Mrs. Annesley. Mother assures me she is a genteel, agreeable-looking woman. I am having her references checked as we speak."

"You do that," Darcy said as he took the proffered drink. "And if she is suitable, send her round. I will interview her for the position. If I find her acceptable, then she may start at once."

"My man should have the references checked with his findings back to me by week's end."

"Good! I want this concern settled as soon as possible. I have business in the North. When that is complete, then I am to accompany Bingley in his search for a suitable estate to lease. It is high time he became the gentleman he aspires to be and shakes off the smell of trade from his past. He hopes to be settled by Michaelmas. And perhaps, when he is settled, we will also find him a proper wife as well—one from the right sphere and with the right connections to firmly place him in our circle, as far removed from his origins as possible."

The Colonel laughed as he sipped his drink. "Still grooming the pup, I see. Well, it is all well and good—as long as the pup's littermate does not attach herself to you, that is."

Darcy scowled. "There is absolutely no danger in that prospect. When I do decide to take a wife, it will unquestionably *not* be Miss Bingley." Darcy paused to consider his words carefully. "Fitzwilliam, I do know my responsibility, and I will fulfil it in due time. Just not now. I am not ready for what lies before me. Trust me, Cousin, there is yet time."

The Colonel only shook his head.

The two cousins continued to talk a little longer until the hour grew late. Darcy saw his cousin out and then slowly took the stairs to his chambers. He ordered a tray served in his room and a hot bath prepared as it had been a weary day, and he needed rest. Georgiana was safely placed with his aunt, the Countess of Matlock, thus he could breathe a little easier…almost.

Taking a deep breath, he shook his head as he thought of his sister yet again. Georgiana was badly shaken by the near ruin she had barely escaped, and he was deeply concerned for her fragile mental state and overall wellbeing. She had refused to eat since Ramsgate, only consuming what was forced upon her, and he feared she might collapse from lack of nourishment. He had to constantly reassure her that she was not at fault, nor was she a wicked person for believing the lies of an unscrupulous man. If anyone was to blame, it was him. He had not prepared her for life nor had he told her about the ways of the world, and worse yet, he had trusted the opinion of another instead of doing what he knew he should have done. All of them had been deceived by Mrs. Younge who had hidden her past very well.

Climbing the final steps to the landing, Fitzwilliam Alexander Darcy felt the full weight of his folly. Had George Wickham succeeded in his seduction, Georgiana's dowry, without the protection of a marriage settlement, would have become his. Wickham could have left her penniless. Darcy moaned in misery as the gravity of what had almost transpired tightened his chest like the grip of a giant hand.

However, it had been his own doing, and he thought he ought to feel it, for he had nearly brought about the downfall of the most affectionate and gentle spirit he had ever known. Had that happened, he would have never forgiven himself.

~*~

That night as Darcy lay alone in his cold, oversized bed in the master's chamber of his London townhouse, he thought once more of what had just transpired less than a sennight ago. In fact, it was ever present in his mind. His young sister, all that was left in the world of his nearest relations, had nearly fallen prey to none other than his boyhood friend, George Wickham. She was barely fifteen years old, still a tender shoot of a girl, trusting and kind. He knew George had singled Georgiana out to seek revenge upon him. Darcy was well aware George had felt slighted by his father's will and was therefore more jealous than ever. He had thought he deserved more than was allotted to him. Darcy linked his hands behind his head and stared into the darkness.

George had been his closest friend all throughout their childhood. He was like a brother to Darcy. In fact, old Mr. Darcy had treated him like a second son, sending him to Eton, and then later to Cambridge for his formal education. He had even provided him a living as the rector of Kympton when the living became available. But somehow, things had gone terribly wrong. George had spurned the living, claiming he did not wish to take orders, and so a cheque for three thousand pounds had been given instead. The brotherly love they had once shared was now shattered and replaced by bitterness and hatred. How could a brother deceive a brother? Darcy would have taken care of him all the days of his life, seen that his family had never gone without or lived in want, but now—now he hated him more than he had ever loved him.

Darcy nodded as he reflected back over the years. Where had it all gone wrong? Shaking his head, he sighed, for he knew the answer. There had been a root of envy there from the beginning—one that matured and ripened with age.

At some point, George Wickham, son of his late father's steward, had begun to view himself as an equal and not merely a favoured servant's son. Wickham had grown selfish and vain through the years, lacking in gratitude, conscience, and morals, believing that since he was the godson of the wealthiest man in all of Derbyshire, he was thereby entitled to all the privileges and benefits bestowed upon a *rightful* son. Like so many within their privileged circle, Wickham had become wild and reckless, taking what he wanted and using whomever he fancied to pursue his selfish desires.

As the two boys had grown older, Darcy had quietly gone behind George and settled his debts, often having to arrange accommodations for all the servants and tradesmen's daughters with whom Wickham had meddled. Many a bastard in Lambton bore a strong resemblance to George Wickham, and since the two friends were remarkably similar in appearance and considered as close as any brothers, there was often speculation and rumours swirling around him as well, thus compromising his own reputation. Darcy could not bear for his father, in his then fragile state of health, to know the truth about George, the man who was his namesake and whom he loved enough to elevate far above his station in life. Thus Wickham's habits had become a closely guarded secret, one which that villain had used time and again against Darcy to gain whatever he wanted, which was usually related to money.

Darcy steadied his breath and narrowed his eyes. George Wickham had been given everything a second son could claim. And what good had come of it? George had nearly ruined his beloved sister. For that, he would have called him out had it not been for his sister's pleadings and the danger to her reputation. Instead he had to settle for the Colonel's justice. And after the sound beating his cousin had given George, along with the money he himself had paid him, Darcy felt sure he would never see him again. For surely George would not dare show his face in his presence for fear that he just might beat him to a bloody pulp himself, giving no consequence to what anyone would think or say. He detested the man with a deep rooted hatred that nothing short of a miracle could remove.

Then, as Darcy lay there in the quiet of his chamber, his mind strayed to his conversation with his cousin and the situation at hand. At seven and twenty, he was well aware of what was expected of him—the kind of lady he was to take to the marriage bed. Trouble was he could not abide the empty-headed females who were paraded in front of him in a constant stream to be inspected like the horses chosen for his breeding ventures. And his cousin Anne, whom his family believed he was duty bound to marry, was far too sickly to consider with any degree of seriousness. He doubted she would even survive the wedding night, let alone be able to provide him with an heir. And besides, he felt no attraction whatsoever to her and wondered if *he* could survive the wedding night if she were the bride.

Darcy sighed once more. What he would not give to lie in the arms of a beautiful woman whom he could esteem as much as she would him. A union of love and respect was what he desired and though great beauty was not altogether necessary, intelligence certainly was. Should he meet such a woman—one with an intellect as sharp as his own—he would not hesitate to propose. And though such a woman seemed but a figment of his imagination, he could dream, could he not?

With these thoughts swirling in his mind, Darcy smiled and pulled his pillow closer as he closed his eyes. Tonight he would dream of a wood nymph with dark hair flowing free and emerald green eyes shimmering with mirth—a woman of the night, bright and intelligent, to fulfil his every fantasy.

~*~*~*~

Chapter 2

16 September 1811
Hertfordshire

Darcy thundered across the meadows of Netherfield Park on the back of his white charger accompanied by his close companion, Charles Bingley, the wind blowing in their faces and sod being thrown from the pounding hooves digging into the moist earth. Bingley had come down the previous week to survey an estate his solicitor had found near the small community of Meryton in Hertfordshire. Upon his initial inspection of the park, he had summoned Darcy for his opinion.

Knowing Georgiana was now in capable hands, Darcy had left the following morning to join his friend. A smile crossed his features as he reflected back upon the state of affairs concerning his sister.

Mrs. Annesley had proved to be the perfect solution for Georgiana. The matronly woman was as much a mother figure for his young sister as she was a paid companion. They had gotten on very well almost from the beginning. Having raised six girls, all with different and varying natures, Mrs. Annesley knew exactly how to relate to a fragile girl who had come through a trial such as the one Georgiana had suffered.

When Darcy had returned from Pemberley, he was more than pleased to see that his sister's cheeks had filled out and now glowed with a rosy hue. She was the picture of health. Additionally, her studies had improved to the point where her French and Latin were near perfection, and she was excelling with her music masters as well. Mr. Von Braun could not praise her accomplishments enough, and Darcy had to agree. His sister was blossoming into a very accomplished and beautiful young lady.

His one concern, though, was that she was still painfully shy and sometimes stuttered, something she had not previously done. Mrs. Annesley, however, assured him this would correct itself in due time and that he should be patient. She had also informed him that his sister needed the companionship of her peers; a young gentlewoman closer to her own age with which to associate would do quite nicely. She further noted that should he see fit to take a wife, she was sure Miss Darcy's wellbeing would improve more rapidly, provided the young mistress was of an amiable temperament and willing to be a true friend to his sister.

Darcy drew a deep breath and sighed as he recalled the conversation. *...take a wife...yes, I suppose I must...but who—and where am I to find a woman that I can at least tolerate.* He shook his head to clear his thoughts and concentrate on the task at hand.

Surveying the land, he looked as far as the eye could see over the vast planes, studying it closely. With what he observed, he concluded that the acreage in the southern counties was indeed suitable for farming and could be called tolerable, even pleasant in a prettyish sort of way. But, from what he had detected on a previous visit to this county, Darcy knew that the society was something less than to be desired. He found the local gentry crass and vulgar, the epitome of low class without fashion or good breeding. Why Bingley should want to settle here was beyond him. Many of the young ladies could be seen rambling through the countryside with their bonnets loose and hair blowing in the breeze like bumpkins from the backwaters, and all without proper supervision. The only redeeming quality Darcy could find in Hertfordshire was its location; it was but a mere twenty miles from the outskirts of Town, an advantage of which he would have to avail himself of often should he be unfortunate enough to find himself trapped in this godforsaken area of the country.

Coming to a grassy place in a far pasture surrounded by rolling hills, Bingley slowed his stallion and pulled in the reins. Darcy did likewise.

Turning to look back at the manor house, Bingley cast an anxious eye upon his friend. "What do you think, Darcy? Is it not a good prospect?"

"It's acceptable for what it is, I suppose. The house is spacious with a classic design, and the land is superb for farming—good for both crops and sheep. Cattle will do well here as well, and the stables are as fine as any I've seen."

"Oh, it is nothing to Pemberley, I know, but since you are unwilling to sell and I must settle somewhere, it might as well be here. Do I have your endorsement, old man? Tell me at once. Do you approve?"

Darcy turned his horse back to his friend. "The southern counties are by far the poorest, and I fear you'll find the society something lacking. The people are more like savages than anything else."

"Country manners? Surely you jest! I find them charming."

"Well, if that be the case, then you had better take it before someone else does," Darcy said with a half-smile.

"Indeed, I shall. I shall close with Mr. Phillips directly. He has already drawn up the papers, and my solicitor approves."

Darcy laughed, but then feeling that they were not alone, he glanced up to a mount in the far distance. There stood a young woman looking down upon them. He could not make her out exactly, but he did notice that her bonnet dangled freely behind her and her curls had escaped their pins.

His smile soon faded, replaced by a scowl, as he turned his horse to race Bingley back to the Meryton. Kicking his heels into his mount's sides, he moaned beneath his breath, "Just as I have seen in the village...wild as a March hare!"

~*~

Once the lease was signed, Bingley went about hiring servants: a housekeeper, a butler, several footmen, a cook and kitchen staff, and various and sundry others to complete his establishment. Darcy had collected the estate documents from the country attorney and sequestered himself in the confines of Bingley's study, such as it was, to examine all the particulars relating to the land and determine what improvements, if any, would be needed to bring Netherfield Park up to standard and begin to turn it into a profitable estate. When he felt secure in his findings, he would discuss the essentials with Bingley, instructing him on the particulars of estate management.

A Man in Want of a Wife

Darcy pored over first one document and then another. The irrigation ditches in the northwest section had been neglected and many were filled in. They would have to be re-dug. The crops had not been rotated in many years, and would, therefore, have to be addressed. Turnips, barley, corn, and clover would have to all be planted both for fodder and grazing, rotating as they years went by. The pasture was indeed suitable for sheep, but cattle would have to be kept on another part of the property as the land would not support both in the prime pasture.

There was one shining star in Netherfield's crown, however. It could boast of some of the best shooting and fishing in the county. It was teeming with pheasant and water fowl. Fox were abundant, and the water source was superb with a rather large stream flowing through the heart of the estate, forming a lake near the vast wooded area where Darcy had seen the girl watching them on their first day in Hertfordshire. A gristmill was in order to further increase the value of the land.

He smiled to himself. Sport would be perfect here. He would have to bring Old Sam on his return trip, and he would insist Bingley fill his kennels with shooting dogs and hunting hounds as soon as may be.

Darcy glanced up at the sound of Bingley's voice at the door.

"I say, Darcy, all work and no play make for a very dull boy. Come out man and meet the neighbours."

Darcy groaned inwardly as he noted the short chubby little man accompanying his friend. Why was Bingley so besotted with the backward societies scattered about the countryside, and furthermore, why did he insist on pushing them on him?

Suppressing a frown, he stood.

"Sir William Lucas, allow me to introduce you to my good friend, Mr. Fitzwilliam Darcy of Pemberley in Derbyshire."

Darcy gave a curt bow. "Sir William."

"Mr. Darcy," Sir William returned the bow. "It is a pleasure to make your acquaintance. I have often heard of you and your family when I have been in Town. It seems that not a day goes by that there is not some mention of you in *The Times*. I hope all is well with Miss Darcy and your family, the Matlocks."

Darcy stiffened noticeably. "The Matlocks are well, I thank you. All in good health when last I saw them. My sister, Miss Darcy, is also well."

Darcy gave another short bow. "Now, if you will excuse me, I must attend to these matters of business. I am expected back in Town by nightfall."

"Oh, yes...yes-yes. I quite understand. You are a busy man, not to be interrupted when duty calls. I hope you will visit us again and join us at one of our little assemblies. I have been telling Mr. Bingley all about them, and he seems quite interested. There will be one at The Prancing Fox in a fortnight. Mr. Bingley tells me he is quite fond of dancing and plans to attend with a large party from Town. We would be most honoured if you would count yourself amongst them, Mr. Darcy."

Darcy gave a sharp look towards his friend, and then cleared his throat and nodded as he picked up his quill and dipped it in the nearby inkwell.

"Well, yes," Bingley returned somewhat hesitatingly. "I'm sure we would all be honoured, Sir William. Now," he paused once more, "I shall see you out. When I return from Town with my sister, Caroline, you and Lady Lucas must join us for dinner. Caroline would be delighted to meet Lady Lucas, and of course, your lovely daughters, and I look forward to meeting your son John when he returns from Cambridge."

"Splendid! Capital…capital!" Sir William declared, clapping his hands and bowing low.

Exiting the study, Sir William continued with his animated speech as he walked down the corridor. "Lady Lucas and my Charlotte especially shall be most honoured to make your and Miss Bingley's acquaintance. Yes, honoured indeed. My Maria is quite young yet, but she shall be honoured as well. It is not often that we are in such fine company."

"Indeed, Sir William. The honour is all mine," Bingley said with a smile as they reached the portico.

"Now," replied Sir William, "I shall be off and call upon our mutual neighbour, Mr. Bennet. He has five daughters, all striking beauties, but I must say the eldest Miss Bennet is the prize of the county. Whoever wins her heart should count himself most fortunate. Yes-yes, most fortunate indeed. And I must not forget his second daughter, Miss Eliza. She too is a striking beauty. I think she would suit your friend very well, though the Bennet sisters are all remarkably handsome. Indeed, all five are considered the jewels of the county."

"I look forward to making their acquaintance."

Bingley bowed and waved as Sir William's chaise left in the direction of what Bingley knew was Longbourn Estate. This was not the first time he had heard of the beautiful Bennet ladies, and with so many compliments, he knew he would make an effort to meet Mr. Bennet and seek an introduction to his five daughters, especially the eldest Miss Bennet of whom he had heard nothing but praise for her beauty, and would it not be delightful if Darcy also found one of the other Miss Bennets to his liking as well? Then he and Darcy would be brothers—and that was very much to Bingley's liking.

With a song in his heart and a spring to his step, he turned back to the house.

~*~

Returning to the study, Bingley found Darcy still poring over the stack of papers piled on the desk.

"Sir William is such a fine fellow. Do you not agree, Darcy?"

"I suppose he is, if you like the overly friendly sort. As for me, I prefer the quieter, more dignified type. Men of fewer words suit me better." Darcy returned to his work, his pen moving effortlessly across the page.

"Darcy, there is more to life than all work with hardly a moment spent on pleasure. You did not seem quite so serious when I first met you. I suppose having your estate to manage and a young sister to care for has its disadvantages, but really, Darcy, you must not be so difficult. You need a wife, my friend."

Darcy slowly lowered his pen. "I believe that is quite enough from you. I will take a wife when I am ready. Now, here are the lists of things to which you must attend to. They are in order of most critical to least. Everything is there and laid out for easy comprehension. See to them at once, and should you have any questions, I am always at your service to explain anything you do not understand. Mr. Phillips has acquired a steward for you. I have interviewed Mr. Goolsby and find him acceptable, but as always, the final decision is yours."

"Whatever you say, Darcy, I shall do. I trust you implicitly. If you say this man will make a good steward, then I will accept him."

A Man in Want of a Wife

"Good. Then it is settled. You are to ride into Meryton on the morrow and meet with him in Mr. Phillips's office. There he will go over the particulars, and Mr. Goolsby will begin work immediately."

Darcy stood and came around the desk where he took a decanter of Port from the drinks cabinet and poured two glasses. "Here's to the future, my friend. May we both make the best of it."

"To the future," Bingley said, lifting his glass to touch his friend's.

When they had finished their wine, Darcy left to make ready for his return to London. He had already decided he wanted as little to do with Hertfordshire as possible, and as soon as his work here with Bingley was complete, he would leave, returning only to visit occasionally, for he was sure that infrequent visits would be quite enough for his liking. Soon he would be home…home with his sister where he would have a quiet evening and listen to her play the latest sonata she had mastered.

~*~

Bingley walked Darcy out to his waiting carriage where his friend entered and took his seat.

"I will see you in a fortnight, Darcy. Give Miss Darcy my best, and remember, she is always welcome to come back with you, if she so desires."

"No, that will not be necessary. She is settled in quite nicely at Darcy House with Mrs. Annesley. She has her lessons to attend, her music masters and her drawing, and I am sure she would not wish to leave the comforts of Town for the wilds of Hertfordshire."

"Darcy, you astonish me. I find the countryside to be quite charming. The air is fresh and pure and the society is most agreeable. Everyone is incredibly friendly. Take Sir William and Mr Long, for instance. I find—"

"No, I'd rather not. Enjoy your neighbours, if you will—after all, you are the one settled here. As for me, I'd just as soon remain in the library, or better yet, ride over the fields. Oh, and perhaps do some shooting. You do have a fine assortment of fowl here and some rather good fishing as well."

"That's a fine concession you make. But nonetheless, come back, and we shall enjoy some sport. Perhaps we shall meet some of the local reputed beauties, too. I hear the Bennet sisters are the jewels of the county. I am rather looking forward to discovering the truth of it."

Darcy rolled his eyes. "Bingley, now *you* astound *me*. You fall in and out of love at the drop of a hat. If you are not careful, some matchmaking mama will have you snared for her daughter, and you will find yourself leg-shackled before you know what has happened. Be careful, my friend."

Bingley closed the coach door and smiled widely. "I'll see you in a fortnight, and I will purchase those dogs you mentioned. Sir William tells me Mr. Goulding raises the best in the county!"

Darcy tapped the roof of his coach, signalling the driver to drive on. "I'll see you in a fortnight then."

"Goodbye, my friend." Bingley waved him off as he turned and walked back towards his new home.

~*~*~*~

Chapter 3

Darcy paced back and forth in Bingley's library, sipping a glass of Port and grumbling beneath is breath. He was clearly annoyed. Casting a sharp look at his friend, he chided, "Bingley, you know perfectly well I do not wish to attend this country assembly, so why did you tell Sir William I would be in attendance?"

"Darcy, I did not tell him. He took your nod as acknowledgement that you would be in attendance. If you had not wanted to appear, you should have made your sentiments known. However, if it is such an annoyance to you, I shall make your excuses and all will be well."

Darcy released a deep breath and spoke tersely. "No. I will attend, if for no other reason than I am a man of my word—even when Sir William only *thinks* I have given it, I will keep it."

"Poor Darcy," Caroline Bingley said, looking at her sister, Louisa Hurst. "What agonies he must suffer that he should be subjected to such society. Shall I comfort him?"

"Yes, Sister, I think you *must*. Poor Darcy."

Rising from her seat, Caroline set her tea aside and moved to the window where Darcy stood, gazing out into the distance.

"I see you are as displeased as I in this backward society, Mr. Darcy. There is no sense of fashion and very little breeding amongst the local gentry. The lack of taste among the goods available in the local shops is maddening. The village does not even support a decent millinery shop. Everything is from the last season! However, I fear poor Charles has been bewitched by this wretched place. He will not listen to reason no matter what I have to say. I have been here an entire sennight and cannot wait to quit it."

Darcy turned his gaze upon Miss Bingley trying to hide his disgust at her feeble attempts to garner his attention.

"Yes, well, your brother must settle someplace, and I fear this is his choice. We shall simply have to endure it as best we can."

"But you cannot imagine what I suffer in this horrible place. I have met all the neighbours. How could I not? For they call every day. As soon as the hour approaches, they are being announced. I have met them all—even the *jewels* of the county—the famous Miss Bennets of Longbourn. I see nothing special in any of them, except perhaps the eldest. She is at least tolerable, but the *mother*...she is beyond description, and the younger daughters are absolutely wild! I'm sure you would not want your sister to claim such ill-bred chits as acquaintances, especially with their brazen behaviour."

"If they are as bad as you say, then certainly not."

A Man in Want of a Wife

"If you attend tonight, you shall see for yourself. They will be chasing every man in the room. Stay close to me, Mr. Darcy, and I shall keep you safe from the Hertfordshire ladies."

Darcy glanced down at his arm now in the grip of Miss Bingley's spindly fingers. Reaching down, he gently pried them from his person. Who would keep him safe from *her*?

~*~

Arriving at the Prancing Fox, the footman jumped down and opened the coach door. Lowering the step, he stepped aside and Mr. Bingley exited first, followed by his brother-in-law, Reginald Hurst and his wife, Mr. Bingley's sister, Louisa. Finally, Darcy exited, followed by Miss Bingley.

Darcy took a deep breath as he raised his hand to adjust his bicorne. Caroline slipped her arm in his and snuggled closer, her toilet water almost overwhelming him. "You shall be quite safe, Mr. Darcy. I am here to protect you from the wild denizens of this backwater village."

Darcy raised a brow and once more gently pried her fingers from his sleeve.

"I shall be quite safe, Miss Bingley. I am a grown man capable of taking good care of myself."

Caroline smiled, and then returned her hand to his arm. "Then you shall have to look after me, for I am in need of a protector."

Darcy stiffened. Did she even realize the meaning of her words? Protector indeed! He would *not* take her for a wife. Nor would he have her for a mistress. He released a heavy sigh and shook his head.

Resigned to his fate as her escort, he shrugged and placed his hand upon hers in the crook of his arm.

Entering the assembly room, Darcy glanced around. The place was lively with music and people dancing. The young girls who were not dancing were clustered around the wine table enjoying refreshments while they looked wistfully upon those who were dancing. Old women were huddled in a corner, gossiping, he presumed, while the men were gathered together with their wine and cigars, talking politics. He cared for neither.

Suddenly, the music stopped, and all eyes were turned upon them.

Sir William Lucas noted the awkwardness and immediately came forward.

"Mr. Bingley!" He bowed low. "Allow me to welcome you to our little assembly. We hope you will find things to your liking and have come prepared to dance."

"Sir William," a gregarious, sociable Bingley said with a slight bow. "I'm very glad to be here. And I can assure you that there is nothing I love better than a country dance."

With that, the music resumed, and the gentlemen reclaimed their partners. Sir William escorted Mr. Bingley into the crowd and began the requisite introductions.

As Darcy glanced about the room, he could hear the whispers and assumed that they were the topic of discussion. He caught sight of a crass and vulgar matron who was vigorously motioning for her daughters to come to her. She wore too much rouge and her shrill voice carried across the room. To his horror, he heard his name mentioned, this same piercing voice declaring to the young ladies his fortune of ten thousand a year, how handsome he was, his ownership of a large estate in Derbyshire, and that Bingley's wealth was nothing to his.

To her credit, the fair-haired lady in the group appeared to blush in embarrassment, but the dark haired lass at her side seemed to be amused. He fixed her with a stare as he heard her say, "Perhaps he wouldn't be quite so handsome if he wasn't quite so rich." Darcy rolled his eyes in disgust. He was incensed, and his mood further darkened. He stepped away for a breath of fresh air, and that was when he noticed his friend and Sir William approaching the very lady he had just heard bandying his name about. By force of instinct, he followed.

Sir William bowed to the older woman.

"Mrs. Bennet, Mr. Bingley has expressed a particular wish to be introduced to you and your daughters."

"Oh sir, you do us a great honour, a great honour indeed. Come girls," she said. "Mr. Bingley, this is Jane, my eldest, and Lizzy, my next to eldest, and there sits Mary, my middle one, reading her book, and you will see my youngest, Lydia, and her sister, Kitty, my next to youngest, dancing. Oh, how my girls love to dance! Do you dance, Mr. Bingley?"

"There is nothing I enjoy more, madam, and if the eldest Miss Bennet is not otherwise engaged, I would like to claim her for this next set."

Jane blushed furiously and lowered her lashes. "I am not engaged, sir."

"Good. I shall come directly."

Mrs. Bennet fluttered her handkerchief and spoke with great effusions, spreading accolades upon Mr. Bingley to the point where her second daughter, embarrassed by the display, attempted to check her mother. But Mrs. Bennet would not be deterred, even at the expense of humiliating her eldest two daughters. Finally, the matron settled her sights on Mr. Darcy.

"Sir—sir, how about you, sir? Do you love to dance as does your friend here?"

Bingley seemed to be caught off guard. He stumbled with his speech before finally turning to Darcy.

"I beg your pardon, Mrs. Bennet. Please excuse my manners. Allow me to present my friend, Mr. Darcy."

By pure force of will, Darcy stepped forward and bowed curtly while Mrs. Bennet curtsied.

"Well, sir, have you come prepared to dance as your friend here has. For I doubt you will find more lively music or such pretty partners as you see here before you." She gestured to her daughter, Elizabeth.

"Thank you, madam, but I rarely dance."

"Well then let this be one of the few occasions on which you do."

"No, I thank you, for I do not wish to dance." Darcy gave a slight bow, then turned and walked away, leaving her in mid-sentence.

"Well, I never! Did you ever see a more proud, disagreeable young man? Such ill manners, and he thinks he is above us, does he?"

"Mother, for goodness sake, lower your voice or he will hear you!" Elizabeth exclaimed.

"I don't care if he does, for I will give him a good piece of my mind, should he return for it. Nor do I care for his money and estates, no matter how ever many he has. If he hears my resentment, then so be it. In fact, I prefer it if he does. Who is he that he can think himself so far above us?"

"Well, Mother," Elizabeth answered, "you know very well that the very rich can do as they please, insulting whom they will, but even if he were the richest man in all of England, we do not need the likes of him. There are plenty of agreeable young

A Man in Want of a Wife

men in the world that we need not pay any particular attention to the man from Derbyshire. He may do as he will. Our company is his loss. We need not care for his good opinion, now do we, Mother?"

"No, indeed, we do not. Leave him to himself."

Darcy smirked as he moved to the wine table. Pouring himself a tall measure, he sipped it slowly as he watched from over the rim of his glass. He had heard everything that had been said. Who were they to think he would even care for their good opinion. They were so decidedly beneath him that they were not even worth a second thought. And *these* were the *jewels* of the county? He smirked again. If this was the best Hertfordshire had to offer, then he'd as soon not look any further. His curiosity was well sated. For once, Miss Bingley was right. They were the most brazen women posing as ladies that he had ever seen.

~*~

Darcy walked about the room, watching as his friend and his sisters mingled. Miss Bingley had unsuccessfully tried to engage him in conversation several times, but he had artfully avoided much of her attention for the better part of the evening. She simpered and cooed, complaining about first one thing and then another, boring Darcy to the point that when he saw her approaching, he either moved in the opposite direction or engaged some of the older men in conversation on one of their two favourite topics—politics and the price of corn. When he was not talking to the men, he stalked around the perimeter of the room, watching all before him.

Darcy moved to the far end of the room where he leaned against the wall to continue his observations. The behaviour he observed was deplorable. Young girls not old enough to be out were flirting with any and all who would give them any attention, especially the younger Miss Bennets. They were, perhaps, the worst.

After a few moments he glanced towards the dance floor to see his friend fast approaching. Darcy sighed and shook his head. He knew perfectly well what his friend wanted.

"Come, Darcy," Bingley said, "I must have you dance. I hate to see you standing about by yourself in this stupid manner. You had much better dance."

"I certainly shall not. You know how I detest it. Unless I am particularly acquainted with my partner, I cannot bear the thought of it." Darcy paused and glanced about. "At such an assembly as this it would be insupportable. Your sisters are engaged at present, and there is no other woman in the room with whom it would not be a punishment for me to stand up."

"Darcy, I would not be so fastidious as you are for a kingdom! Upon my honour, I never met with so many pleasant girls in all my life as I have this evening, and there are several of them who are uncommonly pretty."

Darcy sighed. "*You* are dancing with the only handsome girl in the room," he said, looking at the eldest Miss Bennet.

"Oh! She is the most beautiful creature I ever beheld! But look, there is one of her sisters sitting down just behind you." Bingley nodded towards a lady sitting with her hands folded in her lap. "She is very pretty, too, and I dare say, very agreeable. Do let me ask my partner to introduce you."

"Which do you mean, Bingley?" Turning round, he looked for a moment at Miss Elizabeth. Catching her eye upon him, he withdrew his own and coldly stated, "She is tolerable, I suppose, but she's not handsome enough to tempt *me*. Bingley, I am in no humour at present to give consequence to young ladies who are slighted by other men. You had better return to your partner and enjoy her smiles, for you are wasting your time with me."

Bingley shook his head and sighed. "Well, I shall return to my partner. I do hope you will change your mind and join us."

Darcy raised his glass and sipped his wine as he watched his friend depart. He turned his eyes back to Miss Elizabeth Bennet. He was aware that she had heard at least part of his conversation with Bingley, for he could read the expression in her eyes when once again he caught her gaze. She promptly stood up and walked past him as if she had not a care in the world. With a wicked smile she glanced up at him for a brief moment, and that was when he noticed her emerald green eyes. They sparkled with intelligence. Her ebony hair shimmered in the candle light, but those eyes! They were the eyes of the woman who came to him each and every night in his dreams. Well, it was of little consequence. She was a woman so decidedly beneath him that it would not do to let his imagination run away with him.

He turned when he felt Miss Bingley once more latching onto his arm.

"Mr. Darcy, I can envisage what you must be feeling at this point."

"I should imagine not."

Miss Bingley ignored his statement and proceeded on with her outpourings. "How intolerable to be trapped in this dreadful society. Well, soon we shall leave, for I hear this is to be the last set. Would you care to share it with me?"

"Miss Bingley, I have just refused to dance with another. I fear my manners are the topic of much discussion at present. I have already danced one dance with you. Let us not add insult to injury, shall we?" He gave her a curt bow and resumed his occupation of stalking around the tiny assembly hall, listening to the lively conversation he had generated.

~*~

Upon their return from the Meryton assembly, the party from Netherfield settled in the drawing room. Miss Bingley called for tea, and they gathered round the chimneypiece to discuss the ball as they warmed themselves by the fire.

Darcy stood aside from the rest with one hand pressed against the mantelshelf while he stared into the burning blaze, listening to the crackling logs and contemplating the evening, not wishing to dissect it, yet he knew perfectly well what would follow.

Taking her tea to the settee, Miss. Bingley was the first to speak. With smugness, she remarked, "I am afraid poor Mr. Darcy was very disappointed with the evening, Louisa."

She glanced in Darcy's direction. "I heard none of the Hertfordshire ladies could please you, Mr. Darcy."

"Oh! Not even the famous Miss Bennets?" Louisa Hurst added as she took her tea and sat down next to her sister.

"Well, I certainly enjoyed myself," Bingley said. "Upon my honour, I never met more pleasant people or prettier girls in all my life."

Darcy stiffened and turned to face his friend. "Bingley you astonish me. I saw a collection of people in whom there was little beauty and no fashion—the eldest Miss Bennet being the only exception. She is, I grant you, quite pretty, but she smiles too much."

A Man in Want of a Wife

Bingley rose up in his seat. "A fine concession you make. Come Darcy. You can do better than that. Admit it. She's an angel, the prettiest girl I have ever laid eyes upon."

Darcy glanced at his friend but said nothing more.

"Well, I will admit that Jane Bennet is a sweet girl. She is charming and genteel. But her *mother*!" Caroline cried.

Bingley released a deep breath and nodded. "Yes...I will concede that Mrs. Bennet is, perhaps, a little thoughtless, but Miss Bennet—"

Caroline cut him off before he could finish. "I heard Eliza Bennet is reputed to be a local beauty. What do you say to that, Mr. Darcy?"

With his shoulder pressed against the mantelpiece, Darcy raised his cup to his lips and sipped the warm liquid. "I'd just as soon call her mother a wit," he said. "Except for, perhaps, her eyes, she has hardly a good feature in her face."

The Bingley sisters erupted in laughter.

Bingley stood to his feet and shook his head as he approached his friend. "Darcy, I shall never understand why you go through the world determined to be displeased with everything and everyone in it."

"And I will never understand why you are so decided to approve of everything and everyone you meet. You never find fault in anyone or anything."

"Well, your opinions will not lessen mine of Miss Bennet. Dare to disagree with me, but I shall not think less of her," said Louisa.

"No, nor shall I," cried Miss Bingley. "I declare her to be a sweet girl even if she is born to such a disadvantage—her family, Louisa, I shudder to think of such connections."

"Yes," Louisa added, "Jane Bennet *is* a sweet girl. It is, however, unfortunate that she comes with little to recommend her, for I should like to know her better."

Mrs. Hurst cast her eyes upon Darcy. "You see, Mr. Darcy, we are not dissuaded by your disapproval."

"And I should not have you be so. You have minds of your own, and you should use them." Darcy placed his cup back in its saucer and set it on the side table. "Now if you will excuse me, I must retire for the evening. I've had quite an arduous day."

~*~

While lying in bed, Darcy's mind drifted back to the assembly hall and a pair of fine eyes the colour of Indian emeralds. They were the eyes of the woman who often came to him in his dreams, the woman with the long dark hair flowing down her back. Never in his wildest imagination had he considered the possibility that she was real, or that he might someday meet her facsimile. The wood nymph was a figment of his imagination. Miss Elizabeth Bennet was flesh and blood—a country miss from the wilds of Hertfordshire. And there the twain should never meet. Her family had no breeding. Her younger sisters were flirtatious hoydens who defied the essence of common decency and proper modesty, and her mother was the epitome of vulgarity.

However, as Darcy drifted off to sleep, he was forced to acknowledge that Miss Elizabeth Bennet's cheekiness had enticed him. The way she handled his slight was to be admired if for nothing less than the sheer impertinence of it. He chuckled and reached for his pillow, pulling it to his chest with a slight smile etching his features. Perhaps he should strive to know her better.

Chapter 4

The Bennets from Longbourn and the party from Netherfield had now had the pleasure of dining together on several occasions, and Darcy's fixation with the second Miss Bennet was growing with each encounter. Though he had not yet engaged her in conversation, he had watched her every move from a distance, closely examining her. His curiosity in her complex character, and his opinion of her physical appearance had gradually softened.

At first, he scarcely allowed her to be pretty. He had looked at her without admiration at the ball, and when they next had met, he looked at her only to criticise. But no sooner had he made it clear to himself and his friends that she had hardly a good feature in her face than he began to find it was rendered uncommonly intelligent by the beautiful expression of her deep-green eyes. To succeed this discovery were some others equally mortifying.

Though he had detected with a critical eye more than one failure of perfect symmetry in her form, he was forced to acknowledge her figure to be light and pleasing, and in spite of his assertion that her manners were not those of the fashionable world, he was caught by their easy playfulness. She attracted him like a moth drawn to a flame and, furthermore, was quite possibly the first woman to have ever done so, though many a more handsome woman had tried. Then, to his complete astonishment, he often found his eyes tracing over her form while he imagined what might lie beneath her petticoats. She fascinated him, and he began to wish to know more of her.

As a step towards conversing with her, he attended to her conversation with others, paying close attention to every word she uttered and every nuance of her expression. He watched her during dinner at Netherfield, and then when they dined at Longbourn, he was sure to observe how she moved within her family circle. And now at the party at Lucas Lodge, he paid even closer attention, particularly to the way in which she conversed with Colonel Forster.

Admiring her easy manners and how she teased the Colonel, Darcy began to think of his sister and that Miss Bennet could quite possibly be a good companion to her as Mrs. Annesley had suggested. She was about his sister's height and was the proper age to become a close friend. And unlike Miss Bingley and all the others from his sphere, Miss Bennet was warm and friendly. She spoke with genuine kindness. If he were to choose a friend for Georgiana, his choice would be this country lass, though he knew full well they could never be equals in the eyes of the *ton*, nor would his family approve. And truth be told, he could never approve of her either.

Noticing that the conversation with the Colonel had ended, Darcy casually stepped in Elizabeth's direction where she was now speaking with her friend, Miss Lucas.

A Man in Want of a Wife

Approaching them without any intention of speaking, Darcy was utterly surprised when the object of his interest turned to him.

"Did you not think, Mr. Darcy, that I expressed myself uncommonly well just now, when I was teasing Colonel Forster to give a ball at Meryton?"

Delighted to be singled out, he replied, "With great energy, but it is a subject which always makes a lady energetic."

"You are severe on us," she returned with a tinge of sparkle in her voice.

Miss Charlotte glanced between them. "Eliza does enjoy sporting, Mr. Darcy, but it will be *her* turn soon to be teased," Miss Lucas said smiling before returning her gaze to her friend.

"I am going to open the instrument, Eliza, and you know what follows."

"You are a very strange creature by way of a friend, Charlotte! Always wanting me to play and sing before anybody and everybody! If my vanity had taken a musical turn, you would have been invaluable, but as it is, I would really rather not sit down before those who must be in the habit of hearing the very best performers," she said glancing at Darcy.

"Eliza, I will not be dissuaded. You shall perform." Turning to Mr. Darcy, Miss Lucas asked, "Would you not like to hear Eliza play, Mr. Darcy?"

"Indeed, it would be a pleasure," he said, staring at Elizabeth with a closed expression.

"Very well, then. If it must be so, it must." And gravely glancing at Darcy, she added, "There is a fine old saying, which everybody here is, of course, familiar with: 'Keep your breath to cool your porridge', and I shall keep mine to swell my song."

Darcy gave a reserved smile. "A sentiment in keeping with your personality, I'm sure."

As Elizabeth took her seat at the pianoforte, Darcy found the closest chair and moved it near the instrument, intent on catching every note and observing her presentation with a critical eye.

Her performance was pleasing, though by no means capital. After a song or two, and before she could reply to the entreaties of several that she should sing again, she was eagerly succeeded at the instrument by her sister Miss Mary, whom Darcy perceived to have the unfortunate consequence of being the only plain one in the family. Nonetheless, to Miss Mary's credit, she worked hard for her accomplishments and by her air, he surmised, was always impatient for display.

Upon hearing her performance, however, he had just as soon she had not. Though her skill at the pianoforte was tolerable, her song was enough to set the hounds to howling, and if left unchecked, drive every man from the room. Miss Mary had neither genius nor taste, and though vanity had given her application, it had also given her likewise a pedantic air and conceited manner, which might have been acceptable for someone in possession of a higher degree of excellence than she had achieved.

Conversely, Darcy perceived that Miss Elizabeth was easy and unaffected by the opinion of others. Her performance had been received with much more pleasure, though she did not play half so well as her sister.

Miss Mary, at the end of a long concerto, was glad to purchase praise and gratitude by playing Scottish and Irish airs at the request of her younger sisters, who, with some of the Miss Lucases and two or three officers, joined eagerly in dancing at one end of the room.

Darcy stood near them in silent indignation at such a mode of passing the evening, to the exclusion of all conversation, and was too much engrossed by his own thoughts to perceive that Sir William Lucas stood near until that gentleman spoke.

"What a charming amusement for young people this is, Mr. Darcy! There is nothing like dancing, after all. I consider it as one of the first refinements of polished societies."

"Certainly, sir, and it has the advantage also of being in vogue amongst the less polished societies of the world."

"Say again?" Sir William looked on in confusion.

"Every savage can dance."

"Oh, yes. Yes, quite."

Recovering himself, Sir William smiled. "Your friend performs delightfully," he continued after a pause on seeing Bingley join the group, "and I doubt not that you are an adept in the science yourself, Mr. Darcy."

"You saw me dance at Meryton, I believe, sir."

"Yes, indeed, and received no inconsiderable pleasure from the sight. Do you often dance at St. James's?"

"Never, sir."

"Do you not think it would be a proper compliment to the place?"

"It is a compliment which I never pay to any place if I can avoid it."

"You have a house in town, I conclude?"

Darcy bowed.

"I had once some thoughts of fixing in town myself—for I am fond of superior society, but I did not feel quite certain that the air of London would agree with Lady Lucas. But now that Mr. Bingley and his sisters are among us, I do believe our society here in Meryton has perhaps improved."

He paused in hopes of an answer, but Darcy was not disposed to make any.

Miss Elizabeth was at that instant moving towards them, and Sir William, Darcy supposed, was struck with the notion of doing a very gallant thing and called out to her, "My dear Miss Eliza, why are not you dancing?" turning to Darcy he continued, "Mr. Darcy, you must allow me to present this young lady to you as a very desirable partner. You cannot refuse to dance, I am sure, when so much beauty is before you."

And, taking her hand, he would have given it to Darcy who was extremely surprised, and with much pleasure, willing to receive it.

However, to Darcy's dismay, she instantly drew back, and said with some discomposure to Sir William. "Indeed, sir, I...I have not the least intention of dancing. I entreat you not to suppose that I moved this way in order to beg for a partner."

Darcy, with grave propriety, recovered himself and spoke, "I would be delighted to be allowed the honour of your hand, Miss Bennet."

"Thank you, sir, but you will have to excuse me, for I am not inclined to dance at present."

"Come-come! Miss Eliza! Why ever not? You excel so well in the dance that it is cruel to deny me the happiness of seeing you, and though this gentleman dislikes the amusement in general, he has no objection."

"No, I suppose not, for Mr. Darcy is all politeness," Elizabeth said, smiling slyly.

A Man in Want of a Wife

"He is—he is, indeed, but considering the inducement, my dear Miss Eliza, we cannot wonder at his complaisance, for who would object to such a partner, ay, Darcy?"

Darcy gazed at Miss Elizabeth, his eyes intensely studying hers. The game they played of cat and mouse tantalized him, causing him to desire the dance even more than he had imagined.

Elizabeth, however, was not to be moved. She looked at him archly and turned away, much to his regret.

Darcy smiled inwardly. He realized she was mortified by Sir William's boldness, but her resistance had not injured her in his opinion, and he was still thinking of her with some complacency when he was thus accosted by Miss Bingley.

"I'm sure I can guess the subject of your reverie, Mr. Darcy." She chortled smugly.

"I should imagine not."

"You are considering how insupportable it would be to pass many tedious evenings in this manner—in such society, and indeed I am quite of your opinion. I was never more annoyed! The insipidity, and yet the noise—the nothingness—the self-importance of all these people! It is contemptible! What would I give to hear your strictures on them!"

"Your conjecture is totally wrong, I assure you."

Her laughter rang out. "Mr. Darcy, you intrigue me. Pray tell, what were you thinking?"

Darcy's eyes followed Miss Elizabeth around the room as he casually answered, "My mind was more agreeably engaged as I have been meditating on the very great pleasure which a pair of fine eyes in the face of a pretty woman can bestow."

Miss Bingley immediately fixed her eyes on his face. "And which lady is it among our fine society who has captured the attention of the enigmatic Mr. Darcy, thus inspiring such reflections?"

Darcy replied with great intrepidity, "Miss Elizabeth Bennet."

"Miss Elizabeth Bennet!" repeated Miss Bingley. "I am all astonishment! How long has she been such a favourite, and pray, when am I to wish you joy?"

"That is exactly the question which I expected you to ask," he said with a dry wit. "A lady's imagination is very rapid. It jumps from admiration to love, and from love to matrimony, in a moment. I knew you would be wishing me joy." *...and what if I did choose her? What would you think then?*

"Nay, if you are so serious about it, I shall consider the matter as absolutely settled. You will have a charming mother-in-law, indeed, and, of course, she will be always at Pemberley with you."

He listened to her with perfect indifference while she chose to entertain herself in this manner, and as his composure convinced her that all was safe, her wit flowed insufferably long.

~*~

That night in the confines of his chamber, Darcy took out pen and paper and began to answer his most recent letter from his cousin, Colonel Fitzwilliam. He expressed his happiness in Georgiana's latest accomplishments in music and art and then began to tell of his time in Hertfordshire.

It was true, as his cousin had disclosed in his previous missive, that the more time spent with people with whom one has nothing in common, the less one sees of their faults. He went on to tell of the various families in the neighbourhood, listing their qualities to a greater degree than he did their shortcomings. He told of his evening at Lucas Lodge and Miss Elizabeth Bennet, how well she played, and how much he enjoyed her performance. He spoke of her wit and charm and how he thought that if she had been from a more well-connected family, she would make a good friend to Georgiana.

He ended his letter with news of Colonel Forster who was to winter the militia in Meryton before moving to Brighton in the spring. In two days' time he and Bingley would be dining with the officers, and he would give Colonel Fitzwilliam's salutations and regards to him then.

When the letter was sealed, Darcy leaned back in his chair and linked his hands behind his head.

"Miss Elizabeth Bennet," he said out loud. "You have little to recommend you but your charm. From conversations I've had with others in the neighbourhood, I know that your father's estate is entailed away from the female line and that your mother is a spendthrift. Two thousand a year and you should live rather well and yet your mother spends it as quickly as it is made. What will become of you if no one suitable offers for you, and if one does, will your family become an albatross around his neck?"

He sighed. "You are everything I would want in a wife, and I would consider you if not for your low connections, your vulgar mother, and two very silly sisters who would be an embarrassment to me amongst my closest associates. No matter what I might wish, things *are* as they are, and I had best not raise your expectations."

Darcy sighed once more as he extinguished the flame of his candle. In spite of all he knew, he fell asleep with visions of Miss Elizabeth Bennet playing in his dreams, riding his white stallion with nothing for a covering but her long, dark hair.

~*~*~*~

Chapter 5

The morning after the dinner party at Lucas Lodge, Darcy rose early for his morning ride. He wanted to look over the east pastures and survey the work Bingley's steward had begun on the irrigation ditches in preparation for the spring planting season. He also wished to explore Bingley's wooded groves for sport. Whilst riding there two days previous, he had seen a herd of deer near the edge of a dense growth of trees. These trees, he had suggested Bingley cut for lumber to supply the local mills near Town, but at present, they were the home of what Darcy believed to be a large population of fallow and red deer. If that be the case, then he would suggest they host a shooting party and invite the neighbours. Mr. Hurst, he knew, would be very pleased to sport a deer shoot, as shooting and wine were his passions in life. And then again, Darcy reasoned, if he were unfortunate enough to be married to one of Bingley's sisters, perhaps drink and sport would be his passion in life, as well.

Moving down the stairs quickly, he made his way to the small dining room. He had hoped to have his morning meal and exit the house before either of the Bingley sisters rose for the day. But that was not to be. Turning the corner, he met Miss Bingley at the door.

"Good morning, Mr. Darcy. I trust you slept well. Come, sir, please join me," she cooed. "I had Cook prepare all your favourites. We have French toast, dipped in your favourite wine mixed with orange juice, plum cake with sugar on top just the way you like it. There is also a side of orange marmalade spread on fresh bread, and the eggs and ham are cooked to perfection. We even have American white sauce, which I believe your cousin from South Carolina calls *gravy*. His wife was gracious enough to send the recipe when I expressed a fondness for it."

Miss Bingley moved to the sideboard and began filling his plate while he looked on in silence. Had she but read his eyes, she would have realized that he was anything but pleased.

"Come, Mr. Darcy," she said, placing his plate on the table across from hers. "I have fresh coffee from South America. It had only recently arrived from the mountains of Peru before we left Town. I was one of the first to make a purchase when the ship docked. Such refinements one may find only in London, and only if one knows all the right warehouses to shop, which, of course, I do. And do you not think I have set a fine table? Oh, I know the flowers are nothing to those from Pemberley's orangery, but they are the best to be had in this county. Mrs. Robinson grows them in her hot house. And the linens are from India. Louisa and I embroidered the napkins and stitched the edgings on the cloth. What do you think? Is it not elegant?"

Darcy gazed at her in astonishment, and after some moments, he replied with civility, "You set a very sophisticated table, Miss Bingley. I am sure Charles is well pleased. You do him proud."

Caroline's eyes sparkled with delight as Darcy sat down, taking his seat to the right of where Charles would sit.

Miss Bingley poured Darcy's coffee and then took her seat, being sure to do so in an elegant manner.

"Another dull tedious day, Mr. Darcy. I suppose we will once again be visited by every family in the neighbourhood. Mr. Darcy," she hissed beneath her breath, "did you know last evening, Sir William actually offered Louisa and I his assistance in society should he ever come to Town! Can you imagine *him* assisting *us* in society?" She laughed.

"Ay, no, I cannot," Darcy replied, cutting his French toast without looking up. "Nor do I wish to," he said privately.

"Good morning, Charles, Louisa, Mr. Hurst," Caroline said, glancing up as her brother and sister appeared at the sideboard. "It is good of you to join us. I thought Mr. Hurst might wish to sleep in after our late evening. There is a fresh pot of coffee and one of tea. Sugar and cream are on the table."

Darcy stood and bowed while Hurst grumbled as he served himself, piling his plate high.

"Reginald expressed a wish to rise early," Louisa said. "And since he disturbed me in so doing, I decided to join you at breakfast. Perhaps we shall go into the village later and see if there is anything of interest on Main Street." She glanced at her sister. "Caroline?"

"No, I think not. Charles and I have been once, and *once* is quite enough for me. The butcher shop is tolerable, but I have already made the order for the week."

Mrs. Hurst took her seat next to her husband who had already begun consuming his meal, and therefore, paid no attention to the conversation around him.

Caroline glanced between Darcy and her sister.

"What families we were forced to keep company with last evening! What agonies we endured: the Longs, the Gouldings, the Millers, the Thormans, and then there are those Philipses. Do you know, Charles, that Mrs. Philips is Mrs. Bennet's sister and that they have a brother in *Cheapside*?" Her face twisted in an unpleasant manner. "Sir William mentioned it to Louisa and me."

"Umm…yes, that among other things," Mrs. Hurst replied.

"I wonder what sort of shop he keeps." Caroline smirked. "One brother in *trade* and another is a country attorney. Such low connections. There are none of them from polished society. Not at all suitable for our circle, and yet Charles must live here amongst them."

Busily cutting his ham, Bingley never looked up as he replied, "I find them charming—friendly and extremely agreeable—especially Sir William."

"Charming, indeed!" Caroline cried. "I heard from one of the ladies present that Sir William kept a shop before his elevation to the knighthood. I wonder what sort of shop he kept."

Mrs. Hurst burst out in giggles, encouraging her sister in her mockeries of Hertfordshire society.

Darcy said nothing, listening to Miss Bingley's effusions and grating platitudes with complete unresponsiveness while she continued in this manner, which seemed

A Man in Want of a Wife

to satisfy her. But had she been looking, Caroline could have read his disapproval in his expression.

"Charles, I hear you and Mr. Hurst will be riding into Meryton this morning." She turned to Darcy while pouring herself another cup of tea. "Will you be accompanying them, Mr. Darcy?"

"No," Darcy said. "I've plans to inspect the irrigation work Mr. Goolsby is conducting in the east pasture, and then I shall assess the groves. There appears to be plenty of young pines and various hardwoods suitable for lumber, and the forest is teeming with deer, fox, and what all else, I scarcely know. If it is, however, as I believe, perhaps your brother will host a shooting party."

"Indeed, I shall!" Charles spoke up. "Hurst and I have been in great need of some sport, and I wish to exercise the hounds I purchased from Mr. Goulding. What is your opinion, Reggie?"

"Indeed," Mr. Hurst replied. "Damn waste of a day spent doing anything less. Sport, good food, and fine wine, what man could ask for anything more?" he replied, rising for a second helping.

Caroline turned to Darcy.

"If I were of a mind to ride, I would—"

"But you do not," Darcy said, raising his fork to his lips. "And I am not of a mind to entertain when work is to be attended to."

"Yes, but—"

"Miss Bingley, if you will excuse me," Darcy said, wiping the corners of his mouth before placing his napkin beside his plate. "I must be about my business. Scouting the woodlands is no place for a lady, especially when the terrain is unknown." He rose from his seat.

With a bow, he exited the room for the entryway where he took his beaver and riding crop from the waiting servant and left for his morning ride.

~*~

Reaching the stables, he had the boy saddle his horse and asked after his hound.

"Where is Old Sam, Mr. Smith?"

"He left out early, sir and has not yet returned. He must have caught the scent of a rabbit. He does seem to like them."

"Yes, he does. It is a habit I have been unable to rid him of." Mounting his charger, Darcy looked to the boy and took his reins. "When he returns, see to it that he has one of the bones from the butcher. I had hoped to exercise him this morning, but it looks as if he has left without me."

"Aye, sir."

Darcy departed, riding his horse at a full run in the direction of the eastern pasture near the lake. The cool wind in his face served to relieve the tension building in his chest. Last night, much to his mortification, he had dreamed of Miss Elizabeth Bennet. He had had first one dream and then another, each one bordering on the edge of indecency. Many he could not recall with clarity, but the last one, however, he remembered vividly.

They were walking along the lake at Pemberley moving in the direction of Pemberley's cove. She was smiling up at him as he turned to caress her face and remove a loose curl from her brow. Darcy intended to pull her into an embrace and kiss her, and as he reached for her, she reached for him. In his mind, he imagined they would make love under the trees by the waterfall in the cove. But when his fingertips were about to touch her skin, she suddenly vanished, and he awoke in a cold sweat with his heart pounding. He shuddered at the remembrance...the emotion, the desire, the stirrings in his soul. It had been intense, and at the time, seemed *very* real.

He moaned and shook his head as he momentarily closed his eyes. Much to his distress, thoughts and images of Miss Elizabeth were beginning to invade his conscious mind, and he was unsure if he liked the prospect of it; for it was unsupportable to think a man of his distinction and rank could succumb to the charms of a country girl, especially one with nothing to recommend her.

Looking ahead, the men working on the irrigation system came into sight. Taking a deep breath to clear his mind, he slowed his horse and entered the work area. There he found them already busy digging out the soil, debris, and saplings from the existing ditches and replacing the rotten wood with new pine logs. He spoke briefly with Bingley's steward, having noted that the pitch was a little thin, and instructed that an extra measure of tar was to be used so that the seal would last through several planting seasons before having to be redone.

After assuring himself that Mr. Goolsby's work was coming along satisfactorily, he left for the grove he had visited previously when he had had little time to explore. This time he would investigate its offerings more thoroughly.

Trotting in and out of the forest, he saw several deer—many more than he had expected. The herd indeed needed thinning. There were also wild boars and plenty of fox. A shooting party was undeniably in order. And the trees, he noted, were more than ample to generate a good living from the lumber alone. His friend had chosen wisely in his selection of Netherfield Park. In fact, the more Darcy studied the land, the more he approved.

Having finished surveying the wooded copse which bordered the neighbouring estate of Longbourn, Darcy was about to turn back to the manor house when he looked up and saw the same girl from his first visit to Netherfield. She was standing in a grassy field on the mount. He started to look away when something caught his eye. He rose up in his saddle. She was playing with a dog, tossing a stick and running. Darcy narrowed his eyes and focused harder. He instantly recognized the animal. It was his hound! And the girl was none other than Miss Elizabeth Bennet.

Darcy could not say what force propelled his horse forward, but he found himself being drawn to the scene.

Turning to take the climb from a different approach so as not to seem obvious, he travelled up the hill through the wood and eventually came out into the clearing to see her struggling with his hound tugging on a stick.

Miss Elizabeth looked up to see him just as she fell on her backside, having won the battle with the dog.

"Mr. Darcy!" she cried in shock.

"Miss. Bennet," he replied, tipping his hat.

Dismounting from his horse, Darcy walked over to where she sat sprawled in a very unladylike fashion and extended his hand.

Blushing furiously, Elizabeth took his hand and rose to her feet with his help. Her hair was dishevelled with several long dark tendrils falling from their pins. She nervously smoothed the wrinkles from her skirt before forcing her hair back under her bonnet.

"Do you often walk out this early, Miss Bennet?" Darcy asked, admiring her beauty.

She breathed in sharply, and her eyes challenged him. "Yes. I find early morning walks to be an excellent form of exercise. The air is exhilarating. Would you not agree, Mr. Darcy?" she asked archly.

"Yes, of course. I often ride out myself for the very same purpose."

"Indeed. Exercise is very beneficial to one's health."

Darcy took in the scenery. "What is the name of this place? It seems very peaceful."

"It is Oakham Mount, sir, and yes, it is indeed peaceful."

"Do you often come here?"

"As often as may be. It is my favorite place. When I was a child, I would come here to read my book and play. Sometimes I ran among the flowers you see growing here. I would often pick a bouquet for my sister Jane and Mamma."

As she spoke, Darcy glanced around at the flowering meadow of heather growing in thick tufts and envisioned a little girl running in a field of lavender and pink, imagining what she might have looked like then. Was her hair tied up in ribbons, dark and flowing behind her as she ran, or was it lightened by the sun, and did she have a dog for her companion as he often did as a boy?

Just as quickly as his thoughts were lost in Miss Elizabeth Bennet, they were interrupted by his hound coming out of the woods with yet another stick in his mouth. The dog hurried to nudge Miss Elizabeth's hand before laying it at her boots.

Darcy whistled and the hound came and dropped down obediently at his feet.

"Sam seems to have found a friend."

"Is he your hound, Mr. Darcy?"

"Yes. I wondered where he'd gotten off to. He likes to run of a morning, and sometimes he picks up a scent and will be gone for hours. He appears to have caught *your* scent, Miss Bennet."

Once more Miss Elizabeth blushed furiously under the scrutiny of Darcy's piercing gaze, and it amused him to see it. Her eyes sparkled all the more like shimmering emeralds in a pool of milky skin kissed by the sun with a tinge of sweet roses painted on her cheeks. She was lovely, the picture of health and vitality.

"Mr. Darcy, if you will excuse me, I must be on my way. I am expected back at Longbourn for our morning meal. I must not be late."

She dropped a curtsey, and he bowed as she turned and moved quickly down the path.

Watching her go, he caught the faint scent of lavender, a woodsy fragrance he associated with vitality. Darcy paused in his thoughts and took a deep breath. A slight smile crept across his features. As she ran down the winding path towards her home, he also noted that one lone curl had once again escaped her bonnet and was travelling down her back, but little did he realize that in her going, she wore a decided scowl on her countenance.

He looked down at his hound. "So you like her, do you?"

The dog whimpered.

"Come, Sam," Darcy said with a sigh. "Let us go home."

Mounting his horse, the man and his faithful, if wayward, companion left Oakham Mount, cantering through the trails until they reached the dell where they broke into a full run.

~*~

Trotting into the gate of Netherfield Park, Darcy's mind was filled with thoughts of Miss Elizabeth Bennet and the fresh, clean scent of lavender, which he would now and forever associate with *her*: the girl in the meadows. She was unlike any young woman he had ever had the pleasure of knowing. It was clear from casual observance that she had an appetite for living, but had she paid half as much attention to the development of her mind?

Taking the steps two at a time to the portico, his good mood quickly dissipated as he ran directly into the path of Miss Bingley with her dour face.

~*~*~*~

Chapter 6

Pressing his signet ring into the hot wax, Darcy sealed his latest letter to his sister. Georgiana was faring much better, and for that, he was greatly relieved. After placing his missive in the silver salver for his man to post, Darcy collected his letter-paper and pen and put them back in their proper places. When those items were secured in the locked box, he rose from his seat and walked over to the curtains, pulling them back to gaze out onto Bingley's garden. The sky had darkened considerably since breakfast. He shuddered, for he could feel the cold autumn chill in the air and knew rain was likely.

"Umm," he mumbled to himself. "There will be no morning ride today, and I highly doubt *she* will be walking out in this weather either. It is not fit for man or beast. Even Sam will most likely keep to the stable."

Darcy had not been back to Oakham Mount since his meeting with Miss Elizabeth Bennet, for he had no intention of paying her any particular regard. Though she might be engaging enough to arouse his interest, her family with their low connections in addition to her presumed lack of a dowry were enough to drive any affection he might entertain firmly away.

He knew, however, from all of Miss Bingley's effusions at breakfast this morning that the elder Miss Bennet would be calling round for luncheon, and he was much relieved that neither Bingley nor he would be in attendance. It was even more of a relief that Miss Elizabeth would not also be in attendance, though for the sake of her sister, he almost wished she would be. Knowing the Bingley sisters as he did, he could only imagine the interrogation Miss Jane Bennet would have to endure during her visit.

Closing the curtains, Darcy took his great coat, cane, and beaver and left to join Bingley and Hurst in the entrance hall where they would soon be on their way.

~*~

Gazing out of the coach window, Darcy watched the thick, dark clouds roll in across the ever darkening sky. There was a sharp bite in the frosty air as well, signalling that winter was not far behind. He shivered and thought of how a man caught out in this weather could quickly become chilled to the bone, catching his death of a cold.

A loud crack of thunder was heard close by as the heavens opened up, sending the rain down with driving force. Darcy was about to close the curtain when he spied an indistinguishable figure in the distance coming from the direction of Longbourn. *Could it be...Miss...Surely not! Her father would certainly allow her the use of his carriage, would he not?*

Darcy narrowed his eyes to bring the dark unfortunate rider into focus. It was clearly a woman, for she rode side saddle. For a moment, he thought that perhaps it was a servant, but then he quickly put that notion away; for not even a servant would venture out in this, and if one did, it certainly would *not* be a woman.

He drew in a quick breath shaking his head. Nothing would surprise him where the Bennets were concerned—especially Mrs. Bennet. The more he had come to know of her, the more he was convinced that she was allowed to do as she pleased and was never checked by her husband.

Darcy drew the curtain across the window, but kept what he had seen to himself, hoping it was not as he supposed. But if it was, he knew she would soon be at Netherfield where there was at least a warm fire.

~*~

Once they arrived at the makeshift headquarters for the Meryton Militia, Darcy, Bingley, and Mr. Hurst settled in to luncheon with Colonel Forster and the officers. Darcy and Mr. Bingley engaged them on a variety of topics while Mr. Hurst ate heartily with frequent tips to his wine glass for refills, which all the gentlemen declared the vintage to be some of the finest wine they had ever consumed. Colonel Forster prided himself on its quality as it had been seized from the French whilst on a campaign in Portugal. After their meal, the Colonel called for cigars, and he and his guests settled in for more conversation.

"Mr. Darcy," Colonel Forster said, "I understand you are the cousin of my good friend Colonel Fitzwilliam. How is the Old Ironsides these days?"

"Old what?"

"Old Ironsides! You do know how he came to be known as Old Ironsides, do you not?"

"No," Darcy answered with a slight laugh. "I'm afraid I know little of my cousin's life in the army. However, Fitzwilliam is well and sends his regards." Darcy paused. "Colonel, I'm not sure I have ever heard the story of '*Old Ironsides*.' Why don't you enlighten me? What is my cousin about when I am not around?"

Colonel Forster chuckled. "He hasn't informed you, you say. Well, then you are in for a true delight. I am sure you are aware that your cousin has a will of iron when it comes to getting things done—especially when it comes to duty and obligation."

"Of that I am well aware. He also has this implacable habit of reminding others of *their* duties and responsibilities as well," Darcy replied.

"That I would know nothing of, though I am certain of its validity; it surely sounds just like him! Nonetheless, when it comes to military campaigns, that is something of which I can speak with some authority. If I know anything of the matter, and I most certainly do, your cousin should soon become *General Fitzwilliam*; for on the battlefield, he charges when others fall back to scuttle and run. But not Old Ironsides—best damn cavalry leader in the whole damned army! The Dragoon could do no better.

"Unlike others, Fitzwilliam leads the charge himself. Cannons and bullets fly by without so much as nicking his regimentals. Colonel Fitzwilliam exemplifies the best of His Majesty's elite fighting forces. And furthermore, he is a man of deep personal convictions, which, I might add, extends to the field where he adheres to a strict ethical code, offering mercy when he can. And whilst in quarters, he neither drinks nor gambles. Nor does he partake in the traditional spoils of war. He holds his men to the highest level of integrity. He is a man of honour, one I am proud to have served with on the continent, and should we go against Napoleon again, I hope I share the field with him once more.

"But as to how he came to be known as Old Ironsides, well, it is his military name given to him by none other than Major-General Sir William Ponsonby himself when Colonel Fitzwilliam outfoxed the French in one of the most intense battles we ever fought; as a result, his company, which was badly outnumbered, took a key village in Spain for His Majesty. The General says that not since the days of Oliver Cromwell has there been such a commander as your cousin in the regiment of horse, though I must say my friend despises the comparison."

"That is quite a commendation you bestow upon my cousin, Colonel Forster, though being of Irish decent on my mother's side, I perfectly share my cousin's resentment of Cromwell, given how his military skills were perfected on our ancestors," Darcy said. "It is no small wonder Fitzwilliam holds you in such high regard. I shall pass along your compliments."

"Indeed," replied Colonel Forster as he puffed on his cigar.

"What are your plans for the militia, Colonel Forster?" Bingley asked.

"We plan to winter here in Meryton whilst we train. We will run through several drilling exercises meant to prepare us for battle. Then, if all goes as planned, we will spend the summer in Brighton where we will train for defensive tactical support. We could quite possibly be deployed should the need arise with the French, but since we have yet to fill our ranks to the capacity needed for such an engagement, should it come to one, Captain Carter will be leaving for Town in the morning to enlist more men and officers. There is a promising young man who has come to our attention. It would appear that he has come into some rather bad luck and wishes to sign up."

"Do you know his name?" Darcy asked "Perhaps one of us might know him, or possibly have knowledge of him."

The Colonel knitted his brow and shook his head. He turned to Captain Carter who set his wine glass aside.

"It is I who has been in contact with a friend who told me of a friend who has a friend in need of a situation. I have not, as of yet, enquired as to his given name, though I believe it to be Willoughby, or something of that nature. I am told, however, that he is pronounced to be a fine figure of a man with distinguished manners and that he has a gentleman's education. I am to meet with him whilst in Town. If he is suitable, we shall sign him up! As Colonel Forster has said, we are sorely in need of officers, especially those with a gentleman's education. Lieutenant Denny speaks well of him, and Denny is a fine fellow."

"Yes-yes," Colonel Forster added, "He comes very highly recommended. His manners are reputed to be impeccable, and if half of what we've heard is the truth, he carries himself with good regulation. I think he shall add distinction to my regiment and discipline to my men; for my men are in considerable need of training in that area and my officers are in even greater need of society—so much so that I am considering a ball. There seem to be plenty of young ladies quite willing to entertain my officers, would you not say, Mr. Bingley?"

"Unquestionably!" Bingley added in a tone of obvious joy. "In truth," he said, "I enjoyed myself to such an extent at the Meryton assembly that I wish to repay the kindness shown to me by the community. I am considering giving a ball myself."

"Indeed!" the Colonel exclaimed. "That would be a very fine thing."

The men talked and laughed, sharing stories of military campaigns and events in the news until the hour was quite late. Mr. Darcy, Mr. Hurst, and Mr. Bingley bid their farewells and left for Netherfield.

The rain was still coming down steadily, and the wind blew hard, rocking the carriage as they travelled. Winding through the muddy roads, Darcy had two things on his mind: the woman on horseback, unchaperoned in the rain, and the mysterious man Captain Carter was so anxious to meet in Town. If the former was, indeed, Miss Jane Bennet, then Darcy's opinion of her parents had sunk even lower in his estimation of their character, and the latter, with his happy manners, sounded familiar—familiar to the point that Darcy wondered if his *old friend* had decided to try his hand in the militia and pretend to claim an honest living.

Tilting his head, he thought to himself *...Mr. Wickham has most probably run through the two thousand I gave him. He would be in need of a situation by now, and when he wishes, he can exhibit all those things Captain Carter described...happy manners, charming, distinguished... and most certainly a smooth tongue, but surely he would not dare to show his face here...that is... unless he does not know that I am here as well.*

~*~

Arriving back at Netherfield Park, the gentlemen were met with the parting discourse of Mr. Jones. Miss Bingley was obviously distressed, and Mrs. Hurst could not speak badly enough about the Bennets.

"Caroline, what is the meaning of such uproar. Are you unwell?"

"No! It isn't me who is unwell, Charles. It is Miss Bennet."

"Miss Bennet! Miss Jane? She is unwell? Where is she?"

"You are not to worry. I have her comfortably situated in the guest wing where she is being well attended. But her mother! And her father! I cannot believe they allowed her to travel here on horseback and in such dreadful weather! Do they not even own a carriage? Who are these people?!"

Darcy tore his gloves from his fingers and threw them on the entry table. So it had been Miss Bennet, just as he feared.

"I must go to her at once! Come Darcy! Let us see about Miss Bennet!"

Darcy let out a noisy breath as the footman took his coat.

Caroline, paling at the thought of Charles bounding into Miss Bennet's sick room, accompanied only by Mr. Darcy, let out a cry, stating irritably, "Charles you cannot go up alone. Do you want to compromise yourself?"

Hurriedly she climbed the stairs ahead of him and Darcy, turning left as they all proceeded to the second door on the right. Charles gave two knocks and entered to find his angel laying there, a maid applying a cool cloth to her head.

He moved to take the cloth from the woman's hand, but Miss Bingley quickly preceded him and dipped it into the basin of cold water. As she grudgingly applied it to Miss Bennet's forehead Charles enquired, "Miss Bennet, are you much sick? Does it hurt when my sister touches you?"

"No, sir, I am not much sick. I have a cold, and I'm afraid my head aches, but Mr. Jones left a draught of bitter herbs for my cold and a birch tincture for my headache. I shall be well soon," she replied sweetly though her voice was weak.

While Charles and Miss Bennet talked, Darcy stood by the window with his hands behind his back, twisting his signet ring and looking out onto the lawn at the leaves being blown about in the wind and rain. He was incensed. The Bennets were everything Miss Bingley claimed them to be and so much more. It was unthinkable to send a daughter out in this storm. Why would they do it?

He glanced back at Jane who lay there feverish and sick. Was this the machination of her matchmaking mother? Did she hope for Miss Bennet to be stranded here at Netherfield in order to ensnare his friend? The damsel in distress? Was that her mother's plan—to play upon his friend's amiable manners and good heart?

He snapped his head back around angrily and turned once more to the garden. The rain had cleared and the moon moved in and out from the thick billowing clouds. It was well into the evening. Darcy narrowed his eyes. Would they truly risk their daughter's life in order to catch a rich husband? He wondered…

~*~

That evening as they all gathered around the dining table, Miss Bingley and her sister would have their say, disparaging the Bennet family with every breath they took.

"Charles, I invited Miss Bennet to luncheon so that Louisa and I could come to know her better. I had no inkling that she would arrive on horseback. Can you imagine it?" She turned to her sister.

"No. Sister, I cannot imagine anyone coming on horseback even if the weather had been flawless—but for a gentlewoman to ride in such weather? Well, it just isn't done!"

"What do you think, Mr. Darcy?" Miss Bingley asked. "Is it not a…a…" she motioned with her hand as if searching for the precise word to express her outrage at such a notion.

"Neglect on the part of one's parents to look after the welfare of a daughter," Darcy completed for her."

"Precisely!"

Charles slumped in his chair, his eyes never leaving his plate. "I am sure there is a reasonable explanation for it. Perhaps the horses were needed elsewhere, or perhaps the carriage was not available. I'm sure Mr. Bennet did not—"

"Did not what?!" Darcy snapped, putting his knife and fork aside and catching his friend's gaze. "The truth of the matter is, Bingley, that Miss Bennet *did* come on horseback in the cold wind and rain, and now she is sick."

He stood to his feet and threw down his napkin in disgust. "Keep me informed as to Miss Bennet's condition. Should she take a turn for the worse, I shall send straightaway for my physician in Town. Colds can rapidly progress into more serious conditions, and I sincerely doubt this village has a proper doctor to care for one should they become critically ill. Now, if you will excuse me, I must retire for the evening."

"Oh, but Mr. Darcy, will you not join us for cards? Charles has declared he will not play, and thus we will be one short if you do not."

"Miss Bingley, I am not in the mood for cards at present. I have several matters of business I must attend to in my room. So, if you will excuse me, I will join you tomorrow, and be sure to keep me informed as to the welfare of Miss Bennet."

Darcy gave a proper bow and retreated for the privacy of his chamber. It was true. He did have matters of business to which he must attend. There was yet another letter from Georgiana, and one small matter with his solicitor, Mr. Mann, about some property in London he wished to sell. But more importantly, he needed to remove himself from the Bingley sisters and their visceral verbiage as they prattled on about the Bennets. Although he knew they spoke the truth, he tired of hearing it just the same.

After making himself ready for bed, Darcy dismissed his man and went to his desk where he pulled a piece of paper from the letter-box. Placing it aside, he picked up his latest letter from Georgiana. As Darcy broke the seal and began to read, a smile curled his lips ever so slightly. He noted his sister's curiosity about Hertfordshire and the people of Meryton. He had mentioned Miss Elizabeth by name briefly after their dinner at Lucas Lodge, and though he had avoided the subject since then, he knew Miss Elizabeth was ever present in Georgiana's thoughts, for Darcy had never mentioned a woman to anyone before.

Laying the letter aside, Darcy put pen to paper. He knew he could no longer avoid the subject of the locals, especially Miss Elizabeth, or Georgiana would persist until she was satisfied. Therefore, he gave her a brief description of everything she had enquired about along with the best he could say about the village and the people living there. Though Georgiana had improved vastly, he knew she was still on tenterhooks, and for that reason, he weighed his words carefully, for he did not wish to raise her expectations for his felicity any more than he did those of Miss Elizabeth Bennet.

Miss Elizabeth Bennet, he wrote, *is a vivacious young woman whom I would say is about four perhaps five years older than yourself. She seems to have a passion for living and loves to walk out whenever she can. I have met her once on her walks. It would appear that Old Sam has taken a liking to her and that is how I met her. Miss Bennet was walking in the meadows on a hillside about two days previous. When I came upon her, she was engaged in a game of fetch with Sam.*

Miss Elizabeth has four sisters. The youngest, Miss Lydia Bennet, is, I would say, about your age. Then there is Miss Catherine Bennet, the second youngest, Miss Mary Bennet, the middle sister, and lastly, the eldest, Miss Jane Bennet, who at present is ill here at Netherfield from a cold, but recovering, I hope.

Miss Mary enjoys the pianoforte as you do, but I must say that her sister, Miss Elizabeth performs with such feeling in her exhibition, that rarely have I ever heard anyone play better. Her song is very pleasing to the ears and her smile is engaging.

Darcy concluded his letter by sending Georgiana, whom he affectionately called Georgie, all his love.

Dropping his pen on the desk, he threw his head back in his chair and spoke disparagingly to himself. "When I finally meet a woman who fascinates me beyond the first look, it would have to be one with such low connections. A relationship with her is unacceptable; I would be the laughing stock of all of England! My friends would never accept such an alliance. And my family...I do not even want to entertain the idea of what they might think! It's insupportable; that's what it is!"

He winced. "Why, Miss Elizabeth Bennet, did you have to be born into such a family? Your father neglects his duty to his wife and family, allowing them, especially the younger daughters, to run amuck in want of correction. They rule the roost! Has the man no sense of propriety? If Miss Jane should die from this unfortunate excursion, what will they have gained from their neglect?"

A Man in Want of a Wife

Darcy glanced around the room. He would send for his man to enquire after Miss Bennet before he retired for the night. If she were found to be worse, he would then send for his physician and have him here before the cock crowed.

He had seen it often enough. Colds could easily worsen into putrid fever, which was nothing to be taken lightly. It almost always resulted in death and had even taken the life of his mother, Lady Anne Darcy, when he was a youth not more than Georgiana's age. If it were within his power to spare Miss Jane Bennet from that same fate, he would certainly take that responsibility upon himself.

~*~*~*~

Chapter 7

Early the next day Darcy was relieved to learn that the draughts given by the local apothecary had helped Miss Bennet sleep well through the night. Her fever was still higher than was normal, but otherwise her condition could be said to be stable; nevertheless, by Mr. Jones estimation, she could take a turn for the worse at any moment. There was no certainty, to say the least.

The rain had ceased sometime in the night, and the morning proved to be sunny and bright. The air was a bit cold, but other than that, it was a beautiful day, though unfortunately, not one suitable for riding out.

Given the pandemonium in the house, Darcy had decided to take a turn in the garden in order to escape Caroline's harping, sycophantic voice. If she was not criticizing the Bennet sisters, then she was fawning over him: filling his plate with food she perceived he was fond of, refilling his coffee cup before it was empty, and complimenting or affirming his every spoken word. She even parroted any thought she could conceive of to impress him with her wit and suitability as a wife. It tried his patience as a gentleman to remain civil, and if it were not for his deeply held friendship with Bingley, he would put her in her place without hesitation. But his friendship with Bingley meant a great deal to him, and therefore, for better or worse, Miss Bingley came along with it.

Stepping out into the garden, he was soon joined by Sam. The dog whimpered and obediently fell in line at Darcy's feet, looking up in expectation. Darcy grinned and reached down to rub his head, flapping his long ears from side to side.

"Sam, I see you have found me. Well, we shall have to settle for a walk today. In all this dirt, I am afraid a run will not do. What do you say, old boy? Are you ready to explore the gardens?"

Sam pranced about and barked.

"Come along, then. Let us walk."

Darcy and his hound ambled through the graveled pathways past the shrubberies and through the grove of trees bordering Netherfield's gardens until they were out into the open field. They had started up the hill to a tree near a rail fence when Sam suddenly barked and ran. Darcy looked up in time to find himself face to face with Miss Elizabeth Bennet as she jumped down from the fence gate, landing in a puddle of mud.

"Miss Bennet!"

"Mr. Darcy." She curtseyed, dropping her eyes to her feet and blushing furiously.

Darcy smiled inwardly. She was bewitching with her flushed cheeks and dark hair fighting to be free of its bonnet.

"Sam." Elizabeth glanced down at the dog wagging his tail while he licked her hand.

Darcy whistled. "Sam, heel. Where are your manners?" The dog quickly returned to his master and dropped down at his boots, whimpering softly.

A Man in Want of a Wife

"Miss Bennet, might I ask—"

"You may ask, and I may choose whether or not to answer." She jutted her chin upward in defiance as if to challenge him.

Darcy was taken by surprise, but quickly recovered.

"Miss Bennet...what are you doing here?"

"I've come to enquire after my sister."

"On foot?" he asked, glancing down at her boots covered in mud.

She tilted her head as she arched one eyebrow. "As you see."

After a brief moment of silence, Elizabeth enquired further. "Mr. Darcy, if you please, sir, I would ask of you to take me to Jane."

He shrugged his shoulders and turned towards the house.

"Follow me then," he said.

Sam dropped back and walked with Elizabeth, nudging her hand with his cold nose.

"Sam," Elizabeth said in a near whisper, "I don't think now is the time to play, but next time you meet me out, we shall have our game of fetch."

Sam barked and Elizabeth smiled.

Darcy glanced back and gave them both a sharp look before turning back to the path leading to the kitchen.

When they entered through the servants' entrance, Darcy addressed the cook, "Mrs. Ayers, would you see to it that Miss Bennet's shoes are cleaned, and when they are," he glanced at Elizabeth, "I shall take you to your sister's room."

"Lordy, Miss, what have you been up to out in all this dirt? But don't you worry none, Miss. I'll have you good as new before you can turn around," the old woman said kindly.

Darcy smiled. "I found her jumping puddles as she plodded over the countryside," he said. "Have her fit to be seen, Mrs. Ayers."

Elizabeth's eyes glared with anger as they bore into Mr. Darcy's, but she kept her tongue in check.

He then addressed Elizabeth further as she unlaced her boots and handed them to a servant. "Miss Bennet, I have it on good authority that your sister rested well through the night. Mr. Jones has called round and finds her no worse today than was expected. Her fever is still higher than he would like to see it, but I believe her headache is a little better. Rest assured that should she become worse, a doctor from Town will be summoned. Miss Bingley and Mrs. Hurst are doing everything possible to see to your sister's comfort."

"I thank you, Mr. Darcy," she said coldly. "But I am sure a doctor from Town will not be necessary, or at least, I hope not."

Darcy bowed and turned to the servant cleaning Elizabeth's boots. "When she is presentable send her to the breakfast room. I shall be there taking tea with Mr. Bingley."

"Yes, sir. It won't be but a minute more and the lady's boots will be as good as new," the maid said, dropping a curtsey.

But instead of leaving, Darcy remained and watched as he leaned against the wall with his legs crossed one over the other. Twisting his ring, he stared in fascination at the exchange between the servant and Miss Elizabeth Bennet.

"Now, Miss, we shall have you fit to be seen in as quick as a wink. No need to be tracking dirt through the house. The housekeeper is very particular about these floors, and I should not like to be scrubbing no floorboards on this fine autumn morning, cause when me finishes me work here, I gets to go and have me tea and breakfast with me friends, and I wouldn't want to miss it, Miss."

"Of course not. What is your name?" Elizabeth asked.

"I be Molly—Molly McFagan, Miss," the young girl replied.

"Molly, I would not wish to have you on your hands and knees scrubbing floors on my account," Elizabeth said with a smile as her eyes darted to Mr. Darcy, who was sporting an amused grin.

He caught the mirth in her bright eyes and gave a slight inclination with his head. And then, realizing that he had lingered longer than he should have, he bowed and quit the room.

As Elizabeth, ever determined to despise the man, watched him go, she felt a sense of relief to be rid of him. She took his silent stares as haughtiness and was more resolved than ever to avoid his company.

~*~

Standing before the Netherfield party in the breakfast parlour where they were assembled for their morning meal, Elizabeth was unabashed by her appearance as she enquired after her sister. She had not missed the Bingley sisters' eyes as they widened in shock and then narrowed in disdain when she entered their presence, but she was not concerned for their good opinion. Her only worry was for Jane.

On that account, Miss Bingley assured her that the best possible care was being given to Miss Bennet, and that she and Louisa had personally sat with her during much of the night. Pleased to hear this report, Elizabeth requested to be taken to Jane, and a servant was dispatched to take her to her sister's room in the guest quarters.

As Miss Elizabeth departed with the maid, Darcy's thoughts were pleasantly engaged in meditating on the brightness of her eyes and the pretty flush upon her pink cheeks. But no sooner had she quit the room than his attention was abruptly interrupted by Miss Bingley who began abusing her as soon as she was out of sight. Her manners were pronounced to be very bad indeed, a mixture of pride and impertinence; she had no conversation, no style, no taste, no beauty.

Mrs. Hurst thought the same, and added with a derisive smile, "She has nothing, in short, to recommend her, but being an excellent walker. I shall never forget her appearance just now. She really looked almost wild."

"She did indeed, Louisa. I could hardly keep my countenance. Very nonsensical to come at all! Why must *she* be scampering about the country, because her sister has a cold? Her hair, Louisa, so untidy, so blowsy! It's unthinkable!"

"Yes, dear sister, and her petticoat." Mrs. Hurst turned to Charles. "I hope you saw her petticoat, Brother—six inches deep in mud, I am absolutely certain. And the gown which had been let down to hide it, not doing its office."

"Your picture may be exact, Louisa," Bingley said, "but this was all lost upon me. I thought Miss Elizabeth Bennet looked remarkably well when she came into the room. Her dirty petticoat quite escaped my notice."

"*You* observed it, Mr. Darcy, I am sure," said Miss Bingley. "And I am inclined to think that you would not wish to see *your sister* make such an exhibition."

"Certainly not."

"To walk three miles, or four miles, or five miles, or whatever it is, above her ankles in dirt, and alone, quite alone! What could she mean by it? It seems to me to show an abominable sort of conceited independence, a most country-town indifference to decorum. And to think her parents allow such behaviour!" cried Louisa

"It shows an affection for her sister that is very pleasing," Bingley injected.

"I am afraid, Mr. Darcy," observed Miss Bingley, in a half-whisper, "that this little bold undertaking may have affected your admiration of her *fine eyes*."

"Not at all," he replied with indifference as he took his tea and moved to the window, staring out into the garden watching Sam chase a rabbit through the shrubberies. "They were brightened by the exercise."

A short pause followed this speech, and Mrs. Hurst began again.

"I have an excessive regard for Jane Bennet; she is really a very sweet girl, and I wish with all my heart she were well settled. But with such a father and mother, and such low connections, I am afraid there is no chance of it."

"I think I have heard you say that their uncle is an attorney in Meryton," Caroline said, repeating what she had already informed them of the day before, hoping to finally garner Mr. Darcy's attention.

"Yes," replied Mrs. Hurst, catching her sister's meaning. "And Jane herself informed us of the truth of it yesterday before she fell ill," Louisa said. "And furthermore Jane says they have another who lives somewhere near Cheapside on Gracechurch Street I do believe where poets and others of low birth live."

"That is capital," added her sister, and they both laughed heartily.

"If they had uncles enough to fill *all* Cheapside," Bingley cried, "it would not make them one jot less agreeable."

"But it must very substantially lessen their chance of marrying men of any consideration in the world," replied Darcy stoically while he sipped his tea, the expression on his face hard and stern. "That, Bingley, is the material point of it." *...One that I remind myself of daily.*

To this speech Bingley made no answer, but his sisters gave it their hearty assent, and indulged their mirth for some time at the expense of their dear friend's vulgar relations. Caroline was especially please, having archived her desire of lessening Miss Elizabeth's suitability in Mr. Darcy's eyes.

With a renewal of tenderness, however, the sisters repaired to Miss Bennet's room on leaving the breakfast parlour, and sat with her till summoned to luncheon. She was still very poorly, and Elizabeth would not quit her at all, having a tray sent up as needed.

~*~

Darcy kept to his room for much of the afternoon, attempting to entertain himself with a book. He was rather fond of literary philosophy and had brought with him a collection of essays and philosophical writings by Sir Thomas More, written in classical Latin, a subject he found fascinating, especially More's *Utopia*. However, on this particular day, even though his hands held the book, his mind was more agreeably engaged elsewhere.

Recollecting the morning's events, Darcy had to admit that Miss Elizabeth Bennet had caught him completely off guard when she appeared, seemingly out of thin air, in Netherfield's park. His breath had quickened and his heart leapt in his chest at the sudden sight of her. Her appearance had not been the offence to him that it had been to the Bingley sisters. No, it was quite the contrary. He found her to be refreshing and physically stimulating. Her cheeks had been rosy and her lips bright red from the excursion, causing him to desire her in ways not in keeping with his gentlemanly code of honour. It had been a long time since he'd had female companionship of a physical nature, and he was afraid his attraction for Miss Elizabeth Bennet was becoming apparent to those around him, especially to Miss Bingley; that was unfortunate for he knew Miss Elizabeth would pay the price for his misstep.

Darcy pushed his book aside and took a deep breath as he contemplated the object of his obsession further. Miss Elizabeth was a paradox. He did not wish to be in her company, but neither could he resist the urge to do so. She was unlike the women of his circle. They were polished and refined, groomed to look a certain way and behave with impeccable manners which quite often bored him. But with this country miss, it was entirely different. She was impertinent, and yet her manners were always in check. Furthermore, she spoke her mind, something which he admired greatly.

Releasing a long sigh, Darcy knew it was of no use to attempt to bury himself in Sir Thomas More's essays. No matter how much the subject intrigued him, his concentration was broken. Closing his tome, he decided to quit his room in search of some diversion to distract his thoughts from one *Miss Elizabeth Bennet*. A game of billiards should do the trick.

Entering the game room, he racked the balls and began to take his frustration out on a set of fifteen round objects, scattering them about the table and pocketing them, one after the other. He had no more than begun when the very object of his frustration entered the room.

Darcy stood erect and bowed. Miss Elizabeth, clearly flustered by her obvious mistake in entering the room, gave him a startled look and abruptly left. Darcy released a harsh breath and broke the balls once more sending them scattering in every direction. Racking the table, he decided this would not do. He might as well join the others in the drawing room.

~*~

Once Elizabeth had the comfort of seeing her sister asleep, and when it appeared to her rather right than pleasant that she should go down stairs herself, she left Jane's room in search of the members of the house.

Carefully descending the stairs, her mind drifted to Mr. Darcy and their meeting earlier that day. Of all the queer luck, to have *him* be the one in the park when she entered Netherfield's grounds. She had been embarrassed for him to see her boots covered in grime and her skirt splattered in mud. And he would stay behind to mock her when they entered the kitchen. Why could he not have gone about his business and left her to hers? Instead he had stood about staring at her, watching her every move and listening to her every word. It was as if she had sprouted two heads! Though Charlotte thought otherwise, she was certain he looked at her to find fault so that he could ridicule her to Mr. Bingley's sisters as soon as she was out of sight.

Stepping upon the landing at the bottom of the stairs, she glanced about, confused as to where the family had retired to for the evening. The footman pointed her in one direction, but she became disoriented as she attempted to follow his instructions and entered the game room instead where she found Mr. Darcy playing a solitary game of billiards. He immediately stood erect and bowed but said not a word. He had no need to. His eyes said it all; they were piercing and cold, and his stare made her feel even more uncomfortable than did those of Mr. Bingley's sisters. Never in her life had she felt so unwelcomed in a place. Only Mr. Bingley was agreeable.

Taking a deep breath, she shook her head slightly and turned and left the room. Wandering about the house, she was once again greeted by a servant who was gracious enough to lead her to the room where the family was gathered.

~*~

On entering the drawing-room, she found the whole party at loo and was immediately invited to join them.

"No, I think I should much rather read. I can only stay for a little while before I must return to my sister." She went to the bookshelf and gazed at the selections available. Running her fingers across the leather bindings, she stopped when she found something of interest and pulled it from the shelf.

Darcy, who had left his game of billiards shortly after she had departed the room, carefully observed her from where he had just sat down with his own book, curious to see what she would select from Bingley's meagre collection.

"I think I shall amuse myself for a short while with this collection of essays from Sir Thomas More. Then I shall return to Jane."

Darcy was pleasantly impressed. "Miss Bennet, do you enjoy Sir Thomas's work?"

Elizabeth hesitated as if choosing her words carefully. "Yes...I do. In truth, I find his topics on social behaviour to be stimulating to one's mind. Sir Thomas More is one of the most distinguished secular humanist of all times. He addresses a wide range of subjects."

"Indeed. They range from individual meanings to legitimacy of laws."

"Yes." Elizabeth tilted her head and furrowed her brow. "I believe you are correct."

"And what do you know of him, Miss Bennet?" Darcy asked, staring at her in wonder.

Elizabeth smiled. "If you mean to intimidate me, Mr. Darcy, you will have to do better than this, for I am very familiar with the subject."

"Not at all, Miss Bennet. I'm merely curious. I want to know what you know."

"Very well, then" she said with a shrug. "I will tell you. I know that Sir Thomas More studied everything one can imagine: from the social contract to criteria for revolution, and also from functions of everyday actions to the effects of science on culture, and let us not overlook his study of the changes in human demographics nor the collective order of a wasps' nest."

"Indeed." Darcy gazed at her in amazement. Recovering himself, he added, "Do you read Latin, Miss Bennet?"

Elizabeth looked at him in confusion. "Yes...a little, though not very well; therefore, I am fortunate to be able to read Sir Thomas in English. My favorite is his composition, *Utopia*," she said with a smile. "Would you not agree, Mr. Darcy that it is one of the most fascinating works ever written on the human experience?"

Darcy watched for some moments before he replied, "Miss Bennet, who educated you?"

"My father, of course."

Darcy did not reply, but rather stared at her with admiration while Mr. Hurst looked at her with astonishment.

"Do you prefer reading to cards then?" Hurst asked, looking up from the game as he laid a card down. "Such studies for a woman! That is rather singular."

"Miss Eliza Bennet," Miss Bingley said, "despises cards. She is a great reader with interest in *lofty* ideals, and has no pleasure in anything else."

"I deserve neither such praise nor such censure," Elizabeth cried. "I am *not* a great reader, nor could my ideals be described as *lofty*, and, indeed, I take pleasure in many things."

"In nursing your sister I am sure you have pleasure," Bingley said, "and I hope it will soon be increased by seeing her quite well again and able to join us."

Elizabeth thanked him from her heart, and then walked towards a table where a few more books were lying about. Running her fingertips over the various titles, she remarked on their quality. Bingley immediately offered to fetch her others—all that his library afforded.

"And I wish my collection were larger for your benefit and my own credit, but I am an idle fellow, and though I have not many, I have more than I ever look into."

Elizabeth assured him that she could suit herself perfectly with those in the room.

"I am astonished," Miss Bingley said, "that my father should have left so small a collection of books. What a delightful library you have at Pemberley, Mr. Darcy! And the one in London at Darcy House is also splendid."

"They ought to be good," he replied. "They have been the work of many generations."

"And then you have added so much to them yourself, for you are always buying books."

"I cannot comprehend the neglect of a family library in such days as these."

"Neglect! I am sure you neglect nothing that can add to the beauties of your noble homes. Charles, when you build *your* house, I wish it may be half as delightful as Pemberley."

"I wish it may."

"But I would really advise you to make your purchase in that neighbourhood and take Pemberley for a kind of model. There is not a finer county in England than Derbyshire!" Caroline exclaimed.

"With all my heart; I will buy Pemberley itself if Darcy will sell it."

"I am talking of possibilities, Charles. Not the prospect of purchasing Mr. Darcy's splendid estate."

"Upon my word, Caroline, I should think it more possible to get Pemberley by purchase than by imitation."

Elizabeth was so much caught by what passed between the siblings as to leave her very little attention for her book, and soon laying it wholly aside, she drew near the card-table, and stationed herself between Mr. Bingley and his eldest sister, to observe the game.

"Is Miss Darcy much grown since the spring?" Miss Bingley enquired. "Will she be as tall as I am?"

"I think she will. She is now about Miss Elizabeth Bennet's height, or rather taller."

"How I long to see her again! I never met with anybody who delighted me half so much. Such a countenance, such manners! And so extremely accomplished for her age! Her performance on the pianoforte is exquisite."

A Man in Want of a Wife

"It is amazing to me," Bingley said, "how young ladies can have patience to be so very accomplished as they all are."

"*All* young ladies accomplished! My dear Charles, whatever do you mean?"

"Yes, all of them, I think. They all speak French and German, paint tables, cover screens, and net purses. I scarcely know anyone who cannot do all this, and I am sure I never heard a young lady spoken of for the first time without being informed that she was very accomplished."

"Your list of the common extent of accomplishments," Darcy said, "has too much truth. The word is applied to many a woman who deserves it for no other reason than by netting a purse or covering a screen. But I am very far from agreeing with you in your estimation of ladies in general. I cannot boast of knowing more than half a dozen, in the whole range of my acquaintance, that meet my criteria of an accomplished woman."

"Nor I, I am sure," Miss Bingley added.

"Then," observed Elizabeth, "you must comprehend a great deal in your idea of an accomplished woman."

"Yes, I do comprehend a great deal in it."

"Oh, certainly!" cried his faithful assistant, "no one can be really esteemed accomplished who does not greatly surpass what is usually met with. A woman must have a thorough knowledge of music, singing, drawing, dancing, and the modern languages, to deserve the word, and besides all this, she must possess a certain something in her air and manner of walking, the tone of her voice, her address and expressions, or the word will be but half deserved."

"Yes," added Darcy, "and to all this she must yet add something more substantial, in the improvement of her mind by extensive reading and the study of the ancient languages so that she might read the works of great men in their original language—such as Sir Thomas More's letters written in classical Latin." Darcy glanced at Elizabeth. "*That* makes a truly accomplished woman."

Elizabeth's eyes widened in amazement. "I am no longer surprised at your knowing only *six* accomplished women. I rather wonder now at your knowing *any*."

"Are you so severe upon your own sex as to doubt the possibility of all this?" Miss Bingley exclaimed.

"*I* never saw such a woman. *I* never saw such capacity, taste, application, and elegance as you describe, united."

"You are very bold, Miss Bennet, with your assessment of our sex," Louisa remarked.

Elizabeth raised her brow and shrugged her shoulders. "I only speak as I see, Mrs. Hurst."

Caroline smirked. "Perhaps you have not had the advantages we have had, of moving in the first circles and mingling with people of distinction and rank, Miss Bennet," she said. "For there are many *very* accomplished young ladies amongst *our* acquaintance, I can assure you."

Darcy closed his book and sat back, resting his arm over the back of his chair, gazing at Miss Elizabeth. He marvelled at how she held her own with the Bingley sisters as they pressed on with their effusions of accomplished ladies. He also had to admire her audacity in contradicting *him*. That was indeed a new occurrence, and one that might have offended a lesser man, but he was rather intrigued by the experience. He looked forward to the day when he would once again engage her in verbal sword play. Darcy inwardly chuckled. Then he would see if her mettle could stand the test of a true master of the game; for when it came to a sharp mind, his was unmatched.

Finally Mr. Hurst called them to order with bitter complaints of their inattention to what was going forward. As all conversation was thereby at an end, Elizabeth soon afterwards left the room.

"Eliza Bennet," said Miss Bingley, when the door was closed on her, "is one of those young ladies who seek to recommend themselves to the other sex by undervaluing their own, and with many men, I dare say, it succeeds. But, in my opinion, it is a paltry device, a very mean art."

"Undoubtedly," replied Darcy, to whom this remark was chiefly addressed, "there is meanness in *all* the arts which ladies sometimes condescend to employ for captivation. Whatever bears affinity to cunning is despicable."

Miss Bingley, it appeared, was not entirely satisfied with this reply as to continue the subject.

All eyes turned to the door when Elizabeth joined them again only to say that her sister was worse and that she could not leave her alone for the night.

"Of course you shan't leave your sister. I will send to Longbourn directly for your clothes, and we shall send for Mr. Jones this very instant."

"No, Charles! No country advice will be of any service. We must send an express to Town for one of the most eminent physicians," cried Caroline.

Darcy once again closed his book and laid it aside. "If you wish, Miss Bennet, I shall send for my own personal physician immediately. It is but twenty miles to Town. I can have him here before the cock crows thrice."

"Mr. Darcy, I thank you for your kind offer, but that will not be necessary. My sister is not so ill as to importune you to such an extent."

"Miss Bennet, should your sister digress into putrid fever it can become quite serious rather quickly. Madam, in all likelihood, she could succumb to the disease. Please, it is no imposition."

"I thank you, no. Mr. Jones will do adequately, but, should my sister's condition worsen to the point where he feels a physician is necessary, then I will accept your kind offer if it is still available."

Darcy tore his eyes away. For the first time in many weeks he was more than a little annoyed with her. He was incensed, reminding himself of why he held her family in such contempt. Miss Elizabeth might have an enchanting mind filled with wit and charm, able to engage his own in a noteworthy challenge, but this was a part of her nature he did not like so well—her insufferable, stubborn, puffed up, self-conceited independence. However, Miss Jane Bennet was not really his responsibility, and if her family cared so little for her welfare, then why should he?

Although Elizabeth would not hear of sending to Town for a doctor just yet, she was not so unwilling to comply with Mr. Bingley's proposal, and so it was settled that Mr. Jones should be sent for early in the morning. And if Miss Bennet was not decidedly better, then a physician would be called for.

Bingley was quite uncomfortable, and his sisters declared that they were miserable. They found solace from their wretchedness, however, by playing duets after supper, while he could find no better relief to his feelings than by giving his housekeeper directions that every possible attention might be paid to the sick lady above stairs as well as her sister.

Later that night as Darcy lay in his bed, recalling the night's events, he had to wonder if Miss Elizabeth had sketched his character well enough to know what attracted him. Had she come to Netherfield at the prompting of her mother, using her sister's illness as a ploy so that she might be there in his close company, hoping to engage his feelings as he suspected her sister had intended coming in the first place for Bingley's? He wondered.

~*~*~*~

Chapter 8

The next morning, after being assured of Miss Bennet's health, Mr. Hurst insisted that the men go out after breakfast for a round of sport. Sam, though not a field dog, had joined them, sitting obediently by Darcy's side as he watched Bingley's bird dogs bring in one plump pheasant after another, proudly laying them at their masters' feet.

Though Darcy loved to shoot as well as any man, this morning, however, his heart was not in the sport, and he had, therefore, managed to bag only one bird, a miserable showing compared to Mr. Hurst's twenty and Bingley's six.

Darcy's mind was on Miss Elizabeth Bennet. He knew from the maids that she had passed the chief of the night in her sister's room, bathing her sister's forehead with a cold compress. Fortunately, in the morning, just before dawn, Miss Bennet's fever broke, much to her sister's relief. The draughts left behind by Mr. Jones had finally worked, and now that she was on the mend, they were to be discontinued. In their place, he had left a sleeping draught, insisting that Miss Bennet must have plenty of rest and hot bone broth with the marrow intact to make a complete recovery of her strength.

Although Darcy already knew of Miss Bennet's condition, Miss Elizabeth had formally sent word down of Jane's good report to the family while they were still having breakfast. She had also requested to have a note be sent to Longbourn, asking her mother to visit and form her own judgment of Jane's situation. The note was immediately dispatched, and Mr. Jones had agreed to wait for her call, if she chose to come. Darcy had thought it a shame that Mrs. Bennet had to be asked to come. In his estimation, she should have been there the day after her daughter had taken ill. He knew his mother would have been. So why hadn't Miss Bennet's?

For that matter, as Darcy reflected further, he knew that Lady Anne Darcy would have never let her daughter come in the first place—and especially not on horseback with the all likelihood of rain! Darcy shook his head.

After they had killed their fill, bagging enough partridges and pheasants for several meals, they made their way back to the manor house. Darcy, lagging behind the others, spied a coach entering the gate. Mrs. Bennet, accompanied by her two youngest girls, had finally come to Netherfield.

Darcy sighed. "Well," he said privately as he glanced down at his hound, "it is about time she showed *some* concern for her daughter. What do you say, old boy? Should a man like to have *her* for a mother-in-law?"

Sam barked and ran in front of him.

"Yes! I concur. My sentiments exactly! Perish the thought—*run* is what any man should do! And run is what *I* should do."

~*~

A Man in Want of a Wife

Darcy, Bingley, and Mr. Hurst, having just returned to the house, met Mrs. Hurst in the front parlour where they waited for the party from Longbourn to join them after their visit with Miss Bennet.

Miss Bingley, occupied with showing the Bennets to Miss Bennet's room, was not yet present. However, before very long, she, too, joined them, much disgruntled. Stepping into the room, she closed the door and began afresh with her disparaging remarks.

"It is not enough that we should have to endure the eldest Miss Bennets. We now have the mother and the two youngest to suffer! Are we to be imposed upon by every Bennet in the country!?"

She walked over to her sister where Mrs. Hurst extended her hand to offer sympathy.

"Ay, sister. It is too much to be borne. You are too kind with your gracious heart."

Darcy rolled his eyes and took up his post at the large picture window where he once more found solace in Bingley's garden. Leaning against the window frame, he released a hard breath as he listened and watched all that transpired around him.

Caroline took a seat, grumbling with Louisa over what her nerves must suffer in the company of such a family.

After sitting a little while with Jane, the mother and three daughters all made their appearances. Upon their entry, Mr. Hurst rose from his seat and met them with a cordial invitation to enter while Bingley met them with a friendly salutation.

"Mrs. Bennet, you are very welcome to my home, Madam. I sincerely hope you have not found Miss Bennet worse than expected."

"Indeed I have, sir," was her answer. "She is a great deal too ill to be moved. Mr. Jones says we must not think of moving her. Therefore, we must trespass a little longer on your kindness."

"Removed!" cried Bingley. "It must not be thought of. My sister, I am sure, will not hear of her removal!"

Mr. Hurst, sensing that either the obsequious lapping at Bingley's feet was about to begin, or unable to bear Mrs. Bennet's odious shrieking, so offensive to one's ears, darted from their presence, making a beeline for the door as quickly as his feet could carry him. Darcy knew not which it was; perhaps it was both. He only wished he could do the same.

He briefly stared at Mrs. Bennet and shook his head. He himself had enquired after Miss Bennet before coming down to breakfast and knew the severity of her condition was being greatly exaggerated.

Darcy glanced over to Miss Bingley and read the derision in her eyes while Mrs. Hurst had a look of pure disgust in her own. Then he glanced at Miss Elizabeth. Her cheeks were flamed scarlet; she was clearly embarrassed.

Charles glared at his sister until she responded.

Darcy shrugged his shoulders and turned back to the window.

"You may depend upon it, Madam," Miss Bingley said at last with cold civility. "Miss Bennet shall receive every possible attention while she remains with us."

Mrs. Bennet, undeterred by the coolness of the room, was profuse in her acknowledgments.

"I am sure," she added, "if it were not for such good friends, I do not know what would become of her, for she is very ill indeed and suffers a *vast* deal, though with the greatest patience in the world, which is always the way with her, for she has, without exception, the sweetest temper I ever met with. I often tell my other girls they are nothing to *her*."

She paused and Darcy turned back to stare at her, noticing how she glanced around the room in a predatory manner.

"Well, I must say you have a *sweet* room here, Mr. Bingley, and a charming prospect over that gravel walk," she began, walking about the room, turning to take in everything as though it were her daughter's parlour. "I do not know a place in the country that is equal to Netherfield. You will not think of quitting it in a hurry, I hope, though you have but a short lease."

"Whatever I do is always done in a hurry," Bingley replied, "and therefore if I should resolve to quit Netherfield, I should probably be off in five minutes. At present, however, I consider myself as quite fixed here. In fact, I believe I would be happy living in the country forever."

"That is exactly what I should have supposed of you," said Elizabeth, smiling with an expression of joy.

"You begin to comprehend me, do you?" Bingley cried, turning towards her.

"Oh, yes! I understand you perfectly."

"I wish I might take this for a compliment, but to be so easily seen through, I am afraid, is pitiful."

"That is as it happens. It does not necessarily follow that a deep, intricate character is more or less estimable than such a one as yours."

"Lizzy!" her mother cried. "Remember where you are, and do not run on in the wild manner that you are suffered to do at home."

"I did not know before," continued Bingley immediately, "that you were a studier of character. It must be an amusing study."

"Yes, but intricate characters are the *most* amusing. They have at least that advantage."

"The country," Darcy said, stepping away from the window, "can in general supply but few subjects for such a study. In a country neighbourhood you move in a very confined and unvarying society. You would do much better in Town where the audience is more diverse and wide ranging."

"But people themselves alter so much, that there is always something new to be observed in them," returned Elizabeth, quick in her defence.

"The country *unvarying and confined!* I dare say it is not, sir!" Mrs. Bennet cried, offended by his manner of mentioning a country neighbourhood. "The country is far more agreeable to one's enjoyment than Town with all of its crime and riffraff. Regardless of whatever you may think about it, I say the country is far superior. Unvarying and confined indeed! I assure you there is quite as much of *that* going on in the country as in Town."

Everyone was surprised, and Darcy, after glaring at her for a moment, turned silently away. Mrs. Bennet, who fancied she had gained a complete victory over the taciturn man, continued in her perceived triumph.

"I cannot see that London has any great advantage over the country for my part, except the shops and public places perhaps. Even though some may think the theatre in Drury Lane and other questionable activities are a symbol of refinement, I find the country with its unpretentious manners is a *vast* deal pleasanter than Town, is not it, Mr. Bingley?"

A Man in Want of a Wife

Darcy stood stoic, his back to Mrs. Bennet and her affronts upon his character. Apparently she was too ignorant to recognize when *she* had been insulted.

Bingley glanced at his friend. "When I am in the country," he replied, sounding somewhat embarrassed for Darcy's sake, "I never wish to leave it, and when I am in Town, it is pretty much the same. They have each their advantages, and I can be equally happy in either."

"Ay—that is because you have the right disposition. But that gentleman," Mrs. Bennet said, looking at Darcy who had looked back over his shoulder to meet her onslaught, "seems to think the country was nothing at all."

"Indeed, Mamma, you are mistaken," said Elizabeth, blushing in embarrassment for her mother. "You quite mistook Mr. Darcy."

"Did I," Mrs. Bennet replied with indignation. "Did I indeed! No! I think not; for he seems to think the country is beneath polite society."

"No, Mamma." Elizabeth's face was flushed hot. "He only meant that there is not such a variety of people to be met with in the country as in Town, which you must acknowledge to be true."

"Certainly, my dear, nobody said there were; but, as to not meeting with many people in this neighbourhood, I believe there are few neighbourhoods larger. I would have him know that we dine with *four* and *twenty* families."

The Bingley sisters burst out in snickers, each attempting to hold back a full laugh as they dropped their gazes and looked away to hide their mirth.

"*Mamma*," Elizabeth said below her breath, trying to rescue the situation, if not for her own sake, then for that of Jane and her younger sisters who stood by in a stupefied fashion gawking at their mother.

Nothing but concern for Elizabeth could enable Bingley to keep his countenance. Caroline was less delicate and directed her eyes towards Mr. Darcy with a very expressive smile. He was now glaring at Mrs. Bennet, facing her with anger in his eyes, but she paid no mind and prattled on, humiliating even her youngest daughters who appeared to shrink away from their mother.

Darcy shook his head and took a deep breath as he raked his hand over his face. He stood there staring in disbelief at the scene unfolding before him. Revulsion and hostility were the two things that came to mind as he glanced from Elizabeth to her mother. He could read in Miss Elizabeth's countenance that she was mortified by her mother's vulgar behaviour. Furthermore, he truly sympathized with any man unlucky enough to marry one of the *jewels of the county*.

Elizabeth, he sensed, for the sake of saying something that might turn her mother's thoughts away from the present topic, spoke unevenly.

"Mamma, has Charlotte been at Longbourn since *my* coming away?" she asked timidly.

"Yes, she called yesterday with her father. What an agreeable man Sir William is, Mr. Bingley; is he not? So much the man of fashion! So genteel and so easy! He has always something to say to everybody. Now *that* is my idea of good breeding with gentlemanly behaviour, and those persons who fancy themselves very important and never open their mouths, quite mistake the matter."

Elizabeth's bosom heaved from humiliation. "Did Charlotte dine with you?"

"No, she would go home. I fancy she was wanted about the mince-pies. For my part, Mr. Bingley, *I* always keep servants that can do their own work; *my* daughters are brought up differently. But everybody is to judge for themselves, and the Lucases are very good girls, I assure you. It is a pity they are not handsome! Not that *I* think Charlotte so *very* plain mind you, but then she is our particular friend."

"She seems a very pleasant young woman," said Bingley.

"Oh dear, yes—but you must own she is very plain. Lady Lucas herself has often said so and envied me Jane's beauty. I do not like to boast of my own child, but to be sure, Jane—now one does not often see anybody better looking. It is what everybody says. I do not trust my own partiality. Why, when she was only fifteen, there was a gentleman at my brother Gardiner's in Town so much in love with her that my sister-in-law was sure he would make her an offer before we came away. But, however, he did not. Perhaps he thought her too young. However, he wrote some verses on her, and very pretty they were."

"And so ended his affection," said Elizabeth, impatient to end the story. "There has been many a one, I fancy, overcome in the same way. I wonder who first discovered the efficacy of poetry in driving away love!"

"I have been used to consider poetry as the *food* of love," Darcy said, strolling back into the centre of the room as if being pulled by a strong magnet.

"Of a fine, stout, healthy love it may. Everything nourishes what is strong already. But if it be only a slight, thin sort of inclination, I am convinced that one good sonnet will starve it entirely away."

Darcy said nothing, only smiling slightly at her wit.

The general pause which ensued made for an ill and foreboding presence in the room. Darcy noticed Elizabeth trembling and assumed she feared her mother would be exposing herself again. He could see by her appearance, she longed to speak, but could think of nothing to say.

After a short silence Mrs. Bennet began repeating her thanks to Mr. Bingley for his kindness to Jane, with an apology for troubling him also with Elizabeth.

That incensed Darcy even further. Did the woman not have the good sense to know when to shut her mouth?!

Again, he shook his head in sympathy. Darcy pitied the Bennet daughters for having such a mother. Then, glancing at Miss Elizabeth, he pitied her even more. She and her eldest sister had all the earmarks of fine gentlewomen, and, except for the officiousness of their mother, might have had some chance of making a good match.

Mr. Bingley was unaffectedly civil in his answer and forced his sister to be civil also, and say what the occasion required. Caroline performed her part indeed without much graciousness, but Mrs. Bennet was satisfied, and soon afterwards ordered her carriage. Upon this signal, the youngest of her daughters put herself forward. She and her next oldest sister had been whispering to each other during the whole of the visit, and the result of it was that the youngest should tax Mr. Bingley with having promised on his first coming into the country to give a ball at Netherfield.

Darcy leaned his shoulder against the wall by the chimneypiece and assessed Miss Lydia's appearance. Eyeing her from head to slipper, he could see that she was a stout, well-grown girl for her age. She had a fine complexion and a good-humoured countenance. By his estimation, she was also a favourite with her mother. Darcy had overheard Sir William Lucas telling Miss Bingley that the youngest daughter had been brought into the public at an early age, well before the expected time of a girl's coming out. He could also conjecture that Miss Lydia had high animal spirits, and a sort of natural self-consequence. Like Miss Elizabeth, Darcy was also a studier of character, and in his judgment, Miss Lydia had an unwarranted opinion of her self-importance well above that which ought to be, and therefore, felt herself equal to address Mr. Bingley on the subject of a ball.

"Mr. Bingley," she said, batting her lashes, "you promised to give a ball when we addressed the subject back last month, and you know that it would be the most shameful thing in the world if you did not keep your word."

Bingley's answer to this sudden attack was pleasing to Mrs. Bennet's ear as she wailed in delight.

Darcy was disgusted by it all.

"I am perfectly ready, I assure you, to keep my engagement, and when your sister is recovered, you shall, if you please, name the very day of the ball. But you would not wish to be dancing while she is ill."

Lydia declared herself satisfied. "Oh! Yes—it would be much better to wait till Jane is well, and by that time most likely Captain Carter would be at Meryton again. And when you have given *your* ball," she added with enthusiasm, "I shall insist on Colonel Forster giving one also. I shall tell him it will be quite a shame if he does not."

Mrs. Bennet and her daughters then departed, and Elizabeth returned instantly to Jane, leaving her own and her relations' behaviour to the remarks of the two ladies and Mr. Darcy, the latter of whom, however, could not be prevailed upon to join in their censure of *her*, in spite of all Miss Bingley's witticisms on *fine eyes*.

~*~

Once she reached her sister's room, Elizabeth threw herself into a nearby chair and snatched her book from the side table. Opening it, she could only stare at her favorite topic. Jane, sensing her distress, opened her eyes.

"What is the matter, Lizzy?"

Glancing at her sister, Elizabeth smiled and moved to her bed, taking a seat on the mattress and clasping Jane's hand in hers.

"It is nothing for you to trouble yourself over, dear sister. I merely wish that we, superior sisters that we are, should be miles away from here. Only your Mr. Bingley is amiable, dear Jane. We should not remain here."

Jane looked away. "He is not *my* Mr. Bingley, Lizzy."

"Oh, but I think he is, or he very soon will be, for I feel he is soon to be very much in love with you."

Jane smiled and closed her eyes. The latest draught Mr. Jones had given her had begun to make her drowsy. "I'm very tired, Lizzy," she murmured as she turned on her side.

"Then sleep dear Jane…yes…sleep."

Elizabeth pulled the counterpane up over Jane's shoulders and tucked her in. Glancing back at her book, she said to herself. "Sir Thomas, you must forgive me, for at present, I am not inclined to be taken on your wonderful excursion to a faraway island. *Utopia* must wait. I think I had better take a walk and cool my temper…not to mention my mortification." She released a hard sigh and gently shook her head. "Mother, how could you? Have you no idea how you have humiliated yourself…and us? How you've exposed our family to ridicule? No…I don't suppose you have, nor have you ever."

Moving away from the bed, she clutched her spencer and wrap and moved towards the door. Looking back once more on her sister now sleeping peacefully, she turned the latch and quit the room. When she reached the portico, she found Mr. Darcy's hound waiting for her, his tail wagging furiously.

"Would you like to play, Sam? I could use a good run. There is nothing like vigorous exercise to make a body feel better. Go and fetch your stick, and we shall have a time of it!"

~*~

Darcy, feeling the tension in his neck and shoulders, had ordered a hot bath before taking the stairs to his room. In his seven and twenty years, he could not recall ever enduring such an arrogant display of ignorant manners as the one which had just played out moments ago in Bingley's front parlour. The audacity of that woman! She did everything but measure for the curtains and order cloth to reupholster the furnishings.

And then, to add insult to injury, she would have to continue in her stupidity. Elevating Sir William Lucas above *him* in status and gentlemanly behaviour went beyond all that was civil and decent. How dare she! He, the grandson of an earl, placed beneath a Knight of the Royal Order. Unthinkable! If he wanted a title, he could certainly purchase one.

Poor Mr. Bennet, Darcy thought to himself, *to have to put up with such an ill-mannered wife. And her younger daughters, especially Miss Lydia, are just like her. The only good that came from that family are the two eldest Miss Bennets. They, at least, have some redeeming qualities, although they are greatly lessened by their mother's manners.*

There was only one surprising moment during this dreadful event, and it had not gone unnoticed by him. Miss Elizabeth Bennet had tried to defend him against her mother's vulgar display of bad manners.

Having reached his dressing room, Darcy stripped off his clothes and slipped into the sudsy water filled with baths salts and spices for relaxation. The steam filled his nostrils with a pleasant aroma; he breathed deeply, forcing himself to release his anger. His man handed him a bar of French milled soap, but he set it aside, preferring to soak in the soothing waters and allow the tension to ease from his tired body while his mind drifted.

He smiled as he recalled how Miss Elizabeth had come to his defence. "She must care something for you, Darcy, or she would not have spoken up as she did," he stated privately. "She is an attractive young lady; you are a handsome, healthy man. Of course she would desire you. You have everything to offer her...only you mustn't."

He sighed heavily. "I would, Elizabeth, if only I could, but to have *you*, I must be willing to give up everything I have in Town. It is a heavy burden—a difficult decision—one I would not make lightly. I have Georgiana to think of. An alliance with you would severely lessen her chances of making a good match, and *that* I am unwilling to do. My duty to my family, my personal honour, and all that I have been brought up to be, forbid it. I have been bred to be cultured—you have not. And your mother would forever be a reminder of that fact."

Darcy breathed deeply, taking in the rich, spicy scents of sandalwood and myrrh. He had to admire her for the gracious effort she undertook to steer her mother away from ridiculing him, futile though it was. If only she had come from a family of good breeding, he would offer for her in an instant. He could, and often did, imagine the life they might have together. With her vivacious passion for life, they could have one *hell* of a good marriage—a marriage of true minds, as the Bard would say.

Darcy closed his eyes and leaned back, letting his mind go wherever it would, and, as it often did, it led him back to the cove at Pemberley, only this time Miss Elizabeth was with him lying on the mossy ground—naked, her beauty revealed for him to explore. Her breasts were rounded mounds of flesh, succulent and firm, delightful to the eyes and begging to be kissed. He reached out to brush her soft skin with his fingertips and suddenly she was gone.

His eyes flew open.

Groaning, he took the soap and began scrubbing his skin vigorously, trying futilely to steer his mind away from erotic thoughts of Miss Elizabeth Bennet wearing nothing but her hair for a covering, running through the woods like a nymph, dipping her toe in the cool water of the pool in Pemberley's cove, while laughing and beckoning him to follow. The cove was a place reserved for that special woman he would one day love, a place where he planned to take his bride and make love to her by the waterfall in the heat of the Derbyshire summer.

A quarter hour had passed, and the water had grown cool; he called for his man to rinse his hair and bring his robe. Stepping out of the water, he felt relaxed and rested, though frustrated by his unsatisfied carnal lust. Placing the thick, heavy cotton robe about him, he moved to the window and glanced out. As he leaned against the jamb, he felt his lips curl into a small smile. There was the object of his obsession running and playing on the lawn with his hound.

Darcy chuckled. His dog had always been a good judge of character, unpretentious and uncaring of one's rank or place in society. As Sam saw it, all men were created equal—except the scoundrels. Sam always judged them right as well.

"What I would not give to be as carefree as you, Elizabeth. Yes, in the quiet of my room you will always be *my* Elizabeth, for you are everything I could ever want in a wife. How I long to take you in my arms and bring you to my bed. By your very nature, I know you have as much passion for living…as do I, and that will translate into a passion for loving. I could love you with a deep abiding love such as you are not likely to ever know. Oh how I long to taste your sweetness, to hold your body next to mine and make love to you. I can see us in a tender embrace—a lover's embrace—loving one another all through the night and never tiring of it. Only one thing stands in our way…your family and low connections—*that* I cannot abide."

Unexpectedly she looked up and saw him standing in the window looking down upon her, his bare chest exposed. Even from this distance he could see the scarlet spreading from her neckline to her cheeks. She looked lovely, though perhaps a bit flustered.

Suddenly, she threw the stick she held in her hand and turned and ran.

He laughed out loud. "You want me as much as I want you…but I cannot take you for my wife, and I will not take you for my mistress. Though others who felt less would, my honour forbids it…as would yours."

Darcy pulled his robe tight across his chest, securing it at his waist, and then he retreated to his chamber to dress for the afternoon. He wondered how she would receive him when next they met.

~*~*~*~

Chapter 9

After he was dressed, Darcy left his room in search of something new to read, but, before he reached the drawing room where the selections he wanted were kept, the sound of a beautiful melody floated through the closed door and reached his ears. It was Beethoven's "Moonlight Sonata," played in a way he had never heard before.

Even though the notes were not played to perfection, often missed as the artist slurred her way through the most difficult parts, the movement was presented with such feeling that he paused in the corridor to listen. There was no doubt in his mind as to who sat at the pianoforte on the other side of the door, for by the faint scent of lavender, he knew it was Miss Elizabeth Bennet.

How long he stood there, he could not tell. Only when the music stopped and the door swung open, did he come to his senses.

"Mr. Darcy!" Elizabeth cried, flushing furiously. "I…I had no idea you were out here, sir. You should have made your presence known."

"Do not be alarmed, Miss Bennet, for I have only come for a book. Though in all honesty, I could not help but stop to hear you play."

"Yes, well, I was practising for want of something better to do. Jane is resting, and I did not wish to read, so I came down here."

"Yes, I see."

"Now, sir, if you will excuse me, I think I had best return to my sister."

She dropped a curtsey and quickly ran up the stairs.

He turned and watched her go with a smile gracing his countenance. Quickly choosing a book, Darcy soon returned to his room as well.

~*~

Dinner was a rather quiet affair that evening. Miss Elizabeth Bennet had kept to her sister's room for the remainder of the afternoon, not wishing to be parted from her, and so a tray was sent up with beef broth for Miss Bennet and cold meats with cheese and wine for Miss Elizabeth.

After the meal, the party retired to the drawing room for their nightly entertainment, but this night the loo-table would not appear. Darcy had made it clear that he did not wish to play. His sister and his cousin, Colonel Fitzwilliam, had written, and he wished to reply. Another reason why he did not feel inclined to play was because Miss Elizabeth did not play. Instead, she preferred her book; something he thought was a much better way to employ one's time.

Collecting his letter-box, Darcy left for the drawing room in full anticipation of completing the letter he had begun and perhaps engaging in some social intercourse with Miss Elizabeth, who, for some reason, had avoided his company, remaining above stairs after the incident in the drawing room. He wondered if Miss Elizabeth's hesitancy was related to her notice of his watching her from his apartment window. He smiled to himself. Darcy did not regret either encounter one jot, and if he had it to do over again, he would gladly repeat the performances—especially if it gave him another opportunity to watch her from his window whilst standing fresh from his bath, attired in nothing but an open robe.

Entering the room, Darcy was pleasantly surprised to find Miss Elizabeth present with her needlework in her lap. He walked over to where she sat and bowed.

"Miss Bennet, may I enquire after your sister. How is she feeling this evening?"

Elizabeth placed her hoop aside and gave a tentative smile. "I thank you, sir, for your concern. I believe Jane is a little better. Perhaps soon she will be able to join us."

"Good. I'm glad to hear it." He bowed once more and then went directly to the writing table where he took a seat and opened his box. Removing a sheet of letter-paper, he took his pen and dipped it in a bottle of black ink placed on the desk and began to write.

While Mr. Darcy was writing, Miss Bingley took a seat near him, watching the progress of his letter and repeatedly calling on his attention by sending messages to his sister. Mr. Hurst and Mr. Bingley were at piquet, and Mrs. Hurst was observing their game.

Darcy glanced in Miss Elizabeth Bennet's direction to see if her attention was upon him, and it appeared that it was. She had taken up her needlework again and seemed sufficiently amused in attending to what passed between himself and his rather bothersome companion.

Miss Bingley's perpetual commendations on either his handwriting, or on the evenness of his lines, or on the length of his letter, with the perfect unconcern for how her praises were received, seemed to entertain Miss Elizabeth. She might enjoy the exchange, but to Darcy, Miss Bingley's officious fawning gave no such pleasure.

"How delighted Miss Darcy will be to receive such a letter!"

He made no answer.

"You write uncommonly fast."

"You are mistaken, Miss Bingley. I write rather slowly," Darcy said, dipping his pen once more.

Caroline leaned in closer. "How many letters you must have occasion to write in the course of the year! Letters of business, too! How odious I should think them!"

"It is fortunate, then, that they fall to my lot instead of to yours."

"Pray tell your sister that I long to see her."

"I have already told her so once, by your desire."

"I am afraid you do not like your pen. Let me mend it for you," she said reaching for it. "I mend pens remarkably well."

"Thank you," he replied, moving away, "but I always mend my own."

"How can you contrive to write so even?"

He was silent.

"Tell your sister I am delighted to hear of her improvement on the harp, and pray let her know that I am quite in raptures with her beautiful little design for a table, and I think it infinitely superior to Miss Grantley's."

Darcy glanced up and met her gaze. "Miss Bingley, will you give me leave to defer your raptures till I write again? At present I have not room to do them justice."

"Oh, it is of no consequence. I shall see her in January. But do you always write such charming long letters to her, Mr. Darcy?"

"They are generally long, but whether always charming, it is not for me to determine."

"It is a rule with me that a person who can write a long letter with ease cannot write ill."

"That will not do for a compliment to Darcy, Caroline," cried her brother, "because he does *not* write with ease at all. He studies too much for words of four syllables. Do you not, Darcy?"

"My style of writing is very different from yours," said Darcy drily.

"Oh!" cried Miss Bingley. "Charles writes in the most careless way imaginable. He leaves out half his words and blots the rest."

"My ideas flow so rapidly that I have not the time to express them—by which means my letters sometimes convey no ideas at all to my correspondents."

"Your humility, Mr. Bingley," Elizabeth said, finally joining the conversation, "must disarm reproof."

Darcy looked up and placed his pen aside as he turned to face her. "Nothing is more deceitful," he said, "than the appearance of humility. It is often only carelessness of opinion, and sometimes an indirect boast."

"And which of the two do you call *my* little recent piece of modesty?" asked Charles.

"The indirect boast," Darcy replied, glancing at his friend "for you are really proud of your defects in writing, because you consider them as proceeding from a rapidity of thought and carelessness of execution, which, if not estimable, you think at least highly interesting. The power of doing anything with quickness is always much prized by the possessor, and often without any attention to the imperfection of the performance."

Darcy paused and considered his thoughts before continuing.

"Let us examine this further," he said. "When you told Mrs. Bennet this morning that if you ever resolved on quitting Netherfield you should be gone in five minutes, you meant it to be a sort of panegyric, a compliment to yourself, and yet what is there so very laudable in a precipitance, which must leave very necessary business undone, and can be of no real advantage to yourself or anyone else?"

"Nay," cried Bingley, "this is too much, to remember at night all the foolish things that were said in the morning. And yet, upon my honour, I believed what I said at that time to be true, and I believe it at this moment. At least, therefore, I did not assume the character of needless precipitance merely to show off before the ladies."

"I dare say you believed it, but I am by no means convinced that you would be gone with such rapidity. Your conduct would be quite as dependent on chance as that of any man I know, and if, as you were mounting your horse, a friend were to say, 'Bingley, you had better stay till next week,' you would probably do it; yes, you would probably not go—and at another word, might stay a month."

Elizabeth, who had been listening with great interest to their exchange, at last spoke up.

"You have only proved by this," she interjected, with her eyes fixed on Darcy, "that Mr. Bingley did not do justice to his own disposition. You have shown him off now much more than he did himself."

A Man in Want of a Wife

"A fine answer, Miss Bennet! I am exceedingly gratified," Bingley said, "by your converting what my friend says into a compliment on the sweetness of my temper. But I am afraid you are giving it a turn which that gentleman did by no means intend; for he would certainly think the better of me if, under such a circumstance, I were to give a flat denial, and ride off as fast as I could. He thinks I am whimsical, changing my mind with the wind and easily persuaded by the heat of the moment."

"Would Mr. Darcy then consider the rashness of your original intention as atoned for by your obstinacy in adhering to it?"

"Upon my word I cannot exactly explain the matter. Darcy must speak for himself."

Darcy gazed at Elizabeth in fascination that she would challenge him on such a level, though he rather enjoyed the verbal combat. He leaned back against his chair and chuckled to himself.

"You expect me to account for opinions which *you* choose to call mine, but which I have never acknowledged. It is a fanciful game of yours, I'm sure. But, allowing the case, however, to stand according to your representation, you must remember, Miss Bennet, that the friend who is supposed to desire his return to the house, and the delay of his plan, has merely desired it, asked it without offering one argument in favour of its propriety."

"To yield readily—easily—to the *persuasion* of a friend is no merit with you?"

"To yield without conviction is no compliment to the understanding of either."

Her eyes flashed with fire, and Darcy enjoyed the ire radiating therein as she pressed onward.

"You appear to me, Mr. Darcy, to allow nothing for the influence of friendship and affection. A regard for the requester would often make one readily yield to a request without waiting for arguments to reason one into it. I am not particularly speaking of such a case as you have supposed about Mr. Bingley. We may as well wait, perhaps, till the circumstance occurs before we discuss the discretion of his behaviour thereupon. But in general and ordinary cases between friend and friend, where one of them is desired by the other to change a resolution of no very great moment, should you think ill of that person for complying with the desire, without waiting to be argued into it?"

...Miss Bennet, you know not what you speak, for I know my friend far better than yourself, Darcy thought to himself. *He is easily led where anyone who chooses to do so will take him, and while you think it admirable, others call it weakness...his fortune is that it is I who often leads...watching out for his own good!*

Nodding with a smile, he finally spoke. "Will it not be advisable, before we proceed on this subject, to arrange with rather more precision the degree of importance which is to appertain to this request, as well as the degree of intimacy subsisting between the parties?"

"By all means," cried Bingley; "let us hear all the particulars, not forgetting their comparative height and size; for that will have more weight in the argument, Miss Bennet, than you may be aware of. I assure you that, if Darcy were not such a great tall fellow, in comparison with myself, I should not pay him half so much deference. I declare I do not know a more awful object than Darcy, on particular occasions, and in particular places; at his own house especially, and of a Sunday evening, when he has nothing to do. Darcy is a man hard to refuse when his mind is made up—be it for good or ill, he carries the day."

Darcy crossed his legs as he twisted his signet ring about his finger, his eyes boring into hers. He must concede Miss Elizabeth Bennet had surprised him. She pursued her point rather well, and he was impressed, though he perceived that she thought he was offended and therefore checked her laugh. Quite the contrary. He was not offended in the least, but rather fascinated that she possessed the dexterity to know when to persist and when not—a skill not often perfected by most gentlemen of his acquaintance, let alone *any* women. It was a talent very useful in the gaming hells of London. Did she play chess as well?

Miss Bingley, however, warmly resented the indignity she perceived he had received, in an expostulation with her brother for talking such nonsense.

Darcy watched the sparing between siblings and mused to himself. *Perhaps it is time to bring this little battle of the wills to an end. Miss Bennet, you may think you have won the match, but the devil is in the details. Complex minds often call for deductive reasoning where matters of the fainter mind are concerned. You would do well to know this. Perhaps someday I shall teach you. A friend protects a friend, Miss Bennet. And I shall protect mine.*

"I see your design, Bingley," he said at last. "You dislike an argument, and want to silence this one."

"Perhaps I do. Arguments are too much like disputes. If you and Miss Bennet will defer yours till I am out of the room, I shall be very thankful, and then you may say whatever you like of me."

"What you ask," Elizabeth said, smiling, "is no sacrifice on my side, and Mr. Darcy had much better finish his letter."

Darcy took her advice and did finish his letter to his sister, and the one to his cousin, as well.

~*~

After his letters were sealed, Darcy stacked them both together and left them in the salver for a servant to post on the morrow.

Putting his pen and paper away, he applied to Miss Bingley and Miss Elizabeth for the indulgence of some music.

"We would be delighted to play and sing for you, Mr. Darcy. What would you like?"

His gazed fixed on Elizabeth's face.

"Anything will do, but, if you are of a mind, how about 'Moonlight Sonata'? It is a particular favourite of mine."

Elizabeth blushed furiously and turned away.

Caroline glanced between them and stood to her feet moving towards the pianoforte.

"Miss Bennet, would you not like to entertain us first?" Bingley asked, giving his sister a reproachful look.

"I thank you, no," she replied also moving towards the instrument. "I shall peruse your selections and choose one more suited to my ability. I am afraid I would not do Beethoven justice. He is far better left to those who can."

"I would be delighted to perform the piece. It is not too difficult for my skills. Louisa," Caroline said motioning to her sister to follow, "let us play, and when this rendition is over, I shall play another and you may sing."

A Man in Want of a Wife

Darcy smiled and took a seat close to the fire where he might observe the scene more closely. Miss Elizabeth, he mused, severely underestimated her ability, for he had heard her play "Moonlight Sonata" earlier in the day and had never heard it played better.

While Mrs. Hurst sat with her sister, Darcy set his eyes on Elizabeth turning over the music books that lay on the instrument as she stood beside the Bingley sisters. She glanced up every now and again and caught his stare. He noted that she seemed perplexed, but he did not break the contact. He wondered what she was thinking as she tilted her head in puzzlement. He thought to ask, but then remembering their most recent exchange, decided the better of it. He smiled inwardly...*she must wonder at my attention to her.*

Elizabeth, for her part, watched Darcy with interest. She hardly knew how to suppose that she could be an object of admiration to so great a man, and yet that he should look at her because he disliked her was even stranger still. She could only imagine that she drew his notice because there was something about her more wrong and reprehensible than agreeable, according to his perceptions of suitability. He had asked her to play only so that he could find fault with her performance, knowing very well from this afternoon, that she was no proficient. She was quite certain that he thought her beneath any other person present. The supposition did not pain her; she liked him too little to care for his approbation.

Once several moments had passed in this fashion, Darcy turned back to Miss Bingley, and listened to her presentation. Though she played excellently, he gave little thought to the pleasure it was meant to afford him. In fact, so absorbed was he in his thoughts of Miss Elizabeth, that he scarcely heard the melody performed for his benefit.

Miss Bingley noticed his inattention, and after playing several Italian and German pieces, she varied her performance with a lively Scottish air, hoping to draw his notice to her, but it was not to be.

Instead, Darcy's thoughts were even more drawn to Elizabeth as his gaze fell to her feet, which were tapping the floor in time with the spirited tune. Soon afterwards, seeing the opportunity presented to him, he approached her.

Having every expectation of being rewarded, he bowed. "With such lively music, Miss Bennet, do you not feel a great inclination to seize such an opportunity of dancing a reel?"

She glanced up at him with a smile, but made no answer.

He repeated the question, with some surprise at her silence.

"Oh!" she said, "I heard you before, but I could not immediately determine what to say in reply. I know you wanted me to say 'Yes,' so that you might have the pleasure of despising my taste, but I always delight in overthrowing those kinds of schemes and cheating a person of their premeditated contempt. I have, therefore, made up my mind to tell you that I do not want to dance a reel at all—and now despise me if you dare," she said with a pleasing smile as she arched one eyebrow.

Darcy's lips twitched, forming an indistinct, amused curve. "Indeed, I do not, for you have chosen your mode of refusal so well as to tease me in such a playful fashion, characterized only by *you*, that I could not despise you even if I ventured to do so." He bowed. "There will be another opportunity, Miss Bennet, for another time." Turning, he moved back to his seat.

Their eyes met from across the room, and by her expression, he perceived that she had expected him to be affronted by her rejection, but he was not; for there was a mixture of sweetness and mischievousness in her manner which made it difficult for him to be offended. In fact, it was quite the contrary. He found her impudence refreshing and her mode of expression alluring to the extent that he somewhat enjoyed sporting with her.

Her eyes sparkled and danced with the essences of life while his heart pounded from desire. He nodded to himself as he mused:

...Yes, Miss Bennet, there will be another day, and you will dance with me at least once...yes, Elizabeth...at least once... you cannot remain coy forever.

This little game of cat and mouse they played drew him to her like a hound on the scent of a fox. Darcy had never before been so *bewitched* by any woman as he was by her. He really believed that, were it not for the inferiority of her connections, he should be in some real danger of forgetting everything, even going against the very wishes of his family; for had the Bennets been from a more acceptable sphere, he might be willing to forgive some of their vulgarity and savage behaviour, but they were not, and he could not accept things as they were.

Leaning back in his seat, he took a deep breath as he closed the expression on his face, once again keeping his emotions in check.

~*~

Miss Bingley saw, or suspected, enough to be jealous, and her great anxiety for the recovery of her dear friend Jane received some assistance from her desire of getting rid of Elizabeth, who had made her excuses to return above stairs for the night.

Miss Bingley's eyes followed her exit, and when she had disappeared from sight, she turned her covetousness toward Darcy. Trying to provoke him into disliking her guest, she began talking of their supposed marriage and planning his happiness in such an alliance.

"I hope," she said, as she came around to the table beside Darcy's chair, "you will give your mother-in-law a few hints, when this desirable event takes place, as to the advantage of holding her tongue, and if you can accomplish it, do cure the younger girls of running after the officers. And, if I may mention so delicate a subject, endeavour to check that little something, bordering on conceit and impertinence, which your lady possesses."

Louisa eyed her sister in warning. "Caroline, are you not fatigued? I think it has been quite an evening. We should all retire," she said yawning.

But Miss Bingley would have none of her sister's admonishments. "If you are so exhausted, Louisa, then you go to bed. I, for one, am perfectly content to remain where I am."

"Ay," said Hurst, rousing from his nap. "Damn waste of a good evening not to have loo after supper. I might as well call it a day as well if all this talk of marriage is to continue."

"Come, Reggie. Leave them to themselves."

The alarmed look Mrs. Hurst gave her sister as she and Mr. Hurst gathered their things was one of caution, but Caroline was determined to keep her own counsel.

When they had left, Darcy returned his attention to Caroline.

"Have you anything else to propose for my domestic felicity?" he asked, intending to sport with Miss Bingley.

A Man in Want of a Wife

"I think—" Bingley attempted to say, but was cut off by his sister who paid him no heed.

"Oh, yes! I've many more things to say," she interjected with indignation. "Do let the portraits of your Uncle and Aunt Philips be placed in the gallery at Pemberley. Put them next to your great-uncle, the judge. They are in the same profession, you know, only in different lines. As for your Elizabeth's picture, you must not attempt to have it taken, for what painter could do justice to those *beautiful eyes*?"

"It would not be easy, indeed, to catch their expression, but their colour and shape, and the eye-lashes, so remarkably fine, might be copied."

His reserved smile as he poured a glass of wine and sipped it, unsettled her so that she too soon retired for the evening, leaving Darcy and Bingley behind. He grinned copiously as her orange feathers ruffled while she departed.

"Darcy, I am very sorry for my sister's behaviour. It's just that once she begins—"

"Yes, Bingley, I am well aware...but do not concern yourself. I am not offended in the least."

Darcy finished his wine and set the glass aside. "Now, if you will excuse me, I think I shall retire as well. It has been a trying day."

Indeed it had. From Mrs. Bennet's visit, to the afternoon delight in his dressing room and then later in the music room, to their encounter this evening, Miss Elizabeth had proven to be quite a challenge to him...quite a challenge indeed—one to the likes of which he had never before encountered—and he rather enjoyed a good challenge. They were too few and far between.

He smiled a slow, speculative smile as he left for his chamber.

~*~*~*~

Chapter 10

Several days had passed since their last exchange, and Elizabeth had managed to keep to herself, completely avoiding any conversation with Mr. Darcy, though he came with Mr. Bingley to have tea with Jane every afternoon. She had to wonder at why he took the trouble of coming up to her sister's room in the first place when he knew full well she would be in attendance. The man puzzled her to say the very least.

That evening as she prepared for dinner, she took extra care with her toilette, applying lavender oil generously around her pulses, but why she did so, she could not say. Taking a string of pearls from a velvet-lined box in her bag, she gracefully clasped them around her slender neck. When she was ready to go below stairs, she turned to her sister.

"Shall I disgrace you, Jane?"

Jane tilted her head and gazed at her sister wearing the gift their father had given Elizabeth for her eighteenth birthday.

Jane smiled sweetly. "You look very pretty, Lizzy, as you well know. The pearls and your dress are quite elegant. The cut flatters your figure to its best advantage. Papa would be proud to see you now."

"Oh, Jane, I do hope we shall be leaving here soon. I feel quite out of place. I cannot compete with Miss Bingley's elegant manners or her beautiful way of carrying herself. Our gowns are from two seasons back, and hers are the latest fashions, made, no doubt, by the most renowned modiste shops in Town."

"Lizzy, you have never been concerned for such things before. Why are you now?"

"I don't know, Jane. It's just that…that I feel so…so…I don't know. I suppose it has always been left to you and me to set the standard for our family, for if it is left to Mamma and our sisters, then we must surely fall far short of acceptable in the eyes of *some*."

Smiling, Jane took a deep breath and gently shook her head as she reached for her sister's hand.

"Lizzy, you have a grace and beauty all of your own. You needn't worry about Mamma or our sisters, and you need not concern yourself about impressing anyone. If they do not like you for who you are, it is of no consequence; for if they cannot see and judge you for the quality of your character, then the loss is theirs."

"So true." Elizabeth laughed. "What would I do if not for you, dear Jane, to comfort me? I care not one whit for any of their good opinions—not even—and especially *not* Mr. Darcy's."

Elizabeth turned and left for dinner, anxious, but unsure as to exactly why. The Bingley sisters' chiding remarks were bothersome to some degree, for she knew they were made to remind her of her place in society, but Mr. Darcy's constant stare

A Man in Want of a Wife

bothered her even more, to say the least, for she knew he only looked upon her to find fault. Though her gowns might not be the latest fashions from London, they were at least suitable for the country where she lived, and she had rather wear nothing at all on her head than those ostrich feathers so much the latest vogue.

~*~

As Jane watched her sister go, she spoke softly to herself, "Oh Lizzy, you do not know yourself, for I think you protest too much and that you do indeed care for Mr. Darcy's good opinion, though you have yet to discover it."

Smiling sweetly, Jane turned over and pulled her pillow to herself as she sighed in contentment. "Would it not be a good thing, Lizzy, if Mr. Darcy were to fall in love with you and you with him?"

~*~

Coming into the dining room, Elizabeth took a deep breath and found her seat where she ate quietly, speaking only when spoken to. Glancing around the room, she noted that dinner was a relatively tranquil affair. Conversation was light and civil. Mr. Hurst ate heartily, speaking to no one; Mr. Bingley asked quite often about Jane; and Mrs. Hurst and Miss Bingley had an occasional comment about the turn of meat and the goodness of the potatoes when they were not also enquiring about their good friend and if she would be joining them for tea later in the evening. Then, when the meal was finally over, the gentlemen left for cigars and brandy, and the ladies were left to themselves where they talked a little while longer over coffee and dessert before quitting the table.

At long last, when they removed themselves to the drawing room, Elizabeth ascended the stairs and entered her sister's bedroom. Closing the door behind her, she enquired of Jane.

"Do you think you might like to attend us in the drawing room tonight? Miss Bingley and Mrs. Hurst sent their wishes that you would come, and I dare say Mr. Bingley would like nothing better than to see you among the party."

Jane lowered her lashes. "Mr. Bingley sees me every day for tea here in my room, but if you think he would like for me to come down, then yes," she looked up with a smile, "I will come."

"Good! I know he will, for it was all he talked about during dinner. Now let me help you prepare, and we shall join them. But I must warn you, Mr. Darcy can be quite severe in his pronouncements."

"Lizzy, I am sure you are wrong, for when Mr. Darcy comes for tea with Mr. Bingley, he is very kind and attentive, as you well know from observing him."

"Yes, well, who could not be sweet to you, dear Jane? But, he is not so kind to me. It seems every opportunity afforded him, he challenges me with alacrity in a confrontation. I cannot make him out. He surely despises me."

Jane smiled and shook her head. "Perhaps he likes you, Lizzy."

"Likes me? Do you mean that he might be in good humour to give consequence to a young lady slighted by other men? Never! He dislikes me; I'm quite certain of it."

Jane laughed. "Lizzy, that was very wrong of him, but, as you have stated, since then he has asked you to dance twice, I do believe, if you count our time at Lucas Lodge. I think his opinion of you has perhaps improved on closer acquaintance."

Elizabeth chuckled. "Sir William forced me upon him then, and as for last night, you know he was only mocking me. He overheard my very bad rendition of 'Moonlight Sonata,' and then tried to entice me into making a spectacle of myself by repeating the performance for all to hear so they could ridicule me when my back was turned; furthermore, Jane, I am well aware of how much he dislikes dancing. And besides that, I told you about our altercation concerning Mr. Bingley."

"Yes, but Lizzy, I think you might have mistaken Mr. Darcy. I do not think he was trying to make a spectacle of you. I have heard you play before, and it is not the disaster you imagine. Perhaps Mr. Darcy did not think so either.

"As for the other, dear Lizzy, can you not see that even though he might be critical, he is very loyal to his friend? And besides, when I observe him, I find no such offense as you describe. After all, did you yourself not say that he looks at you a great deal, and that you even caught him staring at you from his window when he was a little less than formally attired?"

Both girls erupted in laughter. "I am sure he didn't mean for me to see him, but when I did, he didn't turn away. It was I who left. Though I will say Mr. Darcy is very much a handsome man, and if I were not predisposed to dislike him so much, I might find him attractive. His appearance has not gone unnoticed by me, but otherwise, no. I find him very disagreeable. The only good thing about Mr. Darcy is his dog. Sam is a real treasure, one I would like to own if I could, but he is very loyal to his master, which is another good thing about him. Sam is a faithful friend."

"Then I'm sure Mr. Darcy is a good sort of man to have trained a dog so well and inspire such faith. Dogs are a very good judge of character, Lizzy, and to be as loyal as you say Sam is, Mr. Darcy must be a good sort of man."

"Mr. Darcy, a good sort of man? Certainly not! I have a reasonably good sketch of his character, and I believe I have him marked correctly."

Elizabeth smiled at her sister with a sigh. "*But*, for your sake, Jane, I shall try to be more amenable and keep an open mind. Perhaps I am wrong. However, I seriously doubt that I am, for I have never misjudged one's character so wrongly before, and to allow Mr. Darcy to be as you so believe would indeed be a serious fault in my good judgment. Now come, Jane, let us go downstairs."

Jane only smiled while Elizabeth helped her with her wrap, and seeing her well-guarded from the cold, attended her into the drawing-room.

~*~

When the gentlemen entered Bingley's study, Mr. Hurst went to the drinks cabinet and took out a new decanter of fine French brandy while Bingley opened up a wooden box where he kept cigars from the former colonies of America.

Breaking the seal, Mr Hurst expressed his wishes for a hunt with eagerness. "I think we should have more sport. It seems a damn shame to let so many birds and deer go to waste when we could be enjoying a hunt. When do you plan to have your deer party, Charles?" he enquired, pouring three measures of brandy.

Darcy took his drink and cigar and walked towards the fireplace where he leaned against the mantelpiece while Bingley and his brother-in-law discussed the particulars of the event which was to take place before Christmas. Though he loved the thrill of the hunt as well as the next man, his thoughts were engaged on *another* hunt of sorts. Miss Elizabeth Bennet had appeared at the dinner table looking more beautiful than he could have ever imagined. Her fashion was not frilly or pretentious, but rather modest and simple. The cut of her gown accentuated her alluring curves in a sensual manner as it fell about her hips in a pleasing way, and the string of pearls she wore, resting on her more than ample bosom, had drawn his attention from the moment she entered the room.

But more alluring than her appearance was the faint scent of lavender she always wore. It was a clean, refreshing scent that reminded him of elegance in a genteel lady. His mother had worn it, and though it was not in vogue for their times, he associated it with goodness. All through dinner he could hardly keep from staring. As he drew in a large draw of smoke from one of Bingley's prized Virginian cigars, he contemplated what it might be like to spend an evening at Pemberley with her in attendance. But just as his thoughts were about to run wild, he was riveted back to reality.

"Darcy...Darcy! Did you not hear what I said?" asked Bingley. "Come, man, where is your mind?"

"What? No, I must have been preoccupied. What was your question?"

"I merely asked your opinion on inviting a party from Town to have first a hunt for deer and then a few days later, another for fox. Do you think your cousins, Lord Wexford and Colonel Fitzwilliam, might enjoy a week in the country? Wex may bring Miss Gamble and her brothers if he likes, and I suppose her father might come as well."

"Yes, I suppose they would. If Wex is available, I am sure he would come, but he and Miss Gamble are no longer courting."

"Good! Then it's settled. If your cousins are available, then they shall come. It is too bad about Miss Gamble, but I never thought she suited the Viscount.

"At present, the first week of December I shall go to Town and return with a large party of friends. Yes, I shall invite them to join us. It shall be a great way to introduce all of them to my new home. Now, with that settled, let us join the ladies, and if God's grace is with us, perhaps Miss Bennet will join us."

Darcy tossed his half smoked cigar in the fire and downed his drink; he then turned and followed Mr. Hurst and Bingley to the drawing room wondering what the evening would hold where Miss Elizabeth was concerned. With a smile, he mused to himself *...I look forward to our next encounter, Miss Elizabeth Bennet...indeed I do. What witty exchange will you engage me in next?*

~*~

When Jane and Elizabeth entered the drawing room, Jane was welcomed by her two friends with many professions of pleasure. Miss Bingley and Mrs. Hurst were very attentive to them both, but especially to Jane.

Elizabeth sat back with pleasure and sipped her tea, for she had never seen them so agreeable as they were during the hour which passed before the gentlemen appeared. Their powers of conversation were considerable. They could describe an entertainment with accuracy, relate an anecdote with humour, and laugh at their acquaintances with spirit.

But when the gentlemen entered, Jane was no longer the first object of interest. Miss Bingley's eyes were instantly turned towards Mr. Darcy, and she had something to say to him before he had advanced many steps.

"Mr. Darcy, how good to see you, sir. I have your tea ready just the way you like it, two sugars and one cream. Come. Sit by the fire and warm yourself. I shall attend you there."

Darcy, however, ignored her, leaving Miss Bingley standing there in a stupid manner, holding a pot of tea while Darcy addressed himself directly to Jane with a sincere congratulation.

"Miss Bennet, I am very glad to see you felt up to joining us this evening," he said. "I hope there will be many more occasions for you to do so."

Jane blushed. "I thank you, sir. I am feeling much better."

Mr. Hurst also made her a slight bow. "I am very glad to see you as well, Miss Bennet."

To which Jane responded sweetly, "I am pleased to be amongst you at last. I am truly much better."

However, the highest effusions and warmth remained for Bingley's salutation.

"Miss Bennet!" he said with genuine delight as he made his way to her. "I have never in my life been so glad to see anyone. I'm truly pleased you felt well enough to join us tonight, but then, after our conversation this afternoon, I had hopes that you would. Come. Sit by the fire. Let me pile up the logs so that you are not chilled by a draft."

The first half-hour was spent in this fashion, piling up the fire and stoking it into a roaring blaze, lest Jane should suffer from the change of room, and she removed herself, at his desire, to the other side of the fireplace, that she might be farther from the door and any drafts. He then sat down by her and talked scarcely to anyone else.

Elizabeth, at work on her stitching in the opposite corner, saw it all with great delight so much so that she hardly noticed that the gentleman from Derbyshire rarely took his eyes off her person as he quietly sipped his tea, studying her with admiration twinkling in his dark eyes.

When tea was over, Mr. Hurst reminded his sister-in-law of the card-table.

"There will be no cards tonight, Mr. Hurst. Mr. Darcy does not wish to play, Charles is, it seems, engaged elsewhere, and you know perfectly well Eliza does not play. We've not enough for a game."

The silence of the whole party on the subject seemed to justify her supposition.

"Nay! Nothing to do but useless conversations then—damn tedious way to spend an evening!"

Mr. Hurst had therefore nothing to do but to stretch himself out on one of the sofas and go to sleep. Darcy took up a book; Miss Bingley did the same; and Mrs. Hurst, principally occupied in playing with her bracelets and rings, joined now and then in her brother's conversation with Miss Bennet.

To Darcy's dismay, Miss Bingley's attention was quite as much engaged in watching his progress through *his* book as in reading her own, which he was well aware she had only chosen because it was the second volume of his. She was perpetually either making some enquiry about the subject matter or looking at his page as she stalked about the room. Try as she might, he would not allow her the privilege of drawing him to any conversation; he merely answered her questions and read on. Had she been the only woman in the room, it would not have made one jot of difference; for Darcy was not fooled by her officious fawning. He knew her sole objective was to impress him by her choice of reading material, and by her questions she hoped to demonstrate that she was quite as proficient as Miss Elizabeth in intelligent thought. And although he would not call Miss Bingley stupid, neither would he call her progressive. Miss Elizabeth Bennet need not worry where his thoughts ran when comparing the two.

At length, quite exhausted by the attempt to be amused with her book, Caroline gave a great yawn and sat back down.

Turning about, she said, "How pleasant it is to spend an evening in this way! I declare after all there is no enjoyment like reading! How much sooner one tires of anything than of a book! When I have a house of my own, I shall be miserable if I have not an excellent library."

No one made any reply.

She then yawned again, threw aside her book, and cast her eyes round the room in quest of some amusement. When, hearing her brother mentioning a ball to Miss Elizabeth, she turned suddenly towards him and said, "By the bye, Charles, are you really serious in meditating a dance at Netherfield? I would advise you, before you determine on it, to consult the wishes of the present party. I am much mistaken if there are not some among us to whom a ball would be rather a punishment than a pleasure."

"If you mean Darcy," her brother cried, "he may go to bed, if he chooses, before it begins, but as for the ball, it is quite a settled thing, and as soon as Nicholls has made white soup enough, I shall send round my cards."

"I should like balls infinitely better," she replied, "if they were carried on in a different manner, but there is something insufferably tedious in the usual process of such a meeting. It would surely be much more rational if conversation, instead of dancing, made the order of the day."

"Much more rational, my dear Caroline, I dare say, but it would not be near so much like a ball."

Miss Bingley made no answer, and soon afterwards began walking about the room again. Darcy, for his part, knew her expression of conversation over dancing was made for his benefit and was not her own opinion. Miss Bingley loved to dance as much as anybody, and of late, he had changed his mind about dancing as well. But to her disadvantage, his change of mind was no credit to her.

Miss Bingley continued her walk, swaying her hips as she did. Her figure was elegant, and she walked well, but Darcy, at whom it was all aimed, remained inflexibly studious. He chose to ignore her and her every attempt to engage his attention fell flat. Had she been the last woman in the world, he could not be prevailed upon to care for her in any other way than that of a sister of a close friend, and even in that, she was sorely testing him.

He cast a fleeting glance her way when, in desperation, she resolved on one effort more to acquire what she wanted and turned to Elizabeth.

"Miss Eliza Bennet, let me persuade you to follow my example and take a turn about the room. I assure you it is very refreshing after sitting so long in one attitude."

Though his eyes were decidedly fixed upon his tome, Darcy's thoughts were on Elizabeth. By her reaction, it was clear Miss Bingley had taken her by surprise, but she agreed to it immediately, leaving him to speculate on Miss Bingley's real purpose. However, he wasn't left to wonder long, for Miss Bingley had finally succeeded no less in the *real* object of her civility: Darcy looked up and unconsciously closed his book. If by garnering Elizabeth's attention, she hoped to engage his own, she had succeeded admirably.

"It is so invigorating, a good sort of exercise. Would you not agree, Eliza?"

"Yes…I have always found walking to be a pleasure."

"Mr. Darcy," Caroline said, "would you not join us, sir?"

"I think not."

"And why ever not, sir? Please, pray tell?"

He leaned back in his seat and gave a slight smile. "I can imagine but two motives for your choosing to walk up and down the room together, with either of which my joining you would interfere."

"What do you mean, sir?" She turned to Elizabeth. "Miss Eliza, can you at all understand Mr. Darcy's meaning?"

"No, not at all," was her answer, "but depend upon it, he means to be severe on us, and our surest way of disappointing him will be to ask nothing about it."

He chuckled softly and raised his hand to his face, stroking his chin. Miss Elizabeth had come to know him quite well over the last few days. She was attempting to thwart his pleasure in provoking a sharp rhetorical remark from her. That would not do, but he needn't have worried for long. Miss Bingley would soon take the bait and satisfy his desires.

And he was correct. Miss Bingley was incapable of disappointing him in anything.

"Mr. Darcy, sir what is your meaning? I demand an explanation of your two motives. Tell us at once," she said.

He chuckled inwardly. "I have not the smallest objection to explaining them," he said. "You either choose this method of passing the evening because you are in each other's confidence, having secret affairs to discuss, or because you are conscious that your figures appear to the greatest advantage in walking. If the first is your true purpose, then I should be completely in your way, and if it is the second, I can admire you much better as I sit here by the fire."

He sat back with triumph, relishing in the moment.

"Oh! Shocking!" Miss Bingley cried, turning to her partner. "I never heard anything so abominable. How shall we punish him for such a speech?"

"Nothing so easy, if you have but the inclination," Elizabeth said. "We can all plague and punish one another. Tease him—laugh at him."

"Laugh at Mr. Darcy? Impossible!"

"Impossible? Surely *not*. Intimate as you are, you must know how it is to be done."

"But upon my honour I do *not*. I assure you that my intimacy has not yet taught me *that*. Tease calmness of temper and presence of mind! No, no—I feel he may defy us there. And as to laughter, we will not expose ourselves, if you please, by attempting to laugh without a subject. Mr. Darcy may hug himself."

"Mr. Darcy is not to be laughed at!" Elizabeth cried. "That is an uncommon advantage, and uncommon I hope it will remain, for it would be a great loss to *me* to have many such acquaintances, for I dearly love to laugh."

Darcy sighed. "Miss Bingley," he said, "has given me credit for more than can be. The wisest and best of men—nay, the wisest and best of their actions—may be rendered ridiculous by a person whose first object in life is a joke."

"Certainly," replied Elizabeth, "there are such people, but I hope I am not one of *them*. I hope I never ridicule what is wise or good. Follies and nonsense, whims and inconsistencies, *do* divert me, I own, and I laugh at them whenever I can. But these, I suppose, are precisely what you are without." Her eyes were like fiery darts as they bore into his.

"Perhaps that is not possible for anyone. But it has been the study of my life to avoid those weaknesses which often expose a strong understanding to ridicule."

"Such as vanity and pride," she said, arching her brow in challenge.

Suddenly Darcy was uncomfortable with the turn of the conversation.

"Yes," he said at last, "vanity is a weakness indeed." Then straightening his shoulders, he looked her directly in the eye and continued with conviction. "But pride, Miss Bennet—where there is a real superiority of mind, pride will be always under good regulation."

Elizabeth turned away to hide a smile.

"Your examination of Mr. Darcy is over, I presume," said Miss Bingley, "and pray tell, what is the result of your study?"

"I am perfectly convinced by it that Mr. Darcy has no defect. He owns it himself without disguise."

"Indeed!" Miss Bingley cried. "He is a man *without* fault."

"Is he indeed? A man without fault..." Elizabeth repeated, her lips twisting in mirth. "Umm...now *that* is undeniably an accomplishment!" Her eyes met his and held them in amusement.

"No," Darcy said, his ire rising to meet her challenge, "I have made no such pretension. I have faults enough, Miss Bennet, but they are not, I hope, of understanding. My temper I dare not vouch for. It is, I believe, too little yielding—certainly too little for the convenience of the world. I cannot forget the follies and vices of others so soon as I ought, nor their offences against me. My feelings are not puffed about with every attempt to move them. My temper would perhaps be called resentful. My good opinion once lost is lost forever."

"*That* is a failing indeed!" cried Elizabeth. "Implacable resentment *is* a shade in a character. But you have chosen your fault well. I really cannot *laugh* at it. You are safe from me."

She threw up her hands and turned away, only to halt in her steps when he spoke yet again.

"There is, I believe, in every disposition a tendency to some particular evil—a natural defect, which not even the best education can overcome."

Turning in anger, she replied, "And *your* defect is a propensity to hate everybody."

"And yours, Miss Bennet," he replied, with equal force, "is to wilfully misunderstand them."

By now they had the attention of the whole room. Jane's perplexed gaze darted back and forth between them, unsure of what to make of the exchange.

At his retort, Elizabeth, quite piqued by now, crossed her arms beneath her breasts and turned her face aside.

Darcy leaned back in his seat and placed his arm across the back of his chair as he fixed his gaze upon Miss Elizabeth Bennet's appearance and dwelled on her audaciousness. He marvelled at her boldness, that she felt confident enough to challenge him as an equal. Then, as if by some force beyond him and without a conscious thought for propriety, his eyes slowly fell from her countenance to the curve of her full bosom.

Miss Bingley nervously glanced between the two, realizing the conversation was beyond her control. "Do let us have a little music," she cried. "Louisa, you will not mind my waking Mr. Hurst."

Her sister made not the smallest objection, and the pianoforte was opened.

Darcy, after a few moments' recollection, was not sorry for it. He began to feel the danger of paying Miss Elizabeth too much attention. She was more than a match for his intellect; she had a way of cutting through the chase to the heart of a matter and touching his most vulnerable and guarded feelings—something he allowed for *no one*—and especially not her!

~*~

That night after they returned to their room, Elizabeth threw her wrap on the bed and turned to her sister.

"Insufferable man! You see, Jane, Mr. Darcy is vain and conceited. I told you that he dislikes me!"

"No, Lizzy," her sister said coming closer and placing her hands on Elizabeth's shoulders. "You overstepped. You should not have provoked him. What I saw, when I had occasion to observe you, that is, was a man intrigued by you. Lizzy, he watches your every move. It is clear that he likes you, but as to how much and in what way, that I cannot say. Mr. Darcy keeps his feelings very guarded, unlike Mr. Bingley."

"Oh, Jane," Elizabeth shook her head. "I do not think you are correct in this case, though even Charlotte thinks as you do. I will say this, though; if Mr. Darcy likes me, he has a peculiar way of showing it. But as for me and my feelings, I can certainly vouch for them. I cannot stand the man—even if he does own half of Derbyshire! Come, Jane," Elizabeth said taking her sister's hand, "I've had enough of this conversation. Let us ring for the maid and go to bed. I wish to be rid of this place as soon as may be!"

~*~*~*~

Chapter 11

Elizabeth was up bright and early the next morning, feeling the need for fresh air after taking her morning tea with Jane. She had not slept well last night, and more than ever she wished to leave Netherfield sensing they had long since worn out their welcome.

While strolling along the garden paths, she happened to overhear two very familiar voices on the other side of the hedgerows, speaking in earnest.

"Miss Bennet is more than well enough to return home," Caroline retorted crossly. "What could be the meaning of her staying on? I'm certain, Mr. Darcy, that after Eliza's abominable behaviour last night you must surely be tiring of our guests by now."

He made no answer.

"I do believe, dear sister," Louisa said, "that Mr. Darcy rather enjoys a saucy exchange. Could you not tell?"

They both laughed.

Darcy walked on, staring straight ahead, again without a word to either. His jaw was set firm, and his eyes bore the distinct look of displeasure simmering just below his cool exterior.

"Besides," Louisa added, glancing from Darcy to Caroline, "I'm sure they don't mean to impose upon your generosity, Sister. For if our mother had been anything like theirs, would you not have wished to stay away for as long as you possibly could? And the younger sisters—always chasing the officers—what do their parents mean by letting them out so young?"

Again laughter rang out.

Elizabeth drew in a quick breath and clenched her fists. Anger burned in her chest as hot tears stung her eyes, and she seriously considered making her presence known. But then, thinking the better of it, she quietly turned and took the opposite path, making her way for the kitchen so that she might enter the house discreetly. Fortunately, Sam, who was running in the garden beside her, did not give her presence away. It was as if the dog knew and understood her distress. He approached her, wagging his tail with a soft whimper meant only for her notice.

"Not now Sam. It will not do," she said, fighting back her resentment. "I have other concerns occupying my time. Perhaps you might venture to Longbourn someday, and then we can play at our leisure, disagreeable mother and unruly sisters *notwithstanding*." She glanced down at the dog, so willing to please. "Oh, Sam! If only your master was as agreeable as you. Then I would not feel half so offended, but he is not. I wonder, Sam, what must he be saying now that he has free rein to speak his mind and with such a willing audience to hear it. *Insufferable man!*"

She stomped her foot, and then paused to stroke the dog's head. "I wish all men were as good and faithful as dogs, but alas, they are not, and I have arrived at my destination. Goodbye, Sam," she said with a deep sigh as she reached the back door to Mrs. Ayers' kitchen.

The dog nudged her hand, seeming to understand, and gave one quick bark before he darted away, his attention soon diverted by the scent of a rabbit hopping across the vegetable garden.

~*~

The state of affairs was not at all as Elizabeth had presumed, and had she remained long enough to hear Darcy's rebuttal, she might have found her feelings less affronted. But unfortunately, as it was, she was neither privy to the pleasure of his response nor the comfort she might have received upon hearing it.

~*~

Darcy's patience with Bingley's sisters was wearing thin, to say the least, but for Miss Elizabeth's sake, he would keep his emotions under good regulation for fear that Mrs. Hurst and Miss Bingley be given something else to talk about should he express what he really felt. Reconciling himself to the situation at hand, he released a frosty breath and attempted to alter the direction of the conversation, which he knew had been for his benefit, by raising it to a higher level.

"Miss Bennet," he said at last, his gaze fixed on nothing in particular, "is considerably better, I grant you, but I beg to differ with your assessment of her situation, Miss Bingley. The quiet of Netherfield is far better for her full recovery than the noise of Longbourn." Darcy paused, and then deciding he would answer some of the Bingley sisters' accusations, he cleared his throat and spoke, "And as for her sisters early coming out, well, all I can say on that subject is that the manners in the country are vastly different from those of Town, and while they might not be to your refined taste, I see no harm done in the setting in which they reside. What is there in a country dance to be despised—a few flirtations—a small number of smiles exchanged?" He released another deep breath. "Now, if you will excuse me, I believe I will return to the house."

"Louisa, if I did not know him better, I would say he is utterly smitten by Miss Eliza. Surely you do not think—"

"Perish the thought! You know as well as I Mr. Darcy will only marry from among his own circle He will not choose a country nobody. His honour forbids it! The future Mistress of Pemberley will be a lady of the highest quality—one who has all the polished refinements which are only available from the finest finishing schools and to those who can afford it, such as ourselves. You, dear sister, must learn to control that sharp tongue of yours, or you may lose every advantage you have gained through our brother's friendship with such an illustrious man."

The two sisters looked at one another for some moments and then took the more often used path back to the house. Climbing the steps to the portico, they entered and walked towards the breakfast parlour.

~*~

Elizabeth rushed into the kitchen and asked for a tray to be sent to her sister's room where they would take their morning meal together. She then asked the housekeeper to give her regrets to the family, saying she felt a slight headache and would not be joining them for tea.

Before she could leave, however, Molly approached her and curtseyed. "If you please, Miss Bennet, give my regards to your ailing sister. I hope that she's feeling much better this fine morning, and tell her that I shall have her hot broth to her room directly. Manny had to fetch a fat chicken this morning as the beef bones were all used up."

Elizabeth laughed and smiled kindly. "I shall tell her, Molly, and thank you for being so caring as to ask after my sister. It is very thoughtful of you."

"Oh! It ain't nothing, ma'am. I'd be just as concerned over me own sister—if'n I had one, that is."

"You have no siblings then?"

"Oh, no ma'am! I surely do! Me lot is to have five strapping brothers and all of them younger than me at that. Me da' says that if the Good Lord is willin' and the river don't rise that me ma may yet have another and that one might be me sis, for I so wish for a sis. I would be a good older sis—just like you."

Elizabeth smiled again and shook her head. "I am absolutely sure you would. You are a good girl, Molly," she said, and then turned to leave the kitchen.

Making her way to Jane's room, she ran directly into the path of Mr. Bingley, who, having just had word from Mrs. Nicholls, enquired after her health.

"I am fine; I thank you sir," she said with a curtsey, "I have only a slight headache which I think some warm porridge and a cup of coffee will soon set to rights. I sometimes feel unwell when I walk out so early with nothing but tea on my stomach."

"But of course, Miss Bennet. I do understand. It is a common occurrence for me as well. Give my warmest regards to your sister, and we shall see you directly."

"Ay, sir. I most assuredly will." She dropped another curtsey.

Returning to Jane's room, she pressed her sister for an agreement that they should return to Longbourn this very day, though she kept the exchange she had overheard in the garden to herself.

"Lizzy, if it pains you to such an extent to stay longer, then I think we should go. I realize Caroline is not pleasant to you. I can see the way her eyes follow you around the room, especially when Mr. Darcy engages you in conversation, but I do not think she means—"

"Jane! You do not know the half of it. Miss Bingley is *very much* opposed to me, as I to her. Let me just say that our feelings are mutual, and she need not worry where Mr. Darcy is concerned; for I am sure he prefers her company to mine any day." Elizabeth turned and spoke privately, "And she can have him for all I care!"

Releasing a deep breath, she glanced over her shoulder to Jane as she took a seat at the desk in their room. "I shall pen Mamma a note and send it directly. I must beg that the carriage be sent for us in the course of the day."

After posting the message, an hour had not passed before her letter was answered. Elizabeth tore into it with alacrity.

Lizzy, what do you mean requesting the carriage? Nonsense! You and Jane must remain at Netherfield till the following Tuesday, which will exactly finish Jane's week. I will not hear of you returning a moment sooner, and should you come, you can expect no welcome from me. It is by design that I have Jane at Netherfield and by design she shall stay until a full week has passed. Now, find some excuse to remain, for there is no advantage to either of you here.

Yours, etc.

Mamma

PS: if Mr. Bingley and his sister should press you to stay longer, I could spare you both very well. Stay another sennight.

Elizabeth shook her head as she folded the letter and placed it in her pocket. In regard to staying longer, she was positively resolved against it—nor did she much expect it would be asked. On the contrary, she was fearful that if Miss Bingley had anything to say about it, the opposite would be the case. Furthermore, from the conversation she had overheard just a few hours earlier, she knew she and Jane were considered to have intruded needlessly long already.

She glanced at her sister and released a sigh. "Mamma wants us to stay, but I think we should not. We must leave as we discussed, for I am impatient to be in my own room in our own house. I cannot abide remaining here a moment longer."

"Then we shall request a carriage from Mr. Bingley, for I have a desire to go home as well." Jane paused and looked away. "Lizzy, I know this is not proper. I feel it keenly, and I cannot accept it any longer. We shall indeed go."

~*~

After the breakfast tray was removed, Elizabeth descended the stairs and found the party in the morning parlour taking tea and discussing the day.

"Mr. Bingley," she said, approaching him with some hesitation. "Jane is much improved, and I believe the time has now come when my sister and I must return to Longbourn, and furthermore, since my parents cannot spare the carriage, it is my express wish that we may beg for the use of yours."

"Oh, but you mustn't leave! I will not hear of your leaving and neither will my sister," he said, turning to Miss Bingley. "Caroline, tell Miss Elizabeth that they must stay longer."

"No, we cannot. I—"

"But you must stay till the morrow at least," he cried with quickness. "Caroline…?"

"Yes," Caroline began with less enthusiasm than her brother, "I would not think of your leaving. Miss Bennet must stay at least another day. I insist upon it," she said with a smile that did not reach her eyes.

Elizabeth sighed, realizing that, though his sister might not be so charitable of heart, Mr. Bingley's wishes were genuine and heartfelt. She could not refuse the pleading so vividly expressed in his soft blue eyes. "Well," she said at length, "if it is agreeable to Jane, then it is agreeable to me, *but*, for one day *only*. We are needed at Longbourn to help with the herbs and dried flowers. They must be put away in the herb house with special care, and I'm afraid I am the only one who can oversee the job properly. And then Jane must oversee the distilling of the oils."

Word was sent to Jane who did agree for an extension of one day, and their going was, therefore, deferred. Miss Bingley was then sorry that she had acquiesced to her brother's pleadings and proposed the delay, for her jealousy and dislike of one sister much exceeded her affection for the other.

The master of the house heard with real sorrow that they were to go so soon, and throughout the course of the day, repeatedly tried to persuade Miss Bennet that it would not be safe for her—that she was not enough recovered and should stay another sennight. He stated that the herb harvest could wait another week, but Jane was firm where she felt herself to be right.

When Mr. Darcy returned from the stables, he found the family in the morning parlour having tea, lamenting Miss Bennet's coming departure. Filling his cup, Darcy walked away and stood by the window, gazing out onto the front lawn.

"Well, it is settled," Caroline stated. "The Miss Bennets shall depart for Longbourn on the morrow after church."

She turned to Darcy and walked to where he stood. "I suppose," she said approaching him with glee in her voice, "that you, sir, will be missing a pair of *fine eyes*."

Darcy showed no emotion as his teacup clattered in its saucer. "No, quite the contrary, I assure you."

Stepping away from the window, Miss Bingley smiled and glanced at her sister who raised her cup to her lips and smiled back.

Bingley was engaged with Hurst, who grumbled about another round of sport for the day, but the sky looked of rain and the idea was soon put to rest in favour of another topic which rose to take its place.

Standing there alone while the others chattered back and forth, Darcy continued to sip his tea while he watched Sam go out across the lawn on a hunt, nose to the ground, tail to the air. For his part, Darcy was well pleased with the news, as it was welcome intelligence to him; Elizabeth Bennet had been at Netherfield long enough. She attracted him more than he liked, and Miss Bingley was uncivil to *her* and more teasing than usual to himself.

He wisely resolved to be particularly careful that no sign of admiration should *now* escape him, nothing that could elevate her with the hope of influencing his felicity, sensible that if such an idea had been suggested, his behaviour during the course of their stay must have material weight in confirming or crushing it.

Steady to his purpose, he scarcely spoke ten words to her through the whole of Saturday, and even though they were at one time left by themselves for half an hour, he adhered most conscientiously to his book, and would not even look in her direction, yet he was keenly aware of her presence by the lavender fragrance that always followed her.

Elizabeth, for her part, was much relieved that Mr. Darcy paid her no particular mind one way or the other. She had long since grown tired of their tit for tat, back and forth, verbal sparring, parsing each other's words with meticulous detail. Mr. Darcy believed himself to be of superior breeding with worldly experience and intellect that far outreached hers. She would choose to let him think as he desired. Turning the page in her new book, she would not even glance in his direction, keeping carefully to her own volume, though the lingering scent of sandalwood and myrrh followed him, making concentration on her tome difficult to say the least.

~*~

On Sunday, after morning services, the separation, so agreeable to almost all, finally took place. Darcy had observed throughout the course of the morning that Miss Bingley's civility to Miss Elizabeth had increased very rapidly, as well as her affection for Miss Bennet. In fact, she was positively capricious, and when they finally parted, after assuring the latter of the pleasure it would always give her to see her either at Longbourn or Netherfield and embracing her most tenderly, she even shook hands with the former.

Darcy smiled at the duplicity of it all as he noted how Miss Elizabeth took leave of the whole party in the liveliest of spirits. All appeared to be joyful. Only Bingley, it seemed, was not so well pleased as he lamented the loss of Miss Bennet's company.

From his bedroom window, Darcy had watched it all. Never in his life was he so glad to see someone go as he was Elizabeth Bennet. He could not deny that she attracted him, nor would he deny that, with very little provocation, he could have her hand if he wished it, and that was reason enough to put an end to his fantasy, even if she was the flesh and blood replica of the wood nymph that often visited him in his dreams. It was time to put away childish desires and behave as a responsible man of his station.

~*~

Upon entering the gate at Longbourn proper, they were not welcomed home very cordially by their mother. Mrs. Bennet wondered at their coming, and thought them very wrong to give so much trouble to Mr. Bingley by requesting his carriage and not adhering to her commands. She was sure Jane would have caught cold again, but their father, though very laconic in his expressions of pleasure, was really glad to see them. He missed them dearly and had felt their importance in the family circle. The evening conversation, when they were all assembled, had lost much of its animation and almost all its sense, with the absence of Jane and Elizabeth.

They found Mary, as usual, deep in the study of thorough base and human nature, and had some new extracts to admire and some new observations of thread-bare morality to listen to. Catherine and Lydia had information for them of a different sort. Much had been done and much had been said in the regiment since the preceding Wednesday: several of the officers had dined lately with their uncle, a private had been flogged, and it had actually been hinted that Colonel Forster was going to be married. And so the merry party was once again established at Longbourn.

~*~*~*~

Chapter 12

Soon after the ladies of Longbourn had departed Netherfield Park, Darcy found that he sorely missed Miss Elizabeth Bennet and her pert opinions though he would scarcely admit it to himself, and most certainly not to any member of the household. He aimlessly wandered about the house expecting to hear her merry laughter or the sound of music coming from the drawing room but only silence hung in the air. More times than he cared to remember, he entered the room where they had spent many hours only to find it empty, devoid of anything pleasurable.

Unfortunately, Miss Bingley noticed his melancholy, for she and her sister enthusiastically approached him as he stood aimlessly by the pianoforte and begged that he join them in the gardens for a stroll. He declined. Instead, he gathered his volume of Sir Thomas More and left for his room where he could read in peace. But even as he read through the passages of philosophy and critical thought, he found himself wondering what Miss Elizabeth would think of More's opinion of first one subject and then another, as he knew she most certainly would have a judgment of her own.

Finally, bored with Sir Thomas More, he gently laid the volume aside and went to find Hurst and Bingley in the hopes of engaging in some sport. Perhaps shooting would relieve his growing anxiety.

~*~

The next morning, Darcy was even more restless, and after his morning meal, he decided exercise was in order. Taking his gun, he set out with Sam, riding hard and fast over the pasture lands, exploring all they could find. At the border of Longbourn and Netherfield, Sam caught the scent of a deer, which man and dog proceeded to hunt for several hours, but the animal proved too elusive for them and thus was granted a reprieve to forage in the forest for another day.

Wandering through the wooded paths, Darcy and Sam soon found themselves atop Oakham Mount. Trotting into the open area where he and Miss Elizabeth Bennet had met once before, he glanced around, but Miss Elizabeth was nowhere to be seen. Sam, he knew, was looking for her as well, sniffing every trace of the open meadow where they had on one occasion played, but Darcy was rather pleased that she had chosen not to walk out this particular morning, for he had no real wish to meet her here and had no idea why he had come, except that he had followed his dog. Taking a deep breath, he shook his head as he dismounted and tied his horse to a nearby low-hanging branch.

"Well, Sam, here we are. You miss her don't you? Well, I suppose I miss her, too, but we must not tell anyone."

Sam barked and frolicked about. Sighting a stick, he fetched it and laid it down at his master's feet.

"So you want to play just as you did with her, do you? Then play we shall."

Darcy reached down and picked up the stick, throwing it as hard as he could across the field. Sam dashed after it.

"I cannot marry her," Darcy spoke chidingly to himself. "It would be unsupportable. I must think of my sister and prospective heirs—my children. With a mother like hers and family in trade, they would never be accepted in the top tiers of society. Am I willing to give up everything it took generations to build…I, the grandson of an earl?"

He looked down at the unpretentious dog wagging his tail as he once more laid the stick at his feet.

"What do you say, Sam? Would you like to breed with a mongrel—a dog that is not a foxhound? Of course you would take no thought not to. You're a dog, and if a bitch is in heat, you would most certainly avail yourself of the opportunity."

Sam barked almost angrily.

"Yes, I know Miss Bennet is a gentleman's daughter and not a dog, but what of her *mother*? That is one woman, Sam, that I cannot abide. Once my circle met her, I'd be the laughing stock of all of London."

Darcy reached over and stroked his dog's head. "You do not care for such things, do you? And perhaps I should not either." Remembering what he had thought to himself many months ago, he spoke again. "Yes…I did say I would propose in an instant if I were to ever meet a woman who could fulfil my desires, but when I said that, I did not intend for it to be someone from trade or with Miss Elizabeth's inferior connections. She is so decidedly beneath me in all things that matter in my world—and need I mention what my family would think? It would be an abhorrence which my better judgment has always opposed. No, Sam," he glanced at his dog as he tossed the stick once more, "I cannot give over to my own foolish desires with one reckless decision. I have a duty and an obligation to the Darcy name, and I cannot forget it."

Sam did not hear the last of his master's words as he was long gone once the stick left Darcy's hand.

"It is just as well," Darcy muttered under his breath while he moved to retrieve his horse. "I'd just as soon talk to you, Calibus. You'd be just as likely to understand my dilemma as Sam." Darcy chuckled. "I must be fit for bedlam. I have just had conversations with first my dog, and now my horse."

The horse whinnied and raised his head as Darcy turned him towards Netherfield. "Come," he said, giving a shrill whistle for Sam. "Let's go home."

~*~

Five days had passed from the time when the ladies of Longbourn had departed, and since his outing with Sam, Darcy had put away thoughts of Elizabeth Bennet and stilled his emotions, placing them under good regulation while finding other things to occupy his mind. That was during the daylight hours, but at night, in the quiet of his room, it had been another situation entirely. There he could not even open his favorite book without images of Miss Elizabeth and their spirited conversations dominating his consciousness. He smiled softly as he relived each and every conversation while he sipped his brandy and smoked a cigar. There was no way to

A Man in Want of a Wife

deny what his heart spoke to him: she was the perfect woman in every possible way. He took a deep breath and raked his hand over his face.

"What are you going to do, Darcy? You want her like you have never wanted a woman before." He glanced around the room as he exhaled a stream of smoke. "Am I in love?" he asked himself.

He threw back his head and gave a hearty laugh. "The thought has crossed my mind—and more often than I would like at that. Good God, what am I going to do?"

"Excuse me, sir," his man said, stepping into the room, "Could I get you something before I retire for the evening?"

Darcy looked up, his eyes fixed on the older gentleman standing before him. "Yes...you can."

"And what might that be, sir?"

"Advice," he answered.

"Advice, sir?"

"Yes," Darcy said, matter-of-factly, "advice."

The man cleared his throat, stood straight, and nodded.

"Winfred Cunningham, my good man, have you ever been in love?"

"In love, sir?"

"Yes...in *love*. Has a woman ever captivated your thoughts so that you think of nothing else but her?"

"Yes, sir. I was once in love."

"Did you marry her?"

"Yes, sir, I did and was quite happy whilst it lasted."

"And...what, if I might enquire, happened?"

"She died in childbirth four and twenty years ago last December—the third to be exact."

Darcy furrowed his brow. "I never knew."

"No, sir, I never told you."

"And you never remarried?"

"No, sir. I have never seen the need to marry since my Molly. The thought of replacing her was reprehensible. I could never conceive of it. When you have loved and been loved in return, sir, you will understand."

"Loved..." he breathed out on a whisper.

"May I be so bold as to speak freely, sir?"

"Speak."

"Is Miss Elizabeth Bennet the object of your affections, sir?"

Darcy laughed. "How very perceptive of you."

His gentleman cleared his throat yet again. "Sir, if I may be so bold for a second time, I would speak and offer you my humble opinion on the matter."

Darcy raised a brow and motioned with his hand. "By all means, speak!"

Stepping away, his man walked about the room. After several moments of contemplation, he turned and fixed his gaze upon his master. "Mr. Darcy, love is a many splendored thing. It's like the roses that bloom in Pemberley's gardens in early summer, fragile and lovely with a sweet fragrance, giving a man a reason to live. It is the costly jewel set in a golden crown that makes a man a king in his own home, and it is also an illusion that many seek but few find. But, however, if you are fortunate enough to find the right female to accompany you through life's difficult pathways, then you are indeed blessed and should seize the opportunity at once, for love is rare—precious beyond all comprehension. Do not let it slip through your fingers, sir, or be the fool who thinks one woman is as good as another. It simply isn't true. It is a false assumption."

Darcy threw back in his chair and reached for his decanter of brandy. He poured another drink and set it aside as he gazed at the older gentleman before him. Raking his hand through his thick, dark curls, he released a breath and spoke tersely. "Thank you, Winfred. That will be all."

"As you wish, sir."

Mr. Cunningham moved to the door, but as he put his hand to the latch, he turned and gazed at his master. "Have a good evening, sir. I will see you at six o'clock sharp."

Darcy raised his glass. "Six o'clock sharp."

As the door closed behind his gentleman, Darcy downed his drink and slammed the glass on the side table. He moaned out loud. "What a romantic soul my man has! I must be in my cups to have had such a conversation with Winfred." He glanced at the half empty decanter of drink and shook his head. "I will regret this in the morning," he said as he rose for bed.

But sleep did not come so easily for Darcy. He tossed and turned all through the night with restless dreams of Elizabeth Bennet. He saw her walking in a meadow, and she would turn to smile at him. He approached to walk by her side and reached out to take her in his arms, longing to kiss the lips that taunted and teased him, to feel her lovely breasts in his hand, but she would vanish just as his fingertips were about to caress her beautiful face.

Darcy's eyes flew open, his heart pounding. He glanced at the clock barely visible in the moonlight streaming in from his window. It was four o'clock, and in the distance he could hear a cock crowing. Moaning, he clutched his pillow to his chest.

"Elizabeth Bennet, what have you done to me...and what will become of me if I do not offer for you?"

~*~

The days passed by slowly, and while Darcy could not vouch for his hound's whereabouts, as Sam had not followed him when he and Charles had ridden out to see about estate matters, he himself had not returned to Oakham Mount since the morning after the Miss Bennets left for Longbourn. And furthermore, though Darcy had managed to keep Bingley's time occupied with the business at hand: Mr. Goolsby had made good progress on the irrigation ditches, the men had begun to repair the stone walls for the outlying pastures, and Hurst, to his credit, had managed to keep his brother-in-law entertained at night with loo, he knew Charles Bingley felt the loss of the Longbourn ladies most acutely.

However, with all that Darcy strived to achieve for his friend, Bingley's thoughts were still occupied with one object: Miss Jane Bennet. He had expressed on more than one occasion how he sorely missed spending his afternoons with Jane, taking tea in her sick room while they talked. In fact, Charles missed Miss Jane so much that it had been all Darcy could do to keep his friend from galloping to Longbourn to *see about* Miss Bennet's health, as he would say, each morning after breakfast. But the various and sundry projects Darcy had used to keep his friend distracted had managed to lessen the necessity of calling on Longbourn...until today. As they rode back from the fields where the men were working, Bingley turned to him.

"Darcy, I think it would be fitting and proper to call on Miss Bennet this morning. It has been six days, man! She will think I have no care in the world for her wellbeing. I must call. I insist, and I will not be dissuaded."

"Well, if you insist, then let's call."

"You mean it, Darcy? You will ride over with me?"

"If you wish it, then certainly I will," Darcy replied with a half-smile as they turned their horses in the direction of the village. Though he would never own it to his friend, he too longed to see a *certain* lady once more, to catch the mirth in her beautiful eyes as she laughed, to smell the scent of lavender he now associated with only her, and last, but certainly not least, he simply wanted to be in her presence one more time. Darcy smiled a contented smile. Yes...he was more than willing to accompany his friend.

Darcy glanced over at Bingley as they entered the main street of Meryton with all its clamour and hustle and bustle. Carriages were going to and fro with people coming and going while they moved in and out of the many shops along the busy street. Riding down the thoroughfare, both gentlemen caught sight of a small party standing on the corner laughing and talking together very agreeably in happy readiness of conversation. Darcy heard Elizabeth's merry laugh ringing out and instantly recognized her there among those gathered together. She was with all her sisters, several officers he recognized, a rather large man wearing a vicar's collar, and one unknown person who looked oddly familiar. However, the man's back was turned to him, and therefore, Darcy could not place the acquaintance.

When the sound of their horses drew the assembled group's notice, they looked up. Darcy and Bingley rode directly towards them and began the usual civilities. Bingley was the principal spokesman, and Miss Bennet the principal object.

"Miss Bennet!" he spoke, raising his beaver. "How good it is to find you out and about this splendid morning. Darcy and I were on our way to enquire after your health. How are you this fine day?"

Jane blushed and lowered her lashes. Glancing up she said in a soft genteel voice, "I am quite well, sir, as you see."

"Well, yes, I can see that you are," he said, looking in his friend's direction.

Darcy acknowledged the ladies with a bow of his head, determined not to fix his eyes on Elizabeth, but before he could school his emotions, they got the better of him; and for one brief moment, his eyes locked with Miss Elizabeth Bennet's. However, his attention was suddenly diverted by the sight of the man standing next to her. He rose up slightly in his saddle and narrowed his eyes. The man in the blue coat turned slowly and faced him fully.

Darcy's body tensed. Both gentlemen changed colour; one white, the other red. Mr. Wickham, after a few moments, touched his hat—a salutation which Darcy was forced to return.

Darcy cast a fleeting look at the expression of astonishment on Elizabeth's countenance as she glanced between them, and then he turned back and glared at his enemy, hatred most assuredly displayed in his eyes while fear clearly showed in the eyes of the other.

Not wanting to prolong the awkward situation a moment longer, Darcy turned his horse and trotted off in the direction from whence they had come. In the next awkward moment, Mr. Bingley spoke a few words and took leave to ride on with his friend.

When they had cleared the town limits, Bingley glanced over to his companion.

"Darcy, what happened back there? I thought we might visit with Miss Bennet."

"Bingley, if it suits you, you may turn your horse round and return, but I have little use for the company."

"Company?"

"Yes. Did you not observe the gentleman in the blue coat standing among them?"

"No. I'm afraid he quite escaped my notice. I saw the sisters, Lieutenant Denny, and a parson, but who was that other man? I've never seen him before."

"That gentleman, though I use that term loosely, was none other than Mr. Wickham."

Bingley looked confused.

"Wickham, man! He's here," Darcy spat out.

"Wickham…here? Your old friend from Cambridge?"

Darcy shot him a look; his lips narrowed in disapproval.

"Ah, yes…I do remember you telling me much about him; he was not discreet in his behaviour as a gentleman should always be, but I am sure he has improved. Surely he has. You paid him quite handsomely to study law—that is after he refused the living bequeathed to him by your father's will. Surely Darcy he has improved since then. I mean—"

"You think that do you?" Darcy cut him off in irritation. "Well, let me simply say that though he may have the outward appearance of a deserving gentleman striving to make his way in the world, he most decidedly is *not*. He has betrayed me in the most infamous manner—one that I shall never forget. I will not give you the particulars at this point in time, but I will say that he nearly brought about the ruin of my family through his treachery. No," Darcy shook his head, "I shall never forgive his betrayal. We were once close friends, but never again. I was nothing but kind to him, and yet he would betray me—and not just recently, but all through our youth with his lecherous living and gaming debts, and my father, God rest his soul, never knew."

"Darcy, I know not what to say, except I am deeply sorry for the pain he has caused you and your family and—"

"That is enough, Bingley, please. If you wish to return to the village, then do so. I will find something else to divert my attention."

"No. We shall return to Netherfield together. I need to speak to Caroline about the arrangements for the ball. Nicholls needs several pounds of mutton and some beef from the butcher's shop. When that business is seen to, then I shall speak with Hurst. Perhaps he would like some sport. We've not gone shooting in several days. The dogs could use the outing, and I dare say so could you."

The two gentlemen turned their horses in the direction of Netherfield Park, but Darcy's mind was far from shooting and pheasants. He wondered if Elizabeth would be taken in by Wickham's charms, but it was only a passing thought. If he knew anything about her, he knew she was not so easily fooled. No, Elizabeth, he was certain, could hold her own with anybody. She would not be deceived by the likes of *him*.

~*~

That evening after dinner, Darcy excused himself from the usual night of cards and conversation. Tonight Bingley's ball would be the topic of discussion, and Darcy had just as soon *not* take part in the planning of such an event. The invitations were engraved and preparation of white soup enough to feed the county was well underway. And therefore, Darcy chose a book from Bingley's meagre selection and retired to his chambers claiming fatigue, although he was not in the least tired.

Instead, he was tense and desirous of a hot bath, a good bottle of wine, and to be rid of Hertfordshire once and for all. The sight of his nemesis had opened old wounds, and the more he thought about it, the angrier he became. Elizabeth and her sisters, the two youngest in particular, had appeared to enjoy Wickham's attentions, and though he did not believe Elizabeth could be taken in by the libertine in the long run, he was not so sure, as he had originally presumed, about the present.

As he soaked in the relaxing waters of his bath, his thoughts returned to the scene on the corner of Main Street in the village. He recalled the expression on Elizabeth's face as she glanced between him and Wickham. She appeared to have been confused. What had that rake been telling her? And worse yet, what would Wickham tell her now that she had seen his own reaction to their meeting? Darcy wondered.

Wickham had the ability, with his charming manners, to present a pleasing persona. He was, as men go, handsome, and his words were smooth like honey pouring forth from a silver tongue. She could very well *be* deceived, caught up in the moment before she knew what had transpired. Only God knew how many other innocent women had fallen for his lies. But if she were so easily taken in, then perhaps she was not as good a judge of character as she presumed herself to be. Only time would tell.

Dipping the sponge in the soapy water, he ran it along his shoulder and arm as the soothing steam rose up and filled his senses with its relaxing aroma.

"Ahh..." he said aloud. "There is nothing like a hot bath to soothe a man's body...unless it is a good woman to satisfy his soul and quench his lustful hunger."

Darcy leaned back and breathed deeply as he smiled to himself. Bingley's ball was to be in less than a fortnight. He would have his dance with her if it was the last thing he did, and then he would put away all thoughts of Miss Elizabeth Bennet *forever*.

~*~*~*~

Chapter 13

The Netherfield Ball

Darcy dressed for the evening in his best black woollen dress coat and crisp white cotton lawn shirt, both of which he had chosen specifically for tonight. He knew that whatever *she* wore, black would complement it, and he intended to look his best for this ball.

Standing before the large looking glass, he gazed at his reflection as his man went about putting the finishing touches to his appearance. He had been anticipating this evening's festivities for several days now, for this night he would claim the dance he had set his sights on all those many weeks ago at Lucas Lodge.

After his man had adjusted his cufflinks to suit him, he walked over to the window where he took his station of observer and drew back the heavy brocade curtains, carefully monitoring the activities below.

Inspecting the guests one by one as they arrived in the courtyard of Netherfield Park, Darcy was looking for one coach in particular. When that carriage finally rolled to a stop, and a footman opened the door, his eyes found the object of his imaginings. He breathed deeply as Miss Elizabeth Bennet stepped from the carriage. She was wearing a simple, yet elegant, gown of cream coloured silk and a dark green velvet wrap. Her hair was styled with tiny sprigs of baby's breath and lavender mingled amongst small light yellow rosebuds scattered about her locks, with one pale yellow ribbon and pearls interwoven in her hair, holding it all together. Her dark curls hung gracefully down her back slightly past her shoulders. He stared at her in fascination. Though her gown and coiffure were not of the latest fashion from the continent, she looked lovelier than any woman he had ever seen dressed for a ball.

She glanced up and caught his gaze, and from the expression on her countenance, he surmised she was perplexed to find him observing her. Breaking the connection they shared, he moved away from the window and approached his man.

"Winfred, I shall have the sandalwood with musk, lavender, and oak moss for tonight—the one I keep for special occasions."

"*Very good*, sir! It is a fragrance that most becomes you. I dare say the ladies will most certainly be fond of it," he said as he went to retrieve the bottle of costly blended oils and spices from the wardrobe.

Darcy gave a dry response as he took the amber bottle from his valet's hand. "Perhaps, but there is only *one* lady I want to notice me tonight, and *she* will be wearing lavender."

"Then you and the lady will surely complement one another very well with this one. Good luck, sir."

A Man in Want of a Wife

With a sharp look to his valet, Darcy replied, "It is not what you assume. The lady owes me a dance. That is all it is, and, therefore, I trust you will keep your thoughts to yourself."

"Umm, yes sir. It was only a misstep on my part; I simply meant to—"

"That'll be all."

"Yes, sir." His gentleman bowed and took his exit.

Darcy placed the bottle on his dressing table and left the room with one purpose in mind: to find Miss Elizabeth Bennet. He would observe her, and when the opportune moment presented itself, he would ask for her hand for *one* set.

~*~

Darcy descended the stairs and entered the room with confidence. He moved in and out of the crowd and found a place by the mantelpiece where he stood and leaned against it, watching the guests as they mingled, searching until his eyes finally rested on Miss Elizabeth as she came through the archway with Bingley and her sister Miss Jane Bennet. As he observed her, he noticed that she appeared to be looking for someone, and for a brief moment, he wondered if she were looking for him; but then she was approached by a redcoat, and by her expression, he knew it was not so. Darcy had since learned that Wickham had been the man Captain Carter had spoken of that day he and Bingley had dined with the officers, for he had later joined the militia stationed outside the village.

Thinking back to the day he and Bingley had come upon Wickham in Meryton, he remembered the great pleasure he had seen in Miss Elizabeth's eyes as she and Wickham had talked, and, therefore, he presumed it was *he* whom she sought and not himself as he had originally hoped. Darcy sighed in dissatisfaction, and for a fleeting moment, a twinge of disappointment mixed with jealousy seized his heart, but he quickly rejected it.

Darcy had agreed that Bingley should issue a general invitation to the officers, which he was well aware would include Wickham, but he seriously doubted the reprobate would have the audacity to attend. He stared and gently shook his head. Lieutenant Denny turned in Darcy's direction with a look of contempt which was followed by Miss Elizabeth's gaze, and by the disappointed look upon her face, he knew he was correct in his assumption. Elizabeth was looking for Wickham, but apparently he was not in attendance. Once more, he was saddened and wondered if he should still ask for her hand in a set, but yet again he dismissed the thought as preposterous. For he was more than assured of his abilities as well as his self-confidence with respect to his person to obtain her good opinion if he wished it. He was Fitzwilliam Darcy of Pemberley in Derbyshire, and that alone would grant him any woman he chose for any *reason* he chose.

Darcy turned away and moved towards the refreshment table where he took a glass of wine and resumed his observation.

Lieutenant Denny was soon distracted by Miss Lydia, and Elizabeth was left to herself. She looked about the room until she found the familiar face of her friend, Miss Charlotte Lucas, and made her way towards her.

Darcy watched her from over the rim of his glass. She was talking with her friend most agreeably when suddenly they were interrupted by the officious looking parson he had seen with her and her sisters that day in the streets of Meryton. Darcy frowned but made no move. Elizabeth looked as if she were uncomfortable, but then she quickly recovered until the music began, and the vicar led her to the dance floor for the first two dances.

Darcy set his glass aside and moved towards the dance line where he strolled around the couples so that he could better examine Elizabeth and the parson as they performed the set. What he observed caused him to barely contain his amusement, though he truly sympathized for her condition. Her partner proved to be as big of a buffoon as he looked. The rather large parson was awkward and solemn, apologising instead of attending to the dance, and often moving in the wrong direction without being aware of it, thus bringing himself into rather forceful contact with the matronly dancers who moved within his circle, much to their distress. He gave Elizabeth all the shame and misery which a disagreeable partner for a couple of dances could give. Darcy chuckled to himself as he observed the horrendous display before him. It was obvious that Elizabeth was mortified, and he wondered if her toes would survive to dance another set.

She glanced in his direction, and her gaze caught his for a brief moment as he walked about following her every move. She coloured from bright pink to deep crimson. Darcy chuckled even more. Clearly she deserved a better partner and one who could do her justice, for her steps were elegant and graceful, befitting a lady of the highest circles. Finally the exhibition ended, but before Darcy could make his way to her, Elizabeth was approached by an officer for the next set, and instead of dancing, he was forced to once again watch from a distance. However, at least this time her toes were safe, and she was spared the mortification of her last partner.

Darcy was well aware that if he was not quick on his feet for the next set, he might never have the chance, and therefore, when those dances were over, Darcy saw the opportunity afforded him and seized it.

Approaching her and her friend, Miss Charlotte Lucas, he bowed before them.

"If you are not otherwise engaged, Miss Bennet, would you do me the honour of dancing the next with me?"

With a look of complete astonishment, she responded, "I…I…had not…" she bit down on her lower lip and then spit out, "I thank you, yes."

Darcy bowed, and then turned and walked away.

When the music began, he and Elizabeth took their place in the set. They stood for some time without speaking a word until finally she spoke.

"I believe we must have some conversation, Mr. Darcy," she said with an artful smile.

She made some slight observation on the dance when they came together, but he made no reply as they moved through the line. The scent of lavender filled his senses, and Darcy's mind was too full for conversation. He was not so distracted, however, as to be unaware of his surroundings, for he did not miss the stares from the townspeople nor did he misinterpret what they meant. It was indeed a great honour that he had bestowed upon her to stand opposite him for the set, and reading her neighbours' expressions, he saw their amazement in beholding it. But the only thing he wanted was the pleasure of the moment. He had no intention of raising her expectations.

"If you will, sir," she pressed, "a very little will suffice."

They were separated again and then came back together.

"You should say something about the dance perhaps."

After a pause of some minutes, she addressed him a second time.

A Man in Want of a Wife

"Come, Mr. Darcy. It is *your* turn to say something now. *I* talked about the dance, and *you* ought to make some kind of remark on the size of the room or the number of couples."

He smiled. "Whatever you wish me to say, I will say."

"Very well, then. That reply will do for the present," she said as they moved in the line. Coming together again, she smiled. "Perhaps by and by I may observe that private balls are much pleasanter than public ones. But for *now* we may be silent."

Struggling to think of something to further the conversation, Darcy finally responded, "Do you talk by rule, then, while you are dancing?"

"Yes, sometimes it is best. One must speak a little, you know. It would look odd to be entirely silent for half an hour together; and yet for the advantage of *some*, conversation ought to be so arranged, as that they may have the trouble of saying as little as possible."

"Are you consulting your own feelings in the present case, or do you imagine that you are gratifying mine?"

"Both, I imagine," Elizabeth replied mischievously, "For I have always seen a great similarity in the turn of our minds. We are each of an unsocial, taciturn disposition, unwilling to speak, unless we expect to say something that will amaze the whole room and be handed down to posterity with all the éclat of a proverb."

"This is no very striking resemblance of your own character, I am sure," he said. "How near it may be to *mine*, I cannot pretend to say. *You* think it a faithful portrait undoubtedly."

"I must not decide on my own performance."

He made no answer, and they were once more silent till they had gone down the dance line.

At length Darcy thought to turn the conversation in another direction more suited to his desire and hoped she would oblige his curiosity.

"Do you and your sisters very often walk into Meryton?" he enquired.

"Yes, quite often." She paused as they turned in and out of the dance line. When they once again came together, she continued. "When you met us there the other day, we had just been forming a new acquaintance," she said sweetly, almost with pleasure in her voice.

Though he desired to know the particulars, her deportment and the lightness of her response enraged him, but he said not a word as he fought to swallow back his anger and hatred for the man who appeared to have found her favour.

After some time Darcy composed himself and spoke in a constrained manner. "Mr. Wickham," he said, "is blessed with such happy manners as may ensure his *making* friends, but whether he may be equally capable of *retaining* them is less certain."

"He has been so unlucky as to lose *your* friendship," replied Elizabeth with emphasis, "and in a manner from which he is likely to suffer all his life."

Darcy made no answer, now desirous of changing the subject. He had no wish to explain or defend his actions. His character spoke for itself, and when Wickham's was fully known, it would define him as well.

In another moment, to his relief, Sir William Lucas appeared close to them, meaning to pass through the set to the other side of the room, but on perceiving Mr. Darcy, he stopped with a bow of superior courtesy to compliment him on his dancing and his partner.

"I have been most highly gratified indeed, my dear sir," he said with all officiousness. "Such very superior dancing is not often seen. It is evident that you belong to the first circles. Allow me to say, however, that your fair partner does not disgrace you and that I must hope to have this pleasure often repeated, especially when a certain desirable *event*, my dear Miss Eliza," he said, glancing at her sister and Bingley with a sly happy look, "shall take place. What congratulations will then flow in?!"

"Sir...I..."

"Nay-nay, say no more, I understand. I appeal to Mr. Darcy—but let me not interrupt you, sir. You will not thank me for detaining you from the bewitching converse of this young lady, whose bright eyes are also upbraiding me." Sir William clapped his hands together. "A great pleasure it is, sir. Capital-capital," he said as he walked away.

Darcy scarcely heard the latter part of this address. Sir William's allusion to his friend struck him so forcibly that his eyes were directed with a very serious expression towards Bingley and Jane, who were dancing together. Recovering himself, he turned to his partner and said, "Sir William's interruption has made me forget what we were speaking of."

"I do not think we were speaking at all. Sir William could not have interrupted any two people in the room who had less to say to one another. We have tried two or three subjects already without success, and what we are to talk of next I cannot imagine."

"What think you of books?" Darcy said, smiling.

"Books! Oh no! I can never talk of books in a ballroom; my head is always full of something else."

"The *present* always occupies you in such scenes, does it?" he said, pressing his brows together.

"Yes, always," she replied, softly without thought.

Suddenly she turned and spoke again. "I remember hearing you once say, Mr. Darcy, that you hardly ever forgave, that your resentment once created was unappeasable. You are very cautious, I suppose, as to its *being created*."

"I am," Darcy said with a firm voice, wondering at the turn in the conversation and raising his guard, for he knew her tactics well enough to know when a trap was about to be sprung.

"And never allow yourself to be blinded by prejudice?"

"I hope not."

"It is particularly incumbent on those who never change their opinion to be secure of judging properly at first."

"May I ask to what these questions tend?" he asked, finally tired of their tête-à-tête.

"Merely to the illustration of *your* character," she said. "I am trying to make it out."

"And what is your success?"

She shook her head. "I do not get on at all. I hear such different accounts of you as to puzzle me exceedingly."

"I can readily believe," Darcy answered gravely and with caution, "that reports may vary greatly with respect to me, and I could wish, Miss Bennet, that you were not to sketch my character at the present moment, as there is reason to fear that the performance would reflect no credit on either of us."

"But if I do not take your likeness now, I may never have another opportunity."

"I would by no means suspend any pleasure of yours," he replied with cold civility.

Darcy was more certain than ever that Wickham must have given her some perverse intelligence of their dealings.

Miss Elizabeth made no response, and they went through the other dance and parted in silence.

Darcy walked away with his mind full, and though he held a powerful resentment for Wickham, there was an equally powerful feeling towards Miss Elizabeth. He could not find it within himself to resent her, for he was now certain that the black-hearted villain had filled her head with his lies, and unfortunately, she had apparently been deceived by them. But, however disconcerting it was to know the truth, he was not sorry he had ferreted it out of her, for now he knew that she was not as knowing as she thought herself to be.

Supper had begun, and the guests were finding their places as they gathered around the table elegantly set with fine bone china and displaying a feast fit for the occasion. His card had been placed across from the Bennets. No more had he taken his seat and begun to dine, than the parson who had danced with Miss Elizabeth approached him and bowed low in solemn humility.

Darcy turned in his chair and stared at the man so imprudent as to break from propriety.

"Mr. Darcy," the man said, "I have made a *remarkable*, I must say an *amazing* discovery. I understand that *you* are the nephew of my noble patroness, Lady Catherine de Bourgh of Rosings Park. Well, Mr. Darcy, I am in the happy position to tell you that her ladyship and her lovely daughter, Miss Anne de Bourgh, were in the best of health..." he paused and glanced aside for a fleeting moment, "yesterday, a sennight ago."

Appalled by the man's forward behaviour, Darcy restrained himself as he spoke. "I'm glad to hear it," he said with coldness as he rose to his feet. Towering over the obsequious man still bowed low at the waist and looking up at him, Darcy asked, "And may I ask," he pressed, "what is your name?"

"I, sir, am her ladyship's humble servant, parson of Hunsford Parish, William Collins, Mr. Darcy. And I am very, very honoured to..."

Darcy turned and walked away before Mr. Collins could finish his speech, leaving the fawning subservient toad with his grovelling manners standing there alone, looking as senseless as he was large.

He joined the Bingley sisters, who looked on with horror, making signs of derision as the evening rapidly deteriorated into a comedy of errors. Bingley had asked for some music and had requested that his sister Caroline play, but before he could finish his request, Miss Mary Bennet had risen to the occasion, much to everyone's surprise and distress, and all but ran to the pianoforte. Taking her seat, she jutted her jaw and arranged her sheet music. She began to play and sing a laborious piece, her voice shrill and grating as she banged on the instrument with more force than was necessary.

Darcy, impenetrably grave, glanced at Miss Jane and then Miss Elizabeth. Both were staring in mortification, especially Miss Elizabeth, as the entire room seemed to be made uncomfortable by the performance. Even her father was embarrassed. The display was crass and discordant—much worse than he had remembered from before.

When she had finished, she began anew, and, at this point, her father interrupted her before she could proceed, humiliating the girl who then gathered her music and ran from the room. Darcy breathed deeply, the hair on the back of his neck standing on end at the display. It was clear that, as a father, Mr. Bennet showed little consideration for his duty as master of his house. What had he accomplished over the years? His wife was unrestrained in her tongue, and most of his daughters showed little regard for proper decorum.

Then, just as Darcy thought things could not possibly become worse, they did. Waxing eloquent with a speech of self-importance, Mr. Collins approached the pianoforte.

"If I," said Mr. Collins, "were so fortunate as to be able to sing, I should have great pleasure, I am sure, in obliging the company with an air; for I consider music as a very innocent diversion, and perfectly compatible with the profession of a clergyman. I do not mean, however, to assert that we can be justified in devoting too much of our time to music, for there are certainly other things to be attended to. The rector of a parish has much to do. In the first place, he must make such an agreement for tithes as may be beneficial to himself and not offensive to his patron. He must write his own sermons; and the time that remains will not be too much for his parish duties, and the care and improvement of his dwelling, which he cannot be excused from making as comfortable as possible. And I do not think it of light importance that he should have attentive and conciliatory manners towards everybody, especially towards those to whom he owes his preferment. I cannot acquit him of that duty; nor could I think well of the man who should omit an occasion of testifying his respect towards anybody connected with the family."

Happily, before he reached the instrument, Louisa Hurst rescued the moment and rushed to the bench where she took her seat and began to play an Italian song, her hands moving rapidly over the keys with perfection.

Walking through the crowded room, Darcy could not help but hear the hum of conversation. Everyone, it seemed, anticipated the wedding of his friend to the eldest Miss Bennet. The vulgar display of her mother, stuffing food in her mouth while talking, was easily seen as well as heard over the din as she declared that the marriage of Miss Jane would throw her remaining girls into the paths of other rich men. She even alluded to the fact that Elizabeth might soon be engaged to the overly officious *parson*. Mr. Bennet, though he appeared to be embarrassed, made no effort to check his wife.

Next Darcy glanced at the eldest two Miss Bennets, and from their flushed expressions, he could see that they were further humiliated with shame for a situation which they could not control. He heard Elizabeth endeavour in vain to check the rapidity of her mother's words, or persuade her to describe her felicity in a less audible whisper, but it was to no avail. Her mother only scolded her for being nonsensical.

Darcy shook his head in disgust.

Turning to walk away, he was nearly knocked from his feet by Miss Lydia who was sporting an officer's military sash over her head as the young man gave chase. Miss Catherine was no better, for she, too, was being chased by an officer while she waved her ribbon as a prize to be caught. The evening was quickly digressing into a calamity; even the local gentry appeared to be made uncomfortable by it all.

Stalking about the room, unable to return to his seat, fire burned in his eyes. He was incensed. On no previous occasion in his life had he witnessed such a display of

A Man in Want of a Wife

ill and *offensive* manners by one single family. If it was the last thing he did, he was determined to put an end to this charade between his friend and Miss Bennet. For he had no doubt that she, at her mother's bidding, would accept his friend's addresses regardless of her true feelings and have him leg-shackled before Charles realized what had happened.

~*~

Climbing the stairs to his room, Darcy reflected back on the events of the evening. It had begun well enough with great expectations, but just as quickly, it had disintegrated into a complete disaster—one that would embarrass anyone with good sense.

The Bennets had been the last guests to depart as Mrs. Bennet seemed in no hurry to leave, nor would she refrain from making a further spectacle of herself, fawning and flattering Miss Bingley and Mrs. Hurst, making assertions about her daughter and their brother. From his stance by the fireplace, he had observed it all.

He knew by their contemptuous expressions that the Bingley sisters were just as appalled as was he. And while Mr. Bennet had given the impression of being embarrassed, he never once made an attempt to curb his wife's vulgar behaviour. Instead, he had seemed reconciled to accept it with complete indifference, if not, even, with a measure of humour. This angered Darcy even more.

Whatever feelings he had for Miss Elizabeth must surely be put away now. By no reasonable means could he consider making her an offer of marriage or ever entering into a courtship after the total want of propriety he had witnessed by her family this night. If he *should* condescend to do so, this evening's improprieties would only be repeated in his own house with Miss Lydia and Miss Catherine creating a scene so distasteful as to chase after every *single* man in attendance—especially his cousin Colonel Fitzwilliam! What example would they set for his sister?

And then there was Charles. After Sir William had called it to his attention, Darcy had carefully watched his friend with Miss Bennet throughout the course of the evening. It was obvious to the casual observer that he had been drawn in by her and fancied himself in love, but by the serene expression on Miss Bennet's face, Darcy could not see any sign of real affection.

Reaching his room, he found his man cheerfully waiting for him.

"May I enquire after your evening, sir?" Winfred asked, rising to meet his master.

"You may," Darcy said, ripping his cravat from his throat and throwing it across the back of a chair as he stalked into the room, "but I doubt you will be pleased with the answer."

"That bad, was it? Sir, I am truly sorry."

Darcy gave him a sharp look.

"And the young lady…did you have your dance?"

"Yes. That was perhaps the only *good* thing to come of the evening, but it was *not* enough to make amends for the rest. Winfred, her family is appalling," Darcy said, as his gentleman removed his coat. "I've never witnessed such a display of vulgar and disrespectful manners in all my seven and twenty years as I saw this night. Any man unfortunate enough to find himself shackled to one of those girls must be either insane or lacking in good judgment. Never have I been so thankful to see an evening end as I was *this* one."

"Oh, I had hoped it would prove to be an enjoyable evening for you, sir, but I can sympathize with your predicament. My Molly's family was somewhat of a disgrace as well, and I had to think long and hard before overcoming the obstacle of her *less* than desirable relations and make her an offer, but I have found that love will find a way if it is meant to be."

Darcy furrowed his brow and glanced at his man. "What were they like?"

"Oh, sir, they were the most horrid family that you could imagine. They came from a prosperous English family on the island of Barbados. But they were very wild, their manners fixed with such commonness. Some of them displayed such savage behaviour for which *I* had never seen the likes. Rude and loud accompanied by riotous living, gambling away their fortune in the gaming hells of London, and there were several family members in trade at the time with less than honourable dealings. They have since gone the way of men of such disrepute, but then it was to be expected, you see, for their grandfather was hanged in the Americas for piracy—Stede Bonnet, if you recall his reputation."

"Stede Bonnet—the gentleman pirate?" Darcy asked in astonishment.

"The very one, sir, and the Bonnets carry his stigma to this very day. They seemed to have had an aversion towards respectability, but my Molly was a true lady in every sense of the word. Though she had no dowry, she was virtuous and pure—gentle as a dove, even if the family reputation was tarnished." The older man continued with a twinkle in his eyes, "So you see, sir, you must never judge a book by its cover. I fear that if you do, you will do it and yourself a great injustice."

"I'll keep your counsel in mind," Darcy said as he pulled his nightshirt over his head.

"Will there be anything else, sir?"

"No. That'll be all. Do not come for me until seven o'clock. It has been a long day."

"Very well, sir. Seven o'clock it is."

~*~

That night as Darcy lay in bed tossing and turning, he thought about everything his valet had said, but no matter how he struggled, he could not reconcile the evening's events or, for that matter, everything previous from Miss Bennet's illness to her mother's behaviour, with his obligation to his duty towards his family, his position in society, and need he add, *himself*. For Mr. Cunningham to align himself with a reprehensible family was *one* thing, but for Fitzwilliam Darcy of Pemberley and Derbyshire to do so was quite *another*.

Then his eyes narrowed as his thoughts turned to his friend. If Charles were to marry Miss Jane Bennet and settle at Netherfield, Darcy would be forced to either choose between his friend's family and being thrust into Miss Elizabeth's path whenever he was in Town, or parting ways, for surely Bingley would insist on his company at every opportunity and *that* he could not abide. Yes, Elizabeth Bennet was a true danger to him and that truth he could no longer ignore.

~*~*~*~

Chapter 14

Darcy made his way to the breakfast parlour a little late the next morning. He had slept longer than was usual for him, and therefore, had expected to find the other members of the household long since finished with their morning meal, leaving him to take his in peace. But it was not to be. Caroline and Louisa were fretting about Charles in miserable conversation when Darcy entered the room.

"Oh, Mr. Darcy, you must lend us your assistance in this matter of great urgency!" Caroline cried, wringing her hands in severe agitation as she turned her head in his direction.

"Yes—you must," Mrs. Hurst added, "for if you do not, I do not know what will become of us—of our poor brother. Charles has gone to London on business, but it is not just business that calls him away. He intends to purchase a ring for Miss Bennet! We cannot let him throw his life away on someone with such an offensive family and such vulgar manners!"

"You are perfectly right, dear sister," Caroline interjected, turning back to Louisa. "And speaking of vulgar manners, did you not see how Miss Lydia behaved last evening? She had Lieutenant Denny fetching grapes from her bodice—grapes from her bosom, dear sister! Can you believe one would display such a wanton act of impropriety and in view of the whole room! And if that were not enough, I do believe her sister Catherine had spilt wine on her bodice while frolicking with *another* officer. I have never seen such vulgarity as we witnessed last night."

"No, nor I," said Louisa with great animation.

Darcy said nothing as he took his coffee to the window and gazed out into the courtyard where just the night before he had watched, with great anticipation of a pleasurable evening, Miss Elizabeth exiting her carriage.

"It would be simply insupportable to be aligned with such a family. Do you not agree, Mr. Darcy?" Caroline asked.

Darcy turned and strolled to the sideboard. "Yes…I concur wholeheartedly. It would indeed be a degradation."

"Then you must do something to help us."

He gave no immediate answer, but instead, filled his plate and took his seat. As he began to eat, he glanced between the sisters and asked, "What would you have me do about it? Your brother is a grown man in possession of his own fortune. Charles is his own master, Miss Bingley."

"Yes, but you could at least talk to him—persuade him to think the better of it. He listens to you and holds your opinion in very high esteem."

"Yes," Darcy nodded, "he does at that, but I am not sure it is my place to intervene in such personal matters. Selecting a horse or buying a dog is one thing, but choosing a wife is quite another."

Caroline and Louisa simply looked at one another with stunned expressions.

Darcy was silent on the subject as well. Although he agreed with the Bingley sisters and would like nothing better than to separate Bingley from Miss Bennet, he was hesitant to do so for the expressed reason that it gave nothing more than the appearance of a haughty intruder who would do so for purely selfish reasons. But there was one point on which he could feel justified in interfering: from his observations, Miss Bennet held no true regard for his friend, and *that* was reason enough for him to act.

Miss Bingley must have also had some reservation on the matter for it was a little while before she spoke. Finally she swallowed in trepidation and did so.

"Yes," she stated at last, "but you must admit, Mr. Darcy, that a wife is a far more permanent attainment than a dog or a horse. If either of those should prove to be unsatisfactory, one can simply dispose of them—sell them to someone else. It is not so with a wife."

"You make a valid point, Miss Bingley," he said looking up at her as he returned his cup to its saucer. "Allow me to consider your request. I have to ride out this morning to check on the work in the fields. It should be complete in a day or two, and then perhaps, if it is all that important to you, you should close up the house and proceed to London. No matter what you choose to do, I am leaving for Town in the morning. I've had quite enough of this savage country. I am impatient to return to society and see my sister. My cousin, Lord Wexford, will be back from his travels and I am anxious to see him, and then perhaps I shall take Georgiana out for an evening at the theatre. Though some in this country may not think so, there is much to be said for the pleasures of Covent Garden and Drury Lane."

Returning to his meal, he said nothing further as the two sister exchanged pleased looks.

When he had finished, he threw down his serviette, rose to his feet, and left the room. He needed time and space to unclutter his mind so that he could think more clearly. Interfering in a man's life on such a personal level was insupportable, and yet he found himself considering it, if only for the noblest of reasons. In *that* he could justify his actions. And besides, it was no secret that Charles fell in and out of love at the drop of a hat. Surely he would overcome his infatuation with Miss Bennet and go on to the next lady who caught his fancy. Such was the way of things with Charles Bingley.

~*~

Once Darcy had cleared the room, Caroline turned to her sister.

"Louisa," Caroline said with confidence, "It is obvious that Mr. Darcy will indeed aid us in getting rid of Jane Bennet, and any hope she and her mother might possess of an alliance with our brother will be crushed. After last night's display, I do not think even a pair of fine eyes is incentive enough for Darcy to overlook the disparity in our respective classes."

"Hum…yes, sister, I quite agree. But it is too bad Jane has such relations and low connections, for I do fairly like her."

"But not enough for our brother!" Caroline cried.

"No, indeed not. While it is true I am fond of Miss Bennet, I do not like her well enough to claim her as sister, especially with all the baggage that must accompany that appellation."

A Man in Want of a Wife

"I quite agree, Louisa. I am desirous that our brother will form an attachment to Miss Darcy. It would be far more beneficial to us."

"You mean to *you*, Caroline, for if he *does*, that will throw you into the path of her brother." Mrs. Hurst laughed. "How very clever of you, my dear sister...very clever indeed."

They both burst into giggles as they followed Mr. Darcy's example and quit the room.

Caroline went about her household duties, giving instructions to Mrs. Nicholls and the butler to close up the house, explaining that it might be some time before the family returned, if at all. They were all given generous compensation for the short notice and wished well. Caroline then sat down to pen a letter of explanation to her *"dear friend,"* giving subtle hints such as to dissuade Miss Bennet from any further hope of a connection with their brother while offering Jane all her deepest sympathies and regrets for the loss of her friendship at this particular time, though she alluded that they would visit again in the yet to be determined future. When she had concluded her missive, Caroline sealed it with satisfaction and handed it to a footman to post on the morrow, long after they were gone. Afterward she went about having her things made ready to leave for London at the break of dawn on the morrow.

~*~

Riding out to the fields where the men were working, Darcy thought about his conversation with Miss Bingley and her sister. It was certainly not in keeping with his character to interfere on such a personal level. But in this particular case, he could justify it because he knew, or felt reasonably certain, that Miss Jane Bennet would do her mother's bidding regardless of what she felt, and securing a rich husband to raise the family's fortune was her mother's only consideration.

And yet something from deep within urged him to desist, affirming that in doing so he would commit a grave wrong against both his friend and Miss Bennet. Darcy took a deep breath of the chilled air blowing in his face as he tried to reconcile himself to the conflicting feelings fighting for dominance in his troubled mind.

Reaching his destination, he slowed his horse, entering the work area at a trot.

"Good morning, Mr. Darcy," Mr. Goolsby said, looking up from his work. "Is Mr. Bingley not with you this fine morning?"

"Is it a fine morning, you think?" Darcy asked with some doubt.

"A bit cool, I'd say, but fine nonetheless."

"Yes, it is rather cold, but it is the twenty-seventh day of November, and that is to be expected. As for Mr. Bingley, he had pressing business in Town which called him away."

"Ah, I am sorry to hear that as I wanted to tell him that I think one more day will do it, and this job will be complete."

"Yes, well, it could not be helped. But as to the job," Darcy glanced around, "it looks completed to my specifications exactly and very well done at that. You and your men are to be commended. How are the walls on the other side of the estate coming along?"

"Splendidly, sir. The men finished up yesterday."

"Good. See Mr. Phillips in Meryton, and I will see to it that you are all paid by tomorrow. Until Mr. Bingley returns, that will be all that is needed for the present.

When you are required, you will be contacted again. Mr. Bingley will, of course, keep you and the principal men on retainer. See the attorney for the particulars."

"Thank you, sir."

Darcy tipped his hat and mounted his horse, riding off in the direction of the village to settle things with the attorney for the men's wages. Bingley had given him carte blanche to hire workers, dismiss or pay them, and do whatever else was needed on his behalf, and thus Darcy intended to use it.

~*~

When Darcy returned to the house, he found, much to his disappointment, that Miss Bingley was waiting to greet him.

"Mr. Darcy, all the arrangements have been made to leave in the morning at first light. I am closing up the house. If I have my way, Charles will not be returning to this wretched place any time soon. But you must help Louisa and I to convince him of it, for I fear he may not be so easily motivated unless you assist us."

Darcy glanced at Caroline while the footman helped him with his greatcoat. His valet had appeared in the vestibule to hand him a letter, and by the look on his man's face, he knew Winfred was aware of what was taking place, and why.

Taking the letter, he dismissed his man and sent him on his way with instructions to prepare his trunks to leave at first light on the morrow. Then, turning to Miss Bingley, he said, "There is only one way in which I will assist you, and *that* is if I am certain that it is for the best."

She was taken aback.

"Surely you cannot think that an alliance with the Bennets is a good thing; you would not want your family in such a … a disadvantageous situation, would you?"

"Certainly not, but what of your brother? Are his feelings not to be of any consideration?"

"Mr. Darcy," she reaffirmed, "you know as well as I that Charles falls in and out of love on a notion. He will not be as affected as you seem to imply. This is for the best…for all of our concerns, for if he were to marry Jane Bennet, you know as well as I that all of us would be tainted by the association."

Darcy stared at her and gave a deep sigh. Although he hated how she presented her argument, he knew that she was most probably right. While in Derbyshire society it might not matter; in London, it most assuredly would.

Releasing a terse breath he finally spoke. "If you need my assistance, then you shall have it, but I am doing it for one reason only, and that is because I do not believe that Miss Bennet's heart is so easily touched. If I thought for a moment that it was, I would not interfere. At some point your brother must make his own way without my assistance."

"Agreed!" Caroline cried.

Taking Darcy's arm, she led him toward the dining room. "Now, let us have our evening meal and retire for the night so that we may take our leave at first light. Our trunks are already loaded onto the carriages. When yours are ready, I will have Simmons fetch them down as well."

~*~

A Man in Want of a Wife

Winfred Cunningham stood at the top of the stairs in disbelief at the conversation he had just overheard, and though he knew he should not, the man felt a strong compulsion to aid his master, even if his master did not *wish* his assistance. But alas, realizing that everyone must be allowed to make their own mistakes, even Fitzwilliam Darcy, he left to do his master's bidding with a heavy heart.

Once behind closed doors, he went about packing Mr. Darcy's trunks with misgivings, for he was quite certain that his master was making an immense mistake—one that he might one day regret when it came full round to bite him firmly on his posterior.

"Meddling in your friend's affairs is serious business," Mr. Cunningham grumbled to himself. "You should not listen to Mr. Bingley's ruthless sisters. They are harpies of the worst kind, better left to men who will enjoy *their* qualities—though I doubt Mr. Hurst is very enthused over *his* jewel."

Having overheard the conversation below stairs, his opinion of the Bingley sisters was decidedly fixed. In his estimation, they had neither good breeding nor good sense. He could hardly believe that they would consider intruding in their brother's personal affairs, but he knew what they were about. Their own selfish interests drove them. However, then to involve Mr. Darcy was beyond common decency. It was a damned shame. And even more than that, Mr. Cunningham was sorely disappointed in Mr. Darcy; for he knew the real reason his master would consider stooping so low as to help Mr. Bingley's sisters. His master was afraid of something he could not comprehend. *That* was a failing indeed.

Mr. Cunningham looked up from his work and glanced around the room to make sure all of Mr. Darcy's articles were packed and ready for tomorrow's journey. Satisfied that they were, he sighed and took one remaining suit from the wardrobe and began to press the coat as he continued to mumble to himself.

"And so you are stumbling headlong into another grave mistake. For a man of sense and education who has lived in the world, it astounds me how you could be so damnably *stupid* in matters of the *heart*!"

He had seen Mr. Darcy's longing gazes as he stared at the lady from Longbourn, and he knew what they meant. Mr. Darcy was in love—and it was not merely a lustful love, though Winfred was certain there was plenty of that. Mr. Darcy was a healthy male in possession of a virile appetite with all that those urges demanded; but it was more, it was a longing he recognized from his own days as a young man struggling over his Molly.

It grieved the older gentleman to see the young man he had come to love and respect throw happiness away with both hands, all in the name of duty and honour; for what did those things matter on a cold winter's night when you lay alone in an oversized bed? The older man shook his head in sorrow as he continued to press Mr. Darcy's travelling clothes.

"You will regret this day, sir," he said to himself. "You have made a grievous error in judgment. One with the spirit and intelligence of Miss Bennet is a rare jewel not often found, and you are too blind to see it. Nevertheless, I shall pray for you and ask our Lord and Saviour to intervene on your behalf."

While Mr. Cunningham was putting the final touches on Mr. Darcy's shirt and cravat, his thoughts were interrupted by the sound of his master's voice.

"Winfred, is everything ready to be loaded on the carriage for tomorrow's trip?" Darcy asked as he entered the room.

"Yes, sir," the elderly gentleman said as he turned to face Mr. Darcy. "I shall send for a footman directly to take your trunks down."

"Winfred," Darcy said as he walked over to the side table and poured himself a glass of brandy, "you do not approve of our leaving on such short notice, do you, my good man?"

Mr. Cunningham looked away and gave no answer.

"We've been together since I was a youth," Darcy pressed. "You can speak your mind. I know you think I am wrong in my decision."

"Mr. Darcy, sir," Mr. Cunningham replied, catching his master's gaze, "it is not my place to say whether you are right or wrong. Only you and your maker can judge that, but if I may be so bold, sir, I will say this: do not let other people involve you in their misdeeds, for trouble will surely follow, and on that I must now be silent and not speak further. I have said all I will say."

Darcy looked down into the glass of brandy in his hand and sighed as he swirled it around. He knew better than to push the issue, for when he wanted to, his valet could be more stubborn than a jackass laden down with burdens and refusing to move.

"Is there anything else you desire before I retire for the night? Shall I help you with your nightshirt?"

"No, that'll be all," Darcy replied, shifting in his seat. "I will undress myself. Call for me at four o'clock. We are leaving at dawn."

"Very good, sir; I shall see you at four o'clock sharp, then."

Without a word more, Mr. Cunningham quit the room, closing the door with a resounding click, leaving Darcy alone to consider the situation at hand and his involvement in it. For some hours his mind was engaged in a personal war, but in the end, his stubborn pride carried the day.

~*~

The next morning, as the sun rose in brilliant colour over the eastern sky, the Netherfield party boarded their coaches and set out for Town. The family rode in Mr. Hurst's rather elegant coach, and Mr. Cunningham, along with the personal servants, followed behind in Bingley's less comfortable carriage while Darcy and Mr. Hurst rode alongside the carriages.

Sam, running alongside Darcy's horse, barking and frolicking, seemed delighted to be once more travelling with his master.

Coming to the crossroad between the village of Meryton and London, Darcy took one last look back in the direction of Longbourn, and then turned his head towards London. He could almost see her eyes bright with laughter, but the relentless pounding of the horses' hooves against the hardened road served to remind him that he was leaving *her* behind forever. Furthermore, if she chose to marry that sycophant of a parson, it was no concern of *his*.

~*~*~*~

Part Two

The London Chronicles

Chapter 15

November 29, 1811

Darcy, along with Sam, had no more than stepped through the door of his house at Number 15 Grosvenor Street, than a jubilant Georgiana rushed down the stairs to greet him, followed by her companion, Mrs. Annesley. "Brother!" she cried as her steps quickened, intending to embrace him before remembering herself and slowing her approach to a more sedate pace. Blushing, she glanced back at Mrs. Annesley who only smiled and nodded her approval in return.

Dropping a curtsey, she smiled shyly. "Brother it...it is unexpected—though I am not without pleasure that you have come home. I thought from your last letter that you would be some time in Hertfordshire."

Darcy broke into a grin, almost laughing, as one footman removed his greatcoat while the others went to retrieve his trunks. "Georgie! My heart has longed to see you, and, therefore, I could not resist the opportunity to return when Bingley left for Town on business. Letters are a fine thing, but nothing can replace being in the presence of a dear one. I've missed my baby sister's smiles." Turning to the footman, he said, "Take Sam to the kitchen and have Mrs. Whitmore feed him. Then order a bath. He's to stay in the house tonight." Returning to Georgiana, he continued. "Come," he said, motioning for her to step forward.

Taking her into his arms, he hugged her tightly, for he truly had missed her.

She looked up at him and furrowed her brow. "Brother, I am no longer a baby. I am soon to be *sixteen*."

"And so you are! And I should do well to remember it. In fact, Georgie, it is soon to be Christmas, and I want us to spend time together. I am going to have two portraits commissioned to celebrate the event—one for Darcy House and the other for the gallery at Pemberley. I'll tell you more when I've hired a master."

He stepped back and held her at arm's length as he looked her over. A soft smile spread across his features. "My little sister is indeed growing up," he said with a twinkle in his eye. "You are a young lady now. It is time to step out into society. In two years you shall be presented at court and have your coming out ball for your first season."

Georgina lowered her gaze. "But Brother...you have not married yet. Should you not have a wife before that special time? I should like to have a sister, and please do not let it be Miss Bingley!"

Darcy laughed. "It will decidedly *not* be Miss Bingley. On that I am very certain."

"Good, for it is plain to see that she only likes me because she wants to marry you, and besides, she makes me feel...well...I feel somehow inadequate in her presence; but Brother, who shall you marry? For you must marry. I want to be an aunt."

Darcy sighed and passed his hand over his face. "Yes, I should...but Georgiana, I have not met a suitable lady, and I do not want to marry someone who...." Darcy glanced away.

"Someone who...?" she asked.

Darcy turned back to his sister. "It is nothing for you to concern yourself over. When the time is right, I shall choose a wife."

She looked confused. "But...I...I had thought from your letters, that is...that—what about Miss Elizabeth Bennet? I—"

"If I led you to believe that she and I were more than friends, then my words were badly chosen. While Miss Elizabeth Bennet is a remarkable young woman, we are not suitable for one another. The matter is closed. I will see you tonight at dinner, and then afterwards, I want you to display your latest accomplishments for me on the pianoforte and harp. Now, if you will excuse me, I must freshen up as I have business at my club."

He gave a slight bow and turned to leave, taking the stairs at a rapid pace.

"But..." Georgiana's voice trailed off in a soft whisper. She glanced at Mrs. Annesley with a worried look.

The older woman moved beside her, gently laying an arm across Georgiana's shoulder.

"There-there, child. You know your brother is a very busy man."

Georgiana looked to her companion. "But I thought my brother was in love. He rarely mentions any women and never the way he spoke of her. I read the passages to you. Did you not think he had met someone who suited him?"

The two women walked into the front drawing room where Mrs. Annesley called for tea. As they both took a seat on the settee, the motherly woman took her young charge's hand and spoke in a gentle voice.

"Miss Darcy," she said with wisdom in her eyes, "the way of men and women is...well, complicated. It is clear from his many letters that your brother *liked* the young lady from Hertfordshire, but whether or not he felt that he should make her an offer of marriage, or even enter a courtship, is another matter entirely."

"But I don't understand. If you like someone, then what could possibly be wrong with going further? And Mrs. Annesley, I do believe he feels more than friendship for her. My brother has never spoken of any woman the way he spoke of her."

"Miss Darcy, it is difficult to say, but I cannot stress it enough when I tell you that there are many things that come between people. Perhaps the lady could not return your brother's affections, or—"

"Impossible! My brother is the best of men. He is kind and generous and caring. He always tells the absolute truth. There is no one better than Fitzwilliam!"

Mrs. Annesley smiled. "That, I am sure, is true, but there is also your brother's social status to consider. Ladies and gentlemen of your sphere do not marry people of another. Like keeps to like."

"Oh," Georgiana said softly. "I do understand that. But she is a gentleman's daughter. My brother said so, and her father owns an estate. I believe Fitzwilliam said it was called Longbourn. They are equals. My brother is a gentleman; her father is a gentleman. I see no conflict."

To this Mrs. Annesley shook her head and laughed.

"In that sense they are, but in wealth, most likely they are not. However, it is not our concern, and we should be mindful of it. Your brother's personal life is just that...*personal*, and, as ladies of good breeding, we mustn't meddle."

"No, I suppose we should not," Georgiana said despairingly as a servant entered the room with her favourite tea service on a silver tray. Dismissing the servant, Georgiana's smile returned as she poured herself and her companion a cup of Christmas tea. Mrs. Annesley said she should not meddle and she would not. But what harm would there be in asking Brother to tell me more?

She saw no harm at all, and therefore, she determined to ask him about the young ladies of Longbourn. Fitzwilliam loved her, and consequently she felt confident enough to enquire.

And if that fails, I shall swallow my misgivings and ask Miss Bingley!

With a contented smile, she turned to her companion and sipped her tea.

~*~

Darcy washed the dirt from his face and hands and changed his clothes to make himself presentable. He was fairly certain that at this time of day he would find Bingley at White's, either with friends or alone. He hoped for the latter. After his man had put the finishing touches on his favorite coat, Darcy left for his club.

Since Mr. Hurst had expressed a wish to join him, Darcy set out on foot for Hurst's townhouse, which was but two down and across the street from his own. Both homes were situated in the heart of London's exclusive Mayfair District, the most elite section of the Old City, with Hyde Park nearby. Once he arrived, they would travel together in Mr. Hurst's carriage.

~*~

The short ride to St. James's Street gave Darcy time to think and reason through what he was about to do in the coming evening. Although Reginald Hurst was a man of few words, he and Darcy had talked much about the events over the last several months. Hurst had been as appalled as he and Bingley's sisters over the Netherfield ball and stated as much openly. This gave Darcy a greater sense of justification in taking responsibility for his friend's happiness, but he still questioned whether it was the right thing to do.

Staring out the window deep in thought, Darcy stroked his chin while he pondered further the implications of his actions. The irrevocable choice he was about to make had long-ranging consequences which would affect the lives of more than just one person. He gave himself all the reasons why it was a good and sensible thing to do, and yet, something from deep within his inner being told him it was wrong to interfere.

Although his given reason was his friend's wellbeing, which it was, he knew perfectly well the *true* reason for his concern was his *own* wellbeing; for if he were to spend much more time in Miss Elizabeth's company, then *her* family might actually become *his* family. No matter how he tried to deny what he felt, Darcy knew he had never wanted any woman as much as he wanted her. His need to feel her warm body beneath his and to have her lying next to him after they had made love had almost become an obsession—one which very well could make him forget everything but his desire to have her.

A Man in Want of a Wife

The coach jerked, snapping him out of his trance as it came to a stop. He shuddered and turned his attention back to Mr. Hurst who, in that short span of time, had fallen asleep.

"Hurst," Darcy said, nudging his companion. "Hurst...we are here."

"What? Oh," he replied looking around. "Louisa kept me up last night with her incessant babbling about her brother, and that, fixed with being up at the crack of dawn, I'm afraid I am a little tired. Ah, well, let's be about our business."

When the gentlemen of Grosvenor Street entered White's, Mr. Bingley, who was sitting alone, stood to greet them.

"Darcy! Hurst! I thought you were at Netherfield," Bingley declared, his expression puzzled.

"Yes, we were, but your sisters decided to follow you to Town. I had business here as well, and so they closed up the house and here we are."

"Caroline closed up the house?! Blast! I'd planned to return by the end of the week."

"Yes, but since we are all here," Hurst interjected, "perhaps we should stay for at least a fortnight."

"Perhaps maybe a sennight, but I must get back to see Miss Bennet. She will be expecting me. I said I would return in five days."

Darcy coughed and then cleared his throat. "Bingley, there is something we must discuss, but not here. We'll do so tonight over dinner. You, along with your sisters and Hurst, are invited to dine with me at Darcy House—unless, of course, you have other plans."

"No, no other plans. I was going to dine here at White's and then return to my hotel."

"There is no need to remain in a hotel, Brother; you may bring your things to Hurst House and reside there with us. Louisa and Caroline would not have it any other way, and I will have no peace until you do," Hurst said with a deep laugh.

"Well, since you put it like that, then I shall remove myself today to your home, but come, man, you and Darcy must sit and take tea with me. I just ordered a platter of cold meats, some cheese, a small loaf of bread, and cucumber salad. It would be a shame to let it go to waste."

The three gentlemen took their seats and began to eat while engaging in casual conversation. Darcy conveyed that the work at Netherfield was now complete to his satisfaction, to which Bingley expressed his gratitude for his friend's diligence on his behalf.

While they were talking, several friends stopped by their table to give their salutations. One, in particular, was a jolly sort of fellow.

"Fitzwilliam Darcy!" The gentleman cried, approaching the table with a bow. Turning to Bingley and Hurst, he bowed again. "Charles Bingley and Reginald Hurst! Fancy meeting the three of you here. I've been looking for you. Viscount Wexford said you had taken an estate in the country...ah...where did he say?"

"Hertfordshire," Bingley answered brightly.

"Yes, quite right. Hertfordshire. Dreadful country! But never mind that. I was going to call round to invite you to our yuletide ball. My wife would have my head if I did not. Your cousins will be there," he said, turning to Darcy. "The ball is the twenty-first of December, and you are all invited. I shall send the invitations round directly."

Charles's features skewed, and he went to speak, but Darcy raised his hand to silence him.

"Randal Pennington...it has indeed been a while. I have not seen you since your wedding last Christmas."

"Yes...I do believe that is correct. Marital felicity and family duties have consumed my time. My father keeps me busy at Sandalhurst and Greensward, and my wife keeps me busy elsewhere."

They all laughed.

"I understand, but nonetheless, I am glad to see you just the same. Send round your invitation. We'll be there. I think I might enjoy a ball in this festive season," Darcy said, glancing at Bingley.

"Well, I should hope so. Susan has two unmarried sisters here from India with their father, and they each come with a dowry worth a fortune the likes of which is only to be seen in a princess," he said with a wink at Darcy and Bingley. "But I'll not have either of you breaking Kate's or Millie's hearts—especially you Bingley. Poor Miss Carter. You quite broke her heart last year, you did. It took her all of a fortnight to recover from her disappointment. Jolly well, I must be on my way. Susan expects me home for tea. You know how it is when you are newly married, Reginald! Remember, all of you are invited, and send my best regards to Mrs. Hurst."

"I will at that, Rand," Mr. Hurst replied.

When Mr. Pennington was out of hearing, Bingley spoke. "Darcy, why did you accept that invitation as if it were a settled thing? I presume you know I came to London to buy a ring for Miss Bennet. We are as good as engaged."

"Have you asked for her hand?"

"Well, no, but there is an unspoken understanding. I can tell she holds an affection for me, and I certainly do for her. I plan to be at back at Netherfield in no later than a sennight. I've already selected the ring I wish to purchase."

Hurst, wanting to avoid an unpleasant situation, took his watch from his waistcoat and said as he glanced at Darcy, "Five o'clock. If we are to be at your house by eight, we had better leave.

"Bingley," he continued, returning his gaze to his brother-in-law, "I will send round for your things in half past the hour. Be ready and then we shall talk tonight. Come, Darcy," Hurst said, rising to his feet.

Once they were outside, Darcy turned to Hurst.

"Reginald, I owe you a debt of gratitude. It would not have done for Bingley to know too much before we speak tonight."

"Think nothing of it, Darcy. I was glad to be of service."

Riding back to Grosvenor Street, Darcy sighed and closed his eyes as he thought to himself. *...well, whatever hesitations I might have felt, I am now committed and there is no turning back.*

~*~

**Later that Evening
Dinner at Darcy House**

When dinner had concluded, instead of the gentlemen separating from the ladies for brandy and cigars, as was the custom, they all joined together in the drawing room where Georgiana played for them on the pianoforte. Darcy sat in a state of

A Man in Want of a Wife

peaceful contentment as he listened to his sister's performance, and for the briefest of moments, he was once again back in Hertfordshire at Lucas Lodge. He could see Miss Elizabeth playing at the pianoforte with an expression of sweetness on her countenance as she sang. She smiled at him, and his eyes flew open. His heart pounding, he swallowed hard and reached to loosen his cravat which had suddenly become very constrictive.

Sitting up straight, Darcy shifted in his seat. Georgiana had finished her piece, and Miss Bingley and Mrs. Hurst could not give her accolades enough. Even Charles admired her performance. Recovering himself, Darcy spoke.

"Georgiana, your performance was magnificent, perhaps the best I have ever heard you play," he said with true joy. "But now, if you will indulge your older brother once more, I would have you play the harp. I feel that I need the comforting music only your talent can bestow."

"Very well, Fitzwilliam; though I do not excel, I shall play, but only one song."

"Nonsense!" cried Miss Bingley. "No one plays as well as you, for I have heard many performances in the great halls of London, and I can assure you of the justice of my words," she said, glancing at her sister.

"I, too, quite concur, Miss Darcy," replied Mrs. Hurst. "Your performance is sublime. Do you not agree, Brother?"

"What! Oh, yes-yes. Please play a sweet melody for us, Miss Darcy," Charles said, rather distracted. "I would love to hear you exhibit."

"You are very kind, Mr. Bingley," Georgiana answered softly, rising from the pianoforte to take her place at the harp.

As his sister began to play, Darcy closed his eyes and smiled absently. Georgiana's playing served as a balm to his troubled soul much like young David's music had soothed King Saul.

Darcy breathed wearily. He had always been a man of conviction, and tonight would be no different. His duty to his friend was as great as his duty to his family.

After the music was over, he opened his eyes and smiled once more.

"That was lovely, Georgiana. You have truly grown in your accomplishments. I am very proud of you."

Georgiana blushed and lowered her lashes. Lifting her eyes, she caught Darcy's soft gaze. "Thank you, Brother. I have tried very hard to become the kind of lady that would please you."

"And that you have done."

Mrs. Annesley, who was sitting in a chair by the fire with her needlework, spoke in a gentle voice. "Mr. Darcy, your sister has indeed accomplished much in such a short period of time, and I, too, am well pleased with her progress—especially in music, but now," she said, glancing at Georgiana, "Miss Darcy, it is time for you to retire for the evening. Tomorrow's masters will be here very early, and you would not want to disappoint them by being tired."

"No, I would not," she said, rising from her seat. "I am eager to excel in Latin as well as music, and Mr. Emerson is quite the demanding taskmaster with his lessons. Therefore, I bid you all a good night."

"Goodnight, Miss Darcy. I hope to see you soon. Do call at Hurst House when it is convenient and we shall spend the day on Bond Street shopping," Caroline said with an artificial smile.

The Hursts and Mr. Bingley gave their regard, and with a curtsey, Georgiana left the room with her companion.

Darcy stood to his feet and followed them to the door, closing it behind them. He then turned to Bingley who was seated on the settee beside Mr. Hurst.

Miss Bingley, seeing the opportunity accessible to her, seized the moment and rose to her feet, coming to stand in front of her brother.

"Charles," she said in a firm voice, "there is something of great importance which Louisa and I must discuss with you."

Bingley glanced between his two sisters who were both now standing over him. "Here? What could be on your mind that we must discuss here, Caroline?"

"You cannot be serious in offering for Miss Bennet," Caroline said.

"Yes, I am perfectly serious."

"But Charles, did you not see and hear what was so obvious to all the night of the ball? Her mother is the most vulgar woman any of us have ever seen. What could you mean by such an alliance?" asked Louisa.

"I don't see it as such a degradation when one is in love; nor do I see it as any business of yours. After all, it is I who will be marrying her," he said with conviction.

"But it *is* my business when it affects you and your good standing in society," Caroline responded with vigour. "You cannot align yourself with her!"

"I do not understand this passionate reaction of yours. You and Louisa *both* admired and liked her, pronouncing her to be a sweet girl, one whom, as you both have stated, you should not object to knowing better. 'Miss Bennet,' you said, 'is a sweet girl, one of fine deportment and polished manners,' and, therefore, I felt authorised by such commendation to think of her as I chose; now you are telling me otherwise?!"

"But, Bingley," Darcy interjected, strolling over to stand next to his sisters. "You have always told me that you wished to marry for affection, have you not?"

"Yes! And I love Jane dearly!"

"But what does *she* feel for you?"

"Well, I think she feels the same. She seems to enjoy my attentions whenever we are together."

"*Seems* to!" Darcy cried. "And that is the material point, isn't it? You are not certain how she really feels, are you?"

Bingley started to speak, but then released a breath and fell back against his seat, doubt written in his expression.

Darcy folded his hands behind his back and paced in front of Bingley. Turning, he looked his friend directly in the eye and asked, "Has she ever told you or even alluded to you how she might feel? Or are you so blinded by your own infatuation that you cannot discern the truth of hers?"

"Well, no, we have never discussed it, but I think—"

"You think, but you do not know. I, on the other hand, have observed the two of you together, and while she clearly enjoys your attentions, I sense she has no real affection for you. But, what I have *heard* and *seen* is that her mother wants this match very badly, and Miss Bennet, gentle and compliant as she is, will do whatever she is told. She will marry you out of duty to her family, as so many other young women do every day in this country. Is that what you want, Charles…a wife who will be nothing more than her mother's instrument in securing a rich husband so that not only Miss Bennet, but her sisters, as well, will benefit from the connection? Can you not see this?"

A Man in Want of a Wife

"Charles, listen to Mr. Darcy. I know you, as well as everyone in the whole room, heard Mrs. Bennet the night of the ball. You are the prize—the catch—to deliver them from their present circumstances, and if that suits you then, by all means, do as you will, but before you even consider it, think of Caroline. Her chances of making a good match will be severely damaged, even with her dowry of twenty thousand pounds! Think of us all!" Louisa cried.

A great sorrow overcame Bingley, and he turned first to Mr. Hurst and then to Darcy.

"Is that what you think…that Jane does not love me, but is rather a pawn of her mother's machinates…nothing more than a device to secure not only me, but other rich husbands for all her daughters? Yes, I heard Mrs. Bennet that night, for who could not? I doubt even the dead escaped her voice; it was loud enough to wake them…and yes, I was embarrassed by the display—but for Jane's sake—not mine."

"Bingley," Mr. Hurst said, "many a man has entered a marriage of convenience. You know it is expected amongst our circle, but I have known you for a long time, and that sort of situation, convenience coupled with unequal affection, would crush your spirit. You possess neither the strength nor the will to endure it. Think long and hard about your decision; for you will not only acquire Miss Bennet, but also her *mother*, and her father and sisters as well, and while Mr. Bennet and his two eldest daughters appear to be sensible, the others most certainly are *not*. Is that what you want?"

Bingley dropped his head. "No," he breathed out.

Looking up, he caught Darcy's piercing gaze. "Is this what *you* truly believe?"

"It is."

"Then I had better take my hat and leave. I'll send a message to Nicholls in the morning and tell her to close up the house for long storage as it is unlikely that I will return."

Darcy felt the severity of his friend's pain like a blow to the chest as he watched Bingley amble from the room.

Once the door was closed behind him, Caroline and Louisa celebrated in triumph.

"Thank goodness! We prevailed," Caroline said. "For I feared we would not!"

"Yes, I know. I thought it might be more difficult than it was, and I don't think it would have been possible at all but for you, Mr. Darcy. We are in your debt." Louisa smiled.

Darcy acknowledged her with a nod, but said nothing.

Instead, he watched with disdain as Miss Bingley and Mrs. Hurst continued their attack on the Bennet family. Gazing at them, he shook his head in contempt for what motivated them. Their behaviour was calculated to please when it suited them, as it had been with Miss Bennet at the time, but he clearly saw it for what it was. They were proud and conceited, their only concern was associating with people of rank and moving in high society, and, therefore, they thought well of themselves and meanly of others. Bingley's sisters cared not one jot for their brother's feelings or whether or not he married for affection. All that mattered to them was themselves and their position in society. And though Darcy could not recommend the Bennets, he knew the eldest two Miss Bennets did not deserve the harsh derision at the hands of Miss Bingley and Mrs. Hurst. He glanced away as he began to feel sorry for his role in this entirely sordid affair, though he firmly believed it was for the best.

~*~

Unable to sleep, Darcy sequestered himself in his study, watching the flames crackle and pop, with a bottle of brandy for his comfort. Pouring himself another drink, he sat there stone cold in his chair. Sipping his drink slowly, he thought about the evening and all that had transpired, reliving the events that had led up to this moment as he gazed into the fire. The image of Bingley's face suddenly appeared in his mind's eye. Charles looked like a caged animal about to be taken to the slaughter. Darcy downed his drink and shook his head as he reached for the decanter of brandy.

Pouring his next drink, he was alerted to the small knock on his door.

He turned his head and called out. "Enter," he said, thinking it was his man.

Peeping round the corner with her fingers gripping the door, Georgiana said shyly, "Fitzwilliam, may we talk?"

"Come." He motioned with his hand for her to take a seat. "I thought you were Winfred, but never mind. What do you wish to speak of?"

"Well...I was wondering—if it is not too presumptuous of me, that is...if you might tell me a little more about...about...Miss Elizabeth Bennet. You spoke so well of her in your letters. You said she is lively and kind and has a great affection for her sister. I have always wanted a sister to love—and to love me back like Miss Elizabeth loves her sister...one whom I could tell my deepest secrets to and she could tell hers to me. Please...if you will, tell me more."

Darcy stared past his sister's shoulder, fixing his gaze on the picture of their father and mother above her head, contemplating what she had asked. He understood her need better than perhaps she thought, for he had always wanted a brother—one that he could respect and confide in. That was possibly why he had felt the betrayal of George Wickham so acutely. In George he had hoped to find that bond he longed for in a sibling and yet never had. It seemed but an illusion, like sand slipping through one's fingers when clutched tightly; and furthermore, perhaps that was why his friendship with Bingley meant so much to him. Bingley needed him like a wiser older brother to think of his needs, to keep him from getting himself into the sort of scrape he had just escaped. Darcy turned his gaze from their parents' portrait and caught his sister's intense blue eyes.

"I will tell you all that I know," he said at last. "She is kind, as I told you in my letters," he nodded, "but she is also stubborn when she feels she is right. She is not afraid to speak her mind, something I admire greatly in a woman. Did I tell you that she walked three miles through the countryside in the dirt after a rainstorm, her petticoats six inches deep in mud, to attend her sister when she was ill at Netherfield?"

"No," a shocked Georgiana replied, "you did not. You only said that she came to care for her sister." Georgiana paused. "Were you not affronted by her appearance when you saw her?"

Darcy smiled and shook his head. "No, not in the least, for she was absolutely beautiful. I met her on the far end of the lawn as she jumped the fence onto Bingley's property. I was so stunned by her sudden appearance that I could scarcely draw breath. Her green eyes, brightened by the exercise, shone like polished emeralds, and her face was flushed with a warm glow. I saw no fault in her at all."

"What else? Go on; tell me more."

"Well...she is the first woman to have ever challenged me in an argument with the confidence to win—which she almost did on several occasions. I would say at least some of them were a draw with neither of us defeating the other. And she plays the pianoforte with such feeling that I find myself spellbound in a world of my own when I listen to her performances. She does not play with perfection like you and Bingley's sisters, but the emotion she puts forth is truly remarkable. Her singing is also very beautiful. With the right masters, she could become a great performer—much better than Miss Bingley or Mrs. Hurst.

"And then there is one other thing. She has made a close friend of Sam."

"Sam?" Georgiana laughed. "Why Sam, I wonder? Though you did mention him in your letters."

"Did I?" He laughed.

"Yes, you did, but I would still like to know why he would choose her?"

"I don't know for certain, but I think she and Sam are kindred spirits. Sam loves to play and can recognize when a person is amiable or not, and she is a studier of character who can also discern goodness or folly in people...and apparently dogs. Besides myself, I've never seen Sam so taken with another human being as he was with her."

Darcy was unaware that he smiled in quiet reflection.

"The first time I ever spoke to her was when no one was around to distract us. She and Sam were playing a game of fetch in a meadow covered in heather. Miss Elizabeth is playful and carefree, and Sam was delighted to have the attention. After that I caught them frolicking quite often. In fact, I really believe she would like to have him for her own if I were willing to part with him."

"Umm...I wish I could play in a meadow of flowers. It sounds so...so simplistic. I am predisposed to like her already. What else! Tell me more!"

"Well, let's see. Miss Elizabeth is a great reader, though she would tell you otherwise. She enjoys Sir Thomas More."

"Sir Thomas More? Is that not a favorite of yours? I think he is your most favorite author, for you are always reading his work."

Darcy laughed. "That he is...one of them, at least. I once tried to engage her in conversation concerning books while we were dancing, hoping to learn more about her tastes, but she would not speak of books in a ballroom."

"So you danced with her then...that is very good. Is there anything else you might tell me? What is her family like? Are they rich? You said her father was a gentleman. Is he like our father was—a gentleman in high standing in their community?"

Darcy breathed deeply as he lifted his glass for a swallow. Setting it back down, he met his sister's curious gaze.

"They are perhaps not rich, but well off, I would say—and yes, Miss Elizabeth is the daughter of a gentleman who is perhaps the wealthiest in his sphere, but, unfortunately, his estate is entailed away from the female line, and thus it will be lost upon his death as he has five daughters and no sons."

Georgiana's hand flew to her mouth. "Oh! How horrible. That means either she or one of her sisters must marry well."

"Yes," Darcy said, nodding his head slowly. "One of them must marry well."

"Perhaps the eldest Miss Bennet will marry Mr. Bingley and then maybe—"

"Georgiana that is enough for one night. It is well past your bedtime, and Mrs. Annesley is correct; you will be in no condition for your Latin master tomorrow if you do not go to bed."

"I suppose so." She sighed. "But when we talk next, I want to know all about her sisters—especially the younger sisters. Are they close to me in age?"

"Close—especially the youngest, but you have nothing in common with them. Now off to bed."

"But—"

"***Georgiana!***"

"Yes, Brother." Georgiana dropped her gaze and rose to her feet. Before she left the room, however, she turned and said, "I only want your happiness, Fitzwilliam. Your felicity is my only concern. I love you dearly, Brother."

With that, she closed the door behind her leaving him alone once more, and Darcy did feel alone…alone in a way he had never felt before.

He downed what was left of his drink in one swallow and left for his own bed, praying tomorrow would be a better day.

~*~

In the quiet of her room, Georgiana Darcy dropped to her knees and said a simple prayer.

"Please, dear Father, help my brother. I know he cares for Miss Elizabeth Bennet, but something is terribly wrong. I fear my brother has carried the weight of the whole world upon his shoulders for so long that he no longer recognizes his own needs. He always puts everyone and everything before himself, and that is wrong. Please help him to understand that simple truth can overcome whatever it is that would keep him from her, and not only for Fitzwilliam's sake, but for mine as well, for I so need and want a sister, and I am certain it is Miss Elizabeth that I want. Goodnight, dear Lord. Amen."

Georgiana slipped under her warm covers and fell asleep with a contented smile on her lips, secure in the Lord's goodness.

~*~

The next day, any regrets Darcy might have had on separating Bingley from Miss Bennet were quickly put away. In fact, he congratulated himself on having saved his friend from the inconveniences of a rather imprudent marriage.

Donning his greatcoat and beaver, he grabbed his walking stick and set out for the day. Strolling down the sidewalk, he twirled his cane and griped the handle tighter as he tapped it against the bricks and mortar. *…what's done is done, and done for the best! I am protecting everyone's future, especially Georgiana's. …**Her** future is paramount to everything else!*

~*~*~*~

Chapter 16

December 12, 1811

The following days had passed by rather quickly. Darcy had called on Charles twice, but his friend had not felt like company, and Darcy had been forced to put up with the displeasure of spending the calling hour with his sisters instead. Having conveniently found somewhere else to be, even Hurst had not been available for his relief. It was a most unpleasant experience, one he had just as soon not repeat; and therefore, he had no plans to call on Bingley again anytime soon. When Charles was ready, he could call round to Darcy House.

Since he had yet to call upon his cousins, Darcy's plans were to visit Viscount Wexford, and if Richard was in town, perhaps the three of them might spend the afternoon together. Then this evening, he and Georgiana would make use of their private box in Covent Garden Theatre. This evening's production promised to be one of the best of the season. *Macbeth*, featuring Sarah Siddons as Lady Macbeth, was being performed, and when he first mentioned it to his sister, her excitement was the only gift he needed in this Christmas season; for it had given him great pleasure to see the light return to her clear blue eyes.

Gathering his beaver, coat, gloves, and cane, Darcy left for the short walk to Number 10 Brook Street where his cousin, Viscount Wexford, lived with his parents in Matlock House.

Raising the heavy lion's head knocker, he gave three sharp raps.

"Good afternoon, Mr. Darcy," the butler said as he opened the door. "Won't you come in? Lord and Lady Matlock are not in at present, but the Viscount is in the drawing room with his brother, Colonel Fitzwilliam."

"Thank you, Robinson; my cousins are precisely whom I have come to see. Do not bother announcing me, I know the way."

"Very good, sir."

Moving into the great hall, he turned left and took the corridor to the front room with the wall of windows facing the gardens.

"Darcy!" Colonel Fitzwilliam cried, jumping to his feet, followed by the Viscount, as they both went to greet him. "I had quite given up on you," the Colonel said. "Have you been in Hertfordshire all this time?"

"I arrived back in Town a little over a week ago, but have only now had the time to call round."

"And what of Bingley? I had rather thought from your last letter that he would be leg-shackled by now. You seemed distressed at the prospect."

"Yes...well, things took a turn in a different direction—to everybody's satisfaction." Darcy moved to gaze out the window at the large Spanish oaks towering over the shrubbery. Murmuring under his breath, he said privately, "Satisfaction and *relief*."

"What did you say, Darcy?" Colonel Fitzwilliam asked, looking rather perplexed.

Turning, he answered, "I was about to ask after your parents. I trust they are well and in good health."

"Yes, quite well. In fact, we are all in good health at the present."

Lord Wexford laughed. "For the present *yes*, but soon my brother may be in some danger."

"Danger?"

"What Wex is referring to," the Colonel spoke up, "is the post I received from the commanding general of the horse regiment earlier this morning. It seems that I am to return to Sandhurst on the tenth of January for training exercises."

"Training exercises…what does this mean?"

"Simply that I am needed at Sandhurst to train a Regiment of Horse making them battle ready. The war with Napoleon is heating up, and if my intelligence is accurate, a war with our former colonies is also brewing."

"The Americans?"

"Precisely. There is still bad blood between us and the Yanks over the rebellion. Due to trade restrictions because of our on-going war with the French, our ships are seizing their trade vessels and abducting their sailors, pressing them into service in the Royal Navy—not to mention British support given to the American Indian tribes against American expansion into their lands, or the American's outrage over insults to their national honour after we humiliated them on the high seas. The Yanks will not stand for it much longer, I fear. Wex and I were just discussing how on earth we can fight a war on two fronts. It cannot be done. The cost in British lives will be immense."

"This is a heavy burden indeed. Do you think you will be deployed?"

"Only if it explodes on two fronts, but at present, I am only to be used in training as my good friend Colonel Forster is doing in Meryton. And I know what you're thinking, but there is no need to worry. I am training until early spring. I will accompany you in March to Rosings. Only out and out war with the Americans can prevent that."

"That is good to know, as I'm not sure if I would make the trip without at least one of you. It is bad enough to put up with Lady Catherine's officious interference, especially where our cousin Anne is concerned, but to do so alone, I do not think I could endure it. Why doesn't one of *you* marry her? Especially you, Wex. I dare say it would suit Lady Catherine, and it would be a great relief to me."

Wex gave a hearty laugh and threw up his hands. "Not me. I desire a woman a little less…how do I say it?"

"A woman with a little less overseeing from her *mother*, perhaps?" Darcy asked.

"That, and one a little less sickly. One with more of a healthy *appetite*, if you understand what I mean."

"I do indeed." Darcy smiled.

Walking over to the wine table, Lord Wexford poured three drinks and handed one to his brother and another to Darcy. "Why don't you both join me at The White House in Soho Square tonight? We can celebrate the season and my brother's eminent removal to Sandhurst after the New Year. They have some very delectable French courtesans that I am told are very skilled in the art of love making."

A Man in Want of a Wife

"I think not," Darcy said, "Fitzwilliam may join you if he wishes, but I am taking Georgiana to Covent Garden Theatre tonight." Darcy paused for a sip of wine and then glanced between his cousins. "Instead of spending your time in a brothel, why don't the two of you come with us? Georgiana would love to see you both."

"I love Georgie as much as either of you, but a French courtesan in high demand waits for no man. I can see Georgiana at another time. I have an appointment."

"I think I would much rather take Darcy's offer, Wex. My taste for French *anything* has waned over the years."

"As you wish, Brother," the Viscount said, sipping his wine. "Your tastes have certainly become priggish, if you ask me."

Colonel Fitzwilliam laughed. "And I certainly did not ask you, but maybe you, good Brother, need to give up your association with Prinny's set. Lord Bryon and Beau Brummel and their Whig friends will be your bane. What you need, Wex, is a good woman and an heir, lest I have to find a wife and produce one in your stead."

Lord Wexford smiled. "In good time, Brother...all in good time."

"Topics of marriage and courtesans are not why I am here," interjected Darcy. "Let's go to White's and have luncheon. Then we can discuss whatever you like over a decanter of good Italian wine—as long as the subject is *not* one of the aforementioned. I'd rather discuss war to women."

They all laughed and set out for White's Gentlemen's Club. Once they arrived, Lord Wexford found a secluded table in the far corner and ordered a bottle of their best Toscana wine along with a platter of cold meats and all that went with it. Pouring three glasses, they each took their drink and began to talk as they ate.

"So you think war is inevitable, do you?" Darcy asked Colonel Fitzwilliam.

"I do, and as I said before, it is coming on two fronts. We are already at war with the French, and before this next year is out, we will be at war with the Americans, as well. They are a stubborn stiff-necked people—the best and the worst of the motherland, and as they have proven, they know how to fight. It will take all the forces this country has to offer and then some to wage war on the American continent and at the same time engage the French."

"Then Colonel Forster will get his wish," Darcy replied softly.

"And what wish is that?"

"To join you on the battlefield one more time...*Old Ironsides*."

"What?! Did he tell you about Ponsonby?"

"Indeed he did."

The Colonel rolled his eyes and Lord Wexford laughed. "Brother, no matter where you go, you shall never escape the association with Cromwell. Cheer up. You cannot help it if you are as skilled and cunning as our worst enemy from the days of the English Civil Wars. Think about it. You bring balance to the record."

"I'd just as soon not. You know how I feel about that Puritan butcher. The stories have been passed down from one generation to the next, how he came into our villages offering peace only to turn and kill our women, children, and old men, and what he didn't kill of our children, he sent to the sugar plantations in the West Indies as slaves. I will hear none of it—no praise associated with him will I share. Now, if you please, no more talk of me or Oliver Cromwell."

"Darcy," the Colonel said, changing the subject. "You have piqued my curiosity over this country miss you've found in the wilds of Hertfordshire. You spoke so well of her in your letters that I am eager to know her better. You said she had dark hair and emerald eyes—a striking beauty, I'd say, and one who plays and sings. What is she like?"

"Humm...has our cousin met a woman who captivates him enough to write home about? Eh, Darcy?" Lord Wexford winked.

Though he was a man who kept himself under good regulation, this question caught Darcy completely off guard and caused him to blush. "Miss Bennet is a singular woman," he said at last, composing himself, "much different from the ladies of the ton. But she is nothing to me other than a friend, I assure you."

"Ah, our cousin has met his match. What a safe answer, Darcy! Even I know when you are avoiding a subject which evidently causes you distress, but if you do not want to share the particulars of your country lass, then so be it. I have a good imagination."

"Imagine what you will, Wex, but that is all it is—a fabrication of your fancy."

The Colonel chuckled. "If she is all that you have written to me in your letters and you truly have no interest, then perhaps I shall get to know her better. How much is her dowry?"

"If she has one, it would be a paltry sum. I'm told her father's estate is entailed away from the female line. She has no brothers."

"That is a great misfortune. She will have to rely on her charms for there are few men who can, or are willing to, take on such a burden," said the Colonel.

Lord Wexford studied his cousin carefully. "An entail is a nasty thing that plunges our women into poverty, leaving them little choice but to go into service or *worse*. I may talk lightly about brothels and such, but I know it is a deplorable plight many women face, and it should not be forced upon them. Our own third cousin, Lady Mary Fitzgerald of Ireland and her sisters, would have been reduced in circumstances to the point of living in the parish poor house had it not been for Father.

"His cousin, the Earl of Derryberry, thinking he would preserve his properties by entailing them to his earldom, placed his son's family in grievous danger when no sons came of his heir's union with Lady Lyndon.

"When I take my seat in the House of Lords I intend to push for legislation to do away with such cruelties as the entail. The only reason Father hasn't opposed it is because the Lords resist change, and he has had so many other important changes for which to fight that he has not had the strength to add entailments to the battle. However, I intend to fight them when it is my turn."

Darcy stared at his cousin for some moments as he sipped his wine. He had all but forgotten their distant cousins from Ireland, but now that Lord Wexford had called it to his attention, he remembered his parents talking about their piteous plight. And if Lord Matlock had not stepped in, George Darcy had intended to. Entails were indeed a mockery of justice.

Setting his glass aside, he bristled. "Yes...I remember poor Lady Mary and her sisters well. I was just a boy when they were turned out of their home with no remorse or respect from the heir when he came to claim what was his. Your father gave them each a dowry of ten thousand pounds and the dowager cottage at Matlock where they lived until they were respectfully married. It was a sad situation."

"Here-here, let us speak no more of such serious business," the Colonel said. "It is depressing, to say the least. Let us speak of something more cheerful. What say you of Pennington's ball? Are you coming, Darcy? Wex and I plan to attend, and I hear there are to be some extremely pretty—*and eligible*—young ladies in attendance. There certainly won't be a question of dowries there. Pennington also promises to extend the invitation to a foxhunt as well to be held in mid-January, which, unfortunately, I will not be able to attend." The Colonel sighed. "His family raises some of the best hounds in all of England. I only wish I could be here for that. Say you will attend the ball, Darcy. It will be my last time in society until Easter when I travel to Rosings with you. If you do come, we can ride to Cavendish Square together."

Darcy answered in the affirmative, and after the topics of the ball and Pennington's fine foxhounds were exhausted, they talked of other things: the current bets on the books at White's, which of their friends were next to be married, and the politics of the day. When the hour grew late in the afternoon, Darcy pulled out his fob and made note of the time.

"Three o'clock. The hour draws near to tea time. I had best be off to Darcy House to take tea with Georgiana and her companion. Do you wish me to meet you at Covent Garden, or shall I come for you in my carriage?"

"I'll meet you at the theatre. Look for me in the lobby."

Darcy snapped his watch shut and the three gentlemen left for home.

~*~

The Darcy coach pulled up and rolled to a stop at the entrance of Covent Garden Theatre. Darcy exited the coach first and gave Georgiana his hand to help her down. The look of awe in his sister's eyes warmed his heart and gave him cause to smile, something he had done a great deal of these past few days in her presence. Except for an occasional slip, he now managed to hardly think of Miss Elizabeth, or of his stay in Hertfordshire. It was a memory just as soon forgotten and put away as a foolish inclination.

As they entered through the great doors, Georgiana turned to her brother and said, "Oh! It is such an elegant place. It glitters like a thousand diamonds shining all at once. The chandeliers are magnificent! Thank you, Brother, for bringing me here. It is truly a wonderful sight to behold and the best present you could have given me. Shall we now find our box, or shall we wait?"

"Colonel Fitzwilliam is to join us. Once he arrives, then we shall find our box. Patience is a virtue, Georgie," he teased with a smile.

Georgiana returned his smile as she glanced up at him. "You are perfectly right, Brother," she said in confidence, tightening her grip on his arm as they moved into the lobby. "I must learn to be all things gentle and good."

They had not gotten very far when a fashionably dressed party approached.

"Darcy! Fancy meeting you here! And Miss Darcy, too! Susan and I were just talking of you, and well, here you are." Mr. Pennington bowed.

"Rand, it is indeed good to see you. And Mrs. Pennington, it is always a pleasure to see you." Darcy bowed.

Susan Pennington laughed. "I am always glad to see you Mr. Darcy. Please, do not be a stranger. Call on us."

Darcy smiled and nodded.

"Yes, of course!" Randal Pennington said, "You must call at Cavendish Square and bring Miss Darcy with you. Now," turning to the two young ladies standing beside his wife, he continued. "If you will, allow me to introduce you to my wife's sisters, here lately from India: Miss Kathryn Singleton and Miss Millicent

Singleton," he said with a sweep of his hand, "This fine gentleman, ladies, is Mr. Fitzwilliam Darcy and his sister, Miss Georgiana Darcy of Pemberley. They own an estate next to ours in Derbyshire."

Each young lady curtseyed, the dark haired one batting her lashes as her intense green eyes searched Darcy's countenance. He noticeably stiffened and drew a deep breath. "Miss Kathryn, Miss Millicent, it is a pleasure to make your acquaintance," he said with a bow.

The ladies smiled. "We are pleased to make your acquaintance, Mr. Darcy," Miss Kathryn spoke up. Tearing her eyes away from Mr. Darcy, she continued. "Miss Darcy, I am pleased to make your acquaintance as well. My sister, Susan, speaks well of your family, and it is indeed an honour to place the faces with the names."

"I am honoured, Miss Singleton," Georgina said, returning a curtsey.

"The pleasure is ours, Miss Darcy. But you must call us Kate and Millie, for we are twins and are not inclined to follow formal protocol," the fair-haired girl replied.

Kate's eyes flew back to Darcy. "I understand you are to attend my brother and sister's ball, Mr. Darcy."

"Yes. My cousins and a good friend will be in attendance."

"Perhaps I shall see you there, then," she said with a coquettish smile.

Georgiana's eyes darted between the two, shock and surprise written in her expression. When they departed, she whispered to her brother. "They are quite unusual, are they not—and rather forward?"

"Unusual, perhaps, but not in an unpleasant way," he muttered as his eyes followed their leaving. Then, as if on impulse, Miss Kathryn Singleton looked back over her shoulder and smiled.

Darcy's lips lifted in a gentle curve as he stared, taking in her beauty. She had an uncommonly beautiful shade of hair which he found striking; it especially complemented her dark forest-green eyes, rendering her even more handsome in a daring way.

Her hair is unusual...a shade of black cherry red. I've never seen anything like it. ...She reminds me of Miss Elizabeth Bennet in an odd sort of way, only more polished and refined in her address, and her sister is equally lovely. I wonder? Perhaps Bingley might find the fair-haired lady as agreeable as I find her sister...yes...he might indeed!

About that time, Colonel Fitzwilliam came through the entrance. "Darcy, I am exceedingly sorry for being late, but we have not missed the opening scene, I see. Let us hurry to your box for the curtain is sure to soon rise."

They arrived at their box and were seated comfortably. It was a front box situated for the best viewing, and Georgiana was seated between her brother and cousin.

Darcy glanced over to Georgiana, who was well pleased with the performance of the first act, which consequently pleased him. However, before he could return his gaze to the stage, his eyes locked with Miss Kathryn Singleton's from across the gallery. She was seated with her sisters, fanning herself—desire clearly written in her eyes.

Turning back to the stage, Darcy smiled softly. *...perhaps they will indeed do ...yes...perhaps they will at that...*

~*~*~*~

Chapter 17

December 13, 1811

While Georgiana entertained Miss Bingley and Mrs. Hurst in the drawing room, Darcy sat alone in the library. It had been a fortnight since he had last seen Charles, and he was beginning to worry after his friend's health. The other morning when he had called round for the morning calling hour, Miss Bingley had said Charles rarely left his room and often had a tray sent up for his evening meal. If Charles did not come soon, then Darcy was determined to go over and drag him from his room if need be.

When the footman entered the library, Darcy jumped to his feet, hoping it might be Bingley, but it was not.

"The mail, sir."

"Thank you, Mosley," Darcy said, taking the letters and strolling into the centre of the room.

Shuffling through the post, he finally found one which held some interest. His aunt, Lady Catherine de Bourgh, had written in their last exchange that her parson was to be married to a local girl from Hertfordshire, and Darcy had answered her, asking for the name of the "fortunate" woman.

Breaking the seal, his eyes quickly ran over the words, and as they did, a small smile lifted his lips. He looked up and let go of the breath he had been holding. "Miss Charlotte Lucas." ...*Miss Elizabeth is safe.*

Crumpling the missive, he moved to the chimneypiece and tossed it into the fire, watching the flames consume it as it burned to ashes. He was deep in thought, his mind once again dwelling on Miss Elizabeth's fine eyes and lively manners, when his butler came in once more and announced Mr. Bingley. Darcy looked up in relief.

"Good morning, Darcy. How are you this fine morning?"

"As well as can be expected, and how, may I ask, are you?"

Bingley drew in a deep breath. "I am...much better," he responded with less assurance than he displayed, "and looking forward to Pennington's ball. It is the Saturday before Christmas, if I recall correctly."

"Yes, that is correct—the twenty-first of December."

"If you will have me, I'd like to ride with you, if you are attending, that is."

"Yes, I am riding over with my cousins, and of course, you may accompany us, but what has made you change your mind? I thought you were not interested."

"You are my closest friend, Darcy, and I trust you implicitly. If you say that Miss Bennet held no real affection for me, then I owe you a debt of gratitude for having saved me from a most impulsive marriage...one which I most likely would have regretted," he said, his voice cracking as he spoke.

Darcy began to speak, but Bingley held up his hand. "No, Darcy. We shall speak no further on the subject. Yesterday is gone, and tomorrow may never come. *Carpe diem*—seize the day, they say. Let us go to White's, and I shall buy you lunch."

Darcy smiled. "I'll get my coat."

~*~

Georgiana sat quietly in the drawing room, listening to the overly flattering effusions pouring forth from Miss Bingley's mouth. She smiled softly as she lifted her cup to her lips and glanced at the mantel clock, praying the hour would soon end, but as usual, Miss Bingley was anything but ready to leave.

"Oh! Georgiana, it is so refreshing to be back in civilized society. You have no idea what the wilds of Hertfordshire were like, and I pray you never have that displeasure. The fashions are two years behind those of London, and there is not one decent shop to be found in the entire village. The people of the county are not of our breeding, especially one particular family in the neighbourhood," she said, cutting her eyes across to her sister who smiled in return.

"I am sorry you found it…it not to your liking, Miss Bingley. I—"

"Caroline! Call me Caroline. We are on intimate terms after all."

"Yes, very well…*Caroline*." Georgiana, flushed with embarrassment, momentarily lowered her lashes, and spoke tentatively as she raised her eyes to Miss Bingley. "I…I was about to say that…that I find country manners are often less formal than town manners…but they are by no means less gracious."

"Oh! I quite agree, if you are speaking of the northern counties, but my dear Georgiana, had you seen the inhabitants of Hertfordshire, then you must own that their manners are very savage—especially the family from the estate neighbouring Netherfield. The younger girls were positively wild, chasing after the officers in the local militia at every opportunity afforded them; one of the older sisters possessed a conceited sort of independence which I found offensive, and their mother was crass and vulgar. I could not believe how she pushed her daughters towards every eligible man she saw, your brother included. Only one of them had any sort of good breeding, but then it was materially lessened by the rest. I would not want my brother to become attached in such a way that he would find himself forever linked to that place.

"Charles is a great deal too apt to like people in general. He never sees fault in anyone he meets. The entire world is good and agreeable in his eyes; never does he see them as they are truly seen by polite and refined society. I was worried he might align himself with one of the country ladies he seemed to fancy. You must trust me when I say it would not have been in anyone's best interest, but alas, that dalliance seems to have gone the way of his other infatuations, and that is just as well. When Charles marries, it must be to a refined and accomplished young lady such as *yourself* or any of the other acceptable ladies of our circle—not someone from a place of no consequence. Do you not agree, Louisa?"

"Umm…yes, you are quite right. One must always marry upward. To do otherwise is simply not done. It is unconscionable!"

For assurance Georgiana glanced to Mrs. Annesley who was smiling as she sipped her tea. The woman gave a gentle nod and returned her cup to its saucer, though Caroline had no way of knowing that Mrs. Annesley was smiling because she did not consider Caroline a suitable young lady either.

"Well," Caroline said to her sister, "it is getting late in the morning, and if we are to call upon Lady Granford, then we must be on our way." Turning to Miss Darcy, she continued, "Georgiana dear, give our warmest salutations to your brother and do express our deep heartfelt regrets on having missed his company, and when we next gather for the evening, you must play for us, for nothing gives me more pleasure than to hear your beautiful music—especially on the harp. No one plays or sings so well as you. Your playing is always the crowning note to an evening well spent in such distinguished society."

Rising to her feet, Georgiana saw her guests to the door and bid them farewell. When she returned to Mrs. Annesley, she took her seat and sighed deeply.

"They make me weary. I know they mean not a word of their false prattle. They are always expressing opinions which are not their own. Must I really put up with it without at least one word of contradiction? They are not at all agreeable."

Her companion smiled. "I am afraid you must, Miss Darcy. It is the way of fine deportment in a gentlewoman, but you must recognize their faults for what they are and dismiss them from your thoughts as soon as they are out of sight, for it is a very common fault between those who are established in society and those who wish to be. In other words, Miss Darcy, they insinuate themselves into your circle with words of flattery by telling you what they think you wish to hear, and unfortunately, it is effective on those of a lesser mind, which you, thankfully, do not possess."

Georgiana sat for some moments contemplating Mrs. Annesley's sensible words of wisdom, and, after she considered them more thoughtfully, she began to understand her brother a little better.

"That is what you were trying to tell me when my brother returned from Hertfordshire, and we spoke of Miss Bennet, is it not?"

The older woman folded her hands in her lap. "Yes, it is."

"After all the disparaging things Miss Bingley said of the families there, especially the one family which she did not name—though I believe from my brother's letters that I know who they were—I began to wonder about it. If the family she spoke of is Miss Bennet's, then I can see my brother's hesitation, and I am greatly sorry for it. What he wrote in his letters, however, contradicts Miss Bingley's account of the Bennets, or at least that of Miss Elizabeth Bennet. And Fitzwilliam never said anything about her mother or her sisters—except for the one who was unwell at Netherfield."

"Miss Darcy, you must consider that your brother would never disparage anyone to you."

"Yes…that is true. My brother never speaks unkindly of anyone, and I should hope he would never think such thoughts either."

While Miss Darcy was speaking, a footman entered and announced another set of callers.

"Miss Kathryn Singleton, Miss Darcy, and her sister, Miss Millicent Singleton," he said, "have sent their cards. Will you be attending to them, Miss Darcy?"

"Yes, of course, Mr. Foxmoore. Please send them in."

The footman left and returned shortly with the two young ladies and an Indian servant who quickly walked past him and made their way into the centre of the room with considerable confidence.

Georgiana rose and greeted her guests. "It is a pleasant surprise, Miss Kathryn Singleton, and Miss Millicent Singleton." She curtseyed to each. "Won't you please join us for tea and biscuits?"

"Indeed we shall, but you must call us Kate and Millie," said Miss Kathryn. "That is what all our friends call us, and I am certain we shall soon become fast friends."

"I know you must think us presumptuous," said Miss Millicent, "but after our introduction last night at Covent Garden Theatre, and since our brother and yours are such good friends, we thought it would be fitting and proper to avail ourselves of the honour of calling on you as soon as possible, and to express the hope that we might further the acquaintance."

"The honour is mine, Miss—*Millie*, and you may call me by my Christian name, Georgiana."

Miss Darcy almost gave them permission to use the pet name her brother and cousins often called her, but upon subsequent consideration, she thought the better of it.

"I want you to know," Miss Millie said, "that my sister and I were quite glad, almost giddy even, to meet someone closer in age to ourselves—so much so that we were positively determined to further our acquaintance with you. We just passed our nineteenth birthdays last summer, and it has been difficult to find proper company for our station while we pass our time here in London. You see, we are newly in England from India, and, having spent the better part of our lives there, we know absolutely no one in Town except for Susan, our older half-sister. She was reared in England, but Papa did not see fit to allow us the same privilege."

"Well, really, Millie, it was our mother who could not part with us."

"Kate, you must let me tell it, or tell it yourself," her sister snapped.

"By all means, Millie, tell it! But do get it right!"

Both sisters smiled with giggles and turned their eyes to Georgiana whose own eyes were wide with surprise.

"Your father is in the army then?" Georgiana asked recovering herself.

"Oh no!" they both laughed. "Our father is Jacob Phillip Singleton, Governor-General, Viceroy to India, as well as Governor of the Far Eastern Trading Company," Kate said.

"And our grandfather is Lord Bradford in Twickenham," Millie added.

"Far Eastern Trading Company..." Georgiana furrowed her brow. "We often buy imported things in the shops on Bond Street from the Far Eastern Trading Company. Isn't your father's trading company one of the oldest in the kingdom?"

"Oh, indeed it is, but it is not *solely* Papa's. It is owned by shareholders and is governed by a board of directors of which our father is the governor," Millie said proudly. "The charter was formed in the days of Queen Elizabeth. You see, the first governor was our ancestor, the Earl of Cumberland. He oversaw the charter just as our father does today. Papa is very proud of the fact that the line has been unbroken from then until now. Teas, coffee, cottons, silks, indigo dye, spices, and opium—anything one could want from the Orient, the Far Eastern Trading Company imports it."

Georgiana set her teacup in its saucer and folded her hands in her lap. Completely caught up in her guests, she found the sisters' enthusiasm catching, and soon she became alive with the conversation.

"Oh, it does sound interesting, especially since you have lived abroad and seen the world, but I think I would miss my native England. It must have been difficult being raised apart from your heritage—and your older sister," Georgiana replied.

"Yes," Millie lamented, "it was in one sort of way."

"Indeed, for we may have had the excitement that accompanied living abroad, but there were other things we did not have," Kate said with a sigh. "I understand from Susan that you sing and play very well. We can do neither. While others had the privilege of an English education in the finest seminaries, we had Indian tutors and our *Ayah*."

Georgiana frowned. "*Ayah*? I've never heard of such. Pray tell, what is an *Ayah*?"

The twins laughed and exchanged looks.

"You have no knowledge of the far east, do you?" Kate responded. "An *Ayah* is anyone in female service from a maidservant, to a nursemaid, and even to a governess. Ours served as all three, changing occupations as we aged, and she travelled with us to England. We could not get on without her." They cast a glance at the dark-skinned woman seated by the fire wearing what Georgiana supposed to be a *sari* similar to the ones she had seen in her geography books.

"I've never been outside of England, and I would dearly love to know of other places. What was it like to grow up in India?" Georgiana asked. "My only knowledge is from pictures in my geography books."

"Oh!" Kate cried. "India is *wild* and *exotic*."

"Indeed!" Millie said. "We have tigers and elephants, and there are extremely large snakes that swim in the rivers, and therefore, it is not safe to go into unknown waters as they are known to attack and *eat* people. It is dreadful. But, India is also very beautiful—especially in the high mountains where tea is grown. People live in bungalows—little huts. It is very hot and sometime uncomfortable. And during the monsoon season, it rains for weeks and weeks. It never stops until it is over. Kate and I had many adventures there."

"We have many fascinating stories if you care to hear them," Kate said.

"Oh yes, please, do tell them."

"Very well then," Kate said. "I shall tell you, though it may shock your sensibilities." She giggled. "When we were ten, Papa bought us our very own elephant. We rode her into the village whenever it pleased us, and it pleased us often until one day a mouse frightened her so badly that she destroyed the marketplace, and we had to give her up, though I must say we did revel in the scene of people scattering about in all the excitement. You see, Georgiana, I'm afraid we were quite wild back then and did some very ridiculous things. I am almost ashamed to admit it, but I once put a snake in Millie's millet. She had crossed me, you see, and I set my sights on getting her back, and, I must say, it worked quite well. You should have seen her. She was scared out of her wits!" Noting the shock on Georgiana's face, Kate quickly added, "Oh! But it wasn't poisonous—it only looked as if it was."

"*Kate*! You mustn't tell such things! I was not frightened in the least!"

"Oh yes, you were!"

"Well, perhaps a little, but I soon returned the favour, if you recall properly." Millie turned to Georgiana and laughed. "I put a spider in hers. She is terrified of the eight-legged, wiggly things, and this was a huge one."

Georgiana's eyes widened and she had to suppress a gasp at such light-heartedness. The Singleton sisters were so unlike most English ladies in her acquaintance that she began to worry what her brother would think as she studied them more carefully."

They were tall and slender and wore such pretty gowns, thin and floating and full of lace with silk ribbon embroidery along the hem, very unlike the modest designs that she wore. Her eyes lifted to their hats and stylish hair. Georgiana rather thought their bonnets were beautiful and unique for the season's fashion.

They were of woollen felt, trimmed in lace and feathers, and their hair was styled in a most unusual manner. Millie's was like spun gold. It was shining and pretty and hung in ringlets gathered to one side, while Kate's hair was arranged similarly, only her ringlets hung down her back and were like burgundy silk in the muted light of the room, and yet the colour changed when the light caught it differently.

Kate and her sister Millie had small, rather delicate, turned up noses and large laughing eyes that sparkled with life. The more Georgiana heard and saw, the closer she found herself drawn to their liveliness, though she secretly wondered if they were too energetic for English society.

In any event, she smiled at their accounts sincerely given as the two girls spoke in glowing terms of life in India. They relayed one mischievous adventure after another. At times Georgiana listened with an astonishment bordering on alarm at their lively, sportive manner. Never in her life had she heard such gay frivolity. Was their conduct unladylike, or was this what it was like to have a sister? Occasionally lifting a brow, she continued listening attentively to the two young ladies.

While her sister was talking, Millie raised her eyes to the mantelpiece. "Oh! Look, Kate. It is half past the hour. We must hurry if we are to meet Papa at the chocolate shop. He promised after luncheon to treat us to an afternoon of shopping in the bazaar. I would be *so* disappointed if we should be late, and therefore, miss our outing." She turned to Georgiana. "With his duties, we rarely have the opportunity to see our father; consequently, his taking the entirety of his afternoon for us is indeed a treat."

"It is, indeed," Kate said, "but I am having such a lovely time that I am loath to leave."

Kate turned to Miss Darcy with pleading eyes. "Georgiana, you must call on us as soon as it is convenient. We are staying with my sister in Cavendish Square. I'm sure your brother knows the address as he is quite good friends with our brother-in-law. Therefore, you must call."

"Yes, you must," Millie begged. "Our father is only in England for a little while, and except for Susan and Rand, we know not a soul here."

Georgiana smiled. "If you will leave your card, then Mrs. Annesley and I shall call. I know what it is like not to have many friends. I have often felt the loss."

"We shall see you soon, then, and please do not think us too impertinent. We have matured since our youth. I would like to think we have become sensible young ladies," said Kate with a sly wink.

The two women, with their most peculiar manners, then gathered their things and left with their Indian servant following at what Georgiana thought was an unusually far distance. Since she had never treated Mrs. Annesley as anything other than a dear friend, she was unaccustomed to seeing the reverse.

When Georgiana returned from seeing them out, she approached her companion and said, "Are they not the most extraordinary girls you have ever seen? They are so different from Miss Bingley and Mrs. Hurst. I almost forget myself when they laugh. What do you think of them?"

"On first appearances they may seem very nice, especially when they converse with you as they have today, but you need time to sketch their characters. Only a closer inspection will reveal their true selves."

"Then you do not yet approve of them?"

A Man in Want of a Wife

"Only time will tell me that, Miss Darcy, but for now, if you wish to call, then we shall call."

~*~

Darcy took the steps to his townhouse two at a time. He was in a very good mood. Bingley seemed to have improved from when he had seen him last, further convincing him that it was as he had suspected; his friend's attachment to Miss Bennet had been nothing more than a thin inclination—a boyish love like the many others before it.

What his friend needed was to be around more suitable young ladies like the ones he had meet last night, and since they were the sisters-in law of his old boyhood friend, Randal Pennington, they would be at the ball.

Entering the house, he gave his cane to the butler. Tearing off his gloves, coat, and scarf, he laid them on the calling table.

"You are in a very good mood, sir. I trust your day has been a productive one."

"Indeed it has, Mosley," he said. "Would you mind telling me where I might find Miss Darcy?"

"Miss Darcy is in the drawing room, sir. I believe I heard her playing the pianoforte."

"Very good. I shall find her."

"Georgiana," he said, approaching his sister as he entered the room, "how was your day?"

She turned and smiled up at him from her seat. "It was very good. My lessons went well, Miss Bingley and her sister called, and there was one other who called, or I should say *two* others."

"Who?" he asked.

"The young ladies we met at the theatre—Miss Kathryn Singleton and her sister Miss Millicent."

"The Singleton sisters? They called?"

"Yes. We had a delightful morning. They are quite interesting, to say the least. I find that I enjoyed their singular personalities very much and was amazed by their talk of India. Brother, did you know that their father is a major importer from India and the Orient, and that they have lived there for much of their lives?"

Darcy wrinkled his nose. "They are in trade? I thought Pennington's wife was the granddaughter of an earl."

"Oh, they are the granddaughters of an earl, and I wouldn't say Mr. Singleton is in trade exactly, only that he is the governor of the Far Eastern Trading Company, and the Governor-General to India."

"I see." Darcy nodded. "The *Governor-General...Viceroy* to *India*...Then that would explain why they seem so different. Rand failed to mention that last year when he and Susan married. I'll have to speak with him about it. Did you enjoy your time with them?"

"Oh, yes, very much. I am to call on them next. They have a liveliness about them that I almost envy, though I could never be like them."

"But that is the beauty of the differences in people, Georgiana. The Miss Singletons have a certain vitality which you admire, and Bingley has a goodness that I esteem. He is a trusting, good-humoured, lively sort of gentleman, which is something that I highly regard, but I could never have his ease in society as I am much more reserved and less trusting in the good of humanity," Darcy said staring off into the room.

Turning his attention back to his sister he continued. "I am glad you seem to like the Miss Singletons. Perhaps we shall see more of them. But now I must tell you that I have a special surprise for you. Mr. Bingley and his sisters are to dine with us tomorrow."

Georgiana dropped her gaze. "I must practice more than usual then. Therefore, I shall retire early after dinner."

"Why?"

"Because...when Miss Bingley called today, she said that I must play for them when we are next together. It has been an exhausting day, and if I am to play, I will need to spend tomorrow in practice."

"Georgiana, nothing would give me more pleasure than to hear you play, but if you do not wish to perform, do not think that you must."

She smiled. "I will see you at dinner."

When Georgiana departed, Darcy went to the calling table and found two embossed calling cards, one with gold lettering and the other silver. He lifted Miss Kathryn's card from the silver salver and ran his fingers over the gilded letters.

...the Viceroy's daughter...hmm... connections... money...suitability...perhaps she would do... I almost wish I had been here to see her...

Chapter 18

Darcy parted the curtains and stared out into the night, his mind full of wandering thoughts as he watched the street. Although Bingley had seemed cheerful enough while conversing with friends on their outing yesterday, Darcy had not been deceived by the congenial appearance of his friend. Bingley's smile did not reach his eyes, and often enough Darcy noticed him staring off, completely oblivious to his surroundings.

He sighed. "I suppose it will take more than a few days to revive his spirits," he said privately, "But I think an evening spent here, and then Pennington's ball ought to do the trick…especially when I introduce him to Miss Millicent Singleton. She has many fine qualities that I think he will find agreeable, and then Miss Bennet will be all but a faded memory. And Miss Kathryn," he further said, "should do the same for me." Suddenly he smiled. A carriage had rolled to a stop in front of his townhouse.

Releasing the heavy brocade drape, he moved away from the window and turned to leave for the front entrance.

As he entered the foyer, Georgiana appeared, stepping lightly down the stairs. "Brother," she said, "do I look pleasing enough for this evening?"

He smiled as he went to meet her at the foot of the stairs. "Georgie, you look lovely," he said. "The colour of your gown is most becoming. It enhances your blue eyes beautifully."

He moved to hug her and froze in his steps. "What is that scent you are wearing?"

Georgiana blushed furiously. "It…it is my…my lavender sachet. Mrs. Annesley said to wear it close to my heart. She said other ladies wear them and that I should do so as well. Is it wrong, Brother? Do you think it too strong?"

"No," he said in an almost whisper. "It is very pleasing…a favourite of mine." He paused and then smiled. "Do you have any other scented sachets?"

"Of course," she said with a quizzical look. "I keep them in my wardrobe to scent my clothes. I have several; lavender is my favourite."

Hesitating, he enquired, "Would you mind if I had one—for my closet, I mean? It reminds me of mother and…"

"And?"

"Someone I once knew."

"Very well, then. I shall have Sally send one to your valet."

"Also, there is one other thing. I commissioned Sir Thomas Lawrence to paint your portrait. He will begin on Monday."

"Splendid! I will choose my best dress and sit for him."

"Wear the soft blue silk morning dress. It most becomes you and enhances your eyes." He paused as he glanced at the door and smiled. Returning his attention back to his sister, he continued. "Our friends have arrived; therefore, we will speak at another time if you wish to know more."

Turning to the sound of their visitors at the front door, Darcy and Georgiana moved forward to welcome their guests.

"Miss Darcy, it is indeed a pleasure to see you! And, Darcy," Bingley said. "I am delighted to see you as always. It felt very good to be out of the house yesterday. I enjoyed our day immensely, and I am equally glad to be here tonight."

Darcy smiled. "Bingley, you are always welcome in my home." He turned to the others in the party. "Mr. Hurst, Mrs. Hurst, Miss Bingley," he said with a bow, "I am pleased to see you as well. Dinner will be served in half an hour. Shall we adjourn to the drawing room for some wine and fruit?"

In the drawing room, a table was set with bowls of fall and winter fruits: apples, grapes, pomegranates, as well as figs and oranges from Italy. Cheese and bread were also sliced and placed on serving trays.

After they had filled their plates and taken their wine, they sat down for conversation. Georgiana took her place with Miss Bingley and Mrs. Hurst while the gentlemen sat by the window where the gas street lights shone in through the sheer curtains.

Georgiana's reception of her companions was civil, though she gave the appearance of being uneasy. Every time she went to speak, she was overrun by one or the other of Bingley's sisters. Darcy pitied her for he knew how uncomfortable they made her.

At last, the time came and they were called to dinner.

~*~

The first course went without much provocation, leaving Georgiana time to think of all that had happened since her brother had returned to London. Although he seemed his usual self, she sensed that something troubled him, and though she felt comfortable enough to approach him on some matters, she knew better than to press things he did not wish to discuss, especially after their discourse over Miss Elizabeth Bennet.

The second course was served, and as she ate, Georgiana observed her brother more closely. Fitzwilliam was exceedingly handsome with a distinguished jawline and dark curly hair. He was also a good and honest man. He was kind and thoughtful in his care of her and others and was all that she could surmise in an honourable man. Her brother deserved to be happy, and yet she knew he was not.

She smiled as she glanced between him and their guests. He seemed to be enjoying himself with Mr. Bingley and Mr. Hurst, though she noticed he tried, unless importuned, to ignore Mr. Bingley's sisters, but then she could perfectly understand why. They were exasperating, to say the least.

The servants had come and cleared the dishes, and while the third course was being served, she reflected back on her brother's strange application at the foot of the stairs. The fact that her sachet reminded him of their mother pleased her, for she also often thought of her mother whenever she wore it, yet Fitzwilliam had also mentioned another when making his request. This bit of intelligence served to puzzle her exceedingly, for the only woman he had ever mentioned to her was Miss

A Man in Want of a Wife

Elizabeth Bennet, and now that seemed a hopeless case. She thought the entire conversation quite odd and wondered if he knew that women wore the sachets in their corsets between their breasts. However, before she could reflect further on the subject, her thoughts were interrupted by Miss Bingley.

"Georgiana, dear, I forgot to enquire after the table you were painting when Louisa and I were here yesterday. Those delicate roses against the backdrop of pale green would be absolutely lovely. Nothing Miss Grantley could ever do can compare to your stylish designs. Have you by chance finished it? I would love to see it."

"Yes...I have. It is in my sitting room above stairs. If you would like, I shall take you and Mrs. Hurst there for tea and lemon tarts once we part from the gentlemen."

Caroline glanced at her sister. "We would be delighted," she said. "And then, after we have seen your latest design, we can talk of far more interesting things than politics or whatever it is that gentlemen prefer. They never appreciate the small details that concern a lady's feelings and apprehensions—those *delicate* little matters that only ladies can share...*sister* to *sister*." She cut her eyes across to Mr. Darcy, but if he heard her artful banter, he gave no credit.

Georgiana flushed furiously. She would much rather confide in her brother's horse than speak to *Miss Bingley* about anything, let alone those *delicate little things* she could only imagine Miss Bingley meant. And besides, if she needed a confidante on personal affairs, she had Mrs. Annesley.

Georgiana smiled benignly, however, and replied, "Of course."

Caroline turned her attention back to the dinner. "Mr. Darcy, you must give my compliments to your cook. The fish and sauce were sublime, and the roast was turned to perfection. I have never tasted anything better, especially when served with roasted potatoes and sautéed apples the way Mrs. Whitmore prepares them. Oh, and the plum pudding with chocolate sauce is divine. In fact, all in your service seem to perform their duties to the highest standards. No doubt this is a compliment to your generosity. There is very little left to be wanting in your household, except perhaps, a mistress of the house to oversee it all. Do you not agree, Louisa?"

"Oh! But, of course," Mrs. Hurst cried. "However, one must admit Darcy House *is* run flawlessly; though, I find that good help is very difficult to come by these days. Seeing that everyone is doing what they ought is the sort of thing that a good mistress of the house should attend to. It is definitely a skill better left to a woman." She turned to Darcy and enquired further, "How do you manage, Mr. Darcy, and what an odious burden it must be?"

"My housekeeper, Mrs. Rawlings, sees to such things. I hardly have a hand in anything. Whether one has a mistress or not, management is best left to a trusted and faithful servant whenever you can find one, and I am fortunate to have found many," Darcy said.

"Quite true, and when Charles has a house of his own, I am sure I will manage equally well in overseeing the tasks of finding such men and women in service. He shall have a housekeeper capable of the task of managing everything properly under appropriate supervision. For it is a true mark of an accomplished lady not only to sing and play well, speak the modern languages, and attend to her family's connections through extensive entertaining, but to also manage the household well. I intend to adhere to the *strictest* of proprieties. Everything will always be *perfect* and up to standard. Charles will have no reason to concern himself over the little details. I shall see to them all."

Without an answer to Miss Bingley's remark, Darcy turned to his friend. "Charles, Pennington sends his gratitude to you for accepting his invitation to his yuletide ball. He was most disappointed when he thought you would not come. Over the years, the Penningtons have always strived to accomplish the best in entertainment, and though it is his first season presiding over the festivities, Rand will be no exception to the rule. His wife seems to complement her husband well in that regard, but then it *is* a love match, and thus the incentive to please is greater with pure motives that come from the heart." He glanced at Miss Bingley momentarily before returning his attention back to his guest.

"I am looking forward to it, Darcy. I have always loved a dance whether in Town or in the country, and I am sure I will enjoy this one. I hear everyone will be there, and that Pennington has two uncommonly pretty sisters-in-law. Perhaps we shall dance with them."

"I'm sure we shall. I met the Singleton sisters the other night at Covent Garden Theatre, and I assure you their praise has not been exaggerated."

"I'm looking forward to it then. Perhaps she will…will…I am sure Miss Singleton is a lovely young lady, but…"

"But what, Charles?" Caroline snapped.

Bingley looked at Darcy with vacant eyes and said, "I find that I miss the simple society of the country. In Town everyone is so refined that they do not shine, and I don't—"

"Nonsense, Charles!" Caroline cried. "From what I know of it, one can never be *too* rich or *too* refined. How could you even think otherwise! I think—"

"*I* think we should retire to the library for brandy and cigars, and you ladies should see my sister's table. It is quite lovely and speaks well of Georgiana's tastes and abilities." Darcy threw down his serviette and left the table, leaving Caroline to gawk after him.

Hurst and Mr. Bingley exchanged surprised looks and soon followed suit, leaving the ladies to themselves.

Georgiana coughed and cleared her throat. "Perhaps we should see the table. It is really nothing special, but it is my first attempt at painting on wood, and I am pleased with the results. I shall have refreshments sent up."

"I think it will be lovely; lemon tarts are an absolute favourite of mine," said Caroline.

After making her request to the maid clearing the table, Georgiana led her guests out into the hall and up the stairs to her sitting room where the table was presented. Mrs. Hurst and Miss Bingley could not compliment the item enough, and Miss Darcy found herself barely able to contain her embarrassment at their faux devotion.

~*~

Moving over to the side table, Darcy poured himself a drink and downed it. He had seen the grief and remorse reflected in his friend's eyes at his sister's sharp retort and wondered why Charles continued to allow her the upper hand when he was supposed to be the head of the family. Someday there would be a reckoning, and he himself would rise to the occasion and curb Miss Bingley's sharp tongue if Bingley did not.

Pouring himself another drink, he held it up and looked at it. "And this is what men do who are married to a harpy. What did King Solomon say? Ay, yes, 'It is better to dwell in a corner of the housetop, than live with a contentious woman in a whole house, and a quarrelsome wife is like a constant dripping.' No wonder Hurst prefers his wine. If I were leg-shackled to one of Bingley's sisters, I'd drown in a bottle, too! And that is why I am reluctant to marry unless I feel certain of my intended's affections."

Footsteps alerted him that his guests would soon join him. He released a sigh and shook his head.

Looking up as Bingley and Hurst came through the door, he held up two glasses. "Brandy or wine?" he asked, and with a slight tilt of his head, he added, "The cigars are over there in their case. Please help yourselves."

"I'll have a brandy," Hurst said, moving to the wooden box where Darcy kept his fine cigars.

"I shall have brandy as well," Bingley answered, "but I think I will decline the cigar. I find smoking no longer satisfying."

Darcy smiled and clapped his friend on the back. "Someday you shall have an estate and all the things you desire, and then we shall both smoke by your fire and enjoy a bottle of Cognac—the best Brandywine known to man. Here, have a brandy and come sit by my fire."

Mr. Hurst and Mr. Bingley took the proffered drinks, and each settled into a seat by the mantelpiece.

Staring into the flames, listening to them crackle and pop, Darcy said in a low voice, "I am to journey into Kent in the spring and attend my Aunt Catherine's estate with her overseer. I should be there no longer than two weeks—three at the latest if things warrant it. When I return to Town, I will be here for most of the summer, and then I want to take a large party of friends to Pemberley for Georgiana's sixteenth birthday on the seventh of August. I would like to invite all of you to come. I'm having her portrait painted for the occasion, and I have ordered a grand pianoforte to be delivered before she arrives."

"I see no reason why I cannot attend. I plan to leave soon after the New Year for Yorkshire to see about my father's mills. I will visit with my Aunt Martha and then return to town by midsummer. I should be here by the first of August. Caroline will not go with me as she can barely stand the business or Aunt Martha. Therefore, I should be here for the journey, and you can depend upon Caroline being in for it, too."

"Very good, then." Darcy turned to Hurst. "How about you, Reginald? Will you and Mrs. Hurst attend?"

"Louisa may do as she pleases, but I spend my summers on my family's estate in Hampshire. My brother Horace raises foxhounds for sport, and summer is the whelping season. It is when we take the new pups and begin to teach them to track by scent; 'tis a critical time in the business and I cannot miss it."

Darcy nodded. "I understand perfectly."

Turning back to Bingley, he said, "My cousins believe Pennington is going to host a foxhunt in mid-January. If that is true, would you be up to the sport?"

"Foxhunt? I would be delighted. I cannot remember the last time I have run with the hounds. I shall delay my trip North until after the hunt."

"And you, Hurst?" Darcy asked. "Would you be interested?"

"Come, Darcy. When have you known me to miss an opportunity at some sport?!" He grinned. "Of course I will! It will almost make being forced to put up with a damn ball worth it! Damn tedious evening that will be. The only good thing is the wine and food they serve, and I know Pennington will have the best."

Darcy smiled, pleased to see the life return to his friend's eyes.

The men sat by the fire and talked for some time exchanging tales of sport and drink until the ladies returned. Then, after Georgiana had played several songs, a few more pleasantries were exchanged and the party departed, leaving Darcy and his sister to themselves.

Returning to the drawing room, Darcy took a seat and bid his sister to join him.

"Did your time spent with Miss Bingley and Mrs. Hurst try your patience too terribly much?"

"Not *too* much, but it is perfectly clear to me that Miss Bingley only desires *my* attention because she desires *you*, and Brother, she would like nothing better than to see an alliance between her brother and me. I think she believes it would insinuate her further into your good graces because then you would see what an amiable hostess and companion she would make. If I heard it once, I heard it ten thousand times: 'I have been educated in the finest seminaries and have the knowledge to make the perfect wife.' But she lacks two important elements."

"And what are those?"

"Compassion and modesty. I fear she would not treat our tenants and servants as Mother did. I know I was quite young when Mother died, but I remember how she worked very hard to see after their needs. She was always there when a baby was born, and when they were sick, she attended them with Mrs. Reynolds, nursing them until they were well. I could never see Miss Bingley in that role. She has compassion for no one unless it is to her advantage. I may not know much of the world, but I know she is no friend, and yet she pretends to care for me."

Darcy took in a deep breath and released it slowly. "Yes, our mother was all those things, and though Miss Bingley will never be mistress of this house or Pemberley, I am not sure I would want my wife to be too much like our mother." He turned and looked at his sister with intense eyes. "You do know how mother died, don't you?"

Georgiana made no reply.

"She caught a fever from a dying woman, and it turned putrid. Had mother not attended Mrs. Malone that night, she very well might be with us today."

Darcy rose to his feet. "I am very tired. Tomorrow promises to be a long day. I think it is time for us to retire for the night," he said as he turned to walk away.

"Brother?"

"Yes," he answered turning back.

"Must I always entertain Miss Bingley alone? She makes me feel embarrassed. I am naturally shy and reserved, and I…I feel even more so whenever I must sit with her and Mrs. Hurst. I know her accolades and friendship are false."

"Where is Mrs. Annesley?"

"She is there, and it does help, but I had just as soon not entertain them without you. They dominate the conversation with praise of me and you and say disparaging things about those they feel are beneath them."

Darcy closed the distance between them and took her close to his chest, hugging her like a father would. "No. You do not have to entertain them if you do not wish it. Keep Mrs. Annesley close by, and I will not leave you if I can help it. Now," he said, holding her at arm's length, "you must go to bed, and so must I. It is very late."

A Man in Want of a Wife

~*~

After his man had helped him dress for the night, Darcy dismissed him and went over to his side table where he pulled out a calling card from the drawer and brushed his fingers over the raised lettering. Taking a seat in the chair beside his bed, he cast his eyes on the small lavender pouch lying on his bed. Georgiana had sent it to his room before coming downstairs with Bingley's sisters, and his man had placed it there so that he would find it. He set the card aside and reached for the sachet.

Running his fingers over the lace and satin, the gentle fragrance of lavender wafted upward. He breathed the clean scent of the herb in deeply and closed his eyes. It was indeed his mother's fragrance, and he remembered it well, but it was not his mother that came to mind as the fresh scent filled his senses.

Suddenly, without consciously thinking about it, he found himself back at Netherfield with Miss Elizabeth Bennet. His memory replayed their every conversation, and he smiled at her expression as she pressed her point. The memory swirled, and he could hear the sound of Beethoven's "Moonlight Sonata" once more coming from the drawing room. His breathing was controlled and relaxed. There in his mind's eye was the impertinent face of Miss Elizabeth smiling in a coquettish manner. With one eyebrow raised she said more than most said with a thousand words.

...Miss Elizabeth Bennet... whenever I least expect it, you are there...everywhere...you are in my mind and in my soul. Even my sister's perfume reminds me of you...

Opening his eyes, he laid the sachet aside and picked up the calling card from the table beside him. He held it to his nose, inhaling deeply. It was not the scent of his sister, nor was it his mother's, or even Miss Bennet's. This was a scent he had never encountered before. It was sweet, like an orchard in spring, and yet it held a sensuous note, deep, and perhaps even faintly erotic—one that played with a man's senses. Miss Kathryn Singleton was close in age to Miss Elizabeth Bennet, but was she close to her in other ways? He would explore the possibility and see.

~*~*~*~

Chapter 19

It was late morning when the last master departed, and since Sir Thomas Lawrence was not due back for their sittings until tomorrow, Georgiana was free to do as she pleased for the remainder of the day. Walking over to the calling card table in the foyer, she searched through the cards left there from a few days back. Frowning, she turned to Mrs. Annesley.

"Did you perchance remove one of the cards from the calling salver?" she asked.

"No, Miss Darcy, they should all be just as they were left."

"But they are not. Miss Kathryn's card is missing. Only Miss Millicent's is here."

"Oh…well, it may have fallen and somehow gotten lost. But it is of no consequence. The address is the same on both cards."

"Yes…I suppose you are correct. I want to return their call today. It has been put off for far too long. But then Sir Thomas is such a demanding painter. I've not had any time to myself since he came. I shall call for a carriage."

"But the painting is so lovely, Miss Darcy. I think he captures your spirits quite well."

"Perhaps, but I must call, or the Miss Singletons shall think me rude, and I cannot have that."

"No, we cannot have them think ill of you. Therefore, I think it would be fitting to call today since you have the time."

The carriage was ordered, the ladies boarded, and soon they were off for Number 15 Cavendish Square. Georgiana sat quietly, staring out the window, her thoughts wandering in great anticipation of greeting her new acquaintances with the hope that they would soon become fast friends. She was eager to hear what interesting tales they might recount today. In all her life she had never met anyone quite like them. They were so full of life that they made her feel more lively just being in their presence. She had always longed for a sister, and if at some point she acquired one, she hoped that they would laugh and tease one another as the Singletons did.

Georgiana turned from the window and looked over to her companion. "What do you suppose Miss Kate and Miss Millie are doing today? I am sure that whatever it is, they are enjoying themselves."

Mrs. Annesley smiled. "I am sure they are, Miss Darcy. But you must remember, young ladies should never act too forward. It is unbecoming of a fine gentlewoman. I fear that the Miss Singletons have not had the advantage of a proper English upbringing. In that, they are sadly lacking."

Georgiana frowned and returned her gaze to the window. No they had not had that advantage. They had said so themselves. But as Georgiana saw it, at least they were not unfriendly and aloof like many of the debutantes she had occasion to meet.

A Man in Want of a Wife

~*~

The girls had not come down for breakfast with their brother and sister, having slept later than was the custom, and so a tray had been sent to Miss Kathryn's room where the two broke their fast together while they shared much conversation over the events of the last few days.

Kate, still in her dressing gown, walked over to the window and parted the curtains. She turned to her sister who wore nothing but her petticoat, and said, "I wonder why she hasn't come. It has been *five* days. Don't the English return calls promptly? I've always been told it is proper decorum to call within two days."

"Kate, do not fret. She will come. If I am a judge of anyone's person, I know Miss Darcy was intrigued by us. She is so dull and shy, and we are the opposite. She needs our friendship much more than we need hers."

Kate released the breath she was holding with a loud sigh and flung the curtain closed. "Yes, I suppose you are right."

"You know I am right. I've never been wrong—especially about things so important as sketching one's character."

"Well, I wish you had been wrong about why Papa dragged us to England."

Millie lifted one brow. "And why would you doubt me, sister dear? Have I not always told you he would do this?"

"Yes. I know, but...well, it's just difficult to believe that Papa would replace Mother so soon. She is hardly cold in her grave, and you know how he is about keeping up appearances."

"Mother has been dead a week short of twelve months, Kate. It is within Papa's rights to remarry. Besides, in India, nobody cares about those sorts of things."

"I don't care. I cannot stand the woman! An outing on Bond Street at the *Western Exchange* and chocolate in Piccadilly Square were what I expected—not the surprise that accompanied it. Why did he not just simply take a mistress? Why did he remarry? Who is this dowager countess of Waterford Abbey anyway?"

"She is Lady Crofton, and you had better make yourself accustomed to calling her such, or she will make us miserable. She is not like Mother who hardly gave a care about our comings and goings. Lady Crofton will not be so amenable. She will insist on the strictest decorum, and therefore you, and *I*, will give our new mother her due respect. Else she will give us grief!"

"Humph!" Kate stamped her foot. "I will not, for I do not like her! She thinks she can come in and change things—change us. Well, she cannot! Hateful woman!"

"Then we shall just have to find husbands before she finds them for us," Millie said with little emotion while she rubbed her ayah's blended coconut oil into her nails, polishing them until they glowed.

"Yes. The thought has crossed my mind, but I refuse to give up my money! ...or my freedom," Kate replied in a soft whisper.

"Who says we have to give up either? Find a man, make him fall in love with you, and then instruct him as to how the marriage contract will read. Afterwards, we can live as we choose. It will be like picking gooseberries in India. Remember that colonel in New Delhi? You had him full in love with you. I've never seen one more besotted as Colonel Brockton was. Were you in love with him?"

"What is love that I should be mindful of it? It is nothing more than a foolish inclination that soon passes when the next man comes along."

"Well, you certainly had the good colonel eating out of *your* hand."

Kate perked up, laughing. "Indeed I did, and I shall have the next one similarly smitten."

"Kate," Millie said, putting her polishing cloth in her pocket. "I know you well. You've already chosen the next one haven't you? I saw the way you looked at Mr. Darcy the other evening. And furthermore—"

"Yes! That is why I insisted we call upon his sister! We need *her* to secure *him*. He *is* marriage material, after all, and you must admit he is very easy on the eyes."

"Why Kate, aren't you the clever one. And to think all this time I thought you liked the timid little mouse, but it is her *brother* you like. I do believe you have set your cap on *him*."

"Umm…yes, perhaps I have, but I am fond of Georgiana even if she is rather shy. I believe she will make as good a friend as any, and she is not like the social namedroppers we have had the displeasure to meet so far," Kate replied casually. "Millie, do you think he might like my new gown?"

Kate went to her dressing table and searched for her newly stitched frock designed by the French modiste she kept in her entourage of servants. Not finding what she was looking for, she turned in an angry temper.

"Arpita-Arpita—where is my new gown? I had it just this morning. Where is it?"

"I put away, Missy Sahib," the ayah replied from the sofa where she sat. "You no want Memsahibs to see that dress. They not approve if they see, and *that* you should know."

"Hang Susan! And hang my new mother too! Fetch me my gown this very instant! I could not care two straws for what my sister *or* the countess thinks. I shall be the judge of who sees what and when! How shall I catch a fish without appealing bait?"

Displeased, the ayah slowly rose to her feet and shuffled over to her mistress's wardrobe at the far corner of the room. Digging through the many selections of beautiful gowns and accessories, she finally found what her mistress desired. Lifting a finely stitched evening dress from the hook, she folded it over her arm as she shook her head. It was made almost entirely of netted lace. By any stretch of the imagination, *this* was a scandalous dress.

Kate moved to where the older woman stood and snatched it from her.

The ayah stepped aside and lowered her eyes.

"What do you think, Millie?" Kate asked, walking back into the centre of the room. "Will Mr. Darcy like it? I know Edward would have. Colonel Brockton was very fond of my sense of fashion even if it was *scandalous* as they say!"

"I should think any man would be driven to distraction with that design—especially if you wear nothing beneath it," Millie said. "You really should stop reading those French journals and Gothic novels. They are corrupting your good morals. What would Reverend Fordyce say to that?"

Both girls laughed and Millie added, "I only wish I had thought of it first, but then I have no potential suitor; however, if I did…?" They collapsed on the bed with more giggles.

Recovering, Kate fixed her eyes on her sister. "But when will I have such an occasion to wear it? Not here in Susan's house surely! She wouldn't have it!"

"Susan and Rand will leave for the country shortly after the ball to prepare for that silly foxhunt. They are not likely to return anytime soon."

"But what if Susan doesn't go after the ball? She may not, you know. There is Christmas to consider. They will not leave before then, and besides the holiday, she

A Man in Want of a Wife

may wish to remain in Town and have more parties to introduce us to suitable men," Kate replied.

"I do not think it likely, but if it is, we shall find a way to overcome any obstacle thrown in our path, come what may."

"And what of Papa?"

"Oh, you need not worry about *Papa*. He will be too busy with his newly-won countess, and we shall be left to our own devices just as we have always been," Millie said with a sigh.

Kate smiled. "Then, when all is settled, and we are engaged, I shall invite Mr. Darcy over for a private tea, and on that occasion, I will wear the dress just for him. Oh won't he get a shock!"

"Indeed! I saw the way he eyed you at the theatre, and if that look means anything, Saturday's ball will tell," Millie said. "Then, my dearest Kate, if my perception is correct, the rest is up to *you*, but you will have to make haste of it, for Susan and Rand will not miss all the season. They will eventually return to London—especially since Susan feels she must sponsor our coming out."

"I am well aware of what I must do, so you needn't worry about it!" Kate countered with a sharp look.

Millie placed her hands on her hips and tilted her head. "We shall see, dear sister. *You* are the reckless one. *I* am the sensible one."

Kate rolled her eyes.

Returning her attention to her dress, Kate held the lace gown up to the light and sighed. "Yes...it is beautiful, but I couldn't dare wear it with nothing at all underneath. I must appear at least a *little* tasteful. He shall think me a harlot if I am not careful. I will wear my finest silk petticoat—the pale green chiffon one. It complements my beautiful green eyes, and it is so sheer it is hardly visible." She laughed. "Together the layers will conceal just enough to whet one's appetite, but not allow the treasure hidden beneath to be *too* discernible. Umm...tease and tantalize like we did with those ostrich fans in New Delhi."

"Kate, do not speak of that!" Millie snapped. "It was a private masquerade party at the garrison officers' quarters. No one has any idea that it was *us* behind those fans, and it must remain as such."

"Oh, very well; you can be so dull at times, Millie. It was the most fun I have ever had." Kate giggled. "And that's not the half of it. Papa would have been knocked for six had he known—"

"But *that's* the *point*, Kate; he does *not know*, and if you wish to keep your inheritance, he must *never* know."

Kate sighed. "Yes...I suppose you are correct. But it will all be of no consequence if we marry well, which brings me back to the subject at hand. If I should capture Mr. Darcy's heart and he marries me, then you do realize that a man like that will require an heir, and you know what we promised one another sitting under the tulip trees in Kolkata, and yet, I will have to give him one. You know I must, or he will not have me. *But*...as I said, he is easy on the eyes, and I suppose I could be prevailed upon to have a second. I might even have three if he should prove to be tolerably good in the art of lovemaking. But no more than three, for I will not ruin my figure for anyone—not even one I suspect is as good a lover as Mr. Darcy," she said with a satisfied glow in her expression.

"And if he is not?"

"Not what?"

"A good lover, of course!"

"Then I shall take one who *is*."

"Oh Kate! You cannot possibly mean that! I know we have had our wild times, but this is now very serious. You cannot create a scandal! You must be faithful."

"What? Like Papa and all the other men in high society? This is a man's world, Millie. Marriage is not about love. It is a game of chance and societal contracts—the *do*s and *don't*s— and separate lives once the heir is produced. The best a woman can hope for is a comfortable existence with little more than dinner parties for her husband and a few flirtations for herself," Kate said. "I would imagine that Mr. Darcy is like any other man of his sphere, and therefore, I am convinced that my chance of happiness with him is as fair as most people can boast on entering the marriage state. I don't expect *much*, and consequently, I will not be disappointed *much*."

Handing the gown back to her ayah, Kate turned and went to the window for a second time and parted the curtains.

"Oh look, Millie. Miss Darcy and her companion have arrived," she said, letting the drapery fall back into place.

Turning to her ayah, she snapped, "Arpita! Put away that dress; put it away now!"

"Yes, Missy Sahib."

Returning to her sister, she protested, "That woman—Mrs. Annesley—is too prim. I don't like her at all. Did you see how she watched us when we called on Miss Darcy the other day? She doesn't trust us, so we shall have to conveniently lose her for the afternoon, for I cannot speak freely to our dear friend with her in attendance."

"Yes, well, we had best make ourselves presentable." Millie said as she moved towards the door separating her room from her sister's.

"Arpita, call for a servant to remove these breakfast trays, and help me dress. I want to wear my blue frock."

"Yes, Missy Sahib."

~*~

Miss Darcy and her companion had entered the great house of Pennington Hall and were shedding their wraps with the aid of the butler when another footman approached and bowed.

"Miss Darcy, Miss Kathryn Singleton and her sister Miss Millicent are in the drawing room. If you will follow me, I shall make your presence known."

Turning to the left, they moved through a short corridor and into one of the grandest rooms Georgiana had ever seen. From the decor, to the furniture, to the art hanging on the walls, the entire room spoke of wealth and distinguished taste.

Upon entering the drawing room, Kate was the first to approach her. "Georgiana! How *good* of you to come. Millie and I were just talking about you. Were we not, Sister?"

"Oh! Indeed we were. I was telling Kate how I longed for you to visit, and well, here you are. Please take a seat while I ring for tea."

Millie moved to the inglenook and pulled the embroidered bell cord, and within minutes a servant appeared carrying a tray filled with a variety of sweets and a pot of tea.

A Man in Want of a Wife

"Mrs. Annesley," Kate said as she lifted the steaming pot, "Do you take one sugar or two, and do you prefer cream or plain?"

"I take my tea with cream only, please."

"Georgiana?"

"One sugar with cream."

Millie fixed the cups, and Kate poured the tea.

Sitting back with a small plate of sweets, Kate said, "Millie and I have been so bored of late what with parties and such. We would like to get out in the fresh air. There is a pretty sort of park nearby, and we have longed to walk in it. After we have visited for a little while, would you like to join us for a stroll, or would you prefer to ride? If you do not own your own horse, my sister Susan has plenty. She would not mind in the least if we should borrow them."

"Is your sister in the house? If so might she join us, perchance?" Georgiana asked.

"Oh no, Susan is out most mornings with Mrs. Pennington—planning and making arrangements for Saturday's ball and all. It keeps her quite busy, and since we are essentially guests, we are not included, which is just as well. I prefer to have my mornings to myself."

"Umm...as do I," Millie added. "I find planning parties such tedious work. I'd much rather spend my time with friends riding in the park or shopping. I bought the most exquisite bonnet the other day. You must see it. I shall wear it should we go out. It matches my riding habit to perfection."

"Oh, but it is not as pretty as mine," Kate said. "Mine is white silk covered in crepe and trimmed in white satin with delicate Pinks and Sweet Williams set in the band."

"Yes, but it not for riding," Millie returned. "More like a wedding bonnet if you ask me. Oh, but never mind that. What say you Georgiana? Would you like to take a turn in the park or perhaps a ride?"

Georgiana looked to Mrs. Annesley who smiled and nodded.

"Yes, I would love to ride in Hyde Park. There is nothing I like better than to take my mare out, and it has been some time since Aries has had the privilege. We shall enjoy it."

"Excellent!" both girls said at once.

The young ladies sat and talked for half an hour while they enjoyed their tea. Georgiana talked more than Mrs. Annesley had ever seen her do before, and though she was glad to see her participating in conversation, something about these two young ladies bothered her. Yet she could not seem to figure it out. They came from a good family, had excellent manners when it came to protocol, and were modestly, though stylishly, dressed. Nevertheless, there was a certain independence about them that did not bode well with her. Thus, she sipped her tea and watched them carefully.

Finally, Millie said, "It has been such a good visit, but if we are going to make time for a ride in the park, we had better get on with it."

Georgiana placed her teacup aside and rose to her feet. "I shall see you in half an hour's time. Meet me by the large Spanish chestnut near the grove of elms in the centre of the park. There is a pretty little shrubbery there with benches. Mrs. Annesley and your companion can sit and talk while we ride," she said with a warm smile.

The Singleton sisters walked their guests to the front door, and after seeing them out, went to their rooms to make themselves ready for their outing.

~*~

Georgiana sat upon her grey mare in the centre of the park gazing out over the distances, waiting expectantly for her friends.

Though the air was cool and crisp, it was a beautiful sunny afternoon for this time of year. Children's laughter could be heard as they played by the small frozen lake, and men and women were either out for an afternoon stroll, or circling the park in their open carriages.

Mrs. Annesley sat on a stone bench by the walkway with her book, not reading but observing. Her pleasure at the outing was plainly expressed on her features.

Miss Darcy's face lit up with a smile when she spied a chestnut mare and a black, Kate riding the latter in the most beautiful indigo blue riding habit Georgiana had ever seen, and her sister on the former dressed in burgundy red.

Georgiana kicked the side of her mare and urged her forward, meeting her new friends under a grove of trees.

"Have you been here very long?" Kate asked. "We were delayed in leaving. Our ayah could not come and, rather than disappoint you, we came alone."

"Not very long," Georgiana said, "though I was worried something had detained you, or worse, that you could not come."

"Yes, well something did keep us," Millie said, fretting with her reins. "You see, our papa stopped by and…"

"What Millie is trying to say is that Papa has lately married. We are all a good bit upset over it. Even Susan is displeased."

"Yes, though if you ask me, she and Susan will soon become fast friends. She's not all *that* displeased."

"Hush Millie!"

"But why…why are you displease?" Georgiana asked.

"Because our mother has not yet been dead a year," Kate said. "We've not even been out of mourning but a week, and he has taken a new wife! It is one of his reasons for our coming to England—that and his yearly meeting with his company's court of directors. He married the Countess of Crofton, whom we had never met, and who does not seem very happy with us. I am afraid she scolded us severely. Poor Arpita was beside herself!"

"I am sorry to hear that you are upset," Georgiana said, "but had he known Lady Crofton for very long?"

"No, not at all," Millie replied. "They met through correspondence. He saw her for the first time about a sennight ago. One of the directors encouraged the match, and Father married her."

"Then it was not likely a love match."

"Oh, goodness no!" Millie cried. "Love has nothing to do with it. Status, connections, wealth, empires—those are the reasons men marry. Because she was a widow with no issue, Father will claim her late husband's entire estate. There is no one to contest it. Waterford Abbey and all that it entails is now Papa's. Lady Crofton carries the title since Lord Crofton was also her cousin, but Papa owns everything else. Although, to be fair, she does gain the status of being married to the Viceroy of India and that in itself is something grand."

A Man in Want of a Wife

Georgiana took in a deep breath and shook her head. "It does not seem fair that a woman must give up all she owns when she marries, especially when there is no affection for one another by either party."

"Indeed it is not, but this is a man's world and men rule it," Kate interjected. "I'm afraid love is not an option for many of us in our circle."

Georgiana dropped her head and spoke softly. "I should like to marry for love, and I believe my brother would, too."

"How remarkable," Millie cried. "So should we! Kate and I talk of nothing else. But we must be careful, for unscrupulous men abound, stalking about like savage animals, seeking to devour a young woman's fortune and then leave her in a loveless marriage—her happiness dashed to bits!"

Georgiana stiffened. "Yes...I know," she said, thinking back to her own near disaster; had it not been for her brother, her life would have been ruined. She turned to Kate and asked, "If you would not mind telling me, what was your mother like, and how did she die?"

"No, I do not mind. Our mother was very beautiful and loved to entertain. She was often invited to parties and such. Our father was rarely at home, business keeping him away more frequently than not, and so Mother was often alone in our little village. I remember quite well how it happened. Father was in Kolkata on business when the cholera broke out. There was a dinner party that Mother was supposed to help host, so she did not heed the warning to vacate the hamlet, thinking there was still time. By the next morning, however, it was too late. She was dying. Fortunately, Millie and I did not catch the disease, but we saw its devastation as everything, bodies and all, had to be burned."

"How horrible it must have been to lose your mother in such a dreadful way. I am sorry."

"Thank you," Millie said. "Though we were in the care of our ayah and tutors for most of our lives and we did not see Mother every day, it was very hard to lose her."

"What about your papa?"

"He is Viceroy to India and has the Far Eastern Trading Company to occupy his time."

Done with explaining, Millie kicked her horse and cut across the centre of the park headed for the far end. Kate followed and Georgiana trailed after them. When they came near the south entrance, they pulled back and came to a stop.

"Fitzwilliam! Mr. Bingley! What a pleasant surprise," Georgiana said. "How did you know I would be here, or is this an accident of chance?"

Darcy tipped his beaver. Smiling he said, "It is no accident of chance. Your maid said that we might find you here and the Miss Singletons would be with you. Therefore, I thought we would join you."

"I'm glad you did."

"As am I." Glancing between his friend and the ladies, he further stated, "Ladies, this is my good friend, Mr. Charles Bingley. Charles, these are the Singleton sisters I spoke of the other night at dinner. This is Miss Kathryn Singleton, and the fair haired lady is Miss Millicent Singleton. They are Pennington's sisters-in-law you've heard so much about. They are lately here from India with their father, the Governor-General."

"I am pleased to meet you, ladies," Charles said. "I have heard much of you from my friend here, and I must say none of it has been exaggerated." His eyes met Millicent's soft grey ones and, for a brief moment, they locked.

Tearing them away, he said, "Shall we ride round the park, ladies?"

"Yes," said Millie, dropping in beside Bingley. "I hear you are to come to my brother's ball on Saturday. Do you like to dance, Mr. Bingley?"

"At times I have enjoyed it. Do you dance, Miss Singleton?"

Millie smiled, and she and Bingley joined in conversation while Darcy rode beside Miss Kathryn with his sister on the other side of her. He said not a word as they rode side by side, but instead, he studied her and his sister who was chatting animatedly. Georgiana smiled and laughed. She seemed to come alive in Miss Kathryn's presence, showing a confidence Darcy had not seen since their father's death. This was the most he had heard her speak without being prompted since last summer. And then there was Miss Kathryn Singleton herself.

He had not missed the coquettish turn of her countenance, or how her eyes caressed him as if she were drinking him in with her smile. It was also not difficult to see that her blue velvet habit suited her well and showed her figure off to its best advantage.

Looking further, he noted that she wore a fashionable felt indigo-blue women's beaver with just enough blue and black ostrich feathers to be stylish, yet not overdone. There was no uncertainty of her physical beauty or her style and deportment. By her expression and the way she carried herself, he could tell she was a woman fully grown, one who possibly had some experience with life in general, though undoubtedly innocent with gentlemen. But would she be a good mistress for Pemberley? That he had not decided, nor would he until he knew a great deal more about her.

Those things he pondered as he rode by her side without one word passing between them. And if there was a fly in the ointment, it was a fleeting thought that took up residence in his mind and would not be dismissed—Miss Elizabeth Bennet would have looked lovely in that indigo blue riding habit.

~*~*~*~

Chapter 20

Darcy stood in front of the looking glass, staring at the man who solemnly gazed back at him. His mind was fixed on his situation in life. He had put it off long enough. Though he would probably never have what his father or his friend Randal Pennington had, it was time he married. It was not the custom among his peers, but, like his father and friend, he had desired to marry for love. But alas, after searching the debutante balls and soirées, attending numerous dinner parties, and visiting family estates of the nobility and very rich for years, it had all been in vain. He had found no one who met his ideals—or at least no one who met *all* his ideals.

He reached up and reworked his cravat, adjusting it to suit his meticulous style. Staring at his reflection, he gauged his appearance as he turned from side to side, remembering another ball and the great anticipation and desire he felt back then for the pending dance, but there was little expectancy for this ball. No. For with this ball he would go through the motions and pay his due to society. He would single out Miss Singleton and test her. If Miss Kathryn Singleton proved to be acceptable, then he would spend more time with her, perhaps pursuing the relationship further. He sighed and shook his head.

...why could fortunes not have been reversed and Elizabeth have been Miss Singleton? ...had circumstances been different, and Mr. Bennet fathered a son...and grown a spine to curb his wife's tongue—better yet, had he married a woman of good sense!

Suddenly he realised what he was doing and narrowing his eyes, he murmured to himself, "If I do not put away this obsession, I'm in danger of making the most disastrous decision of my life! I will get out from under her spell. I *must*!"

"Mr. Darcy, sir."

Darcy turned to the sound of his name. "Yes."

"I have your black coat read—"

"No-no—the blue one. I wore black at the last ball. I do not wish to wear it again."

"Very well, sir, the blue one it is then, but it is less form..."

Darcy gave his man a warning look which silenced him in mid-sentence.

Clearing his throat, his valet spoke again. "Sir, which cologne do you want for tonight? The one you wore for the last ball or something else?"

"Bring me the musk."

Mr. Cunningham's eyes widened. "The musk, sir?"

Darcy turned with a sharp look. "Have you become hard of hearing, Winfred? I said the musk, and the musk is what I want."

"But the musk has a more raw, animal scent. I think it highly unsuited for a ball, sir."

"Nevertheless, that is exactly what I want."

"Very well, sir. I shall fetch it."

Once his man had left, Darcy turned back to his reflection.

"Mr. Darcy," Cunningham said, approaching from his dressing room. "Here is what you requested, but be advised, sir, that a very little will do. Musk tends to become stronger as it ages."

"I know what it does."

"Very well, sir. Call me if you should need anything else. I shall busy myself tidying up a bit."

Darcy uncapped the bottle and despite the warning, applied a generous amount. Placing it on his dressing table, he turned and left the room. Moving down the stairs at a rapid pace, he went to the foyer where the footman helped him with his greatcoat, and he was soon on his way—first to his cousins, then to Hurst's townhouse, and finally to Number 15 Cavendish Square. Leaning against the posh cushions of his coach, Darcy's mind drifted to the two women that attracted him in such diverse ways: one a challenge to his heart and everything he had been taught since a youth…and the other? She challenged something else entirely.

…From the scent of her card I know Miss Kathryn has high animal spirits, and a sort of natural self-consequence that shows confidence in her ability to attract any man she chooses. Miss Bennet had a similar self-assurance in another turn. Elizabeth played the game of wits; Kathryn Singleton plays the game of allurements. I will match Miss Kathryn in her own game…just as I did Elizabeth in hers!

~*~

The Darcy coach pulled up to the carriage step of one of the largest and most magnificent houses in Mayfair. Candles glowed in the windows, and sprigs of pine and wreaths of fir with festive apples and pears garnished the doors and window frames. The lamps were lit and decked with holly, and gay music could be heard coming from the open doors on the veranda of the ballroom. Darcy was the first to exit followed by Bingley, Miss Bingley and Mrs. Hurst, and then Mr. Hurst and Darcy's cousins.

"What a splendid house, Mr. Darcy. Quite an improvement from the assembly hall of Hertfordshire, don't you think?" Caroline Bingley observed with practiced conceit.

Darcy looked around not bothering to reply to her prompting.

Miss Bingley placed her hand on his arm.

He glanced down and shrugged, but this time he did not remove it as he had done at the Prancing Fox in Meryton. It would not matter if he did, he reasoned, as she would only persist as she had then.

"I think we shall be quite safe here, Mr. Darcy. We are far away from Hertfordshire this time."

"Indeed we are…a good distance, indeed," he said more to himself than to her.

Entering the house, Darcy glanced around as they moved through the receiving line. The elite of the ton were present: lords and ladies, dukes and duchesses, and the finest families from high society. Only the royal family appeared to be missing. The interior of the townhouse was as festively decorated as the exterior with holly and mistletoe tastefully placed throughout. He made a mental note not to be anywhere in the vicinity of the latter with Miss Bingley in sight when the clock struck midnight.

"Darcy, Bingley, and Hurst, I am glad you came. Colonel Fitzwilliam and Lord Wexford, and Miss Bingley, Mrs. Hurst, it is a pleasure to see you again," Randal Pennington declared. Mrs. Pennington and the elder Mr. and Mrs. Pennington also greeted their guests, making them feel welcome.

Once the greetings were exchanged, Darcy broke away from the others and entered the ballroom through a large archway that was likewise covered in greenery. He glanced around taking his measure of the guests. There were many people he knew, but only one in particular he was seeking. His eyes roamed over the crowd in earnest pursuit until they finally rested on *her*. She stood with her sister and a couple whom he presumed were her father and stepmother.

As soon as she turned fully round, their eyes locked and held for some moments. Miss Kathryn Singleton was stunning. She wore a deep blue silk gown that hung in folds swirling around her hips as she moved, but there was something more that caught his notice. His eyes, as if by their own volition, fell from her face to her ample bosom. They were pushed up, out, and over the top like French fashions of the day.

Moving quickly to the refreshment table on the other side of the room, he poured a glass of wine and leaned against the wall positioning himself comfortably so that he could watch her from over the rim of his goblet as she talked and smiled with the many gentlemen who came by to pay their regard. Every now and then she would turn and tilt her head as she caught his stare. It was obvious by her expression that she desired his notice, but Darcy made no move to accommodate her; he only continued to slowly sip his wine. With very little effort on his part, he knew he could have her attention all to himself if that was what he desired. Lifting his drink, he emptied the glass and set it aside. Folding his arms over his chest, he continued to stare.

Finally the music began, and she lined up with her first partner. Darcy pushed away from the wall and stalked around the room following her through the dance, his eyes never leaving her as she moved in and out of the line.

Her chin was held high as she glided over the floor with ease and elegance, her skirt moving to reveal her figure to be light and pleasing. Kathryn Singleton was captivating, much as Elizabeth Bennet had been at Netherfield. And just like Elizabeth, she was robust and lively—everything he was not. That Miss Kathryn had money, connections, the right pedigree, and came from a family as old as his own with ties to the Crown, served as confirmation of his wisdom in seeking a woman of his own sphere.

Several sets passed, and just as it had been with Miss Elizabeth Bennet, Miss Kathryn Singleton was never in want of a partner. At length, however, she was finally without attention from the other gentlemen, and so Darcy approached her while she was in conversation with her sister.

With a curt bow, he said, "Miss Singleton, if you are not otherwise engaged, I would like to request the honour of your hand in dancing the next with me."

"I am not engaged, sir, and I would be honoured."

He again bowed, and abruptly left.

Millie smiled, taking her sister's hands in hers. "Kate, I told you he would ask. From the time he entered the room, he has done nothing but watch your every move. You followed my instructions and made him mad with desire. Flirting with the other gentlemen has shown him you can have any man in the room, so play it to your advantage, my dear sister. I was correct. This dress would be the allurement to draw him in, now use your arts to secure him. Remember, do not say too much. Mr. Darcy is a man of few words."

"Millie!" Susan, their older sister scolded, "You should not talk such nonsense! Where are your manners?! If you and Kate do not control yourselves, your reputations will soon be fixed and the two of you will be known as the biggest flirts to—"

"Susan!" Millie's eyes flashed in warning. "You are anxious for nothing. I believe that we shall have the reputation of being remarkably sensible and clever in our arts, for I have found that if you are nice to the gentlemen, the gentlemen will be nice to you." She turned to walk away, but her sister grabbed her arm and spun her around.

Grabbing Kate's arm as well, she leaned in and spoke firmly. "Millicent! Kathryn! I must speak plainly to you both, and you had better listen to what I have to say! If you do not take the trouble of checking your exuberant spirits, your characters and reputations will be fixed as the most determined flirts who ever made yourselves and your family look ridiculous. No gentleman, and hear me well, *girls*, for I do mean *no gentleman* of any quality will have you. They will think you ill bred. Then Mrs. Singleton and I will have to find you husbands who will take you without any consideration for what you may want or desire. Do you understand me, girls, for I am speaking to the both of you equally?!"

"Perfectly!" Millie spit out as she turned and stomped off.

Susan turned to Kate and was about to say something more when Kate arched a brow and smiled. "I hear the music. Mr. Darcy of Pemberley awaits me." She started towards the dance floor, but then turned back. "Dear sister, if I were you, I'd worry about keeping my own husband happy instead of what your sisters do in pursuit of theirs." She laughed and walked on.

Moving to her place in the line opposite Mr. Darcy, she smiled and curtseyed when the chord struck and the dance began. They came together and moved in and out, circling and swaying, but neither said a word. When their hands touched, Miss Singleton's eyes fixed on his with a look that was intense and full of desire, and when the dance brought them close, he could smell the scent of her perfume. As he suspected, there was a hint of musk in the fragrance—musk and something else, sweet and exotic and unknown to him.

He made a casual comment about the Christmas decorations, but she said not a word. Circling out and in once more, he remarked on the number of partners as they came together.

"You are quite popular this evening, Miss Singleton. Is it always this difficult to catch you between partners?"

"Yes."

"Do you dance often at balls and assemblies, then?"

"Yes."

"Do you speak while dancing as many other young ladies are fond of doing?"

"No."

"Miss Singleton, I am not a man of many words, but I believe it is customary to at least have *some* conversation."

"What would you have me say, Mr. Darcy? Tell me, and I will say it."

A Man in Want of a Wife

The corners of his mouth lifted slightly. "I'm more interested in what *you* think and not what you think I want to hear."

Coming together, they turned and moved to the side. "Very well, then. I do believe that dancing brings out the best in people in a more refined and polished society."

"And in unpolished societies what would you say it brings out?"

"Animal behaviour in some, I would imagine," she replied without any reservation as she arched a brow.

Darcy stiffened, and she smiled. They were separated again by the dance and then came back together.

"Have you not ever seen the peafowl in their mating dance? They are common in India," she said. "It is quite arousing to watch." Moving in close and twirling around, she continued. "They move in and out as we do here. The peacock displays his colourful plumage to the peahen in the dance, hoping to impress her, but it is the *female* that chooses the *male*. It is not so different with other species which, I believe, would include humans."

It was now his turn to arch a brow. "Do you speak of such things as a rule, Miss Singleton, or do you seek to amaze me with your knowledge of cocks and hens?"

After a brief moment of silence, she smiled, and her eyes locked with his once more.

"Come, Mr. Darcy. You asked me to speak, and I spoke. I grew up in India. I have seen many dances...both civilized and *uncivilized*. But perhaps you think the illustration of the peafowl was not appropriate for ballroom conversation."

"I am certain that most young women would not have thought to mention the mating rituals of any animal. However, I am amazed that, for a lady of your sphere, you speak your mind at all, and so boldly. It is quite odd for one so young."

"Why would that be?"

"Because, it is uncommon. Most ladies, I fear, feel they should wait until they know what a man wants to hear and parrot it back to him. They do not speak as they see—if they have a mind at all."

"Pity, then."

"What think you of books?" he asked as they separated in the line.

When they came back together, she replied, "Books? I think little of books, unless you speak of gothic novels or ladies' fashion journals. They are all I read. Everything else I find quite boring."

Darcy drew in a deep breath as they separated again.

Coming back together, she enquired, "Have you happened to read Ann Radcliffe's *The Mysteries of Udolpho*?"

Darcy's astonishment was such that it was all he could do to keep from rolling his eyes.

"No, I have not," he flatly stated and changed the subject. "Ah, Miss Kathryn, do you ever walk out when you are in the country, and do you like rocks and hills or fields of flowers. In particular...do you like lavender?"

"Walk? Oh goodness no! Why would one *walk* when they can ride? And the only flowers I care for are the lotus and night blooming jasmine of India. Jasmine is sweet and intoxicating. It speaks of beauty. The lotus flower means purity and perfection in Indian culture. Who could care for lavender? The scent is very dull, and it is such a common bloom that only those who can afford no better would consider it."

Darcy took a deep breath and released it slowly. "I happen to like lavender," he murmured to himself as they turned and each took the hand of the partner beside them.

"Did you say something?" she asked moving to his side in the dance.

"No...nothing at all."

"Mr. Darcy," Miss Singleton moved beside him and leaned in close, the scent of her perfume once again assaulting his senses. "I do not speak words I think you want to hear. I speak my mind, and if it pleases you then I am pleased; if it does not, then you will be displeased, but I will not. I am who I am; certainly nothing less, but so much more."

Darcy tried to smile, but made no response. His mind was too full for further conversation, and so they passed the remainder of the dance with little conversation exchanged. He had heard enough to satisfy his curiosity. Like Miss Elizabeth, and unlike every other woman he had known, Miss Singleton did not simper and fawn, and neither did she speak solely to please him. Fully aware that her personality was strong, he considered that he would have to make some allowances for the shortcomings in her education and proper English decorum; for what she lacked in the improvement of her mind, could easily be made up with a little instruction from a husband with sense and education. And furthermore, what she lacked in one capacity, she more than made up in quite another. Her self-confidence recommended her well. When the dance was over, they parted in silence, leaving Darcy with a lot to consider concerning his future.

Quitting the dance floor, Darcy spied the prominent gentleman he had seen earlier standing by the refreshment table with his wife and Mr. and Mrs. Pennington, and supposed him to be Rand's father-in-law—Miss Kathryn's father. He seemed amiable enough and was fashionably dressed, and his wife was attractive, polished and refined—the complete opposite of Mr. and Mrs. Bennet.

His uncle, Lord Matlock, approached him with a smile and a slap on the back.

"I noticed you dancing with the Governor-General's daughter, Darcy. She and her sister are probably the most eligible matches for this season, and they are uncommonly beautiful...especially the one you were dancing with, nephew. She and her sister seem to have the spice of life in their souls. Perhaps you noticed?"

"I noticed. I fear one could not help but observe their beauty and liveliness—especially Miss Kathryn's. It seems to flow from her to everyone in the room."

"And have you met their father, perchance? He is an old friend of mine."

"No, I've not had that pleasure."

"Then, by all means, let me introduce you. He is lately married to Lady Crofton of Waterford Abbey."

After making their way to the wine table, the Earl of Matlock approached his old friend and bowed. "Singleton, How good to see you old fellow. It has been many years since we last met."

"Matlock!" the Governor-General cried. "It has indeed been too long since we last spoke. I had hoped to meet up with you in Westminster Abbey, but I suppose you have not been present when I was there. Is it not a pleasant ball my son-in-law has given? Lots of food and dancing for the young people."

"Indeed."

"Matlock, do you know my wife, Lady Crofton?"

A Man in Want of a Wife

Lady Crofton smiled. "Dear, of course I know the distinguished Earl of Matlock. My late husband and Lord Matlock were colleagues, often arguing on the same side in the House of Lords."

"Then I am well pleased. But Lord Matlock, might you introduce the gentleman with you. I've seen him dancing with one of my daughters and wondered who he might be."

"Yes, of course." The Earl smiled and turned aside. "Phillip, allow me to introduce my nephew, Fitzwilliam Darcy of Pemberley in Derbyshire. Darcy, the Viceroy, Governor-General to India."

Darcy bowed. "It is a pleasure to finally meet you, sir. I've heard much of you and your family."

"Oh!" The Viceroy laughed softly. "I trust it was all good."

Darcy smiled. "It was."

"And I see you are acquainted with my girls," he said, his eyes intently searching Darcy's. "You've danced with Kate, and I believe you spoke with Millie."

"Your daughters are indeed handsome young ladies, and Miss Kathryn is an enjoyable partner."

"Umm, they are handsome at that," Mr. Singleton said, glancing between his eldest and the twins. "Take after their mothers, they do—except Kate. She is like my mother in many ways." He sighed. "We've been too long in India. My girls are so vivacious, but either of them, I'm sure, will make a suitable wife when the time comes. I have settled one hundred thousand pounds a piece on them, but if I know they are settled well and happy, then it is a small pittance to pay." His piercing gaze held Darcy's eyes for several moments.

Breaking away, the Viceroy glanced towards the entryway. "I see one of my directors is here, so, if you will excuse me, gentlemen, I have a small matter to discuss with him." He set his wine glass aside and moved on.

Darcy watched as the Viceroy walked away. "A hundred thousand pounds…and he thinks it a *pittance*!"

"Darcy, what is a hundred thousand pounds when you have millions? Jacob Phillip Singleton is quite possibly the richest man in the kingdom. His money and pedigree are not only quite old, but his line has a propensity for making money—lots of it. Anyone who marries one of those girls is fortunate indeed. I see no impediment if you wish to pursue the connection with either of them, and Lady Catherine can be made to see reason on the subject as well. Truth be told, she will embrace it once it is settled. It would be a most fortunate match for you, which I hope you will consider, and from the way that lass looked at you, I doubt you would have a difficult time winning her hand."

"Yes…it is a considerable amount of money *not* to consider, and it would secure Pemberley for many years to come, though it is not simply the money I would consider. We must be compatible."

"Compatible? With a hundred thousand pounds what is not to be compatible? I am pleased to hear you are at least more sensible than before." the Earl laughed and then continued. "Am I to assume you've given up that Shakespearean notion of a love match?"

Darcy diverted his eyes and shrugged.

"Good! Too many passions are not good for the heart. No dignified Englishman would admit to such foolishness. Affection for one's wife, perhaps, but *love*? Never!

Better to have a good wife to bed and bear your heirs than have one tangle you up in all that passion the poets speak so highly of," Lord Matlock said.

Glancing to the left, he noticed his wife signalling him. "Well, Darcy, I'd best be off. Lady Matlock is beckoning me for some damn fool thing or another. And when you are my age, you know it is wise to come when *she who must be obeyed* calls."

Darcy took a deep breath, attempting not to roll his eyes. "We'll talk again."

As Lord Matlock left, Rand Pennington approached. "I see you've met the Viceroy."

"Yes, a most unusual sort of gentleman, but I must say, not unpleasant. You failed to mention at your wedding that your father-in-law was the Governor-General to India and the chief director of the Far Eastern Trading Company. Why were he and his daughters not present for your wedding?"

"Umm…yes…that. Well, my wife and her father have not always been on good terms. It seems that Susan and her stepmother were at odds for many years, and then there was that nasty cholera epidemic last year. The Viceroy missed his annual meeting with his directors and the Crown because of it. The Viceroy and his late wife were not on good terms. From all accounts I've heard, the second Mrs. Singleton was a narcissistic sort of woman who thought mostly of herself. She came down with the disease because she refused to leave the village when the evacuation was ordered, deciding to stay until after her dinner party with the garrison officers' wives. That night, while they were eating, cholera broke out in the village and the Viceroy's wife fell victim to the pandemic. She died the next day. This is Phillip Singleton's first opportunity to return to England since her death. I must say Susan gets on much better with his third wife than she did the second."

"Refused to leave because of a dinner party?" Darcy looked on in astonishment. "I'm surprised she had a choice in the matter."

Mr. Pennington laughed. "Darcy, you must understand that Millicent Singleton was not a woman to be ordered to do anything. The last evacuation was to be the next day, and so all the wives decided to go on with their plans, expecting they had time enough for their gaiety. Many of them are not here today to have a second opinion on the matter. Anyway, you have met him now. He's a very accommodating sort," Rand Pennington said with a smile as he glanced towards the dance floor. "Darcy, if you will excuse me, I must be getting on to see about the next dance with my wife before someone else decides to partner her. Carry on, old chap."

Darcy smiled as he watched his friend leave. He took a deep breath and shook his head. *…you've done very well for yourself, Pennington…very well indeed…you have a good match and love…*

Moving over to the far corner where the game tables were set up, Darcy took a seat beside a large bay window. The fragrance of Miss Kathryn's perfume still hung in the air, and once again his thoughts drifted to Miss Elizabeth and the lavender which always surrounded her. He took a deep breath and closed his eyes as two women played in his mind. *…love is a many splendored thing…that's what Winfred said…if that is true, then what is Miss Kathryn? …can I so easily replace one woman with another?*

"Darcy…Darcy…?"

Darcy's eyes flew open.

"Bored with the evening or too much excitement for an old man?" Bingley asked. Both men chuckled.

A Man in Want of a Wife

"I'm neither bored nor tired. I was meditating on the great pleasure a pretty woman's company can bestow."

"I see that you have singled out one of Rand's sisters-in-law for your attention. She is exceptionally pretty, I will admit, but as for the others, I couldn't say. I haven't noticed."

Noting the reappearance of sadness inhabiting Bingley's expression whenever he spoke of available women, Darcy said, "What about Miss Millicent? She is very pretty; would you not agree?"

"Yes…I've danced with her, and I suppose she is handsome enough."

"But not handsome enough to tempt you."

"I'm afraid no one can compare to Miss Bennet. Forevermore, she shall be the standard which I fear few, if anyone, could ever meet."

Darcy was stunned at his friend's statement, but did not have sufficient time to think of a reply before he heard his name being called again.

"Darcy, Bingley!"

Bingley turned and smiled. "Colonel Fitzwilliam, Lord Wexford."

"Have a seat, Wex, and you as well, Richard," Darcy said.

"No-no. I only came by to see how the evening has been for the two of you," Lord Wexford said. "I've a set reserved with one of the Viceroy's daughters. Pennington was right. His sisters-in-law are surprisingly pretty—especially the dark haired beauty. She certainly has a way with the gentlemen. You can hardly have a dance with her thanks to the long line of her many suitors."

Darcy glanced past his cousin and saw Miss Kathryn sitting in a chair with several young gentlemen surrounding her, and surprisingly, it was they who were fawning and simpering.

He glanced back to the Viscount. "Excuse me."

Colonel Fitzwilliam exchanged looks with Bingley and his brother as they noted Darcy's abrupt departure. "What is this with Darcy? Has some lady caught his attention?"

"I don't know, but I think it would be great fun to watch," replied Lord Wexford.

Darcy approached where Miss Singleton was holding court and bowed. Never looking at anyone but her, he said, "If you are not otherwise engaged for the supper dance, I would be honoured if you would accept my hand."

Kate glanced at the four young men standing around her and replied, "Mr. Darcy, I would be honoured to dance with you."

He bowed and left but not before overhearing: "Kate, you promised the supper dance to me."

"Do not pout, Mr. Hardwick; you shall have the next," she said tapping him with her fan.

When he returned to his friends, the Colonel smiled. "I suppose that is how a man of fortune has his way with the beautiful girls. Even the Viceroy's daughters are at your service. But let's dispense with the pleasantries," the Colonel said. "What if she had turned you down? From the looks of it she already had a partner for the supper dance."

"If I thought she would refuse, I would not have asked."

They all laughed.

"Well, I think I shall partner her sister," Lord Wexford declared. "She is an uncommonly intelligent woman and very beautiful. It is a rare occurrence amongst the debutantes and very refreshing."

After the Viscount had departed, the Colonel spoke with a smile. "Everyone seems to be having a good time, except your sister, Bingley. I have danced with Miss Bingley, but for the most part, she seems to have been ignored. Darcy, perhaps you should dance with her."

"Darcy will not dance with Caroline, and I could hardly blame him. If she is not finding pleasure here, it is because she won't take the trouble to be friendly. I've never in my life met anyone more sour than my own sisters, Caroline being the worst of the two."

"Yes…she has spent the entirety of our time tonight complaining about you, and…well, she does not like your partner, Darcy. I would say she is jealous of Miss Singleton."

"I am sorry to hear it, but she was also jealous of someone else I knew. Now, if you will excuse me, I've a dance to attend."

"I think Darcy might like the Viceroy's daughter," the Colonel said as he watched his cousin approach Kate.

"Perhaps he does, but I rather thought he liked Miss Elizabeth Bennet when we were all together at Netherfield, and evidently I was wrong. I am finding it hard to understand Darcy lately."

"Well, one thing is for certain, he needs to choose a wife soon. Georgiana's coming out is in two years, and he needs a wife to oversee it, but more importantly, he needs an heir and a mistress for his estate. So does my brother, for that matter. Perhaps he will choose the Viceroy's other daughter. Would that not be a triumph—my brother and cousin married to the toasts of the season?"

Bingley turned to study the woman to whom Darcy was speaking without replying.

Richard continued, "Care for some wine and cheese, Bingley?"

"I think it an excellent idea."

~*~

When the supper dance ended, the guests began to move towards the dining hall, ambling about as they searched the cards to find their places at the extravagantly decorated tables. When everyone was seated, Randal Pennington called them to attention. Standing at the head of the family banquet table, he looked out over the numerous people seated in the great hall.

"Here-here!" He clapped. "Listen up! I have something of great importance to announce. It is something that will cheer you all immensely. As a gift to my friends and neighbours, I shall host a foxhunt, and you are all invited. It will be held at Greensward Estate, our horse and foxhound manor on the outskirts of London. It will be held on the twentieth of January. And, as you all know, Pennington horses, which are bred and raised on this estate, are some of the finest in the country; so, if you do not own a horse, do not let that be an impediment to this event. Invitations will be sent around shortly."

Applause was heard throughout the room as everyone clapped and cheered. Rand took his seat and the dinner began with the serving of the white soup.

As he ate, Darcy noticed the Viceroy watching him from the elevated platform where the family dined. He saw him lean in, talking privately with Rand and old Mr. Pennington, and from the subsequent glances in his direction, Darcy assumed he was the topic of conversation. At least, he reflected, in this instance the whole room was not party to their conversation as had been with Mrs. Bennet during the last ball he had attended.

In fact, this ball bore no resemblance at all to the Netherfield ball. A master played at the pianoforte for the dinner, and when the supper was complete, traditional carols were sung up to the midnight hour where couples then gathered under the mistletoe.

As Darcy watched the festivities, he began to wish he had a love of his own, and once again his heart ached as the memories of Miss Elizabeth Bennet rushed forth, flooding his mind with her essence. He swallowed past the lump rising in his throat and hurried away.

Suddenly finding himself in need of fresh air, he fled through the large double doors to the balcony. Leaning against the great stone banister, he looked out over the finely manicured garden lit with gas lamps and sighed.

"If only I was a man of lesser means without so many lives depending on me...if only I had a family that understood. I would follow my heart and ask for the woman who has stirred my soul like none other instead of the one I must settle for. It isn't how it should be, but it is as it is. Elizabeth Bennet...what have you done to me?"

He stood there for some minutes with his hands forming into fists—twisting and gripping—while visions of Miss Elizabeth swirled through his mind. A small tear escaped his eye. He reached up and wiped it away. "If only your father had been a Viceroy...Elizabeth," he whispered into the night air.

Finally, shaking his head to clear his thoughts, he stood erect and turned to walk back into the world to which he belonged, his jaw set with the determination to forget her once and for all.

~*~

It was well into the early morning hours when Darcy arrived home. Everyone in the house except his butler, Mr. Moseley, had gone to bed. He had even told his valet not to wait up. Climbing the stairs to his room, Darcy thought of the evening and the turn of the events. Miss Singleton's tale of the peafowl was indelibly pressed into his mind. He wondered if she actually understood the double meaning of the tale. ...*the female chooses the male indeed!*

It made no difference. He and *he* alone would choose his destiny. Still, a smile played upon his lips as he stepped upon the landing and moved towards the master suite. He had danced two sets with Miss Singleton and none with anyone else, much to Miss Bingley's disappointment. Yes, it had indeed been a good night. Even Caroline Bingley and her endless prattle had not affected him during the dinner hour.

He entered his room and went to his dressing table, his determination set. He would do his duty to his family, to Pemberley, and all that was necessary for his station in life.

With a singleness of effort, he tugged at his cravat, his fingers working the knot until it finally loosened. Ripping it from his throat in one fluid motion, he tossed it aside as he thought out loud, "Miss Kathryn Singleton, you are exactly what I need to forget Miss Elizabeth Bennet. No one in my family could object to you. Like Elizabeth, you are beautiful, intelligent, spirited, and Georgiana is already very fond of you. My uncle thinks highly of you. Your father is a Viceroy of our most prosperous colony and the general director of the largest and oldest trading company in the kingdom. With your family's fortune and status, who could protest the match? Everything is in your favour to recommend you."

His fingers quickly ran down the length of his linen shirt unbuttoning it as he went. Stripping it off, he threw it over the back of a chair. Next he removed his boots, stockings, and breeches. Within minutes he was under the counterpane, his hands folded behind his head, staring into the dark of his room.

"Yes...I think you will do quite well. Maybe in time I might even grow to love you."

He rolled over and pulled his pillow to his chest and closed his eyes in sleep. Tomorrow, there would be church at St. Paul's and Christmas Service on Wednesday, and then, sometime within the next two weeks, he would call at Number 15 Cavendish Square to pay his regard to Randal Pennington, and if the Viceroy was present, then all the better.

~*~*~*~

Chapter 21

December 27, 1811

As Darcy sat in his study taking his morning coffee, Sam lay sprawled on a rug in front of the fire, watching his master with diligent eyes while said master read the early edition of *The Times*. The sound of a knock at the door alerted the dog, and his ears perked up as his eyes shifted in that direction. Setting his cup in its saucer, Darcy folded the paper and put it aside.

"Enter," he called out.

Georgiana peeked around the corner of the door. "Brother, if I may, I would like to speak with you before my morning session with my Latin and history master."

"Come in and have a seat," Darcy said, motioning to the settee in front of the bookcases near the hearth. "What would you like to talk to me about?"

Georgiana moved into the room and glanced towards the fire. "Oh, good morning, Sam," she said pleasantly.

The dog whimpered in response, and then rested his head between his paws.

Taking her seat, she folded her hands in her lap and looked at her brother, her eyes slightly larger and more inquisitive than usual. "Well," she said somewhat hesitantly, "it is Miss Kate and Miss Millie. I am to call on them this afternoon, but I do not think Mrs. Annesley approves of them, and I am so confused about it all. They seem nice enough to me, and I truly enjoy their company, but they are so different from most of my acquaintances. The last time I called on them, they told me of things they did when they were children, and I was taken aback. I cannot imagine you acting in such a way when you were a boy."

"And what way would that be?" Darcy asked crossing his legs and leaning back in his chair.

"They played with the native children and collected insects and lizards and snakes. I cannot imagine such activities for boys, much less girls. You never did such things…did you, Brother?"

Darcy laughed. Passing his hand over his face to hide his smile, he looked up and cleared his throat. "Georgie, you were barely six years of age when Mother died, and naturally, with no siblings or cousins of your own age to play with your life was far more sheltered than that of most children. Girls—and children in general— do tend to frolic with one another in what some might consider improper settings—such as playing with children of lesser rank and getting into mischief, as you've described. I would add that *certain* adults would not approve, but, to answer your question, *yes*, I did do similar things."

Her eyes widened. "What sort of things?"

"Well, once on one of our Easter trips to Rosings when I was ten and your cousin Richard was twelve, we did something we should not have done. He took a small garden snake to church in his coat pocket. He had found it in the roses that morning and, naturally, was fascinated with it. Wex, who was thirteen at the time, was teasing us about it, saying he didn't believe Richard had a snake as it was still early in the season for such creatures to be out. Richard, not to be gainsaid, took it out to show him. I asked to see it, and when he handed it to me, it bit me and I dropped it. The snake then went slithering down the aisle toward the centre of the church before any of us could react."

Georgiana gasped. "You did not!"

"Yes...I did," Darcy said with a grin.

"What happened?"

"Let us just say that the church service was the shortest Reverend Smith ever held. The congregation awakened from their usual Sunday slumber and thought they were in a Methodist revival instead of an Anglican Easter service. There was shouting and jumping—some even knocked over the benches in their hurry to escape while Richard and I slumped in our seats and Wex laughed. During the excitement your Aunt Catherine figured out what had happened and dragged us both out by the ear. When we returned to Rosings, we were thrashed soundly while your cousin, Lord Wexford, stood in the corner and laughed until he nearly doubled over. But we repaid him the next day, exchanging the sugar in his bowl for salt. His tea and porridge were a little less than he expected that morning, but he said not a word."

Georgiana laughed. "I never knew. I find it...*pleasing* to know my brother once did such things. You are certainly nothing like that now."

"No, but one day when you and I have children of our own, I suspect they will be getting into their share of mischief and will have to be corrected, just as your cousin Richard and I were. It is how we grow and become responsible adults."

"Then it is not unusual to be silly when one is young?"

"No. It is not. In fact, I once knew a young lady not much older than yourself who walked three miles across a field after a soaking rain to see after her sister who was unwell. When she arrived, her petticoat was six inches deep in mud. Some thought it was impertinent, accusing her surreptitiously of showing a form of conceited independence."

"It was Miss Bennet, was it not? You told me about it when you first returned from Hertfordshire."

"Did I? Well, then you have an excellent memory, Georgie."

Georgiana's lips curled slightly. "I always remember everything you say, Brother," she said softly. "But, did you think it was...was...disrespectful, I mean, of Miss Bennet to come so far in all that mud knowing her dress would be ruined."

"No. I thought it showed a great affection for her sister—and perhaps a bit of mischievous wilfulness and an independent spirit." *...and so much more which a brother does not tell a sister...*

Georgiana giggled as Darcy unknowingly smiled at the memory.

"I should truly like to meet Miss Bennet someday."

"Perhaps you shall...someday, that is." Darcy glanced away momentarily. Turning back with a gentle smile, he continued. "But, back to our topic of discussion, Georgiana. When we grow up and become ladies and gentlemen, then it is time to put away foolish things. If it concerns you, I shall have a word with Mrs. Annesley."

A Man in Want of a Wife

"No, I do not think that will be necessary. I shall go now and practice my music whilst I wait for my Latin and history master. After my appointment with Sir Thomas Lawrence, I shall then call on Miss Kate and Miss Millie, if it is agreeable with you, that is."

"I see no reason why you should not. I think they do you good," Darcy said. "And how is Sir Thomas coming along with your portrait?"

"Very well, I think. We will finish the first sitting by the end of February, and then the second by early spring. It is tedious, but I don't really mind. I find I can daydream whilst I sit."

"Very good, then; they shall be ready before I leave for Kent. Now, off with you. I have some figures to go over, and then I have to pay my respects to my friend Mr. Pennington. I've yet to give my regards to his family for the ball," Darcy said as he unlocked his desk drawer and took out a record book and opened it.

Georgiana stood to her feet but hesitated.

"Yes?" Darcy asked looking up from his ledger.

"I was wondering…well, I mean to say…do you like her, Brother?"

"Like whom?"

"Miss Kathryn. You seem to, but then I…I mean…well, you don't speak of her like you did Miss Elizabeth Bennet."

Darcy placed his pen down and folded his hands. "I like Miss Kathryn as well as I like any young lady. She is fashionable, handsome, and appears to be pleasing. Miss Elizabeth was a young lady whose company I also enjoyed for the time we spent together. She was well read, impertinent without being offensive, amiable to all around her, and she had a pleasing smile. Anyone in her company could not help but feel comfortable…and then there was her laughter. Her eyes were always bright with laughter and that never ceased to make me smile. I consider her a friend."

"I see," Georgiana said, nodding as she continued. "Miss Kate's laughter makes me smile, too, and I like her very much. Should I ever chance to meet Miss Bennet, I am sure I will like her as well, especially if she is like Miss Kate and Miss Millie."

Contented, Georgiana turned and left the study feeling much better about her new found friends. On her way out, she met her cousin Richard and winked.

"It is so delightful to know my cousin had his share of mischief," she said, not stopping as she moved along the corridor.

Colonel Fitzwilliam tilted his head and furrowed his brow. Turning, he knocked on the open door and entered, finding Darcy with a small smile threatening to become a full laugh.

"What was that about?" the Colonel asked.

Darcy raised a brow as he looked up at his cousin. "Georgiana wanted to know if we were normal boys."

Now it was Colonel Fitzwilliam's turn to laugh.

Darcy shook his head. "It seems she is becoming friends with the Viceroy's daughters, and they have told her of their adventures as girls in India. Since Georgie did not have such an animated childhood as they apparently have had, she was wondering if girls really did such things as play with insects and reptiles."

"And you told her about the time I put a frog down Wex's back during the Spanish chestnut season in Lambton—or perhaps the time I slipped a newt into your soup at Pemberley when all the family came for the harvest festival?"

"No. I told her of the time you brought a snake to church."

The Colonel laughed harder.

Darcy smiled and then sobered. Clearing his throat, he spoke in a serious tone, "Richard, I was just reading the morning paper before Georgiana came in. They say all crucial military personnel are being asked to report for duty. Am I to assume you are here to say your farewells?"

Richard nodded.

"Well then have a seat and let me send for more coffee," Darcy said, ringing the bell.

When the footman returned with a fresh server of coffee, he poured the Colonel a cup and another for Darcy.

Making himself comfortable, the Colonel said, "I am to leave for Sandhurst on Monday, but I will return in less than three months for a thirty day furlough—just in time for our annual trip to Kent. There has been another incident on the high seas with the Americans—thus the reason for my early departure. War is coming."

"Yes…I've been reading all about it. It is front page news, I'm afraid. The Americans claim we have meddled in their affairs long enough. Mr. Madison speaks of war if we do not repeal the Orders in Council restricting their free trade. And the Tory position is very clear on that. They intend to send more troops to Canada as a precautionary measure in the event of an actual war, though according to the paper they can scarcely come up with the additional troops. It does look very bad, but England will protect its colonies in Canada. We cannot afford to lose them." Darcy paused, studying his cousin's grave look. Finally he spoke again. "And you disagree. You think the Crown should bend to their wishes."

"I am a solider. I do as I'm told. But…"

"But what?"

"But I regret the loss of life that will follow." The Colonel sighed heavily and glanced away. Returning with a smile, he said, "I am not here to talk about me, but rather you and Pennington's ball. It seemed to me that you enjoyed yourself more than usual."

"Perhaps I did. It was one of the better balls I've attended. People behaved civilly and the society was excellent."

"Darcy, when have people not behaved civilly? And you know what I want to know. You danced two sets with Miss Kathryn Singleton and *only* with her."

"You want to know if I am considering her."

He nodded.

"Of course I'm considering her, but, as of yet, I do not know enough about her. She is the daughter of the Governor-General to India, she has a dowry of a hundred thousand pounds, and she is very pretty, but that is all I have learned."

The Colonel laughed. "What else is there to know, Darcy? I would think her family and their money and connections to the Crown would be all you need to know in order to decide."

"Not quite. I know nothing of her character, the turn of her mind, or if she is willing to be the kind of wife that I desire. I don't want a cold fish in bed—a marriage in which I sire an heir and a spare and then my wife and I go on to live separate lives as so many in the *ton* are known to do. I want something more…" Darcy said softly as he dropped his gaze to Sam resting on the rug beside the fire.

The hound raised his head and the dog's eyes met his. Sam seemed to understand his master's conflicts and appeared to speak as thoughts played in Darcy's mind.

…You knew a lady once who was your ideal of what a truly accomplished woman should be in every possible way, and you spent a good deal of time studying her. You

159

said you couldn't choose her, and so you determined to marry a woman just like her...but will you ever find such a woman, Master...will you...?

Sam laid his head back down and closed his eyes, stretching out as he released a small whimper.

"Darcy, are you unwell?" the Colonel asked, furrowing his brow.

"No...I was merely thinking," he said, returning his gaze to his cousin. "Richard, I want a lover—a companion, if you will—not a broodmare. And that is why I am going to be very careful. I will get to know Miss Kathryn, and if she proves to be suitable, then I will ask for a courtship, and marriage could follow after that—but not until I know all these things with certainty."

"Well then what are you going to do about it? Have you paid your regards to Pennington for the ball yet?"

"No. That is the first order of business later this morning. Care to accompany me, or have you already paid your regards?"

"I have not. Wex did before Christmas, but I thought I would wait until today, and therefore, I would be glad to accompany you. Perhaps we will have the opportunity to see the Viceroy's lovely daughters. They are the talk of the town down at White's. In fact, the bets are already on the books concerning Wex and Miss Millicent. I just imagine that it shan't be much longer until you and his other daughter are a speculative venture."

Darcy threw back his head and laughed. "Let them. Now, if you are ready, shall we call on Rand and perhaps the Viceroy himself?" Darcy turned to his hound as he stood to leave. "Come along, Sam. Let's see what Mrs. Whitmore has for you in the kitchen."

Sam rose and shook his head, flapping his long ears and yawning. He then followed his master and Colonel Fitzwilliam from the room.

~*~

Lady Crofton sat on the edge of her large four poster bed and gazed at the man whom she had recently married as he fussed with his cravat. She had met him through correspondence. Her brother sat on the governing board of the Far Eastern Trading Company, and when he had told her of their governor's loss in India, she, having only recently lost her own husband of twenty years, requested permission to write to him and express her sympathy. For many months they wrote to one another, first while she was in England, and then whilst she took holiday in Naples where her family owned a villa near the sea.

From there a friendship began which soon blossomed into affection and then into love, so, when he came to England for his yearly meeting with the Crown and the governing board, they met and decided to marry. She smiled to herself. Jacob Phillip Singleton was a firm man, very much the perfectionist, and used to getting his own way. She had also come to know that patience was *not* one of his virtues.

"Cora," he called. "Cora!"

"Yes, dear," she answered, rising from the bed.

"Bradley did not get this damned neck cloth knotted to suit me. Would you take the trouble to see if perhaps you can? I am to meet with the Lord Chancellor later today down at White's, and it's important that I look presentable. Several of the other governor generals and a few of the colonial governors will be present. If I have the chance, I mean to have a private word with the current First Lord of the Treasury, as well."

"Mr. Perceval, you mean."

"Yes, that's the one—the Tory leader."

"He is not a Tory, my love."

"Oh! I forgot. Mr. Perceval and his ilk are Independent Whigs, or *Friends of Mr. Pitt*, as they like to be known. He doesn't like to be referred to as a Tory—but Tory he is as far as I am concerned. Nevertheless, please assist me with this wretched thing!"

"I would be delighted, Phillip, but pray tell, why would you want to meet with Mr. Perceval? I rather thought you preferred the Whigs at Brooks's?"

"I don't especially care for either of them, but I know who it is that serves my purpose at the present, and that, my dear, is whom I associate with when I have a mind to do so. For the time being, we have a conservative government, and therefore Mr. Perceval is important to me."

Cora smiled as she went to her husband and began to move her slender fingers in and out of the stubborn cloth until she had the cravat tied once more.

"Does that suit you, my dear?"

He glanced down at her, beaming. "Perfectly,"

"Now, Cora," he said taking her by the hand and leading her to the settee by the fire, "we must discuss Kate and Millie as they are ever present on my mind. I want you to watch the girls judiciously. Make sure they are properly instructed and presented to society. The ball was a success with numerous possibilities, but I want several candidates to choose from. So, if you spy any young men interested enough in my girls to be a possible candidate, point them out to me.

"Lord Matlock has already given me some information about his nephew, Fitzwilliam Darcy of Pemberley, who danced two sets with Kathryn, and with that I have managed to discover a little more. He comes from an old family in the North of England which, unfortunately, is untitled. I do like him, however, and if I see that a marriage is probable, then as a wedding present I intend to purchase a title for him. My daughter deserves nothing less than to be a countess.

"And then there is Millicent. Lord Matlock's eldest son singled her out for two sets, and since I am well acquainted with the family, I know that he is a suitable match. If Lord Wexford shows additional interest, I will be speaking with Matlock on a possible arrangement. However, the other gentlemen my Millicent danced with are, for one reason or another, definitely *unsuitable*—especially the one who seems to follow Mr. Darcy around. I've heard they are quite close, but according to Randal, his family's wealth is no more than a generation old. If the young man's income had come from a joint venture with the nobility, I might reconsider—but it did not."

"I quite agree, darling. A match with new money is not suitable; nor is a match with anyone other than one from an old family—with money, of course. A gentleman without a title is unfortunate, but not insurmountable."

"Precisely." He nodded. "My thoughts exactly, love. I hope to interest at least one of the suitable gentlemen, and if we are lucky, perhaps *both* of them, to take the girls off our hands. Help me in this, Cora, and then we can get on with our lives once the girls are comfortably situated."

She laughed. "I will try, Phillip …to please you, but if either Mr. Darcy or the Viscount should come to nothing, and there are no other suitable young men among this season's eligible gentlemen, then there are always my cousin's nephews, the

A Man in Want of a Wife

Dukes of Cleveland and Southampton. They may not be as young as you would like and perhaps not as handsome as the girls would like, but with their estates and titles they would make eligible matches for either of our girls. And let us not forget the things that matter—they have great influence in the House of Lords and with the Crown."

"Yes...I know, but Cleveland is forty and fat, and Southampton is seven and thirty and balding. I would prefer younger men still in their prime. I owe the girls that much—especially since Susan has made such a good match. It wouldn't seem fair to do less for the twins."

Cora leaned in and put her arms around her husband. "Indeed your eldest did marry well, but Phillip, Randal Pennington is *not* of the nobility either. Have you overlooked that one small detail?"

"No...my love, I have not. But his grandfather on his mother's side *is*, and before I leave England, he will have a title as well. That is why I wish to meet with Mr. Perceval. Now, let us not keep Rand and Susan waiting. I am hopeful that Mr. Darcy will call round today."

Lady Crofton smiled. "I hope so, too, love. Susan and I shall spend the morning discussing our plans for the girls' dinner party in three weeks. You enjoy the men."

Smiling, they parted company and left for their respective mornings, each with their own thoughts for the Viceroy's daughters.

~*~

While she went about preparing for her day with her eldest stepdaughter, Lady Crofton thought of another possible suitor for one of the girls: her elder sister's only son, the Marquess of Rocksmore. She hadn't heard from Madeline in many months and owed her a letter. She was yet to tell her sister of her recent marriage and she really should enquire after the health of the Duke who was very ill upon their last exchange. Perhaps she should write and then, as a consequence, she could casually ask about the young Marquess. But then she shrugged and dismissed the thought as quickly as it had come. She doubted her nephew would be interested, for he had just finished Cambridge. Grabbing her wrap, she left for her duties without a second thought of the young Marquess.

Walking past Millicent's dressing room on her way to the morning parlour, the Countess stopped short at the sound of laughter coming from behind the closed door. Suspecting the twins of being up to something, she opened the door without knocking and entered.

"What do you girls think you are doing?" she asked rather crossly. "And what is that disgusting smell?" She narrowed her eyes. "Kathryn Singleton, what is that in your hair?"

Kate huffed. "It is none of your concern, your ladyship."

"None of my concern you say? We shall see about that." She turned to Millie and spoke with determination to know the truth. "Millicent, what has your sister done? And why are you standing about in your petticoat looking stupid?"

Millie looked away and said nothing, her chest heaving in what Lady Crofton presumed to be fury.

The Countess then turned to the maid. "Jenny, what is in Miss Kathryn's hair?! I demand to know this very instant!"

"I be beggin' your pardon, ma'am…oh! I mean your ladyship…but I don't rightly know."

"What do you mean you do not know? From the looks of those orange stains on your hands you obviously have put that disgusting, foul smelling substance in her hair. Therefore, tell me, if you do not know what it is, then what do you *think* it is?"

Jenny looked between her charge and Lady Crofton. "Please, your ladyship, don't make me say."

Lady Crofton breathed deeply. "What is it, Jenny?"

"Goose poop…I think…oh! Your ladyship, if I were to be guessin' that would be me guess, for I truly do not know. I only do as I'm told; it was that Indian woman…she gave me this bowl and told me what to do."

The Countess looked around. "Arpita! Arpita! Where are you?"

"Yes, Memsahib," the old servant said, slipping into the room from the water closet."

"I am to be addressed as Lady Crofton, Arpita. Please remember that."

The ayah curtseyed in submission. "Yes…Lady Crofton."

"That is better. Now what in God's name is that…that…horrible mess in Miss Kathryn's hair? She refuses to say, and the maid is too ignorant to know. What is it, Arpita?"

The servant slowly raised her eyes. "It is henna with indigo and Asian spices, Lady Crofton. It very good for hair. I use special formula from India—Rajasthani henna—the very best. Your husband, he bring it to England. Ladies like it. Makes hair very beautiful."

"For the common prostitute perhaps, but not for my stepdaughters! Oh, Arpita, this is not India. Rinse it out at once!" Turning to Kate, who was standing by Millie with her arms folded over her chest, she said. "You are never to do such a thing again. I wondered how you got that strange colour in your hair. No gentleman would have anything to do with you if it ever became known that you dye your hair. Only those on stage—or worse—do such things. Girls, I am trying to instruct you in the art of being ladies. If you wish to make a good match in the *ton*, then you must listen to me and your sister Susan. We English are very proper, and you must learn our ways."

"My mother never cared," said Kate defiantly. "She dyed her hair, and Papa never said a word. For goodness sakes, he imports henna and indigo into England!"

Walking over to Kathryn, the Countess lowered her voice and looked her stepdaughter directly in the eye. "I don't care what your mother did. This is England—not the wilds of India. There *is* a difference! And if you are to secure a good husband, you will have to adapt to English conventions. You *are* the Viceroy's daughter! I'll not have you expressing any of your outlandish opinions, or behaving like common people with no breeding. Dying your hair indeed! Do you understand what I am telling you, Kate?"

"Perfectly!"

"Now, be a good girl and let Jenny and Arpita help you clean up. Mr. Darcy seems interested in you, and he just might call today," Lady Crofton continued, "but he won't be attracted for long should he learn of this. And remember one thing more, girls. The greater a man is in society the less likely he is to be forgiving of such foolishness. A gentleman's dullness is always in direct proportion to his distinction, and the greater a man is, the better the match. Now, prepare yourselves, and once you are dressed, meet me in the parlour. You father is with Rand in the drawing

A Man in Want of a Wife

room discussing his club, or some such thing, and Susan and I are to plan the dinner party we will host in yours and Millie's honour. Therefore, you need to attend the planning. I also intend to go over proper English etiquette with the two of you."

As she left, she muttered to herself, "What was their mother thinking leaving them to servants their whole lives? Oh, this shall not be borne!"

When the door was shut, Kate turned to Millie. "I shall find a snake and put it in her boot if it is the last thing I do!"

"No, Kate, you will not. We are no longer children." Tilting her head, Millie added, "In one sense she is correct. We must act the part of proper ladies to achieve what we want. I'm sure you can dye your hair when she isn't looking, or once you are married, and I am equally sure it will not be long until you are. Mr. Darcy paid you a great honour at the ball."

"Yes…I know he did, and I do like him in some ways." Kate paused and then said, "Her ladyship is correct about one thing, though."

"What is that?"

"Mr. Darcy is very dull. He likes to read books that I find boring; he even likes lavender, for heaven's sake. Consequently, he must be very distinguished and, therefore, according to Lady Crofton, will make a fine husband."

They both giggled.

"But what about you, Millie? Have you met someone yet? You will marry, will you not?"

"I don't know. I suppose I must, but I have not met one single gentleman, at the ball or anywhere else, with whom I could ever be so overcome with desire as to consider the blissful state with the same enthusiasm others seem to feel upon such contemplation," Millie said with a sharp bite.

Kate glanced at her sister. "You didn't like Mr. Bingley, or the Viscount who paid you particular attention?"

"No, I cared for neither of them. Mr. Bingley is nice, but I must confess that he is *too* nice. He lacks certain qualities which I find essential in a man, and Lord Wexford is an overly confident bore. Oh Kate! Why do I have to marry at all? I don't want to bear children and host parties. Did we not see enough of that with mother? That is all she did—one party after another with never a second thought about us. If it were within my power to choose, I would choose spinsterhood or to be a rich man's mistress. Either is far more agreeable to me than being caged. But alas, it is no more within my power to choose my future than it is for a beggar to become rich."

"How droll you are, Millie! You think being a spinster or an unmarried mistress is *freedom*?! Not me! I *do* want to marry. I want to attend parties and assemblies and flirt and have pretty clothes as I do now. I would be loath to give them up—*or* my money. I'm very determined to have it all. But I do not know if Mr. Darcy would be my choice. I hardly know him at all. And I don't think he likes Gothic novels…or apparently, if our stepmother is to be believed, *henna*."

"Kate…you must be *serious*. We don't have a choice in all of this. We must play our part. Gothic novels and henna be hanged! We are like wingless birds. We wish to fly, and yet we never will." Millie turned and walked away.

Staring out the window, her face resting against the windowpane, Millie was lost in thought. She was a girl who wished to be anything other than what she was. Often she thought of what life might have been had she been born a gypsy or perhaps one of the little Indian children she had played with when she was a child. She sighed and shook her head, knowing that her destiny was fixed forever. Doldrums and a life without love were her future.

Once Kate was bathed and dressed with her hair combed dry by the fire and neatly arranged, she went to the window and stood next to her sister. She observed a coach with an English coat of arms pulling in front of the house. Within moments, Mr. Darcy and an officer dressed in a red coat exited. She pressed her hand against the glass, and Mr. Darcy looked up. She smiled and gave a small wave before turning to walk away.

~*~

Randal Pennington walked over to the side table in the front drawing room and poured himself and his father-in-law a glass of wine. Handing the drink to the Viceroy, he said, "So you think my friend Fitzwilliam Darcy may have an interest in Kate. Well, I suppose that might be so. He did dance two sets with her, and Darcy rarely dances."

"Umm…yes…that is quite interesting to know. My brief exposure to him was pleasant enough, but I want to know more about this young man. I understand he owns the estate that neighbours yours in Derbyshire, but what else can you tell me?"

"Well, he is respectable, has never kept a mistress that I am aware of, and is judiciously protective of those in his care—his friend, Mr. Bingley, for one, and particularly his sister, for another. You see, their mother died when Miss Darcy was six, and Darcy, who was seventeen at the time, has always looked after her as the protective older brother. But when their father died about five years ago, I believe it was, Darcy took it especially hard. Georgiana was all he had left in the world. I remember those dark days well as we were at Cambridge at the time.

"Shortly before graduation, old Mr. Darcy fell ill. Fitzwilliam did manage to graduate, but his father passed on later that week. After that, I would say Darcy, who was more fun-loving back then than he is now, closed off and became more reserved. But, it was to be expected as Pemberley, you see, is one of the largest estates in Derbyshire. And with all that responsibility, in addition to the joint guardianship of a sister more than ten years his junior, which he shares with his cousin, Lord Matlock's second son, he doesn't have the luxury of time that many of us do. He does stay in London more than Derbyshire, but I suspect that is because of Miss Darcy. He provides her the best in education, and, of course, her coming out will be the season after next which will keep him in Town even more."

"I should think he would have married. Why has he not? Surely a young man with such responsibilities as you have conveyed should have married long before now. What is wrong with him? Does he have an aversion for female companionship?"

"Not in the least," Randal Pennington declared, looking his father-in-law directly in the eye. "I believe it is because he is a man of high principles who would not settle for anyone less than a woman he could respect as well as have affection for, if not love. A new-fangled notion, I know, but it is how many of us feel."

"Umm…I like him better and better," the Viceroy said. "And what of the Viscount? Is he of a similar turn?"

"Yes, I believe he is. We are all fast friends having spent much time together as boys and later at school."

A Man in Want of a Wife

"And what about this Bingley fellow? Why would Mr. Darcy, or any of you, for that matter, take an interest in him? Did you not say he was from trade?"

Pennington laughed. "Indeed he is, but his father worked very hard to give him a gentleman's education. Bingley is a likable sort, and, for whatever reason, Darcy has taken a particular interest in him. He has been very careful in helping Bingley transcend the barrier that separates *us* from *them*. Darcy is a progressive in that as well."

"A Whig, then," the Viceroy said matter-of-factly. "And probably a follower of Lord Bryon and his set."

"Not quite, but he does share many of their ideals."

The Viceroy poured himself another drink and walked over to the window. Peering out through the silk sheers, he watched the courtyard as his mind wandered. *...this Darcy fellow sounds interesting. I think he will do quite nicely for Kate...yes...quite nicely indeed.* The Viceroy narrowed his eyes, looking closely to the gate where a chaise and two was entering the square.

Turning, he said to his son-in-law. "We have company. A fine looking coach with a coat of arms—a demi woman holding a clutch of three roses and a white dove—has just pulled into the courtyard."

"Indeed," Pennington said walking over to where the Viceroy stood. "Looks like Darcy and his cousin, Colonel Fitzwilliam, have come." He glanced at his father-in-law. "That is Lord Matlock's second son—the one who holds joint guardianship with Darcy over Miss Darcy."

"Then let us prepare to greet our guests. Perhaps we shall take them to luncheon at White's. I have some business to attend to there, but I never pass up an opportunity to get to know a potential suitor better," the Viceroy said with a sly smile.

A minute more and the footman appeared at the door. "Mr. Fitzwilliam Darcy and Colonel Fitzwilliam, sir."

"Darcy! Good to see you, man! And you as well, Colonel. I believe you have met my father-in-law, Governor-General Viceroy Singleton."

"Yes. We met the other night at the ball." Darcy said as he and the Colonel moved into the room and bowed. "Viceroy, it is a pleasure to see you again."

"The pleasure is mine, I assure you, and do call me Phillip. All my friends do. Here, let me pour you a drink."

"Phillip, it is then." Darcy smiled. "And you may call me Fitzwilliam, or Darcy if you prefer."

The Viceroy moved to the table where the wine decanter was and uncapped it. As he poured each glass with care, Darcy could not help but notice how the older man's eyes twinkled with mirth, much as Mr. Bennet's would when he was amused with something or other and thought no one was aware he was sketching their character. Darcy mused to himself. He knew exactly what the gentleman from India had on his mind, or, at least, he could make an educated guess.

"Colonel Fitzwilliam, I understand you are the younger son of Lord Matlock. Your father is a good friend of mine," the Viceroy said as he handed Darcy and the Colonel each a glass of wine.

"So I understand."

"Come, let us sit by the fire."

"Richard," Randal Pennington spoke up, "I read in *The Times* just this morning that tensions are rising on the high seas. Do you think we will really go to war with the Americans again?"

"Ghastly people those Yanks. I hope we show them not to rise above their betters once and for all. Dumped a lot of our tea in their harbour, they did. Damn Adams, and that Jefferson, too. Damn them both! It cost The Far Eastern Company a near fortune. I was just beginning my career at the age of two and twenty when it happened, but I shall never forget it!"

"Viceroy, with all due respect, sir, war is bankrupting our country, and before we teach the Yanks a lesson, we had best shore up our defences on the home front. Napoleon is the far greater threat than the Americans. Another war must be avoided if at all possible."

"Yes-yes, I suppose you are right. It is a pity we did not put the rebellion down when we had the chance. I would have enjoyed seeing the likes of Franklin, Jefferson, Middleton, and Adams hanged for what they did. And to think my family once considered Arthur Middleton a close friend. He almost married my eldest sister." Turning his attention to Darcy, the Viceroy continued. "And what say you, Darcy? What do you think of war?"

"I think war is a terrible thing best left to military minds, though I will concede sometimes it is necessary to protect our way of life and liberty. The Americans have won their independence. It is best to let them go."

"Well, I will concede they are a rudimentary, unpolished bunch worthy of little respect from their betters—but enough of those damned Americans. I'll not waste another breath on the wilful bastards." Pausing for a sip of wine, the Viceroy glanced between his son-in-law and their guests. "Now, I'd like to invite you both to luncheon at White's. I have to meet with some very important gentlemen, but before that, I'd like to eat and come to know you better. And before I forget, I wish to invite you and the Colonel—his brother, the Viscount, too—to a little dinner my wife and daughters are giving three weeks from Saturday. I shall send the invitations round in a day or two, and then after the soirée, we shall meet at Greensward Estate on the following Monday for the Pennington foxhunt."

"Viceroy, I'm afraid I cannot attend either event," the Colonel said. "I have been called up for training at Sandhurst. I leave on Monday, but I see no reason why my brother, Lord Wexford, cannot attend. As far as I know, he has no prior engagement."

"Good-good...very good then. I am sorry you will miss it, but these things cannot be helped," he said. Turning to Darcy, he continued. "And what of you, do you have any prior engagements?"

"None that I recall," Darcy replied. "I shall plan to attend with my sister, Miss Darcy."

"Then that settles it. Let's go to White's. I'm famished." The Viceroy stood and called to the footman. "Finnegan, fetch my coat and cane and send for the carriage."

~*~*~*~

Chapter 22

January 11, 1812

Caroline Bingley stalked about the drawing room of her brother-in-law's townhouse, wringing her hands in anxiety as she glanced between the door and her sister Louisa. About a fortnight ago she had received a letter from Miss Bennet, stating she was soon to be in Town. Caroline had not answered. Then, a sennight after that, she had received another informing her Miss Bennet was now in London and wished to call when it was convenient. And today, she had received yet another.

"This is not what I envisioned when I penned my letter to Miss Bennet upon arriving in Town. Imagine the impudence of her to think that I actually *meant* to continue our acquaintance! Does she really believe that I *liked* her? I was merely being polite. Louisa, this is the third letter I have received from her. One with good sense and breeding would know that when I didn't respond to her previous posts I did not wish to further the acquaintance. Oh! But not Miss Bennet!"

"Well, Sister, I suppose you should take into consideration that she has not had the exposure to superior society as we have been so fortunate as to enjoy. She simply doesn't understand the rules of propriety. But then, to be quite fair to Miss Bennet, Caroline, you did say in your last letter to her upon our arrival in London that we would be mingling with our many friends and that you wished she might make one of the crowd, and now she has," Mrs. Hurst said matter-of-factly. "I told you not to say that."

"Yes, but I assumed that since I did not answer any of her other letters she would understand—oh, what shall I do! She is actually going to *call*, Louisa. That is what she said. And if she does and finds Charles here, what then will we do?"

"Send her a missive post-haste to find out when she may call. Then we will simply have Mr. Darcy make sure Charles is away. She can make her call, and we can be done with it, but you must be sure she is made aware that Charles is no longer interested in her, and that we no longer want to continue the acquaintance."

Caroline fretted. "Yes, but—"

The sisters turned at the sound of a knock on the door.

"Yes, what is it, Bosworth?"

"A lady and her aunt are here to call, Mrs. Hurst."

The man stepped forward and presented two cards. Louisa took them at once and looked them over. She cast a harrowing glance at her sister. "It is Miss Bennet. Where is Charles now?"

"I believe he is still in his sitting room with Mr. Darcy. What are we to do?"

"You entertain her, and I will see to it that Charles does not come downstairs until she is gone."

Mrs. Hurst flew from the drawing room through the servants' stairs so that she would not meet Miss Bennet in the foyer. Moving up the steps as fast as she was able, she came out in the family wing of the second floor. With a discreet knock, the door opened, and her brother's manservant appeared.

"Perkins, I must see Mr. Darcy at once, and please be discreet about it. I'm in no mood to be gainsaid."

"Yes, madam."

Within minutes Mr. Darcy appeared in the hallway.

"What is so important that it could not wait until Bingley and I came downstairs?"

Louisa pulled him aside and hissed, "It is Miss Jane Bennet."

"Miss Bennet?"

"Yes. She is here calling on my sister, and you must see to it that Charles does not interrupt us until I send word that she has departed. If Charles should discover she is here, it will undo all that we have strived to accomplish."

Darcy stiffened. "Where is she, exactly?"

"In the drawing room by now, I would say."

"And who is with her?"

"I believe the card said Mrs. Gardiner, which would be the aunt from *Cheapside*."

"No one else?"

"No—no one."

Darcy moved to the railing in a dark corner overlooking the drawing room and gazed down to see Miss Bennet sitting on the settee with her back to him. He stared for some minutes before returning to where Mrs. Hurst stood. "Advise me when they are gone. I shall find a way to delay our departure, but be quick about it."

Darcy turned and walked away, and as he did, his chest tightened with discomfort. When Mrs. Hurst had told him that Miss Bennet had come, his heart had leapt into his throat. His first thoughts had instantly gone to Elizabeth. The very thought that she might have come with her sister caused his heart to pound furiously and his blood to run hot. He released a ragged breath and chastised himself severely as he tugged at his neck cloth.

...Get hold of yourself man! This is for the best. She has no connections, no money, and she is not of your sphere. Your friends—and need you be reminded—your family would never accept her.

He stopped short and breathed deeply. Staring off into the distance, he tilted his head in deep thought.

...but then do you really care what anyone thinks, and what need of money do you have? You are your own master. You could be her family's salvation, giving them a home when the entail is finally invoked...Can you really forget her...can you?

Darcy took another deep breath as he put his hand to the latch and turned it. Coming into Bingley's sitting room, he found his friend preparing for their outing at Brooks's and an afternoon of cards with several old friends from Cambridge. He would have to tell Bingley something to explain why he had been called from the room. Contemplating what that might be, he supposed he could say he had received a private message and still speak the truth.

A Man in Want of a Wife

~*~

Entering the drawing room, Louisa Hurst smiled with an effort to display an affection she did not feel. Caroline made the introduction to Mrs. Gardiner as Louisa came close to where Jane and her aunt were sitting and took a seat beside her sister on the settee opposite them. Pouring herself a cup of tea, Louisa leaned back to address their visitors.

"Ah, Miss Bennet, how nice of you and your aunt to join us this morning. Caroline and I were speaking of you only moments ago. How positively wonderful it is of you to call. How long have you been in Town?"

"I have not been long in Town—less than a fortnight, I believe. I am to spend the next few months with my aunt and uncle in Gracechurch Street."

"Oh! How shocking! You should have sent word around that you were in Town. Caroline and I would have called had we only known."

"Yes, Jane, it is very inconsiderate of you to not have written. What a surprise we received when you were announced with no notice. Why Louisa and I are quite beside ourselves with astonishment. We are occupied with the social season, and this is somewhat unexpected for us."

"Oh! But I did write. I wrote *three* letters. Did they not arrive? How very strange; I am sure I addressed them properly."

"Louisa," Caroline glanced at her sister with a perplexed expression, "did you see any letters in the post?"

"No, Sister," Mrs. Hurst returned. "I have not seen any letters, and the post is delivered to me every morning. Miss Bennet, are you absolutely *sure* you addressed them correctly, for we did not receive any letters from you."

"Oh..." Jane cast her eyes downward.

Mrs. Gardiner reached over and took her niece's hand in hers giving it a reassuring squeeze.

"Perhaps they *were* misdirected. It does happen, and London is such a vast city, my dear," said Mrs. Gardiner.

"Yes...perhaps they were," Jane replied, looking up. "I am sorry for the misunderstanding. I assure you it was not intentional." Changing the subject, she further queried, "May I enquire after your brother? I pray he is in good health."

"Oh, Charles is quite well, but he is so much engaged with Mr. Darcy that we hardly see him," Caroline replied coolly. "They are always out and about—from their clubs, to soirées with friends, to balls. They are rather busy, I'm afraid. It is the height of the season, you know. Why, less than a fortnight ago, we were all at the most magnificent ball of the season. It was given by the daughter of the Governor-General to India. The most fashionable people of the *ton* were there. And the beautiful ladies, what can I say about them? They were the most elegant to be seen anywhere, and with the latest fashions from Paris. It was simply magnificent. Charles, I believe, had a grand time. He even entertained one of the Viceroy's daughters—a charming little thing, but nothing compared to Miss Darcy, mind you. I believe it was the pinnacle of the evening for Charles. Our brother does love to dance you know."

"Yes...I know."

Flushed with embarrassment, Jane said nothing more. Finally, after several moments of awkward silence, she spoke. "Was Miss Darcy present?"

"Oh, no!" Caroline stated emphatically. "She is not yet out. But she is to dine with us tonight. She is such a dear girl and so accomplished in every way imaginable. Charles delights in her company at every opportunity. I do believe he is rather taken with her. Jane, could you not wish him well on such a fortuitous match?"

"I see," Jane said, exchanging glances with her aunt. "Yes…of course I could—and do. I desire his happiness above all things and wish him joy."

"Miss Bennet, I hate to put you off, but Louisa and I were about to go out when you called. We are so delighted in your company, but if we do not leave soon we will miss our luncheon with Miss Darcy. We are to call upon her at Darcy House, and then we must hurry home to prepare for our dinner with her and her brother."

"Oh, yes, I understand. We must be going as well. My aunt has some shopping on Bond Street and then we must be home for our own dinner engagement as well. It has been lovely seeing you again, and I do hope you will tell Mr. Bingley that I asked after him and wish him much happiness."

"You can depend upon it, and later this week, Louisa and I shall call upon you."

After showing Jane and her aunt to the door, Louisa gently closed it behind them and leaned against the heavy oak while Caroline stood by the window and watched as the carriage pulled away.

"That was close, Sister—too close. Now that they are gone, I shall send for Mr. Darcy. We cannot take the chance that our brother might discover Miss Bennet's presence in Town. I will tell Mr. Darcy they plan to shop on Bond Street, and therefore, he should avoid that area today."

"I agree," Caroline said. "Everything could be ruined if Charles should see her again. I was most disappointed with him at the ball. Other than the Viceroy's daughter, he danced with no one, and he hasn't the least interest in Miss Darcy no matter what I say or how I recommend her; he will not be moved."

"Well, we must make the best of things, and tonight we shall try again. Charles clearly likes Georgiana, and given time, I am sure he will see her many fine qualities and the advantage she represents, but you must not overdo it, Caroline. There is nothing more unbecoming than fawning." Louisa turned and called for a servant.

After the footman was sent to inform Mr. Darcy their callers had departed, Louisa and Caroline left for the front parlour. Within minutes, Mr. Darcy joined them.

"Charles has sent for the carriage. We will be spending the afternoon at Brooks's with my cousin Lord Wexford and Mr. Pennington. What did Miss Bennet have to say? How long will she remain in Town?"

"She asked after Charles, and we exchanged small pleasantries," Caroline said, "but not much more than that. However, she plans to be in Town for some duration—months at least."

"That is unfortunate."

"Oh, and they will be spending the afternoon on Bond Street, and therefore, you will need to avoid that area of Town," Louisa added.

Darcy took a deep breath as he glanced between the two sisters. "I will see to it that they do not meet," he said, walking over to peer out the window. Turning he continued. "You must return her call, and when you do, make it copiously clear that you do not wish to keep the acquaintance. It is unacceptable to keep Miss Bennet in suspense. She believes you to be her friends, and you clearly are not. That is very badly done. Correct the misunderstanding. Now, I am leaving. Georgiana and I will see you tonight."

Caroline stood almost speechless as she watched Mr. Darcy close the parlour door. Returning her attention to her sister, she said, "I suppose I must call, but not until I am ready to do so."

"I would not put it off too long, and Caroline, Mr. Darcy is quite correct. You must end this. Leave Miss Bennet with no doubt as to where your true feelings lie. You should never have written her after we left Hertfordshire. It is your fault entirely you know."

"My fault? It is not my fault if she cannot understand the nature of things! I only meant to inform her that we, and therefore Charles, would not be returning to Hertfordshire. I meant to end the acquaintance there. I had no idea she would follow us to London."

"Nevertheless, to be forewarned is to be forearmed. Right what is wrong in her understanding, and we must continue our efforts to match our brother with Miss Darcy."

Caroline glared at her sister. "You can depend upon it! I will make things perfectly clear to her. Jane will be left in no doubt as to where she belongs in regard to *us*. Now, if we are to keep our engagement, we must make haste."

The two sisters quickly gathered their cloaks and bonnets and left for their luncheon engagement. They were to spend the better part of the afternoon with their dear friend, Miss Darcy, and with every intention of furthering their relationship with her, hoping to inspire affection for their brother in the process.

~*~

As the coach travelled over the brick and cobblestone, Darcy sat back, sinking into the tufted velvet cushions as he reflected on the recent turn of events. From observing his friend at Pennington's ball as well as their various other social engagements, Darcy knew that Charles was not the man he had once been. There was a burgeoning sadness about him that Darcy had not expected. Darcy twisted his signet ring in agitation. Surely Bingley's affections had not really been engaged by Miss Bennet?

As they turned the corner onto St. James's Street, Darcy glanced over to Charles who sat across from him. "You are unusually quiet today. Is something the matter?"

Bingley shook his head. "No…nothing more than usual." He sighed. "I had a dream last night and it haunts me." He stopped and caught Darcy's gaze. "It was more like a nightmare than a dream."

Darcy furrowed his brow. "What was it?"

Bingley hesitated. "I dreamt that Ja… Miss Bennet was crying. She was upset and calling my name in the London mist. I could hear her cries and pleadings for my help, but try as I might I could not see her, though I searched through the fog and called her name. Something awful had happened, and she was in danger. Darcy, what if she really did love me? Have I been a fool?"

Darcy passed his hand over his face. "Charles, we are all fools when it comes to matters of the heart. Who can really know the heart of a woman? You asked me if I thought Miss Bennet held any affection for you, and I gave you my honest reply. Apart from that, I can say no more—nor will I. Now, here we are," Darcy said as the carriage rolled to a stop. "Let us go inside and see who we can find. Wex and Rand should have a table in the back with a pitcher of ale. Cheer up, Bingley. Times will be better, I assure you."

Bingley laughed with forced cheerfulness. "Ay…yes, quite right. Time heals all wounds, I suppose, and besides a country dance, there is nothing I like better than a pint of ale. Let's have a jolly good time, shall we?"

"Indeed!"

"And tonight I shall enjoy yours and Miss Darcy's company to the fullest!"

Exiting the carriage, the two gentlemen entered the establishment, and just as Darcy had thought, his cousin and Randal Pennington were there to meet them along with a large party of friends and several pitchers of ale.

~*~

Hurst House
Later that evening

Caroline made one last inspection of the dinner table to insure everything was as it should be; for this was to be a very important dinner party. She went from one place setting to another measuring each set of silverware making sure they were accurately spaced and set to perfection, and that the wine glasses for each course were set in their proper places as well. Then she made certain each person's card was placed with care precisely where she wanted it. Charles was to be seated with Miss Darcy, and she was to sit beside Mr. Darcy. When Caroline was persuaded that everything was to her satisfaction, she left to join her family in the drawing room to await their guests.

Moving through the corridor, she thought about her plans. If Charles were to form an attachment to Miss Darcy, then, by association, the two families would be more closely intertwined, and perhaps one happy event would lead to another. Smugly, she entered the drawing room and looked around, surveying the occupants.

Charles was seated by the fire engaged in a game of chess with Mr. Hurst while Louisa sat near the pianoforte playing with her bracelets. Caroline approached her sister and stood beside her chair.

"Louisa," she said as she glanced at their brother, "did you not think Miss Darcy looked uncommonly well this afternoon? I do think the girl is beginning to come into her own. Each day she becomes more lovely and confident than the last."

"Umm…quite," Mrs. Hurst replied, looking in the direction of her brother. "Charles, have you not noticed how Miss Darcy has grown? She is a young woman now, and soon she shall be receiving suitors."

"No, I can't say that I have." He paused for a moment and tilted his head. "But now that you mention it, I do think she has grown. She is certainly not the little girl she was when we first came to know Darcy."

"Really, Charles," Caroline scolded, "sometimes I think you go through the world with your eyes closed. Georgiana will be out in two seasons, and soon after that, she will be married. Of all the young ladies in London, I've yet to meet one more handsome or more accomplished than Miss Darcy. Have you not listened to her play the pianoforte and the harp, or seen the lovely table she painted? Darcy now has it proudly displayed in their drawing room. The elegant vines and pale pink and yellow roses are simply divine. I've never seen one quite like it. Have you not occasioned to notice it?"

A Man in Want of a Wife

"No...I don't believe I have," Charles answered, looking up from his game. "I did see the porcelain she painted in the design you described—a delicately designed little tea set with a serving tray. It is somewhat lovely. Miss Darcy is a remarkable young lady of many talents. I am sure she will make a good match when the time comes, and I will be quite happy for her."

"Here-here," Hurst called out. "Pay attention to the game. It is your move."

"Oh! Quite right." Charles moved. "Check."

"Charles, you must be serious. I am speaking of Miss Darcy as a suitable young lady who is about to come out."

"Oh, I am quite serious, Caroline, and if I don't pay attention to the game, Hurst will best me again."

"But, Charles—"

"Caroline." Charles glanced at the door. "Our guests have arrived."

"Checkmate!" Mr. Hurst beamed. "You should not let your concentration become divided."

Bingley smiled and stood to his feet. "Hurst, you are the superior player as always," he said and then turned and walked in the direction of their guests.

"Miss Darcy! Mr. Darcy!" Caroline cried, moving to greet them. "Charles and I were just talking about you," she said, taking Georgiana's hand and escorting her into the room. "Charles was just telling us how he admired your tea set. It matches your table perfectly. You do exquisite work and are to be greatly admired."

"Yes...you are remarkably talented, Miss Darcy," Bingley said with a smile.

Georgiana blushed furiously. "It is nothing, really. Miss Grantley and I did those together while I visited her at her grandmother's house last winter. It was the first one of that kind I have ever done and will most likely be my last as I am not fond of painting porcelain. I am only now displaying the set as the table is finally finished." She glanced at Mr. Bingley. "I am truly glad you noticed them, but they are nothing really."

"Nonsense! One as talented as you should never give it up," cried Caroline in an exaggerated manner.

Georgiana dropped her gaze and was silent.

"Nevertheless," Louisa said with more genuine praise. "It is very lovely, and you should be quite proud of it. Are you not proud of Miss Darcy's accomplishments, Mr. Darcy?" she asked as Darcy came to stand by his sister.

"Yes, I am quite proud of all Georgiana's accomplishments. She strives to do her very best in whatever she undertakes."

"Of course she does!" Caroline cried, beaming as she eyed Mr. Darcy. "For as you know, I have always been one of your sister's greatest admirers. Georgiana only needs a woman's touch to guide her through the difficult years." She turned her eyes on Charles. "A gifted young girl like Miss Darcy needs a friend who can lead her along to consider the right choices in life. She must choose wisely and learn to entertain as is fitting for her station."

Darcy glared at Miss Bingley. "And that is why I have employed Mrs. Annesley. She does an extraordinary job instructing my sister in all the social graces she will need when the time comes for Georgiana's coming out."

Caroline opened her mouth to reply, but before she could form the words, a footman approached and bowed.

"Dinner is served, madam."

"Thank you, Bosworth," said Mrs. Hurst. Turning her attention to her sister, she continued. "Caroline, I think we should save this conversation for another time." Louisa lifted one eyebrow with a look Caroline understood quite well.

Moving into the dining room, Georgiana found her place and froze. A look of exasperation overcame her features. Though she was quite fond of Mr. Bingley, she was also well aware of his sisters' machinations and strongly disapproved. Glancing at her brother, they exchanged a meaningful look. Darcy nodded, and she could see that he was equally unhappy with the seating arrangements, especially *his* placement.

Taking their seats, Miss Bingley remarked while the soup was served, "I understand the Viceroy is to host a soirée for his two youngest daughters next Saturday."

"Yes, although I believe it is to be hosted by Mrs. Pennington and her stepmother, the Countess of Crofton," said Hurst.

"Well," Caroline sneered, "I don't see anything remarkable in those two girls. They have not even had the privilege of an English education, and to think their father is so rich. One would have thought he would've at least sent them to England for that much! His brother has a house in Town, and Mrs. Pennington was in the care of her grandmother before her marriage. Why did he neglect his two youngest daughters?"

"Perhaps their mother was of another opinion. Many young women of our sphere have little formal education beyond a governess, or, for that matter, past the social graces needed to host a dinner party or to entertain when necessary," Hurst replied, cutting his eyes across the table in warning at his sister-in-law, but she paid him no mind.

"Really, Mr. Hurst. Other than the fact that their father is wealthy and has a governorship in one of the colonies, I see no attraction for them. The only thing that separates them from us is their money. They are boorish and openly flirt with every man in the room. I am sure you noticed it, Mr. Darcy, and would not want your sister to act accordingly. It reminds me of those dreadful people we knew in Hertfordshire. Such ill breeding!"

Georgiana glanced at her brother. Darcy said nothing as he sipped his soup, his expression that of one very disinterested in the conversation. Or perhaps he was more aptly akin to a pot simmering just below the boiling point. Georgiana suspected the latter.

"Oh! I will grant you that they are above the rank of those from our most recent acquaintance, but then that is not to give them much credit, for I never met with a more disagreeable class of people in all my life than those of Hertfordshire, especially that one family Charles seemed to admire."

"Yes," Mrs. Hurst said, "but the material point is, dear sister, that when one has money they are always fashionable…especially when they move in the inner circle of high society. Their manners can be forgiven in proportion to their wealth."

Georgiana dropped her gaze to her plate and fidgeted with her food while Darcy rolled his eyes. Mr. Bingley, sensing Miss Darcy's insecurity, made an effort at pleasant conversation, causing her to give a timid smile.

The servants came to remove the first course, and then the fish and vegetables were served. Darcy never gave notice to Miss Bingley as he ate. He rather wondered if she had any thought to what *he* might think of *her* and where *she* ranked in society. Should a gentleman ever stoop to elevate her, she would become nothing more than the other sycophants from lower society who gauged their self-worth based on the status of their husbands. By the time the third course was served, Caroline had gone on to complain further about the dinner party for the Viceroy's daughters.

"I cannot see why I did not receive an invitation. Why should Charles receive one and not I?" Caroline asked. "And furthermore, why should Mr. Hurst and Louisa? Am I not to be included when I am family, too?"

Mr. Hurst threw down his napkin and looked his sister-in-law directly in the eye. "Caroline, let's get something rightly straight here. You will never be invited to functions of the elite upper sphere of high society because you are *not* one of them. The only reason that Charles or I have an invitation is because *Darcy* has an invitation. Should you become betrothed to one of the *ton's* first circle then you could expect such an invitation, but until you are, respect your place and recognize those of your betters for theirs."

Reginald then picked up his knife and fork and resumed his meal as if nothing was amiss, and Miss Bingley was left to a roomful of silence having forced her brother-in-law to say what gave no one any pleasure, least of all not herself.

After dinner had concluded, the party separated with the ladies leaving for tea and cake and the gentlemen for cigars and brandy. Darcy smiled to himself as the gentlemen had their drinks. Never had he imagined Hurst would be the one to check Miss Bingley's manners, and yet he was delighted that that gentleman had.

When the hour was quite late, Georgiana begged her brother for the carriage feigning a headache, and so the Darcys departed for home. While in the carriage, Georgiana spoke to her brother of her feelings.

"Please, do not make me spend another moment in Miss Bingley's company, for I do not think I can tolerate her constant accolades of my accomplishments. I understand she wants to insinuate me into her brother's good graces, but, Brother, I care nothing for Mr. Bingley beyond friendship, and Miss Bingley does not realize how embarrassing her actions are for the both of us."

"Georgiana, you need not worry. Bingley thinks of you more as a younger sister than a potential wife. But you must not be too unforgiving of Miss Bingley. All her life she has stood on the outside looking in. More than anything she wants to be accepted by the matrons of Almack's and be counted among the most influential and exclusive ladies of London's high society, and yet she never will—unless, of course, she should marry very well which is most unlikely because she is too obvious. Though an older widowed earl or duke might take pity on her, it is very unlikely that any of the rest of us ever will."

"Then I pity her, for I want nothing of the kind. All I want is you and a family one day to call my very own. I want you to be happy and marry the woman you love, whoever that may be."

Brother and sister rode the remainder of the short distance to Darcy House in silence, each too full for further conversation. When Darcy retired to his room that night, he stood alone by the large window in his bedchamber looking out over the city, his mind occupied with thoughts of Miss Bennet as he stared into the night in quiet reflection. She puzzled him exceedingly. She had come to London, but why had she come, and more specifically why had she come to Hurst House? Was it resourcefulness…or was it genuine affection for his friend? Though her back had been turned to him, Darcy had observed her from the shadows of the second floor balcony and had noticed the same languid sadness in her slumped shoulders that had become characteristic of his friend.

Darcy raked his fingers through his thick curls. *And what of her sister?* No matter how he tried to deny what he felt, Miss Elizabeth was ever present in his thoughts.

Gazing at the street lamp below, she materialized before him as a vision. Her sun-kissed face with the wind blowing in her dishevelled hair came into sharp focus. Her lips were ruby red, and her cheeks were flushed with the blush of dew dropped roses. She lifted her eyes and looked at him with a mischievous smile. Nubile and lush, she was in the full bloom of life.

Where is she tonight? He thought to himself. *Could she be in Cheapside with her sister, or has she stayed behind in Hertfordshire? I wonder what she's doing this very hour. Could she be thinking of me as I am her?*

Darcy gently shook his head and then turned and stared at the counterpane, overcome with desire and loneliness. He released the breath he had been holding and slowly returned to the window where he closed the shutters and pulled the curtains. Sighing deeply, he moved towards his oversized bed and murmured aloud, "Tonight I would like nothing more than to have Elizabeth here in this bed with me." He reached down and ran his fingers over the raised pattern of the silken brocade.

Barely beneath his breath, he softly whispered, "Do I dare?"

A morose look of contemplation bore down upon his countenance as his fingers adeptly worked buttons on his shirt. With one fluid motion, he pulled it over his head and tossed it on the stool at the foot of his bed. Turning back to the bed, he stopped abruptly and a slight, self-assured smile tugged at his lips. *Have I spent too long admiring the original to ever even contemplate accepting a replica...?*

~*~*~*~

Chapter 23

"Millie," Kate said, strolling around her room in boredom, "I think I shall go out a little early and enjoy the park before our appointed time to meet Miss Darcy. It is such a fine day that I feel in need of fresh air and a good ride. I shall leave now, if you do not mind my impatience."

"For goodness' sake, Kate, can you not wait a moment longer? I've just a few more adjustments to my habit, and then I shall be ready, and we will go together. Or are you hoping to meet up with a certain someone before Miss Darcy is to meet us? We are a full hour early, you know."

"Shush! Someone might hear you."

"Oh, nonsense! You know as well as I that no one is here but Arpita, and she never tells anyone anything." Millie paused and turned to meet her sister's startled look. "Kate, I know what you are about, and it vexes me to think of it."

"Why, Millie, whatever do you mean '*what I am about*?' I am '*about*' nothing in particular. I simply want some air. I have been in Lady Crofton's school of etiquette for a full two weeks, and I am terribly restless."

"Kate, stop it! You avail yourself of every opportunity to escape the Countess. Do not think that I do not know you have been meeting Colonel Brockton whenever you go to the park for *air*, as you say?"

"And what if I have?" Kate responded nonchalantly as she paced back and forth, twirling a ringlet of her hair around one finger.

"Kate, you are supposed to be enchanting Mr. Darcy, not avoiding him. Is that not the plan we hatched—that you would entice him to marry you?" Millie queried, lifting one eyebrow. "You know perfectly well we must marry favourably if we are to please Papa and keep our inheritance. Why would you take such a chance and possibly ruin everything after all our careful planning?"

"Really, Millie, do you think me such a frivolous fool? I know exactly what is expected of me, and should I choose to see Edward, I know how to be discreet." Kate moved towards her dressing table and lifted a comb as if to examine it. "The hen chooses the cock in the game of love and chance, and I shall choose as I see fit," she murmured quietly.

Turning abruptly, she stated out loud, "And who is to say I will marry Mr. Darcy? I was intrigued with the prospect upon first acquaintance. He is handsome enough to consider, but whether or not I choose to follow through with it is yet to be decided. He is extremely dull for my tastes, and I fear that after marriage he shall want to change me."

Millie shook her head, resting one hand on her hip. "Very dull indeed! Who are we to judge one man from another? It is better to have a dull one rather than a poor one."

Kate shot her sister a look of disdain as she snatched her reticule and riding crop from her desk.

"Very well, then, go without me," Millie said, seeing that her sister was determined. "I shall leave at our appointed time. Just be sure you are *not* found out. I will not fall into disfavour with Papa on your account."

"That is very rich coming from *you* who wishes not to marry at all!" Kate cried. "I shall meet you under the beechwood trees near the centre of the park."

Without another word, Kate turned and quit the room. Moving down the steps at a rapid pace, she exited the house and, with the help of a footman, mounted her waiting horse and left for Hyde Park as quickly as she could. If she wished to see an old flame, no one was going to interfere with her decision, least of all not *Millie*.

Trotting into the park, Kate glanced around. Not finding the one she was looking for, she moved her horse towards the tall elms near the hedgerows. Dismounting, she tied her mare to a branch and loosened her bonnet, letting it fall behind her as she strolled back and forth, grumbling under her breath about the awful chance she knew she was taking. When something alerted her that she was no longer alone, she stopped short and turned toward the sound of footsteps approaching from behind the hedgerow.

"Kate!" Colonel Brockton called as he ran to meet her and they fell into each other's arms. "After our argument, I thought you might not come."

"I almost did not, but at last I did. It was quite a shock to see you in the park on Sunday, Edward. Since then I have seen you at my discretion for the last three days, but we cannot continue to meet like this. Millie knows."

"Has she threatened you?"

"No, of course not! Millie is not like that, but we cannot continue like this. If she has discovered us, then others…"

He leaned down and kissed her. "Is it Darcy? Are you really going to marry him if he should ask?"

"If I wish to keep my inheritance, then I must do as I am told. I have a duty to my family. They expect no less of me, and I have no choice."

He cupped her face in his hands and looked into her eyes. "Yes, Kate…you have a choice. You can marry me. I love you, Kate. I've loved you since that warm night in New Delhi when we held one another close under the mulberries."

"No! You mustn't speak of that."

"And why not? We declared our love for one another." He glanced away in exasperation. "Good God, Kate, we were lovers," he said, returning his gaze to her. "I have ruined you for your future husband. No man will be pleased when he learns you come to the marriage bed spoilt—and Darcy will know. He is no young fool and cannot be deceived into believing you are a maiden when you are not."

"I choose not to think of that."

"But you must think of it. This is England, and everything depends on propriety in an unmarried girl—everything! He will despise you when he finds out the truth."

Tears gathered in her eyes as she paused and bit down on her lower lip. "It is all so complicated. Oh! I simply cannot think of it."

"No, it is not. You know why I am in England. I returned when Father sent word of my older brother's death. Kate, we *can* marry. I am to inherit my father's title. I know a baron is not an earl, nor is the value of the living equal to that of Pemberley, but it is still quite respectable."

A Man in Want of a Wife

Kate pulled away and wiped a tear. "But we will be poor. Father will cut me off, and I will forfeit my dowry. He says I cannot even consider someone below an income of ten thousand a year, which Mr. Darcy is reputed to have, and perhaps even more, though he keeps that information a very close secret. The best we can hope for is that I may become your mistress once an heir is born."

The Colonel released a ragged breath. "No! I will not have it. If I cannot have you for my wife, then I will not have you at all. Have you no concept of what is good and respectable?"

She turned with fire in her eyes. "It is *you* who does not understand! I would rather be rich and comfortable than lauded as respectable. To be cut off from my sisters and my family? It would be insupportable. I am not used to economy. You have an income of two thousand. Mr. Darcy has ten, and father will purchase him a title. I heard him telling Lady Crofton as much. By association, Mr. Darcy will become one of the richest men in England. Father will see to it!"

"And what about us? Have you forgotten the passion that exists between us...the time we spent in New Delhi? Do you think you can ever feel such fervour for the Mr. *Stoic* Darcy? Kate!"

Kate tapped her foot, replying in cold civility, "I think we have said all there is to say. I am to meet my sister and Miss Darcy here at any given moment. Her brother is coming, too. And it is *Miss* Singleton to *you*."

The Colonel laughed. "Ah, but that is not what you said back in New Delhi." He paused and studied her. "Tell me, Kate, did I not mean anything to you...was I nothing more than a passing affair so soon forgotten?"

"You must leave," she said, tears streaming down her cheeks. Looking around cautiously, she continued. "I've told you I am expecting Mr. Darcy and his sister, so if you will, please leave *now*, and do not ever contact me again."

"Not yet. There is one other thing I want to know. Was it really you and your sister behind those feathers at the general's party, and were you *naked*? Because if it was you, Darcy may find out."

Shocked, she reached up and slapped him with her riding crop, leaving an instant welt upon his cheek. "How dare you! Are you threatening me?! Because, if you are, it will come to nothing, and you will be ruined. My father is a powerful man, and he will see to it." With fire in her eyes, she hissed, "If you love me as you say, you will never mention that again. Now, you *must* leave."

His expression was heartrending but Kate steeled herself not to react.

"I do love you, Kate, and I was not suggesting that I will ever tell Darcy, only that there was speculation. Some of the officers at the garrison thought it might have been you and Millie, but I quieted their suspicion. No one knows your secret, Kate...I am not threatening you. I love you...I shall always love you."

With that, he turned and walked away, leaving in the direction from whence he came.

Watching him as he left, Kate hung her head and cried inconsolably. She wept with such bitterness that she was unaware of another horse approaching.

"Kate? Kate! What is wrong," Millie said, sliding down from her mare.

Running to her sister, she flung her arms around her neck. "What has that horrid man done to you? I told you not to meet him! I have never liked him! I shall have him horse whipped and his commission revoked."

"No, Millie," Kate cried, clutching her sister's coat in her fists as she held on to her. "I love him, and he wants to marry me, only..."

"There-there, Kate," Millie said, reaching into her pocket and pulling out a handkerchief. Dry your eyes and blow your nose. Miss Darcy will be here soon, and she mustn't find you in such a state."

"But what am I to do? I love him!"

"I do not know, but you cannot marry him. Should Mr. Darcy ask, you must agree and do not hesitate in accepting his offer. Your best chance at happiness depends upon your securing him."

Kate nodded as she dabbed at eyes. "Yes, I suppose I must," she said. "Marriage is nothing more than deceit and disappointment. I have seen it all around me my entire life. I have only to look to our parents for a primary example of that." She patted her hair distractedly. "Please, help me look presentable."

Millie smoothed her sister's hair, wrapping several ringlets around her finger to secure them back into place, and when she was finished, she tied Kate's bonnet and dusted the wrinkles from her sister's blue velvet habit. Mounting their horses, they turned their mares towards the open field and trotted in the direction of the centre of the park. There they found Georgiana waiting with a smile, her expression glowing with anticipation. Before long, Mr. Darcy and Lord Wexford joined them. By then Kate was laughing and smiling without a trace of her earlier distress, much to her sister's relief. One who did not know her well would assume that Kate was without a care in the world.

~*~

Later that evening
Number 15 Cavendish Square

Lady Crofton entered the dining room with the family butler to conduct her final inspection of the table arrangements. A large vase of pink and white peonies had been placed in the centre with bowls of various fruits arranged around them in an attractive manner. She smiled and nodded in satisfaction. Walking over to the table, she checked each place setting as she ran her fingers over the fine damask, smoothing out a few imaginary wrinkles in the crisp white cloth. Susan had given the instructions of what was to be done, and the butler and staff had carried them out to perfection.

"Mr. Carlton," she said, turning to the butler, "the table arrangements are splendid and do you credit. I can think of nothing more that needs to be attended to."

The older man bowed. "Thank you, madam," he replied with a solemn expression. "I have the wines you wished for and was able to secure the vintage Cognac you requested for after dinner, though not without considerable expense. I'm afraid the blockade does present a problem these days. Runners are rare and their wares expensive."

"Oh, that is of no concern. Apply it to the household account, and I shall make any adjustments that are necessary. I happen to know Lord Wexford and Mr. Darcy prefer it, and Mr. Singleton would spare no expense to accommodate them this evening."

"Yes, madam."

Lady Crofton turned and quit the room in search of her stepdaughters. Finding them in the front parlour with Miss Darcy and Mrs. Hurst, who had just recently arrived, the Countess greeted them with warm salutations.

A Man in Want of a Wife

"Miss Darcy, Mrs. Hurst, we are so very pleased that you were able to come this evening. I hope that you will enjoy yourselves and feel as welcome as we would wish."

"I am sure that we shall," said Mrs. Hurst. "It is a pleasure to be amongst such fine company." She smiled and turned to Miss Darcy who sat between Millie and Kate. "Georgiana, would you not agree?"

"Yes, it is indeed a pleasure," she answered rather timidly.

The two younger Singletons giggled. "Well, of course it is. After all, we are such fast friends," Kate declared. "I was just telling Miss Georgiana how we plan to race our horses in the countryside when the family removes to Greensward next week."

Lady Crofton's eyes flashed in warning at her stepdaughter's exuberance before turning her attention to Mrs. Pennington, motioning for her to follow her for a private conversation concerning the dinner arrangements. Once they were out of the hearing of the others, Lady Crofton spoke to her in a quiet voice.

"Susan, my dear, the table looks splendid. Your choice of flowers and fruit is exquisite."

"Thank you, Cora. I thought they would meet with your approval. The flowers came from my mother-in-law's hot house and the fruit from our own."

Lady Crofton's lips lifted in pleasure, and then she leaned in and lowered her voice, "Now, Susan, I must speak to you on another matter of great importance to me. I do hope that it will not be impractical to have my nephew join us this evening. It was such a shock to see him at Brookmeyer's Clocks this morning. I was not at all expecting it—and to learn of his father's death whilst I was abroad. Such bad business," the Countess lamented as she shook her head, but then she returned with a smile and continued. "I know that it may have been an imposition to accommodate him with such short notice, but I'm afraid, as is common with his station in life, he is unpredictable and expects to be received whilst he is in Town. He plans to stay for a fortnight and will attend the foxhunt on Monday."

"Oh, no! Think nothing of it. His Grace is always welcome," Susan answered with a smile. "Though his arrival was unexpected, it is indeed an honour to have such a distinguished guest as the Duke of Beaumont here with us. I have had one of our best rooms prepared for him in the family wing. I only hope that he is made to feel as comfortable as he would be in his own home. It is not every day one receives someone as renowned as His Grace."

"Yes, well, once the renovations are completed in his London residence, he will remove himself to Brook Street in Grosvenor Square. The house was in dire need of renovations, but the fire was most unexpected, and I dare say nearly ruined the kitchen completely—not to mention the smoke damage to the furnishings. Nevertheless, at least the priceless family portraits from the Elizabethan Era were spared. My nephew's family has had such bad luck over the years."

"Indeed." Susan nodded. "The fire was most unfortunate, but I am sure he will see to it that everything is as it should be before very long."

"Yes, I am sure he will." Lady Crofton paused, and then added, "I must say His Grace seemed to have been much taken with Millie when he arrived, and he is quite handsome. Would you not agree?"

"Yes, he is. No one could deny that," Susan replied with a puzzled look.

"And full *young*." Lady Crofton laughed. "I had not realized just how young he was until about a fortnight ago when the thought came to me that he might be a potential suitor for one of the girls, but then I dismissed the notion as impossible because of his age.

"However, since I was yet to inform my sister Madeline of my marriage, I wrote her a letter, and today in the afternoon post I received a reply. She informed me of the details of her husband's untimely death and of her son's coming into his inheritance. Justin is now two and twenty and has assumed all his late father's responsibilities fully. I'm surprised I did not read about it in the papers or receive her last letter, but then I was in residence at the family villa in Italy at the time and involved with my correspondence and courtship with your father.

"Nevertheless, my sister writes that the young Duke is to open the London house when it is completely redone, and he will remain there for an undetermined length of time. From her letter, I think he might be in want of a duchess. Is that not good news, my dear?! After all, he *is* the *ultimate* marriage material."

"Umm...yet both our girls are soon to be engaged if all goes as planned and—"

"And neither gentleman can trump a duke," Lady Crofton interjected. "My dear, did you not see the way he looked at Millicent earlier this morning at the clock shop? Why he appeared absolutely besotted. Susan, listen to me plainly," the Countess said. "If either of the girls shows the least bit of interest in Justin, and he reciprocates, then I think he should be our first choice; for I can assure you that *he* has an income of eighty thousand pounds a year and the largest estate in Devonshire. It covers half the county, and not only that, his family has a smaller estate in Kent—Croxley Abbey. My dear Susan, think of the distinction brought to the girl he marries, what with his title and family seat."

"Yes...but what about affection and love? Surely that must be taken into account. Marriage is a long business with no escaping it without a host of trouble and scandal."

"Of course that shall be a consideration! I do want the girls to be happy, but I also understand that happiness is often a matter of chance. There is much more to marriage than passion and love, my dear. The girls have a duty and obligation to both themselves and to the family. They must marry *well* in order to prosper—and I might add...for *you* to prosper. Should they not, they will be snubbed by high society; surely you must recognize that."

Susan sighed. "Yes, I am well aware of it. I was fortunate enough to marry a man with whom I fell in love, and he the same. But if the girls can be content in a situation where there is at least *mutual* respect and admiration, then I will be happy for them."

"Very good! Now, come, Susan," Lady Crofton said. "We must return to our guests and then we should move to the library where the men have congregated." She laughed. "We do not want to waste a minute of time in allowing the girls to better acquaint themselves with men of distinction."

~*~

Upon their arrival, Darcy, along with Mr. Bingley and Mr. Hurst, had been escorted to the library where Lord Wexford and the home party were already assembled, while Georgiana and Mrs. Hurst were escorted to the parlour where the ladies were taking tea.

When the gentlemen entered the room, the Viceroy rose to greet them.

A Man in Want of a Wife

"Mr. Darcy, Mr. Hurst, and Mr. Bingley, how good of you to come. Let me introduce you to my wife's nephew, the Duke of Beaumont, who is lately in town for the winter."

The three gentlemen bowed and the Duke acknowledged them with a nod. Lord Wexford then rose and greeted his cousin and friends.

"Darcy," he said, nodding to the Duke, "His Grace has just been telling us of his estate in Devonshire. Do you recall the old castle situated on the cliffs of Teignmouth overlooking the sea towards the channel? It belongs to His Grace."

Darcy's lips curled. "Is that so? Then it is indeed an honour to finally meet you, Your Grace," Darcy said extending a hand. "When we were children, my parents would take me and my cousins to Devon, and we would picnic near the old castle. I remember well how we used to play on the ruins and pretend we were knights defending England against the French."

"Indeed," Lord Wexford said. "We had many good times there conquering the French."

The Duke laughed. "It is not so far from the reality of it, for it was indeed the French, with their ships' cannons, who destroyed it. I was just telling your cousin and the others how I am planning to restore the estate to its former glory."

Randal Pennington moved to the drinks cabinet where he poured three drinks and handed them to his guests. "We have indeed been having a fascinating discussion. Come and join us. I am enthralled with His Grace's tales of valour and conquest throughout his family's history. He has promised that we shall all visit when the castle once again stands tall against the French wind in the channel."

Settling in around the fireplace for conversation, the men became comfortable with one another while the Duke continued to expound upon his plans. As they talked, Darcy sipped his drink, admiring the young Duke as he told them of his family history and his recent debut into society after the death of his father. He included the fact that he was to assume his father's place and responsibilities in the House of Lords in the upcoming session. They talked for some time until they were interrupted by the sound of laughter coming in their way.

Glancing in the direction of the doorway, Mr. Singleton stood to his feet and approached his wife as the ladies entered the library.

"Cora, my dear, your nephew has just been telling us of his family's castle in Devonshire. It was destroyed during the seventeenth century. Were you aware of it, love?" the Viceroy asked.

Returning to his guests with a smile, he continued. "Fascinating young man," he said. "His family is as old as my own, going back to the Conquest."

"Yes, darling," the Countess replied with a warm smile. "I am well aware of Beaumont Castle. It stands in ruins, partially destroyed in 1690 by the French, and then left to decay over the years. Justin's ancestors were able to hold the invasion with cannon fire of their own until reinforcements from the British Navy arrived, but not without considerable cost. In fact, the 5th Duke of Beaumont refused to restore it once the battles were won. It seems that his wife and infant daughter were killed during the siege and grief stricken as he was; he committed suicide from the castle walls some years later."

"You are correct, Aunt Cora," the Duke said. "My great-great grandfather did indeed die on the rocks below, and out of reverence for him, when one visits Devon, the castle appears as it has stood all these years. However, I believe enough deference had been paid, and I intend to change that. I shall move the family seat back to the original location where it belongs. It has been a lifelong ambition of mine since upon first seeing it when I was a mere boy of six. It captured my heart at that moment, and I have been prisoner to it all those years. I visit when I can."

"My dear, I think that is very admirable of you," said Lady Crofton. "I'm sure my sister is very proud of her only son. Beaumont Castle was always a favourite of hers."

"Yes, it indeed is, and, as I was telling your husband and the gentlemen here, the plans are drawn and construction is to begin this summer when the weather permits. I hope to have it done within a year or two, and then I shall move there, but Mother will remain at the dowager cottage in Croxley Abbey. She cannot bear to leave Kent and her many friends."

Lady Crofton smiled to herself and gently nodded. *...then you do plan to take a wife.* Nodding, she added, "That is so like Madeline. She's become comfortable in her old age, but then being a close distance to London, I'm sure, suits her better than sea air."

"Indeed!" the Duke said with a smile.

Lady Crofton and the ladies then moved to the window on the far side of the room where they took seats. The gentlemen continued with their conversation, while the ladies settled in for theirs. It was not long, however, until the butler entered to inform them that dinner was served.

Removing themselves to the dining room, Lady Crofton paid particular attention to her nephew and how his eyes followed Millicent's every movement as the family strolled down the corridor to the formal dining room. She had seated her stepdaughter beside Lord Wexford, but the Duke was seated across from them, and from her position near the head of the table, she could scrutinize both those gentlemen as well as Mr. Darcy and her other stepdaughter. If it was within her power, she would secure the higher rank in place of the lower for Millicent, and, as things stood now, Mr. Darcy seemed an excellent match for Kathryn.

Quiet and cordial conversation circled the table as the party enjoyed their soup and sipped their wine. The Viceroy carried most of the conversation, followed by Mr. Pennington and Susan. Miss Darcy was rather quiet, and Mrs. Hurst hardly spoke a word. Mr. Bingley and Mr. Hurst talked of sport and how they enjoyed the hunt. All were in agreement that Monday would be a splendid day for a foxhunt and how much they were looking forward to it.

Lady Crofton was unusually quiet while she ate. Instead she spent her time observing her guests. First she concentrated on the Duke. He carried himself with all the elegance and grace one would expect from his station, but there was one thing Lady Crofton noticed that might be overlooked by the casual observer. While her nephew was discreet enough not to call attention to his actions, his gaze was never long removed from Millicent whenever he spoke, and furthermore, Millicent was not unaffected by his notice. This caused the Countess to smile with an uplifted brow as she glanced between them. But what was more startling to her was the revelation that while the Duke's interests were clearly piqued, the Viscount's were not. If Lord Wexford noticed either of them at all, outwardly he gave no notice of it.

The Countess then shifted her attention towards her other stepdaughter. Kathryn's conversation with Mr. Darcy was amiable enough; and while she seemed to enjoy his attentions, her eyes betrayed her. Often enough Lady Crofton noticed that she appeared to be in another world whenever her likely suitor spoke, which was seldom, to say the least. And it was not long until complete silence fell between them.

As for Mr. Darcy, and his consideration of Kathryn, it was becoming abundantly clear that he no more favoured her than she appeared to favour him. The Countess gently shook her head as she glanced towards her husband who was so lost in conversation that she was confident all her observations had escaped his notice completely.

While the others enjoyed their meal and wine, which, Darcy had to acknowledge, was the finest he had ever consumed, he glanced around the table. He paid particular attention to the Duke of Beaumont and Miss Millicent Singleton, noticing a very slight interest displayed by the Duke, which, from the shimmer of excitement in her eyes, he assumed she returned. It was just as well, he thought, for he had spoken to his cousin recently and knew Lord Wexford was not seriously interested in the Viceroy's daughter and planned to make his sentiments known after the foxhunt. Wex was nowhere near ready to settle into the married state and had repeatedly told Darcy so.

Raising his wine glass to his lips, Darcy recognised that he, too, must make his sentiments known to the Viceroy before his annual trip to Kent, which would come in a little less than ten weeks. By then, he would have had sufficient time to decide his future concerning Miss Kathryn.

He shook his head and sighed. Although he found her charming and pretty enough, she had failed to stir his emotions the way a certain young lady from Hertfordshire had, almost from their first acquaintance. Setting his glass aside, he glanced at his companion as the second course was served and found her staring off into the room. For a brief moment, he wondered what she might be thinking, but then dismissed it as irrelevant. From their previous conversations, he knew that she was not as well read as Miss Elizabeth Bennet, nor did she seem inclined to improve her mind through extensive reading of materials which might benefit her. Thus, he was sure that her contemplations took a turn in the direction of more frivolous matters.

After dinner the gentlemen separated from the ladies once again for cigars and brandy. When the Cognac was presented, Hurst broke into a smile and Bingley grinned while Lord Wexford shook his head with a laugh.

"How do you like my brandy?" the Viceroy asked as he handed out the glasses.

Darcy sipped his drink and smiled. "It is some of the best I've had."

"That it is," Hurst agreed. "I've never had finer. It is indeed the best."

"Of course it is! It is not *just* brandy; it is *Cognac*—the best Brandywine from the Cognac region of France, smuggled in by some of our best runners. It comes from the private stash of Louise XIII they tell me."

"Then it is a special evening indeed," the Duke said, "for I have heard of it, but never had the pleasure of tasting it."

The Viceroy smiled, very pleased with the evening. "Come; let us have a game of cards. It is not often that I have the pleasure of enjoying such fine company. I cannot tell you how much I am looking forward to Monday when we shall shoot together. Perhaps we shall even shoot pheasants in the afternoon."

Settling in the library, soon a table was produced and a game of blackjack began. The gentlemen laughed and enjoyed themselves with agreeable conversation and a bit of gaming. The cigars and brandy were excellent and the society even better. Darcy could not recall an evening spent in more pleasurable company, and from the looks of it, Hurst and Bingley were just as pleased as he.

When they departed, Hurst declared that it was a fine evening with the best meat and drink he had ever consumed, and his wife was equally pleased with the evening as she had acquired a new friend in the Countess—one of whom she could boast to her sister and their many friends.

And as for Darcy, it seemed a successful evening in regards to furthering acquaintances with those of his sphere. He especially enjoyed his time spent with the Viceroy and his friend Randal Pennington. He also enjoyed the company of the Duke of Beaumont and hoped to further that acquaintance. But whether or not he would deem it a successful evening concerning the decision he must make in regard to Miss Kathryn, he was not prepared to say at this point. The fact that he did not love her or hold any particular affection for her was clear, but what to do about it was not so clear. However, within the coming weeks, he would make his sentiments known to her father and hoped in doing so, the connection would not be entirely broken.

Darcy took a deep breath as he leaned back and closed his eyes while listening to the clip-clop of the horses as the carriage travelled over the cobblestone and brick. One thing he knew with certainty. He was indeed looking forward to Monday with great pleasure.

Chapter 24

Climbing the stairs to their bedchamber, the Viceroy and Lady Crofton could not have been more pleased with the dinner party for their daughters. Phillip Singleton could not remember a time spent with his family in which he had experienced a more pleasurable evening, and Cora Singleton was more than pleased with the progress of the night, namely the object of her newly discovered maternal duty—seeing her stepdaughters well placed in marriage.

A smile spread across her features as they entered their chamber to prepare for bed. She was absolutely certain she had at least one duchy secured, and the fact that the union would blend her dearest sister's family with that of her own newly acquired one was a double plum. If things went as she hoped, she would be sending a letter, post-haste, to Croxley Abbey.

Once they were ready for bed, the Viceroy turned to his wife.

"So, you think your nephew is interested in our Millicent, do you?"

"My darling, if I am any judge of character, I not only *think* he is interested, but means to have her as his duchess. I have known Justin since he was a boy. He has a goodly sort of nature—very serious and caring. He has always been universally kind to all, and the servants and tenants at Croxley Abbey have great respect for him. He is also a god-fearing man, who will be a great patron of the Church. If he had not been heir to the dukedom, my sister has always believed he would have been a vicar. Millicent could not find a finer man if her life should depend upon it!"

"Umm...I would hate that for the Viscount's sake, but a duke is certainly better than a future earl."

"Yes, indeed it is. But you must not worry too much about Lord Wexford, for I do not think his heart is much engaged. He does not look at Millicent the way the Duke does. There is a certain gleam in Justin's eyes that speaks of desire. It will be an excellent match for our Millicent, and Lord Wexford will simply have to get over it."

The Viceroy laughed heartily. "I do love the way you think, Cora. You seem to understand the superior sex far better than most. Now, what say you of Darcy? Once he and Kathryn are engaged, I intend to purchase a title for him. I have set into motion for Randal to have an earldom, but now that I think about it, I do wonder how much more it would cost for the title of a duke? If it is reasonable, then I will purchase a dukedom for them both."

"Darling, I must urge caution there. I do not think Mr. Darcy or our son-in-law will wish to be too grand. Begin with the earldom, then, if things progress of their own accord, we can always find a sponsor for a duchy, but for now, let us not be too hasty."

"Yes-yes, of course, you are right—and very sensible, I might add."

"Indeed. Now, my darling, it is time for us to retire." Lady Crofton paused and took her husband's hand. "Phillip, have you thought about the possibility of our having a child? I am not beyond it, and I would like nothing more than to provide you with an heir."

"Cora? Are you absolutely sure? I thought you…"

"Barren? I may be, but I have no way of knowing for sure. You see, the late Earl of Crofton was not exactly…how do I put it?" She smiled and then nodded. "After our first year of marriage with no issue, he preferred his long-time mistress to me, but that does not mean I cannot bear a child. I've only lacked the means, and I would like nothing more than to bear *your* child, my love."

"Cora, you have made me the happiest of men. I always wanted more children, but Millicent wouldn't have it after the twins, and I was forced to seek my comfort elsewhere. Please, teach my daughters better—that it is not how it should be. Above all things, I desire for them to be happy." He smiled, and further said, "Come, my love, let us practice, and perhaps we shall bear fruit."

~*~

After their parents had left for their chamber, Kate and Millie slowly climbed the stairs for theirs. It had been a mixed night for the girls: one claiming tedious boredom and the other not so much so. And therefore, upon reaching the confines of Miss Kathryn's room, they began to talk as they always did before retiring for the night.

"Kate, did you not enjoy the evening? You looked as if you did not."

"Oh, Millie, no, I did not. I like Miss Darcy well enough, but I find her brother to be quite wearisome. I've no idea what to say to him. He is so solemn. He hardly speaks a word, and he never smiles—much less laughs."

"Yes…I have noticed. But Kate, you must try to find common ground."

"Nonsense! I do not wish to—nor do I wish to speak of me. Instead, I would rather speak of you. Millie, I watched you tonight—after all, I had nothing better to do, and I must say that I believe you *like* the distinguished—and very *dull*—Duke of Beaumont. Really, Millie, did you have to stare so much during dinner?"

"I was not staring, Kate. I only returned his smiles. And he is not dull."

"Well, if you do not think him dull, then you really do like him, but to me he is just as dry and tiresome as Mr. Darcy, maybe even a little more so." She laughed.

"No. He is not dull. And I do think him distinguished and very handsome."

"So you *do* like him," Kate said with a teasing laugh as she began to hum the wedding march.

"Stop it, Kate!" Millie retorted with a sly smile. "And what if I do like him," she further added. "It doesn't mean I am going to marry him nor that he would even want me."

"Oh, but I think he would," Kate said. "He is a single duke with a vast fortune, and therefore, he must be in want of a duchess—and why not you? You're as pretty as any of the debutantes, and far livelier than the lot of them. Such dull and boring, prune-faced little things they are. Only Miss Darcy has any spark—and she is not even out yet. But then, hers is more than likely because of us. She is such a dear, and, at least, does not snub us because we lack the qualities of a '*proper English education*'. How I have come to loathe that expression."

A Man in Want of a Wife

Kate moved to her wardrobe and opened the door. "Millie, would you like to borrow my lace gown? You could wear it with your chiffon petticoat—the blue one to enhance your grey eyes. It would definitely gather the attention of the boring Duke. Oh, how I would laugh!"

"Kate! No! If I *were* to secure the Duke's regard, I would want it to be born of affection—not rooted in lust," Millie replied.

"That is not how you felt a mere month ago. What has changed? Why have you become so insipid? And do not tell me it is because of the Countess, for if it is, I shall scream!"

"Kate, it is time to grow up." Millie hesitated and then spoke again. "My dear sister, you really astound me at times. Have we not both deplored our parents' marriage, with Mother's constant quest for things and parties? When we were children back in our nursery in the village, we would hold one another and cry, wishing our lives were different. Do you not remember?"

Kate said nothing.

Millie took her sister's hand and squeezed it. "Kate, I know you well. You despised their lives as much as I. And now you want to become Mother? Why, after all these years, have you changed your mind? We've talked of freedom—our hopes and dreams. I know there were things I didn't understand, but upon studying our older sister, I've come to the conclusion that it is far better to be loved than not. Mother was proud and self-absorbed—never caring about anything or anyone, least of all her children, so why would you want her life?"

Kate dropped her head and shook it. "I've not changed. I've only become resolved to a life I cannot escape, and thus I must make the best of it." She looked up and caught her sister's gaze. "Millie, how can I marry Mr. Darcy when I love another—another that I cannot have? My fate is sealed. Yes...I will accept Mr. Darcy should he ask...but not because I love him...or even care for him in an affectionate sort of way. It will be out of duty and because I do not want to lose my inheritance or Papa's favour."

"But in time you will come to love Mr. Darcy. I have studied him, Kate. He is a good and sensible man. He will make you happy if you will only let him."

"No, he will not. He cannot...because he...he is...is so different from me. Can you not see that, Millie? We may be of the same sphere—equal in every regard as society judges, but we are not equal of mind. Millie, I've queried Miss Darcy about Pemberley and what might be expected of the mistress of such a large estate. She has told me of all the onerous duties that I would be required to perform. I would not only have to manage the house, which I am sure I could do, and attend to the tenants, nurturing their every need, but also, in the evenings, I would be expected to listen to *music* and read great books. Books, Millie! How dull! Can you imagine the horror of it? For I am sure his opinion of a great book and mine are vastly different! In his mind, I wouldn't know a great book from a naja-naja in the bush! No, Millie. He could not make me happy, and I am most certain that I am the last woman who could make him so. Yes—he is a good man—one who deserves a woman more suited to him, and that woman is not *me*! We would be miserable together."

"Kate, to compare Mr. Darcy's opinion of you to that of a speckled cobra is a bit much, even for you, don't you think?" Millie raised a brow. "You must accept him and learn to please him! If you do not, our stepmother will find a husband for you, and I am quite sure you would like him even *less* than you do Mr. Darcy. As for me, I am quite determined to marry the Viscount, for I have little hope of the Duke."

Millie stopped short and tilted her head. "If you think Mr. Darcy's expectations are high, then what of His Grace's? How would I ever manage to please one such as he?"

"But, Millie, you feel an attraction for him; that is the difference in our situations. I am sure *you* could find that common ground you speak so well of—that is if he should like you in return, I mean.

"Whilst I do not feel any attraction Mr. Darcy—nor do I suppose he holds much affection for me; however, from what I have observed tonight I *do* believe you could care for the Duke in a way that is different from any other."

"No, Kate, I am not like you. I am more pragmatic. I do not reach for things I cannot have. A bird in the hand is worth two in the bush. Now, let us retire. It is very late."

Millie turned to leave, but Kate stopped her.

"And I do? No, Millie, you are quite wrong. I have feelings the same as you or anyone else. The man I love is of no consequence and there is nothing I can do about it. Papa would never allow a match between me and the Colonel. Millie, you know he wouldn't."

Millie sighed. "Kate, I am tired. I do not wish to speak further on the subject. We have church in the morning, and then we are to remove to Greensward in the afternoon. It will be a tiring day, and we must be ready for it." She then stepped away and called for their ayah.

Once they were ready for bed, the girls decided to spend the night together as they had done when they were children. Arpita slept on the bed in the corner of the room watching over her cares as she had always done. Though they might not treat her with the respect she was due, the gentle woman continued to love them just the same. She had wrapped them in swaddling clothes the day they were born and nursed and cared for them all the days of their lives. And now she would see them through until they were married.

~*~

In another wing of the house, the Duke of Beaumont slowly went about making himself ready for bed. He had dismissed his valet early so that he might rise before dawn in order to prepare him for his morning constitutional—a ride in the park before church, something the young Duke would need more than ever to conquer the swelling desire rising up inside of him since he had come to Pennington Hall. The Duke sighed. He was not in the least bit sleepy. All he could think about were his pressing responsibilities coupled with his ever burgeoning desire to find a wife.

Taking a seat by the opened window in his chamber, the Duke poured himself a drink and lit a cigar as he paused to ponder his future.

Only having recently stepped into the role as head of his family and master of their vast estates, he carried a burden of scruples that most men his age would never face. He was not of loose morals; he had never had a mistress or even a dalliance with a woman of the night though he was as virile as any man, and with his tall frame, brooding handsomeness with his dark curly hair and hazel eyes, he was the object of many women's desires. But he attended church faithfully with true conviction to its moral teachings and had kept to those teachings all the days of his life. In all, the Duke was truly a good man who stood above many in his station.

A Man in Want of a Wife

While other young men of a similar age gadded about spending their inheritances on women and wine or squandering it in the gaming hells of London, the young Duke was occupied with other things. Family honour and the care of those under his protection were of the utmost importance to him. Lifting his drink to his lips, his mind drifted back to a time long gone as he stared out into the expanse of the room, recollecting the experiences that had made him the man that he was.

During his boyhood and youth, he had watched the disastrous results of a life lived with little regard for the effects of trifling dillydallies and bad investments on the security of one's family and had determined from a young age that his father's path was not the path that he would follow. The late Duke had not been a man of immorality, nor had he been one to squander money on wine and song. He had been a good man, but not wise. His virtue, or rather his vice, depending on how one looked upon it, had been that of keeping up appearances with his rank and thus neglecting the greater need of his family. With excessive spending on inconsequential extravagances coupled with bad investments on speculative ventures, and traveling throughout the empire, he had hardly known his children at all—especially his daughters. And then there had been the pursuit for the heir and the consequential stress placed on his mother.

Unfortunately, the effect on the Duchess had been costly. In quest of the coveted heir, she had given his father five daughters before his birth, and then three more after that in hopes of providing the spare. This caused her health to be less than desirable for a woman of her age; after bearing nine children, his mother was broken and spent. She had become a bitter old woman well before her time, consumed with duty and the appearance of consequence. The young Duke slowly shook his head as he lifted his glass, caught up in his reflections of the past.

The late Duke's expenditures in the luxuries of fine art and literature had been enormous, and the extravagance with which he had entertained on his estates had burdened him with such debt which his son must be duty bound to repay. His father had also lost a goodly amount of his prosperity in his various capital ventures, participating in such follies as the African Company, the Mississippi scheme, and the South Sea Bubble, and furthermore, he had exhausted much of the family fortune in supplying dowries for eight daughters, providing for their educations in the finest seminaries, and keeping them in fashionable attire while at the same time seeing to the rebuilding of Beaumont Castle. In fact, a significant portion of the family's dwindling cash reserves had been spent on the castle, as his father had allowed no detail to be overlooked, no matter the expense.

His late father had invested heavily in the architectural exploits in the rebuilding of Beaumont Castle. He had employed the best architects of his day to draw up sufficient plans and had set aside a great deal of money to see his dream come to fruition—a dream which his son also shared, and by the confines of the will, was required to complete. But therein lay the material point. The duchy, though supplied with a good income, was in terrible need of funds, and thus his mother's ever incessant prattle to secure a wife for the lone purpose of a large dowry distressed the young Duke greatly.

The Duchess had given many soirées and balls, inviting the top echelon of the society from London, Edinburgh, and various neighboring estates with the primary objective of selecting a wife for her son, and yet, the Duke was determined that he would have none of it. The hunt had become a torment, each event more loathsome than the last, as one heiress after another fawned and simpered over him, vying for his title and family seat as if he were a prize to be won. Though sick of being tracked like prized quarry his mother was insistent, and the Duchess was not a woman to allow her son to forget neither his duty nor his responsibility.

Every waking moment, she constantly reminded him of his father, the will, and his duty as heir to his heritage, of which she need not have reminded him, for he was acutely aware of it. His father had seen to that from the moment he had formed his first words, and had set an example that, as the heir, he not only understood, but desired to fulfill.

The primary difference between the old Duke and the present one was that while the young heir took his ducal duties just as seriously as did his father, he was determined not to neglect his family as he had perceived his father to have done. When he married, it would be to a young maiden of his own choosing, one for whom he could hold a strong, passionate admiration and regard, and one who was of like mind.

And thus, the bickering between mother and son had caused him to flee Croxley Abbey for London where misfortune—or rather in his particular situation—divine providence, had led him to find his townhouse in shambles, partially destroyed by fire. Consequently he sought refuge from his only relative in Town—his mother's sister, the Countess of Crofton.

He knew she had remarried, but had yet to call on her as he was unsure where she was in residence. However, as luck would have it, they had met on Bond Street, thus saving him the trouble of looking her up.

A small smile curled his lips as he sipped his wine and recalled their encounter in the clock shop yesterday morning where she was selecting a timepiece for her husband, and he had brought his family's mantle clock for repairs. His joy in seeing his Aunt Cora had been immense, but nothing compared to the exhilarating feeling that coursed through his body when his eyes shifted to her stepdaughter. Millicent Singleton was perhaps the most beautiful woman he had ever beheld. She was stunning in her pretty French gown and woolen cape. Wispy curls were fighting to escape the confines of her bonnet, and when their eyes locked, his heart began to beat furiously as his mouth went dry.

Quickly recovering, he had bowed graciously and took her small gloved hand in his when they were introduced. In the Duke's mind, he had fallen in love right there on the spot. Her soft grey eyes shimmered with life, and her delicate mouth turned up sweetly when she smiled.

All through dinner and afterwards he had watched her from the corner of his eye and was secretly pleased, as he was not unaware of the fact that she stole a glance his way when she thought he was not looking. He smiled at the mere thought of it. Lifting his cigar, he blew a ring of smoke into the room, forming a circle resembling a heart.

Whatever it took, the young Duke was determined to have Miss Millicent Singleton for his duchess. Whether or not she came with the dowry his mother required, was not important to him. His resolve was not only to make her his wife; he would have her heart as well.

The only problem he saw was that there was another suitor before him. Lord Wexford was ten years his senior and displayed a confidence that recommended him well to a young woman's heart. The Duke would have to consider his options carefully, for he greatly admired the Viscount and his cousin, and if at all possible, he hoped to maintain a friendship that might prosper and grow. For he sensed a certain camaraderie in the two—especially Mr. Darcy, whose coming of age was not so far removed from his own. That pleased the Duke. Whereas Mr. Darcy had the responsibility over only *one* younger sister, the Duke of Beaumont had *three*.

Leaning back in his chair with his head resting on a cushion and his long legs crossed, the young Duke glanced at the chimneypiece as the clock struck two in the morning. Then, turning his gaze towards his bed, he sighed and briefly closed his eyes. Sleep, with Miss Singleton on his mind, would be difficult tonight...very difficult indeed.

Lifting his tumbler to his lips, he downed his drink, and then put out the remains of his cigar. Slowly rising to his feet, he closed the window and extinguished the candle on his side table before making his way to his bed. He was looking forward to church in the morning and Sunday afternoon with the family once they removed to the country. Then there was the foxhunt on Monday; *that*, he very much looked forward to, for he planned to keep one of the Viceroy's daughters well within his sight.

Pulling back the counterpane, he crawled beneath the thick down and closed his eyes in sleep with dreams of Millicent Singleton filling his head. Tonight, in a myriad of fantasies, he would love her, and beginning tomorrow he would woo her.

~*~*~*~

Chapter 25

Monday, January 20, 1812
Greensward Estate, the outskirts of London

The gentlemen and ladies were assembled on the green near the woods, conversing agreeably about first the weather and if one thought it was a good day for a foxhunt, and then whether or not there would be a war with the former colonies. And if there were, would Canada be the next to rebel and join the Americans in independence?

Darcy was there with Sam, who lay calmly by his master's feet. His cousin, Lord Wexford, had brought Delilah, one of the best and fastest bitch hounds in the country, who was also Sam's mate. The Duke of Beaumont, the Viceroy, Randal Pennington, Mr. Hurst and about forty other men, were also present, gathered around the hounds, talking about the news of the day while waiting for the foxhunt to begin. Only Bingley had chosen not to come, claiming his business in the North prevented it.

Millie and her sister Kate, along with Susan, Lady Crofton, and the other ladies present, stood by their horses, apart from the gentlemen, also waiting for the call to signal the start of the hunt. Kate was most eager to forward the match with her sister and the Duke of Beaumont, understanding what her sister did not: the power of physical attraction. While women considered security and affluence when choosing a man; men more often than not preferred physical beauty when left to their own devices. And thus Kate had given her sister her best indigo-blue riding habit for the day, claiming with great animation how her soft grey eyes were brought out to their best advantage by the bright cerulean-blue of the velvet habit.

As the ladies laughed in gay conversation, Kate's eyes cut across to the gentlemen just a few feet away.

"Millie, do not look now, but His Grace is staring at you. Oh, Millie, I think he really likes you. Are you not excited by the prospect?"

"For heaven's sake, Kate, lower your voice, or Susan and the Countess will hear you."

"And what if they do?!" she cried. "I am not saying anything untrue. You are violently in love with him, after all."

"Kate!"

Kate turned and smiled. "Oh! Look, Millie! He's coming! Be quick! Here, let me smooth your skirt. Now smile and look natural."

"Hush, Kate—hush!" Millie retorted in soft tones as her cheeks flamed crimson with embarrassment.

A few moments more, and the Duke with two other gentlemen stood before them.

A Man in Want of a Wife

"Your Grace, Lord Wexford, and Mr. Darcy," Kate said with a curtsey. "Good morning, gentlemen. How good of you to join us. We were just talking about you." She turned and gave her sister a sly smile, to which Millie flushed even more.

The gentlemen bowed. "How remarkable; we were just speaking of you and thought we would come to pay our regards before the hunt begins," responded Lord Wexford.

Spying the hounds beside their masters, Kate went to pet Sam, but the dog growled and moved back, showing his teeth.

"Oh! I don't suppose he likes strangers," she said with a laugh.

Darcy drew Sam's tether tighter. "As a rule, he does not, though there have been a few he's taken to," Darcy replied. "I would advise you not to try to touch him. He's never bitten anyone, but I would not like to play the odds."

"It is no wonder. I am not fond of foxhounds, and they appear to care no more for me than I them."

Darcy and Kate continued to talk while Lady Crofton and Susan engaged the Viscount, laughing and smiling in amiable conversation. The Duke, however, noticed Millicent standing apart from the rest and moved to join her.

"Miss Millicent," the Duke addressed, "do you enjoy a foxhunt?"

"Not particularly. I am not fond of killing anything—especially not for sport. If one means to eat an animal, then it is permissible, but to kill for the sake of killing? Well, that is simply wrong. I always pray the fox will outfox the hounds."

The Duke gave a small smile. "That is quite an extraordinary position for one of the fairer sex. I find it odd that you would care one way or the other." He paused and then said, "Do you often express opinions contrary to established traditions?"

"I speak as I see, Your Grace, and if it brings offense, then I am sorry for it, but that is how I feel. Poor creatures! To be torn apart so that men can boast of the hunt."

"No offence is taken, Miss Millicent. I'm not so sure my opinion on the matter is far removed from your own. The English sport is often overrated, but then we are a people steeped in tradition."

Lord Wexford came to where the couple were standing and nudged the Duke. "Your Grace, we are about to begin."

With a smile, the Duke bowed and left with the Viscount to join Darcy and the other men. As she watched him go, Millie could not help but notice the Duke's long lean figure and how well he carried himself. The Duke of Beaumont cut a fine figure and was quite possibly the most handsome man she had ever beheld.

Mounting their horses, Randal Pennington, as the master of foxhounds, led the procession with the dogs in front, sniffing the ground until the hounds were cast; then the hunt was on. To Darcy, there was nothing more thrilling than the bay of a hound on the scent of its prey, and in this hunt, he was not to be disappointed.

The dogs tracked through the fields and wood, through the thicket and briars, running and leaping, over and under the dense brush. They ran so fast that their masters could barely catch them, jumping fences and streams as they kept pace. Turning, the hounds entered a bushy area so dense that the only recognition of their whereabouts was the musical sound of their lonesome bays carried by the wind.

Millie and Kate trailed behind, and when they came to the dense overgrowth, Millie hesitated to follow, unsure if she wished to enter. Unlike her sister, she was no horsewoman. But Kate would have none of it.

Pulling up beside her, she scolded, "Millie, what are you waiting for? We shall be left in their dust if we do not pursue. Come! Let us be off!" And with that, she struck her sister's horse with her riding crop, forcing the animal forward into the thick patch of heavy brush.

No sooner had they entered, than Millie's horse bucked and reared up on its hind haunches, kicking and crying out in panic. Without a moment's notice, the animal bolted and was off like a bullet. The horse flew like the wind out of the brush and out into the open pastureland with Millie hanging on for dear life. A bone chilling scream escaped her lungs. Kathryn, who was an excellent horsewoman, was now close on her sister's heels, both riding perilously fast, especially for one riding sidesaddle.

Darcy was behind the girls and had seen it all. He jerked back hard on his reins and glanced at his cousin and the Duke, who had also seen the horse break rank. All three men pulled up short and turned their mounts in hot pursuit.

Millie leaned in close to her mount, her heart quickening as she desperately tried not to lose her seat. Clinging to the reins, she dug her gloved fingers into the horse's mane. She wanted to throw her leg over the horse to ride astride, but she feared losing her balance in the process. Her only hope was to stay close to the animal's body and pray her mare tired soon.

The horse ran and ran—for how long she could not tell. Then, at the sound of resounding hoof beats thrumming in her ears, Millie glanced over her shoulder to see the Duke rapidly approaching with Mr. Darcy, Lord Wexford, and her sister close behind. Tears streamed down her cheeks as fear tightened its grip on her heart. Would she be able to hold her seat until they caught her? Never in her life had she ridden so fast and hard.

To her great relief, within moments the Duke was racing beside her, steering his horse ever closer to her terrified mount. Then suddenly, he reached over with one strong arm. Circling her waist, he snatched her from the saddle as if she weighed nothing more than a thistledown.

Lord Wexford came up beside them on the opposite side and grabbed the mare's reins, jerking the horse to a sudden halt.

Heaving a deep sigh of relief, the Duke pulled her closer in his arms, wrapping her in a tight cocoon of safety. "Shush... do not cry, love. I have you now, and you are safe...you are safe," he murmured as he held her close, kissing the blond curls that hung loose from their pins, her hat long gone.

Millie cried all the harder, her mouth resting close to the Duke's while her hands clutched his coat in a fitted grip. "Do not leave me...please. Do not let me go. I am so frightened," she sobbed.

"No, I shan't let you go, love. I will take care of you."

The Duke of Beaumont felt her heart pounding like a frightened rabbit's against his chest, and at that moment he knew he truly loved her, and somehow he would make her his duchess. And as for her dowry, he did not care one whit how much it was or whether or not she even had one. If need be, they would economize until the burden of Beaumont Castle was lifted.

Kate and Mr. Darcy came thundering up from behind. Coming to a sudden stop, they both dismounted and ran towards the Duke and Millie.

"Millie! Oh Millie! Are you well? I shall die if you are not," Kate cried, trembling.

"Your sister is well, Miss Singleton, though a bit frightened."

"Your Grace, that is perhaps the best command of an animal I have ever witnessed," Darcy said. "You have my admiration and respect."

A Man in Want of a Wife

The Duke nodded, still clinging to Miss Millicent.

While Darcy and the Duke continued talking, Lord Wexford examined Miss Millicent's horse. Speaking in soothing tones, he ran his hand over the quivering animal, trying to calm it. As his hand went down the length of the horse's hind quarter, he noticed several prickly spines embedded in the animal's soft flesh. Leaning down, he gently pulled them from the horse's leg.

The mare whinnied and flinched. "It is all right, milady. There-there, you are a good girl. We will get you some liniment for the swelling. I'll see to it that you are given a bag of sweet-feed, and you'll be put to pasture until you have healed."

Approaching the others, the Viceroy held out his gloved hand with several sharp quills. "It looks as if Miss Singleton's mare came in contact with a hedgehog, and from the looks of it, it was a very large hedgehog at that. The horse will need immediate attention when we return to the house. Miss Millicent, do you think you can ride? I'll give you my horse."

"No, she will return with me," the Duke answered with a firm command.

Millie looked up at the man holding her, who now appeared more handsome than she ever imagined, and nodded. Laying her head back down on his shoulder, she relaxed and breathed deeply as her arms slowly circled around his slim waist.

"I want to go home, Your Grace. I have never liked to hunt, and now I wish only to go home."

The Duke said not a word as he kicked his horse in the flanks and turned the animal back towards the manor house.

Darcy turned to Kate with fire in his eyes. "Why did you slap her horse?! It was a very reckless thing to do. Your sister did not want to go into that thicket. It is a difficult terrain for a skilled rider to manipulate, and from the looks of it, your sister is certainly no horsewoman. Miss Millicent is lucky to be alive. For that matter, you are both fortunate to be alive the way you were riding, though you are more skillful in the saddle than she. Your sister might have fallen and broken her neck if not for the Duke."

Tears fell like raindrops from Kate's eyes. "I know," she said shakily, nodding her head. "It was foolish; I only wanted to have fun. That is all it was…a bit of fun. Oh! I am so sorry. Please believe me."

Darcy looked at her in disgust. "Next time *think* before you act. It might save a life." He turned and mounted his horse to follow the Duke.

Lord Wexford came up behind her and put a hand on Kate's slumped shoulders. "Do not cry, Miss Kathryn. My cousin can be rather abrupt."

Kate turned and leaned into the Viscount, and he pulled her into his arms. "What did he say to me that I did not deserve? I have been reckless my entire life. Living for the moment; flinging caution to the wind as if I should live forever with no consequences for my actions. That is how I have been. If I had caused my sister's death, then I would not want to live."

Lord Wexford released a deep breath. "Come, Miss Singleton. We need to return to the house."

"What about Papa and the others?" she asked, looking up with a tear-streaked face, her lower lip trembling as she spoke.

"Never mind them," he answered. "They are too far ahead of us to realise we are missing."

~*~

As they slowly trotted back to the house, Millie's heart was full. She had never before felt the strange feelings that flowed through her at this moment, and she was quite unsure what she should do about it. Glancing up into her rescuer's face, she smiled. "Thank you. You saved my life, and I shall not forget it."

He smiled in return. "It was nothing. I did what anyone would do."

"I must beg to differ, Your Grace. It was something…yes…it was," she said. "You saved my life." And then she reached up meaning to kiss his cheek. But he turned, and their lips met in a soft, chaste kiss which soon deepened into one of passion and need. Millie placed her small hand on the side of his face and pulled him into her.

Breaking free, both were startled at what had transpired between them. Silence reigned for several moments until finally the Duke cleared his throat and spoke.

"Miss Singleton, you must forgive me for my forward behaviour. I did not mean to allow things to breach the bounds of decorum."

"And what about me? I kissed you because it was what I wanted…even desired," she said in a soft whisper.

The Duke's lips curled as he steered the horse forward. "If that is true, and you are so inclined, then I must to speak with your father…that is, if there is no prior understanding between you and Lord Wexford."

She smiled. "There is no understanding between myself and the Viscount."

"Then would you do me the honour of allowing me to court you should your father approve and Lord Wexford does not object?"

"You don't understand. The Viscount and I are merely friends. He has never given me any indication he wishes for anything more, and even should he wish it, I am not inclined to desire it. Your Grace, I would be honoured to have you call on me, and I am sure Papa and Lady Crofton will agree. I do not know if what I feel for you is what they call affection in terms of love, but I feel something I have never felt before, or I would have never allowed you the liberties you have just taken."

"Just the same," the Duke said, "I owe the Viscount due respect both as a peer and a friend. I will speak to him."

He tightened his grip on her waist and smiled as his horse ambled slowly towards the green and home.

~*~

That evening, there was an effusion of joy in the house such that one could not fathom without knowing fully the circumstances which had occasioned it. The Duke of Beaumont had indeed spoken with Lord Wexford, and the Viscount had given his blessing to the young man. Next, the Duke spoke with his aunt and the Viceroy. Both were delighted at the prospect of their daughter becoming a duchess, and everything was in place for a courtship, though the Duke knew it was only a matter of time before there would be a betrothal and then a wedding. He could not have been happier, and the value of his intended's dowry was sure to please his mother as well. And so, when the morrow came, he would dispatch an express post-haste to Croxley Abbey, inviting the Duchess to Town.

Darcy smiled with true joy for his newfound friend and his felicity in his courtship. In the short time he had known the Viceroy and his family, he had come to have a warm regard for them. Miss Millicent had come a long way towards maturing and making her way into English society, and Darcy was sure, with the Duke's help, she would make a splendid wife and hostess in the *ton*. None would dare snub her—the daughter of a viceroy and the wife of a duke.

Now he only had to look for his own happiness, and after today, he knew with certainty it would *not* involve the Viceroy's *third* daughter.

~*~*~*~

Chapter 26

March 23, 1812

The cold, dreary days of January and February had come and gone in the Old City, and winter, with its snow and freezing rain, had given way to a warm and promising spring. It was now the twenty-third of March, and along with the passing of time, came Darcy's anticipated annual trip to Kent. He had been up since before dawn seeing that all was ready. His trunks had been packed and loaded onto the servants' travel carriage the night before, and his valet had already gone ahead to retrieve Colonel Fitzwilliam's luggage before heading to Kent to prepare their chambers at Rosings Park. Darcy, however, had yet to leave. There remained a few last minute preparations to be made before he would follow Mr. Cunningham.

He had gone to the carriage house to have a word with his groomsman, and then there was business to be settled with Mr. Mosley, his butler, before departing. Sam would be coming along, and Darcy wanted his best stallion fitted for the trip as he preferred his own horses to those of his aunt.

Walking back to the house from the stables, he looked around and smiled. The air was a bit chilly with a morning frost still lingering, but otherwise it promised to be a bright and sunny day. By his estimation, it would be an excellent day for travelling, and what was twenty miles of good road?

As the hour drew near for his departure, Darcy said his farewell to Georgiana, and he and Sam entered the carriage. Making himself comfortable, Sam curled at Darcy's feet while Darcy leaned back and settled in for the short drive to Matlock House where he was to meet his cousin. Glancing out the window as the coach moved over the brick and cobblestone, he reflected back over the last several weeks with a series of rambling thoughts as he mused how quickly time had passed. Though the social season would not formally close until the end of May when winter was officially pronounced to be over, several families were already preparing to leave for their country estates where the spring planting season for many would soon begin.

Mr. and Mrs. Hurst had already left, having decided to join Bingley in Yorkshire before Hurst would leave for his family estate for the summer. Caroline, who was rather cross and bad tempered about the turn of events, was forced to go along with them whether she wished it or not, and, from what Darcy could tell, she did not wish it at all. In fact, he quite thought that she still clung to the notion that she might somehow forge an alliance between her brother and Georgiana, if only Hurst would remain in Town long enough for her to work on poor Georgiana's sensibilities such as she had been doing from their first coming to London. But that supposition was even more ridiculous than the one she had harboured concerning himself. Given his thoughts on the matter, he had just as soon marry a fat widow with ten unruly children. Truth be told, it would be an extremely chilly day in hell before he condescended to offer for *her*.

With Bingley and Hurst gone North, Darcy had little else to do except spend his time with his new friends. They dined and socialized either at Pennington Hall or at White's, though they occasionally did dine at Darcy House or Brooks's Gentlemen's Club. There were dinner parties and private balls and nights of supper and cards. Nearly every evening they were together at one place or the other.

The Duke of Beaumont and Miss Millicent Singleton were now betrothed. Darcy had attended their engagement ball, but he had not been inclined to dance more than two sets, and one of those had been with Miss Millicent and the other with the Duke's youngest sister yet to be out, who had been allowed to dance with Darcy because of his friendship with the Duke.

Instead, he and a few of the other gentlemen had chosen cards and cigars. All in all, it had been a good social season for Darcy. He had not thought of Elizabeth Bennet with any seriousness since the day after he had seen her sister at Hurst House. He hoped time and distance would conquer all desire for her. No matter how he reasoned, a marriage contract with Miss Elizabeth was insupportable. All he need do was remind himself of her mother, and that was enough to see the illogic in such a proposal and put an end to the thought, regardless of his desires. He sighed and passed his hand over his face.

The carriage passed a couple on the walkway out for a stroll with their young child in a pram. Darcy smiled at the look of contentment on the gentleman's countenance, and his thoughts shifted to his newfound acquaintance, the Duke of Beaumont.

All the talk of weddings, fashion, flowers, and food had often been more than the young Duke could endure, especially with his mother, the current Duchess, and three younger sisters all in residence in Grosvenor Square. Now that the current Duchess had a future daughter-in-law to instruct, she worried the Duke even more with all the parties and suppers she insisted must be given. On several occasions the Duke had fled his home to the sanctuary of Darcy House where he had related his distress in full to his older friend.

The Duchess and her sister, the Countess of Crofton, were in their element with all their planning for a May wedding. The first order of business had been to secure a special license and then the Duke was to make arrangements for the Archbishop of Canterbury to perform the ceremony, as was desired by his mother. Then there were the wedding clothes. They travelled from one set of warehouses to the next in search of all that was deemed necessary for the most fashionable wedding the Countess and Duchess could arrange, and with each new selection of samples, the Duke was required by the Duchess to bestow an opinion. Even Georgiana, who often accompanied the party, was excited with the prospect of her friend's wedding. The poor Duke, on the other hand, was not so pleased.

Darcy's lips curled as he shook his head. He knew it was much more than he even could ever bear, and therefore, he sympathized with his friend. With designs for clothes and bolts of cloth for the young noble to touch and feel and then give his approval, the young Duke was ready to elope. Consequently, Darcy and Lord Wexford had spent a great deal of time in his company and had concluded that they liked their new, noble friend very much. Moreover, the friendship had developed into a close one, such that the Duke was now known to them simply as Beau.

Furthermore, they had agreed that if time permitted, Darcy would see him in Kent once the Duke and his family had removed to Croxley Abbey for the Easter Celebration in his parish.

Then there was Miss Kathryn. Darcy crossed his legs and rubbed his chin as he thought of her. Since the incident at Greensward, she was not the same and kept mostly to herself. Though she was exceedingly happy for her sister's felicity, Miss Kathryn was more demure and quiet than was her normal self. She hardly spoke a word to anyone and was often seen with either a book of poetry in her hand or stitching some form of needlework, all habits she had only recently acquired. She went for long rides in the park, as the weather permitted, and sometimes Darcy and Georgiana accompanied her. But more often than not, Miss Kathryn preferred to be alone.

Although Darcy had broken his informal courtship with her, he knew that he was not the reason for her present melancholy; for he had no indication from her, or anyone else, that he had touched her heart, much less broken it. She puzzled him exceedingly.

Darcy shifted in his seat, and Sam looked up before adjusting himself and resuming his sleep. Smiling he reached down to caress Sam's head and scratch behind his ears. Sam was a good dog and a good companion. With a deep breath, Darcy returned to the window; they had just turned onto Brook Street. He would soon be at Matlock House.

Darcy was not especially looking forward to this journey and planned to keep precisely to business as he knew his aunt would once again recommend his cousin Anne as a bride. Though he cared for Anne, he had no intention of sacrificing himself by becoming her husband.

Then there was his aunt's new parson, a man for whom Darcy held no respect and very little regard as a clergyman. Lady Catherine's letters were always filled with details about her vicar and his wife. They often took tea with his aunt, and Lady Catherine always had plenty to say where her vicar and his wife were concerned. She appeared to be very involved in their lives, and, from what Darcy could tell, Mr. Collins was just the sort of man Lady Catherine would have in her patronage.

He simpered and fawned, bowing to her every word, and seemed, by his aunt's account, to be very needy. He lapped up her advice, following it to the strictest measure, and was always waiting in the lane to greet her carriage whenever she was out. Every day he walked to Rosings to see what service he might provide for her ladyship's comfort. Darcy rolled his eyes at the thought of it. He did, however, pity the good parson's poor wife, for she seemed a very sensible young lady from his brief exposure to her in Hertfordshire. She possessed a genteel spirit with quiet manners that recommended her well to her station in life. It was a pity her husband did not deserve her.

Lady Catherine had made mention that Mrs. Collins had visitors. His aunt, however, had failed to reveal much about them or even who they were, other than making one reference to Mrs. Collins's father. Darcy was mildly curious as to who the others might be, but had not been willing to enquire. He would know soon enough, he supposed, for by the afternoon they would be at Rosings Park.

Finally, the carriage slowed to a stop at Number 10 Brook Street where he was to meet Colonel Fitzwilliam before continuing on to Kent. He would go in and pay his regards to his Aunt and Uncle Matlock, and then he and Colonel Fitzwilliam would be on their way, but not without one more stop at Pennington Hall. The Viceroy had requested that they come by for tea before departing, and so as a matter of courtesy, they would call upon him and their good friend Randal Pennington, soon to be the new Earl of Ravensbrook. With a little luck, perhaps the Duke would be there as well.

~*~

When Darcy and the Colonel were admitted to the Pennington townhouse in Cavendish Square, they found the place in pandemonium. Servants were scurrying about and the sounds of wailing could be heard throughout while angry voices came from the library. Susan Pennington approached them with quick steps, wringing her hands as she came. Her eyes were swollen and her breath came in quick gasps.

"Good God! What is the matter? Has someone died?" Darcy asked in alarm.

"No," she cried, wiping a tear. "It is worse—much worse. It is my sister, Kate. She has gone off—eloped with a colonel from India." She looked from Colonel Fitzwilliam to Darcy. "Colonel Brockton. My father knows him, but he was unknown to the rest of us. A note was discovered on her pillow about an hour and a half ago when she did not come down for breakfast.

"Papa is now in a closed meeting with the Colonel's father, Lord Brockton, even as we speak. Father summoned him immediately upon his discovery of the deed, and he came quickly with a letter of his own. Millie's betrothed, the Duke of Beaumont, is also with them as are Randal and Lord Wexford who were here at the time Kate's action was discovered. We are all in an uproar, Mr. Darcy, and I fear a duel will result if cooler heads do not prevail. Father has threatened to kill the Colonel for dishonouring our family. And he disparages Lord Brockton with such dreadful language as I have never heard him use. Oh! What will we do? If Father fights Colonel Brockton, he will be killed. I am as sure of it as of my next breath!"

"Brockton...Edward Brockton," Colonel Fitzwilliam said softly as if he considered the name.

"Do you know him?" Mrs. Pennington looked up through her tears.

"Yes, as a matter of fact I do. He is a comrade of mine. We went to the war college together. He is quite skilled as a commander—one of the best swordsmen I know. I think very highly of him. This is most unusual for his general character."

"I don't care about any of that. Four days travelling alone in a closed carriage without a chaperone? He has ruined my sister, and consequently, the rest of us!" Mrs. Pennington cried, wiping back tears. "Her head is full of nonsense to do such a thing!"

"When did they depart?" Colonel Fitzwilliam asked. "And what measures have been made to recover them?"

"From the note she left, it must have been some time after midnight, and what measure can we take? None! Colonel Brockton said in his letter to his father that he hired every single horse at Shap so that his pursuers would find none available for that strenuous part of the journey. Even if we were to find them and drag them back, what good would come of it? Her reputation is fixed! We are ruined! They will be cast off from every family in London, as will we!"

"I can see by your distress that we are intruding." Darcy interjected. "Please give our regards to your husband and father. We shall leave you now."

"No. Please do not go, Darcy," said Randal Pennington as he emerged from the library. I saw your coach in the courtyard and came to find you. I realize that half past the hour of ten o'clock in the morning is a bit early for whiskey, but please join me in the drawing room for a drink. I think a very strong Scotch whiskey is in order. Both of you come with me."

Darcy and the Colonel exchanged looks, and then followed their friend. From the looks of him, he needed more than a drink. He needed a friend as well.

~*~

Lord Brockton glared at the man standing before him, his features twisted in anger as he gripped the glass in his hand. The Governor-General stood over him, the veins in his neck bulging, as he spoke in fury through gritted teeth.

"Your son has raped my daughter's innocence with his happy manners and smooth tongue—so happy indeed that they disguise the true nature of his black heart. He has disgraced my family! If you and your son think that you will collect one shilling of my daughter's fortune, then you are sadly mistaken. He will take her penniless if he takes her at all! I'll not give a farthing to this sham of a marriage."

"I will not sit here, Viceroy, and have you insult my son in such a malicious manner," the Baron said, slamming his drink down on the side table as he rose to his feet. "We do not want or need one penny of your money. Our estate is secure, and we have enough of our own wealth to manage without one pence of yours!

"My son is a good and decent man! Is your daughter not to share in any of the blame? As far as I am concerned, *she* seduced him with *her* arts and allurements—raping his good and virtuous mind with her flattering and coquettish arts, stealing a young man's heart while she raised a little skirt. If the gossips are to be believed, *your* daughter has perfected the wiles of seduction with her wickedness learned in the wastelands of India." Lord Brockton exploded.

The Viceroy's eyes bulged and his face became dangerously red. "Are you calling my daughter a... a....a whore?! That is an insult I will not overlook! I'll see you with pistols at dawn!"

"Phillip! Please sit down before you have a fit of apoplexy!" Lady Crofton cried rising to touch her husband's arm. "Nothing can be accomplished with such talk, and I will *not* have you fight!"

The Viceroy glanced at his wife and then to the Baron whose eyes bore into his with a lethal glare. Several moments passed, and when he was calmed enough to be civil, he spoke again.

"What have you to say that I should consider you and your son as suitable to be called my family? There is nothing you can say. You are not of our sphere, nor shall you ever be! As for my daughter, this marriage is a mockery of that great institution and must be annulled." Turning to his wife, he continued. "Kate has brought dishonour to this house. She will return to India with us where she can rot in her shame. I am through with her!"

"No, that is not how it will be, Viceroy, for I, as well as you, have a say in this matter. They are now married, or at least will be in a matter of days, and at the very least, they are both compromised; what's done is *done*." The Baron's jaw clenched as he glanced around the room.

"I know what you are thinking, for your snobbery precedes you with your accolades of self-worth. You are proud and think well of yourselves. *But* before you think so little of us, perhaps you should come to know us," Lord Brockton said. "Edward is to inherit my barony upon my death, according to the primogeniture. We are *not* without connections *or* money. I have an income of two thousand a year, which my son will inherit in full when the time comes. And, perhaps, more importantly, we come from a long line of respectable men.

"My great grandfather was the 1st Duke of Chandos[1], and my maternal uncle is an Earl in the Scottish peerage—one of some notoriety in the House of Lords." Lord Brockton looked around the room and knew their disbelief for what it was. He smirked and continued.

"I know what you think. The lineage is too long in the past, or what I say is untrue. And to that I answer…for proof of my words, you may make the necessary enquiries of my cousin, the 4th Duke of Chandos, who is currently in residence at Chandos House in Cavendish Square. I believe it is not far removed from where we are at present."

The Viceroy rolled his eyes and mumbled something under his breath before beginning anew with the bickering that had gone on for the better part of an hour.

The Duke of Beaumont, who had sat quietly by, listening to all that transpired between his future father-in-law and the Baron, finally had had enough. "Gentlemen!" he cried, rising to his feet. "Are you to dispute this matter for the remainder of the morning without endeavouring to come to a resolution? This will not do. Come, let us reason together. Though it seems a hopeless situation, it is not.

"Viceroy," the Duke said. "Lord Brockton is correct. They should not be forced to separate. It would ruin her, reducing her to a life of disgrace and endless shame. Surely you do not want that. With all due respect, sir, it is not as bad as you think; we can hush it up."

"Hush it up? Are you mad! What do you propose we do—have them marry in a church like respectable men and women?" The Viceroy blinked in disbelief.

"That is exactly what I mean, and why not? Misfortunes are sent to test our fortitude, and may often reveal themselves as blessings in disguise."

"Blessings in disguise? Indeed! This is no blessing! It is preposterous. A ridiculous notion if I ever heard one—a wedding over the anvil with the blacksmith priests[2]. I will not have it!"

---

[1] The 1st Duke of Chandos was Jane Austen's great-great uncle through her mother's line. Therefore, Jane had nobility in her lineage. The 2nd Duke of Chandos, Jane Austen's 1st cousin twice removed, actually bought his second wife as chattel at the Pelican Inn, Newbury, on his way to London, when her abusive husband sold her at auction. She was a very beautiful chambermaid who carried herself with dignity, and thus impressed the Duke who eventually married her at Keith's Chapel on Christmas Day, 1744. As you see the 2nd Duke of Chandos broke with the norm of convention for his day and married for love. The 3rd Duke of Chandos died with no male heir to succeed him. The title then became extinct and all properties passed to his second wife, Anna Eliza Elletson, who went mad before her death, and then to his only daughter by Anna Eliza (Jane Austen's 3rd cousin), the future 1st Duchess of Buckingham and Chandos, who also carried her mother's given name.. For purposes of this story, however, a fourth duke was created by the author.
http://www.dukesofbuckingham.org.uk/people/family/brydges/dukes_of_chandos.htm
http://www.berkshirehistory.com/legends/chandos.html
http://www.jasa.net.au/inperspective/family.htm
http://www.janeausten.co.uk/james-brydges-cassanda-austens-princely-uncle/

[2] A wedding over the anvil refers to how weddings in Greta Green were conducted. In coaching days, a blacksmith's shop was usually where coaches first stopped, and since the blacksmith in Scotland held prominence in the local villages, he was often the one who married young couples who eloped. They would arrive at the stop and marry quickly before pursuing parents could catch up with them and stop the wedding.
http://shannondonnelly.com/tag/elopement/

"No, my dear," the Countess interjected, "let His Grace speak." She glanced at her nephew. "Please continue, Beau. I wish to hear what you have to say."

The Duke began to pace with his hands folded behind his back. "This is what we shall do. When Colonel and Mrs Brockton return from Gretna Green, they shall have a wedding in St. Paul's by special license," he said, looking at the Viceroy. "Then, when enough time has passed, I shall sponsor Colonel Brockton in the House of Lords for an earldom. If Lord Brockton is telling the truth concerning his relations, and I believe that he is, then it is a simple affair to correct. With his connections to the Duke of Chandos, whose father was a close associate of my late father's, I would say there is great possibility that this can be resolved within short order without much trouble at all. Through other members of the nobility, myself included, and with Lord Wexford and his father's help, we shall be able to come up with something."

The Viscount nodded. "I will do whatever I can, and I believe my father would be willing to be of assistance, as well."

Lord Brockton indicated his agreement, nodding gently, his brow furrowed in attentiveness. "I think we should listen to what this young nobleman has to say. He appears sensible at least, which is more than I can say for the rest of you."

With fire in his eyes, the Viceroy went to stand, but the Duke stopped him with a raised hand.

He then glanced at the Baron and said, "Lord Brockton, I happen to know your uncle. Lord Herbertshire's townhouse is next to mine in Grosvenor Square. He is very ill and lying on his deathbed this very hour. I also know Lord Herbertshire has no living sons to inherit his title and properties." the Duke stopped and glanced at his future father-in-law to make his point, "And therefore, you and your son are his heirs. Is that not correct, Lord Brockton?" he asked, bring his gaze back to the Baron.

"Yes…that is correct, though I have not seen my uncle in some years and did not realize he was so ill. We are not close. We never were because of a dispute that existed long ago between my uncle and late father. But, from my understanding of the matter, that is the way his title is set up; the next living male relative is to inherit, and that would be me and then my son."

"Exactly! And, consequently, with an earldom in Scotland, I can procure one in England without much trouble at all. And with dual titles, you will be well established within the aristocracy."

The Viceroy stilled himself, glancing from his wife to the Duke. "You would do this?"

"Yes…I would. All is not lost, Viceroy. It will be a very good alliance. Lord Herbertshire, who was a close associate of my late father's, is said to have a castle in Scotland with an income of five thousand a year. Is that correct, Lord Brockton?"

The Baron nodded.

"Yes…well, with Lord Brockton's income of two thousand and the Scottish income of five, they shall be well situated, and I will see to it that they are accepted within the *ton*. With your influence as well as mine, Viceroy, you needn't worry about that, especially when Millicent and I are married.

"Mrs. Brockton will be the sister of a duchess. With such connections, they will eventually be accepted into society. With the passing of time, people will forget the indelicacies surrounding their hasty marriage and move on. There will be no scandal, at least not one of any lasting duration."

A Man in Want of a Wife

The Governor-General's face broke into a large smile as he turned to Lord Brockton and extended his hand. "I think we have come to an understanding, Brockton. Come, let us find the rest of the family and have a drink. I have a bottle of the finest Cognac ever distilled—part of Louis XIII's personal reserve, I'm told. You will stay for luncheon, and we shall have a cigar and talk. I want to meet this cousin of yours, the Duke of Chandos. I have wanted to make his acquaintance for some time. Let us eat, drink, and be merry—a toast to our alliance. You and Lady Brockton shall dine with us tonight, and my wife and yours can plan a wedding. I have always believed people should marry for love. Do you not agree, Cora?" he said more than asked whilst leaving the library with his wife on his arm and the Baron by his other side.

The Countess smiled and arched a brow as she tightened her grip on her husband's arm.

~*~

The gentlemen entered the drawing room laughing and conversing, and Randal Pennington almost choked on his whiskey. Recovering himself, Rand rose to his feet and went to meet the party.

"What is the meaning of this? I thought there was to be a duel."

"Nonsense!" the Viceroy cried. "Why would there be a duel? We have another wedding to plan. Kate is to marry formally in St. Paul's. We'll have a special license and a large party of friends for the wedding breakfast. And let there be cake! There is no need to fight. We have much to celebrate. Lord and Lady Brockton! Oh! How well it sounds!"

Darcy and the Colonel exchanged looks and shrugged while Rand Pennington looked on in disbelief.

After several minutes of smiles and cordial conversation, Darcy and Colonel Fitzwilliam paid their regards and said their goodbyes, but before they could leave, Miss Millicent Singleton ran up to meet them in the vestibule.

"Mr. Darcy," she said, nearly out of breath. "May I have a private word with you?"

"Yes, of course," he said. Turning to his cousin he further stated, "Fitzwilliam, will excuse us?"

"I'll see you outside," the Colonel answered, and with that he left for the carriage.

Turning back to Miss Singleton, Darcy asked, "How may I be of assistance to you?"

"Mr. Darcy, if you will, sir, my sister wanted you to have this. Will you please accept it?"

Darcy glanced at the sealed letter Millie thrust into his hands and then looked up with a furrowed brow.

"Just take it and read it when you are alone, and you mustn't tell anyone what it says, for she has sworn me to secrecy, and should it get out that I have given it to you, well, I think you know it would not go well for me."

"Yes, of course. I shall accept it, and you may be assured of my secrecy."

She smiled. "I know. You are a good and honourable man—one with whom I can claim a proud acquaintance. *À la prochaine. Adieu*! Have a safe trip; we shall see you in Kent. His Grace is teaching me to ride properly. I'm sure we shall see you out, whether it be in the village or at Croxley Abbey."

"Indeed. I wish you and His Grace joy."

Darcy turned and quit the house. Walking down the steps at a quick pace, he slipped the missive inside his coat pocket, mildly wondering what Miss Kathryn—or rather Mrs. Brockton—had to say. Entering the carriage, he took his seat across from the Colonel and ran his fingers over where he had placed the letter, still contemplating the proceedings of the morning. It had been an eventful beginning to a rather ordinary day, and that was expressing it mildly. He gave a small smile and reached down to stroke his hound's lazy head and flap his long ears as Sam yawned. At a quarter of noon, they were getting a late start. But with a bit of luck, they should arrive at Rosings in time for tea, and then he would read Mrs. Brockton's correspondence tonight in the privacy of his room. Leaning back, Darcy crossed his legs and settled in for quiet conversation with his cousin as the coach rolled through the archway of Cavendish Square.

~*~*~*~

Part Three

The Kent Chronicles

To be continued...

Made in the USA
Charleston, SC
17 August 2012